From Winter to Paradise

Jack Coates

Pen Press Publishers Ltd

First published in Great Britain by
Pen Press Publishers Ltd
25 Eastern Place
Brighton
BN2 1GJ

ISBN 978-1-906206-97-0

Printed and bound in UK by Cpod, Trowbridge, Wiltshire

A catalogue record of this book is available from
the British Library

Cover design by Jacqueline Abromeit
Cover photo © Martin Reddy

About The Author

Jack Coates is an award-winning author who served in the Royal Army during World War II. His experiences ranged from participating in the desert campaign in North Africa to surviving behind enemy lines in Italy. During his deployment, he was captured by the Germans three times, was interned in an Italian POW camp, survived a sinking torpeded ship, and had both of his arms broken during combat. He was awarded four medals for his service. Jack is now 89 years old and lives with his wife of 62 years, Ida, in Lossiemouth, Scotland.

Preface

This story is set around the time of Mussolini's fall from power, an event that brought about the Armistice of Cassibile and provided unconditional surrender for the Italian armed forces. The announcement of the armistice over the radio on September 8th, 1943 threw the country into total confusion. With the Allies fighting the Germans up the peninsula, Italy declared war on Germany while the Fascists reorganised and joined the war as an ally of Germany; thus creating chaos.

The National Liberation Army, commonly know as the "Partisans", called on all Italians to fight against Nazism and Fascism, resulting in great sacrifice of life to the resistance. Thousands more were killed in German reprisals against people aiding or sheltering resistance fighters or escaped Allied POWs trapped behind German lines.

These events form the backdrop of this novel. Although it is written as fiction, it is based upon my experiences during the war. Practically everything described herein actually happened. Sometimes the outcome was entirely different, hence fact becomes fiction. The names and places have all been changed, but despite this any character still living would recognise himself or herself absolutely and without embarrassment.

This story remained locked in my head for many decades and there are several people that I must thank for making this book a reality. In the first instance, I'd like to thank my family for their constant support, including my wife Ida, my children, Frances, Harry and Linda, and my grandchildren Martin, Andrew, David, Julie, Joanna and Harry. In particular, Martin transcribed and edited early drafts of this manuscript. Thanks are also due to Lynn Ashman and everyone at Pen Press Publishing for helping me to publish this work. Finally, but most importantly, my undying gratitude goes to all those who sheltered and protected me during the war. Most of these souls offered me help and sustenance without a second thought for their own welfare. This story would not exist without them, and very likely I would not be here today to tell it to you. This book is dedicated to their memory.

Chapter 1

The town was like any of a dozen others he had passed by in Italy, clinging limpet-like to the hillside. The peaceful serenity in tune with the tranquillity in his breast just left of centre. A stream snaked its way through the valley 200 yards below; a bridge of tree trunks and earth spanned the water linking the outlying farms to the town by a good dirt road, a highway of commerce, while the main road ran north to south through the town. Two oak trees stood guard over the bridge like brooding sentinels.

Jim Corner, former Bren gunner, ex-prisoner of war and current fugitive was enjoying the sunshine. Propping up the larger tree, blond hair growing wild to his shoulders, he pushed cheese and bread into his face. He had just hacked three weeks growth of beard from his face with a blade 20 shaves old and he felt refreshed.

Having escaped from the prison camp at Fermo six months ago, food had never been a problem. Shelter from the cold was a little more difficult, and the Germans and Fascists were a permanent threat. Experience had taught him to deal with each in turn: 'Ask and ye shall receive. Seek and ye shall find'. Life was reasonable, under the circumstances. This was as safe a way as any to fight a war. There was always a warm stable or barn to spend the cold nights, somewhere to hibernate through the long hours of darkness, but the Germans were much too active around these parts so he had decided to move north into Marche. After an abortive and almost disastrous attempt at crossing the front line, the experience furnished him with a new resolve and boosted his courage. Upon careful consideration, he had decided to sample the Italian spring: the winter of 1943 had been particularly harsh and he was beginning to enjoy the country and its people. Indeed, he was beginning to speak the language with some authority now, even enjoying the odd conversation, often with himself.

Should he cross the front line, then what? A lot of backslapping, congratulatory handshakes and a couple of weeks' leave. Where do they send an expert Bren gunner with killing experience? The Far East? Maybe the intended second front storming the beaches. He might get lucky and be sent back to Italy. Then why leave Italy at all? The only problem at the moment was the rag he wore for a shirt that was falling off his back. He had been shot at three times with a bullet tear in his coat sleeve to prove it and yet there was something stimulating about conducting one's own war: deploying oneself with masterful strategy simply by moving where the enemy wasn't. It was a safe method of campaigning, cutting down the risks and doubling the chances of life expectancy. Today the sun was shining, his spirits were high and he had a song in his heart. He began singing a song from a Dick Powell film; the *Shadow Waltz* was ever his favourite.

The rattle of small arms fire invaded his festive mood. Women screamed, men shouted in fear, panic reigned in the town spreading into the countryside around him.

"It must be more peaceful further north!" he said to himself and decided there and then to put his plan into practice and seek new sanctuary.

People were scattering through the countryside. He counted four youths racing though the olive groves and fields, running wildly in blind panic.

"What the hell is going on here?" he asked himself.

While the confusion continued, the firing ceased leaving only the sound of high-pitched screams and mocking laughter. The familiarity of that particular sound he knew all too well from past experiences: the Germans enjoyed bullying frightened people. It would be wise to stay here in comparative safety and help the trees guard the bridge. At that point, a youth raced past calling a warning as he desperately tried to beat the four-minute mile.

"Tedeschi!" he called breathlessly, racing across the bridge and away up the hill.

"Tedeschi," Jim repeated, "well, I would never have guessed."

As the excitement and the fear abated, he spotted two German vehicles leaving town, moving north.

"I'll check my luggage and follow the enemy: a half comb, razor and toothbrush. I'm packed. It's much too noisy around here."

As he began to move off he reminded himself, "I really must make an appointment with my hairdresser," as he pushed hair out of his face.

*

Chapter 2

A woman picking her way down the road from town attracted his attention. Normally, he would have just gone about his own business and walked away; he was a busy man.

"My, oh my," he said, watching her approach with more than usual interest.

A big, smart woman several years his senior, she was dressed town-style (in the country, women dressed to a pattern, mostly in black) wearing a white jumper that she filled to bursting point with a blue matching skirt under an open swagger coat. Watching her walk towards him, her hair was so black it gave off a blue sheen in the sunlight. She was almost level and there was a danger she might just walk past. "Speak to her, you silly bugger!" he urged himself, promptly obeying his own command.

"Buona sera, Signora," giving just a hint of a bow.

She turned and smiled, the most beautiful smile he had ever seen.

"Signorina. Buona sera," she replied.

How could anything so wonderful be a signorina? Italian men weren't blind to women. How then had this magnificent animal been overlooked? She had a round face with full lips and white even teeth. He was looking into the brownest eyes he had ever seen; his reflection was there in the coloured retina. All this he took in at a glance. She was quite tall: they stood at eye level, about 5 ft 9 and all of 12 st. They matched one another inch for inch, pound for pound.

"You are English," she said, rather than asked.

Her voice had the soothing effect of a cool, rippling stream.

"Does it show?" he answered, unable to think of anything to say, yet there were a million things he wanted to ask.

"God," he pleaded silently. "Don't let this heavenly creature walk away and leave me."

"Have you been here long?" she asked.

"Long enough to see the show. What was it all about?" He was looking at a nasty bruise on her left cheekbone. Whatever had happened in town, she had been in the thick of the fight.

"Did anyone pass by while you were here?" she asked with concern.

"A boy running as if his life was at stake. He'll be at the coast now."

"Thank God."

She appeared to be somewhat relieved by the news.

"What was all the excitement?"

"'Voluntary recruiting' they call it. Rounding up young men for their labour battalions."

"Oh, something new?"

"It's their second such foray here in this town. They march in firing their guns and we all run like frightened rabbits."

"That's a normal reaction, I'm quite good at it. You didn't run though, I can see that."

He nodded to the mark on her cheek that appeared to have grown in size in the last few minutes.

"Someone has to stand up to them. What on earth has happened to my people? Is everyone afraid?"

He wasn't quite sure whether she was asking or telling him. "I don't know about them," he replied, "I only know that I am."

"I doubt that. You look like a lion with that mane of golden hair."

"I can assure you, I'm no lion."

"No lamb either," she laughed for the first time and it was like a tinkling of chimes.

"Did you achieve anything by your actions?" he asked.

"Oh yes! You have just confirmed it. That boy's safety was my objective."

"Congratulations, you're a better man than I am. I rarely achieve anything. I say, your English is very good. I didn't realise we were speaking it."

"Thank you. I'm flattered, but what about you, have you somewhere to stay?" she asked with concern.

"Not yet, I'm about to go house hunting. I'll probably push in beside some old cow."

They both laughed. He was making progress. His eyes were on her breasts, waiting for the jumper to burst open.

"Would you allow me to help you?" She asked the question as if he would be doing her a favour.

"Am I in a position to refuse?" he smiled.

"I see you have no false pride. Now maybe we can introduce ourselves," she held out her hand, "I'm Rosanna Verde, the local school mistress. That is, when I have a class to teach! They've even disrupted our education."

Her hand was warm and soft, the grip firm. Just keep your hand in mine, he prayed. If you only knew the comfort.

"Jim Corner. What you see is all there is. I'm wearing my complete wardrobe."

"Maybe we can do something about that," she smiled.

He wanted to keep holding her hand. She didn't object but he was carrying the introduction too far. He reluctantly released it.

"Rose Green," he said, smiling into her eyes.

"Rose Green?" she laughed, and the chimes rang out again.

She must have had a distressing day facing up to those strutting cock-sure bastards, yet here she was being pleasant as a guardian angel. He wanted to kiss that bruise on her face, to soothe it, to hold her hand and offer some comfort. That's what he would like to do, but in truth, he wouldn't dare. He had never kissed a woman in his life.

Once in Cairo, walking down a street he should never have been on at all, a very pretty young woman, sitting outside her business premises in bra and panties, teasing trade, spoke to him.

"You want a good time, Johnny?"

He looked at her with longing eyes. She had a nice compact body that would be good to lie with.

"You want a good time, Johnny?" she asked again, "I make you forget the war."

He paused for a while taking in the whole scene: the house, the doorway, the chair she sat on. "Lady," he was speaking to himself, "I would love to! The truth is I'm terrified of what you might transfer into my body, after I've been in yours."

Without warning, she grabbed his hat and ran into the house. He just stood there hatless and clueless.

"Come and get your hat, Johnny. I got love for you. You like," she called from her upstairs window, waving the hat along with two dangling breasts. She had stripped off her bra.

Two soldiers approached looking for a laugh followed by two or three grinning locals.

"Go up and have a go, mate," joked one. "Or you'll lose your hat and your stripes."

"Go on," urged the other, "get stuck in!"

They were laughing, everyone was except himself. The joke was on him. A couple of military policemen drove up.

"Do you want to go up and get it yourself, mate?" one asked.

The happy gathering was beginning to disperse now. It was plain, even to the young woman at the window, that the show was over.

"Well, do you or don't you?" the redcap asked impatiently.

"No," was all that he could say. He didn't like being the focus of attention. The girl dropped the hat at once. That was as close as he had ever been to sexual intercourse.

"Shall we proceed?" asked Rosanna.

They turned and walked away from the town in the direction the boy had taken. He fell in step beside her as they crossed the small bridge that looked as though the dirt track just continued over the stream.

"Any other difficulties outside of food and shelter? The Germans for instance," enquired Rose.

"A couple of careless mistakes. One that nearly got me shot. This was the result." He showed her his sleeve, "That's a bullet tear and it scared me. I've been a good boy ever since."

"Tell me a more humorous incident. I need cheering up," she smiled across at him.

"This was a humorous incident," he pointed to his sleeve. "It was far from funny at the time. I behaved like an idiot, which isn't unusual by the way." Their eyes met, she was smiling. "It happened six weeks ago in the mountains among the refugees from the front line towns below. They were living in caves and communal shelters built mostly from trees. They had firewood; a fire was as essential as food and there was more fuel than food. It was cold and there was no chance of me getting fat. I decided half-heartedly to leave it all behind and cross the mountain to join our own forces whom I was informed had recently occupied a village called Pennipiedamonte." They stopped and turned to face each other. "Am I boring you?" he asked, looking into those brown, brown eyes while the breeze wafted pockets of perfume to further his delight.

She smiled, "How was Pennipiedamonte?"

"I didn't get there and I would have been embarrassed had you witnessed the mess I got myself into."

"Go on, this is getting interesting."

"Leaving out the trivia, I'll take you straight into action. I was no mountain climber but found it stimulating and the sun appeared briefly to help me on my way. Everything was going according to plan until suddenly I walked into a German alpine patrol. Fortunately they were at ease, sitting around talking and smoking. They were as surprised as I was, but not so fearful. Without hesitation, I did a smart about turn. My training sergeant at the depot would have been proud, as would the PTI with the kipper-back; they were good friends by the way. They would have been amazed at my jump from a mountain ledge into a snowdrift that created a mini avalanche that carried me 200 yards down the mountain in five breath-taking seconds. The short journey would have been so excruciatingly painful had not fear dulled my senses. I hit every rock and boulder on the way." He glanced across at her, "I'm glad you didn't come along," he said, smiling, "my ribs, legs, arse and back cracked rocks in flight. I somehow gathered up my numbed senses and continued the journey down through space, sliding and tumbling, while the bullets winged past, ricocheting off snow-covered rocks and drilling into the snowdrifts. The patrol was out as if they were hunting and I was the prey. The ignominious shower of love-begots." He looked across, it was difficult to keep his eyes off her. "Panic lends wings and numbs pain. I was black and blue from head to toe and my body ached for a week. I must have been a ridiculous spectacle rolling down those slopes, no wonder they laughed at me. The climb took three hours, the descent three minutes. You said I looked like a lion; I acted like a clown." They paused for a further inspection. "I bet you got that bruise on your face by standing up to the arrogant baskets while I, poor in spirit, ran with faint heart, inflicting my own injuries. A coward dies many deaths." She was smiling. "You are feeling better now, aren't you?" he asked.

"Yes, much better. You have boosted my spirit and soothed my humiliation. Yes, I think I feel a lot better."

"So do I. So do I."

They rewarded each other with a smile and walked on over the hill where the scene opened up to him. Three farm houses in close proximity, each within equal distance from the well so that no one could claim absolute ownership. As if a lookout had been posted, they were spotted immediately. Everyone poured out of the houses and came to meet her, marching to greet the local heroine.

"I hope you can handle this situation," he quipped.

"They are coming to welcome you," she said, smiling.

"I very much doubt that."

*

Chapter 3

She was engulfed in a sea of admirers and sympathisers as they took her hand, patted her on the back, and examined the war wound. He stood off stage, as it were, trying to glean the story. The boy who had raced past him at the bridge broke away from the throng offering a welcome.

"You met the signorina, I see."

"She came along ten minutes after you. What actually happened in town?"

"They captured six boys of my age and took them to labour camps. I was being led away by two soldiers when the signorina came to my aid, hitting one with her fist and pulling the other off of me. They were taken unaware you see; the action was so unexpected they thought no one would dare oppose them. People were shouting abuse. I didn't stop to see what happened afterwards."

"She hit a soldier with her fist! That's hard to believe."

"Oh, she has done it before. Not a soldier though, she hit the mayor but that happened a long time ago. She's an oldish lady you know."

"I can see that," Jim laughed, "but if it was a long time ago, how do you know what happened?"

"Everybody knows, but nobody talks about it. It's all very hush-hush."

"If it's a secret that isn't discussed, then how can everybody know?"

The boy was becoming confused, realising that he had told tales out of school.

"I don't know why, that's just the way it is. She is wealthy and people respect her. I don't know any more than that."

Rosanna had broken free from all the backslapping and face

inspection. The crowd milled around her as she approached; they were curious to see what she had dragged along.

"I see you two recognised each other," she remarked in Italian. "How do you feel now, Mario? I'm happy to see you safely at home. We were lucky today."

The boy was embarrassed, feeling that he had betrayed a trust, but he had the good grace to thank her.

"Jim," she switched to English, "this is Mario's mother, Anna. You will like her, she is honest and outspoken."

"I'm sure I will, there aren't many of us left," he laughed.

The middle-aged lady hanging on to Rosanna's arm inspected him closely.

"Madre de Deo Rosanna, where did you find this?" Fingering his hair, she said, "I would love to put the scissors through that lot," patting his cheek as one might treat a moron.

Flashing a smile, Rose said, "Why not ask him? I'm sure he would like nothing better."

"It would be a load off my mind, Signora," he chuckled.

Hearing him reply in Italian, she let out a little shriek, hiding her embarrassment on Rose's breast. The crowd, enjoying the display, joined in the laughter. One or two comments were passed; everybody was in a gay mood. Anna's little faux pas had broken the ice; it was just what was needed. Anna too was laughing as she turned to face him, taking his hand in hers and placing the other on his shoulder.

"We got off to a bad start there didn't we, figlio?" she half apologised, looking at him fondly. Turning to Rose, "That was your fault, speaking those foreign languages. Here we speak Italian." Turning back to Jim, she added, "You understand?" with mock severity as she took his arm and linked the other through Rose's, escorting them towards the house.

The whole community gathered in the parlour-cum-dining room, kitchen, living and general-purpose room. He was playing to a full house. Everybody made themselves comfortable, or useful as in the case of the ladies. There was a clashing of pots and pans, the fire was being stoked high enough to roast a pig, questions were being shot at him from all sides without expecting a reply; there was always someone in the crowd prepared to answer for him. Rose sat in the

11

VIP seat, not just by virtue of being guest of honour and heroine of the day, she was accorded status respect. He could only guess why.

Anna came on stage, snipping a pair of scissors in the air and carrying a sheet. Without ceremony or by your leave, she wrapped the sheet tightly around him, imprisoning his arms and tucking it into his collar. Standing facing him, she began combing his hair and putting on a big show. Playing to the gallery, the audience shuffled around for a vantage point amidst laughter and wise cracks.

The sideshow was in progress, with Anna enjoying each snip of the scissors.

Someone cried out in horror, "Look, there's an ear on the floor." One woman screamed in mock alarm.

"That's not important," another replied, "he doesn't wear glasses; he'll not miss that! He has another."

"Not for long!" a wag shouted.

He heard the tinkling peal of Rose laughing amidst the hubbub. Turning his head towards the sound, he caught a fleeting glance as the lady in an adjacent chair laughed helplessly with her head across Rose's knee.

Encouraged by the appreciation, Anna turned his head roughly with her hands, "Keep still, or you'll lose something else!" flourishing the scissors between his thighs. That gesture brought the house down.

"They're off!" someone shouted and nearly stopped the show.

The ladies were rolling in the aisle, the shrieks and laughter redoubled. He sat through it all with excellent good humour, the smile never leaving his face. While Anna combed and snipped the finishing touches, someone brought a mirror. Putting it in front of his face, he screamed in mock horror, putting his hands over his ears. That was the coup de grace: they went wild with delight. Eventually, the laughter died away and everyone calmed down; the show was over. The table was laid and the meal had been prepared by two ladies, probably neighbours, who were reluctantly leaving with the other non-residents. Everyone shook his hand as they left the house. He was being offered the freedom of the city: an invitation to all three humble dwellings.

Finally, when all had been done, he stood there with 50 cigarettes of various brands: Nazionale, Populari and 20 Afrika, the quality cigarette. These small gifts expressed his welcome.

"What do I do with these?" he gestured.

"People usually smoke them but I'm delighted you don't," Rose replied, taking his offerings. "You look smart and clean cut. I'm amazed at the change. Some new clothing might improve things further and make you feel more comfortable. You know, when we first introduced ourselves, I was tempted to say 'Me Jane, You Tarzan'," they laughed together.

Anna was sweeping up the hair, listening with apparent annoyance, "Will you two please speak Italian? You, Goldilocks, what did we agree upon before I allowed you in here?"

"Signora, please accept my apology, it won't happen again. Not in your house." He ventured a kiss on her cheek, amazed at his boldness, while Anna looked at him through half shut, twinkling eyes, smiling.

"What would his wife think about that?" She was fishing but when he didn't take the bait, she let out more line, curiosity goading her on.

"You are married aren't you?" she asked, point blank.

"No," he shook his head.

That wasn't enough. She needed further proof.

"Why aren't you?" she demanded, looking at him. It lacked reason for the continuity of life itself.

"I was never asked," he shrugged, glancing at Rose, an interested spectator who was laughing soundlessly.

Anna had them both under close scrutiny, those narrow slits she had for eyes must have looked fetching once; indeed they still held a magnetic attraction. With greying hair tied in a bun at the back, her face was prematurely lined and care worn. Seeing her from behind, a man could mistake her smart petite figure for a signorina and maybe try his luck. He would get short shrift though; her eyes missed nothing.

"Come, Goldilocks," she said, taking him by the arm.

She walked with him to the table where her husband and son were already sitting, discussing the events of the day. She introduced him formally while he shook each of their hands with both of his.

"My husband, Alvaro, and my son, Mario, you've met I know. Now we all know who is addressing who at the table. You sit there

13

where I can keep an eye on you. Rosanna will sit here as guest of honour."

She seated Rose square to him so that he only had to turn his head to take her all in. Anna sat opposite him, strategically placed to watch them both. That was exactly her intention. Rose had the chair; the topics were widespread, beginning with Mario and his escape to the moment when he was almost in the net. She skilfully shifted the conversation when the actual blows had been struck. Whatever she discussed: events, farming, or livestock, she embraced everyone. He read the words from her lips, listened to the music of her voice, frequently dropping his eyes to her breasts that were trying to push their way out of her jumper. The smile never left her face. Once he met her eyes looking over the wine glass at him and felt a tightening in his chest. She sipped her wine while the others drank theirs. He watched all her mannerisms. She used her hands with good effect. He was mesmerised. Once he glanced across at Anna looking at him and felt that some comment would be appropriate.

"Signora, this food is delicious." And he meant it.

"I'm glad you can taste it. You certainly haven't seen it."

She was sharp.

When the meal was over and the lamps were lit, he listened to the arrangements being made for his safety and comfort. Rose would have a double escort (probably to ensure the escorts would have an escort). She looked more formidable than both. Alvaro and a neighbour, whom he had shaken hands with in the early evening, were ready and waiting for escort duty. Rose picked up her coat and handed it to him.

"Do you mind?" she asked amiably.

As she slipped her arms into the sleeves he found a good reason to touch her shoulders by adjusting the collar and sleeves. She turned to face him and looked straight into his eyes, then looked down at her own cheek.

"It looks like a football to me. How does it really look?"

"Like a football," he replied, laughing, "but that's just because it's been kicked. It's alright. Remember, I haven't seen you any other way. To me, that's how you are. You look good."

She held out her hand.

"Have a good night's sleep. I'll meet you by the oak trees at noon tomorrow. We'll spend the afternoon at your new quarters."
With that she was gone and he felt an empty loneliness.

*

Chapter 4

Anna led him into the storeroom where a bed had been prepared between a heap of grain and a pile of corncobs. Half a dozen hams hung from the ceiling alongside a yard of salami, two sacks of flour were firmly wedged in the corner with dusty footprints outlined on the floor. There was just about enough rations to feed the entire Fifth Battalion Northumberland Fusiliers for a month. The Germans could prolong the war six months with a cache like this.

She carried a small vessel with the wick floating in oil, generating about half candlepower and casting giant shadows on the bare walls. Placing it on a box at his bedside, she instructed him, "Put the light out when you get into bed."

"Very cosy indeed! Sheets for one night: I'm being spoiled."

"Part of the celebration, figlio. Today we have been fortunate so pretend it's your birthday. How old are you?"

"Twenty-six."

"How did you meet Rosanna?"

"She came along after the raid. I was standing by the oak trees."

"I don't think you quite realise your luck."

"Maybe I do, Signora."

She looked at him and made to go.

"Please don't hurry away," he patted the bed, "sit here and give me ten minutes of your time. There is so much I want to ask."

She sat down again immediately, to his surprise. There was obviously something that she wanted to know too.

"Ten minutes? I presume you wish to talk about Rosanna."

"Tell me she isn't rich? That was said among other things."

"No, but neither is she poor. She's too generous to be rich.

Comfortable, maybe. Are you worried she might be out of your reach?"

They could see into each other's eyes despite the dim light. At least she could read his; he couldn't quite penetrate the aperture her eyes afforded.

"I watched you looking at her. You weren't always looking at her face either. I can forgive that, I've often envied those myself," she said with startling candour. For an Italian lady, born in the last century, she was positively daring.

"You watching her didn't surprise me, I expected that. Other men have done so many times, although that was as far as they ever got. She was never interested. No, it was the way she looked at you. You couldn't see that because your eyes were completely absorbed."

"Really, Signora, she is old enough to know better," he was laughing. "Although I admit to being very flattered."

"You should be."

"Can I hold your hand?" he asked, picking it out of her lap. It felt like rough crepe, work-hardened. "I think I'm in love with you, Signora," he said, smiling.

"Well, in that case we should be on first name terms. My name is Anna. Now I'm sure that you want to talk about Rosanna. You have heard a dark secret, except it's no secret. How could it be? You have only been here a half day and you know all but the sordid details. It happened almost ten years ago." He settled back to drink in the legend of Rose Green. "There was a mayor in this town, a lecherous womaniser. Rosanna had recourse to visit his office; her work entailed such visits and she had been in and out many times before. While checking official documents at his desk, the wretched pig put his hand up her dress. Imagine a lady with an immaculate reputation, highly esteemed in the community and a miserable cretin like that attempts to violate her chastity. Feeling the hand on her thigh, she hesitated at first in disbelief, and then filled with blind indignation, she turned and pummelled that evil face with both fists before walking out of his office. She told me later that all she wanted to do was go home and take a bath. Her own hands were swollen for days afterwards."

"How did it end? Does the man still live here?" he asked intently.

"Of course not! Public opinion forced him to move within a month, but a man like that would practice his dirty exploits elsewhere," she concluded.

"She punched a German soldier today I'm told," he was quizzing.

"I don't know the facts about that, all I know is that I got my son back. I'll never be able to thank her enough."

"There has never been a man in her life?" he asked

"Not that I'm aware of. The manner in which she dealt with the mayor scared off all the young men and I rather think that pleased her. Is it going to scare you, I wonder?"

"I'm hardly likely to put my hand up her skirt, so why should it scare me?"

"I don't think you would do that. You would like to though," she challenged him.

"I would like to punch the soldier who bruised her face. It takes equal courage and equal intention. She punched him, whereas I wouldn't dare."

"I'm not so sure that you wouldn't dare. I'll have to give you careful thought. I want to find what she was looking at. I have no doubt she saw something in you that I didn't." Patting his arm, she leaned across and gently kissed his forehead. "Your ten minutes are long gone. Goodnight, figlio. Don't forget the light."

"Goodnight, Anna," he replied as she departed, leaving him alone in the dusky warmth.

He lay between smooth sheets for the first time in four years. Feeling relaxed and comfortable, he wanted desperately to stay awake. The most pleasant memory of this happy day had been watching Rose remove her coat, seeing the frame of her strong shoulders and sturdy arms and how she filled the neat white jumper. He had felt a twinge of jealousy when he saw a couple of the men looking. She had the magnetism to attract, and most certainly the power to defend. He tried to imagine her fists connecting with the mayor's face, smiling at the vision, while a dark cloud passed over him. He passed away into a deep sleep where no dreams came to visit.

When he eventually awoke, it was light; even in the storeroom where the day had access only through a very small window. He had overslept. Folding his bedding and leaving everything tidy, he took a last look around the room. He hadn't left anything because he had nothing to leave. As he entered the kitchen, Anna was moving around business-like. She cheerfully bade him good morning and pointed to his toilet water that was surprisingly hot. Although it wasn't necessary, he shaved again. They were alone in the room; the rest of the family were already about their various tasks. He breakfasted on bread, cheese and figs, while she poured two mugs of coffee; fresh-ground roast acorn, the very best home grown. Their friendship was already sealed; they had established a common trust and slept on it.

Continuing where they had left off, there was much he wanted to know. Anna, he knew, would only tell him so much and he would be happy with that.

"I told you last night that I loved you, didn't I?"

"Last night, but do you still love me this morning?" When she smiled, her eyes narrowed to slits, revealing a sly impishness.

"I'm drinking your acorn coffee. Isn't that proof?"

"You will get a taste for that, as you have acquired a taste for other things around here."

"Rosanna told me you were candid, she wasn't kidding," he laughed.

"Now you want me to tell you more about her?"

"Anna, I'm no match for you. I've been alone too long, but you'll find me a willing listener."

He watched her eyes almost disappear. She was enjoying herself.

"Rosanna intends to take care of you. My husband has gone to make arrangements for your stay with Francesco and Maria Rocco. As you sit here relaxing over coffee, no less than four people are engaged in your welfare. You are a lucky young man."

He laughed, "Anna, my shirt is falling apart. When a man loses his shirt, that is the final straw."

"Without any knowledge of why Rosanna is in town, other than attending her own affairs, I feel you will have a new one today."

"I'm looking forward to a change of fortune."

"It changed yesterday. You don't care about a shirt. You can't wait until noon."

As she sat opposite, teasing him, he could see her clearly; the fine lines around her eyes, her hair still fairly dark with streaks of grey weaving through the knot at the back. No fine fashions there.

"I would like to visit you from time to time, if that's alright Anna?" he asked

"Dear boy, I expect you to. I would like to hear first hand of Rosanna and you. I don't want to hear through idle gossip."

She took his arm and walked with him to the door. Kissing his cheek fondly she wished him luck.

With a couple of hours to spare when he arrived at the little bridge he decided on a stroll upstream.

The desperate croaking of a frog in some distress caught his attention. Suddenly, his eyes focused on a yard of snake, hanging from a bough, with the hind legs of a frog halfway down its throat. He stood watching, completely fascinated. One didn't see a spectacle of nature like this every day. Selecting a large stick, he picked it up and approached the predator. Fortunately, the stream was shallow at this point; he didn't care to start the day with cold, wet feet. With a well-aimed swipe, he caught the snake a couple of inches above the head, the impact hurling the writhing reptile three yards upstream.

The wriggling, twisting, surprised creature was most unhappy at the complete turn of events. The rubber-like jaws must have released some pressure on the frog, its croaking continued with a hint of hope. With the stick in an upright position, he stabbed at and held the writhing coil of energy, pinning it to the riverbed while the rest of the body wrapped around the stick in a spiral. The sheer strength of the squirming, whip-like creature amazed him. The way it fought before finally giving up the struggle was admirable. Indeed, he felt a trifle sad, the reptile was probably having his first meal after hibernation. Did they hibernate? He wasn't sure.

Operation Jaws of Death proved rather tricky and delicate. The mouth had to be opened wide while at the same time holding the struggling frog lest he tear the flesh of his legs on the fang.

"Stop struggling you silly sod! No wonder you got caught. Let's have an inspection. There now, you're not so bad, you lucky bastard."

Placing the frog in the stream, he watched it swim away with the current, his legs were not doing their intended job but the rest of him was working double time. His whole heart was in the escape; to anywhere. Life was real again.

"Sorry about you," he said, picking up the lifeless whip-like creature. Strange how few people liked snakes, something this size couldn't do any harm. "Well it can't now." He threw it into the stream and washed his hands like Pontius Pilate.

He strolled back to the rendezvous with only the scuffing of his boots on the track breaking the sound of silence. He was the only person on earth it seemed. He knew when it was dark, and he knew when it was light but this was the first time he had been called upon to keep an appointment. It made him realise just how little idea he had of time. This was the one and most important appointment of his life; he must not be late. In his heart, or somewhere in his chest, was a joyful ache that couldn't be suppressed. The only outlet was song and so that's what he did. He sang joyously. Two women walking towards him, carrying bundles of firewood on their heads big enough to bring a donkey to its knees, were chatting together and laughing at him while he went on singing. Stepping aside, he bid them good morning with an exaggerated bow. They almost dropped their bundles, laughing. This was a wonderful day, and it had only just begun.

At the oak trees, he didn't have long to wait. She appeared with a companion, each pushing a bicycle. He felt his heart leap as he waved to her. She responded with a most charming smile. The fellow cyclist was Alvaro, Anna's husband. He made a point of being particularly grateful to Alvaro who accepted his thanks graciously. Diplomatically handing him the bicycle and the parcel he was carrying, he bid them farewell, walking away without ceremony.

They stood a few moments in silence while he allowed his eyes to enjoy her presence. They were having a feast.

"Hello Rose," was all he could find to say.

"Jim," she replied, "open your parcel, they are for immediate use."

Standing his bike up against the tree, he proceeded to open the wrapping. With the contents in his hands, he looked at her, looking at him.

"Would you turn your back, please?"

Quickly tearing off his jacket and shirt, he donned first the vest, an actual garment from a Red Cross clothing parcel, original price:

three one-pound loaves of bread sold across the barbed wire of a prison camp. It was wool; someone had obviously stung her for this. He felt the comforting, warm, embracing smoothness. Already he felt good. The shirt came from some other branch of the black market, as did the pullover, both blue in colour. He felt he could survive another winter.

"May I turn round?" she asked, laughing.

He could see the approval in her eyes as she examined her purchases.

"We made a good buy, didn't we?"

"You did. Thank you would be appropriate except that it doesn't sound sufficient, even to my own ears."

"I'm sure it is." She was still looking fixedly at him.

"I feel so clean. You wouldn't believe how difficult it is just keeping clean."

"It will be much easier in future." She had a basket on the front of her bicycle. "You have underwear and toilet facilities in my basket. Oh yes, and socks. Now shall we proceed to your new home? The transport is only on hire, by the way. For the duration," she added, as she pushed away on her bicycle. He followed her immediately.

How exhilarating it was just riding a bicycle as he got the feel of his machine. He raced past her, braked, and turned. A strong desire to touch stirred in his chest, to touch without being deliberate. Gripping her shoulder, he propelled her forward. To his pleasure, she shrieked with delight. At an opportune moment, she did the same. The fun began in earnest; the hills echoed their laughter. Every manoeuvre that entailed physical contact was practiced. Each house they passed, the occupants came out to investigate the merriment and Rose greeted them all by name. He couldn't help noticing the obvious surprise in their returned greeting.

"There goes your reputation."

"Because I'm laughing? They've seen me laugh many times. Today I'm happy, yesterday I was sad. They know all about that too."

"You are excused sadness, but to laugh and fraternise with aliens, that infringes the Italian code of ethics, of that I'm sure. Matthew 7 verse 6 'Give not that which is holy to dogs'."

"St Matthew would never be so cruel," she replied, giving him a playful push.

His front wheel was in a rut at that precise moment. He lay, laughing helplessly on the ground, entangled with his machine. They were behaving like children and having the time of their lives. Whatever they did, laughter invoked more laughter.

Pausing by an olive grove, they leaned on the saddles of their bicycles, faces so close that he could feel her breath when she laughed. The nearness was overpowering, this was as close as he'd ever been to a woman. Leaning forward, he brushed her bruised cheek with his lips. A silence followed, a pleasant, peaceful calm. She didn't black his eyes, but just smiled and didn't even look surprised. They continued on over the hill towards three well-spaced farmhouses situated on a plateau of arable land with the mountains as a backdrop, the sharp peaks looking like cardboard cut-outs against the sky.

Two people approached as they neared his sanctuary.

"Do all your properties come in threes," he quipped.

"You noticed. There are three more, some 14 or so kilometres from here. Here will be much safer for you. Let me warn you that they have two sons, both POWs, in England. Please bear with them if their questioning sounds a little unreal, they have no comprehension. A little patience and a word of comfort would hearten them, and me," she added.

"I will do my very best."

They were an odd looking couple, Francesco and Maria Rocco. A picture-book double of Mr and Mrs Jack Spratt. Rose was welcomed with enthusiasm and respect, her face closely scrutinised amid sympathetic comment. She was duly praised for her bravery in town; Alvaro had already described the action in detail, indeed they knew more about it than she.

His own welcome was no less genuine. Shaking hands with Francesco was an easy and pleasant experience. When he held out his hand to Maria, it was completely ignored as she wrapped both arms around him, enveloping him in flesh. His face was being washed in tears. He was quite unprepared for such a reception and was not really sure if he was being smothered or drowned, but breathing in that embrace wasn't easy.

Francesco took charge of the cycles while Maria, hanging onto

Rosanna's arm and drying her eyes on her pinafore, walked between them into the house.

"You endured the welcome with extreme fortitude, thank you," she smiled.

"Well, I am a special guest, here's the proof." He stood in the doorway. "I'm going in through the front door rather than the stable door. That's a step up the social ladder."

Taking him by the arm, she laughed. It seemed their laughter and delight had only paused for the welcome.

Maria watched with surprised amusement as they walked into the house, arm in arm.

*

Chapter 5

The kitchen was a welcome sight: ivory-white tablecloth, wood fire hissing and cracking in the hearth, and the tempting smell of cooked food mingled with the aroma of herbs. Rose donned her apron, looking completely at home. She and Maria garnished and served the food, Francesco appeared with a huge jug of wine and four glasses; a festive atmosphere was in the air. Rose was beaming; his eyes wouldn't focus anywhere else but the white woollen jumper that she wore like a mould that she had been poured into. Lifting her gaze, she smiled at him while laying out the food, radiating grace and strength from her full figure and stature. There was an abundance of pleasure to be enjoyed from a body like that. At present, he could only feast his eyes while a joyful emotion raced through his chest, creating a pleasant ache; he felt it in each heartbeat. The feeling was different from the urge in his thighs that prompted him to retrieve his hat from that bedroom in Cairo.

The table placings were ideal; he just had to turn his head to look her full in the face. Her nose was perfectly straight and slightly pointed, her face haloed by a cascade of jet-black hair that fell to her shoulders, the bruise on her cheek a purple and blue hue. He was on a sight seeing tour from her waist up.

Francesco and Maria sucked the wine through mouths crammed with food while they tried to talk and laugh at the same time. His opinion was sought on a couple of disputed points; it had been a long time since anyone had bothered about his judgement. The huge jug was taken away and refilled. Rose, he observed, merely sipped her wine and he followed her example. Francesco, on the other hand, poured it down. The room was warm and comfortable, the company just perfect; he hadn't felt so good in years. The new clothing he wore gave an added boost, he couldn't remember enjoying anything so much. It was a great pleasure just to turn his head and watch her lips as she spoke. The POW subject had not as yet been mentioned, but it had to come.

A well-fed stomach is a great contributor to the pursuit of happiness; a little wine can boost the spirit. While the festivities continued, Maria had a quirk of conscience.

"We are here enjoying the best of food and wine, while our two boys might be cold and hungry." She looked across at Jim as the tears were turned to free flow. This was where he had to start earning his keep in the role of comforter.

"Nobody goes hungry where your sons are. Not only do we feed POWs in our country, we supply our own soldiers imprisoned in other lands with Red Cross food parcels. They will probably be better fed than us!"

She looked at Rose, seeking a sign of confirmation.

"He should know, Maria. The boys are in his country."

"You realise, Maria, prisoners in Britain receive the same rations as serving soldiers."

Actually he had no idea, but it was a reasonable assumption. The tears continued but the wheels were turning in her mind.

"I hope for your sake, Maria, they are not being too well fed, they might not want to come home."

Realising immediately that he had planted a fresh seed of doubt, he added, "By the same token, having sampled your cooking, I may want to stay here. This is the best meal I've ever had."

It was too, not so much the food, but the company.

They had been sitting for hours when Rose, rising from her chair, began clearing the table.

"I must get home before dark."

Maria was drying her eyes while Rose dried the dishes and discussed farming arrangements with Francesco. Jim put his hand on Maria's shoulder. It felt like warm dough.

"They really are in the safest place on earth, Maria."

She was composed, but not convinced.

He felt he had done as much comforting as was necessary. He left her to compose her own thoughts and turned to see Rose combing her hair in the mirror. It had been a long time since he had seen a woman practicing natural vanities, he was enchanted. Seeing him watching her through the mirror, she turned, smiling.

"Here, have these," she said, ruffling his hair, "I'm sure you can find a use for them."

"Do you know," he said, combing his hair in the mirror, "I hadn't seen my face for six months until yesterday."

"And you still recognise it?" she asked, laughing.

"Still the same old face."

"That's strange, it looks quite young to me."

"I can stand it if you can," they laughed together.

"Well, I must leave," she said, struggling with her coat.

He helped her find the sleeves while he had both eyes fixed on her breasts; they were like magnets.

"May I escort you to the olive grove?"

"But of course! I was afraid you weren't going to ask. In fact, I told Francesco to bring both bikes, so you see, I intended you coming along. You had better go and help him; he has drunk so much wine. I will dry Maria's eyes."

Francesco appeared from the stable with the bikes, steady as a rock, eyes twinkling with good humour. He knew he was going to enjoy living here.

Rose had her arm around Maria's fleshy shoulders, talking gaily, her strong white teeth sparkling. Their cheerfulness was so fetching that both he and Francesco joined in the laughter. This was a good day.

They duly managed to take their leave, though no one was in any particular hurry, least of all Rose. The jovial chatter and laughter lasted another half hour. They had walked fifty metres still waving and calling greetings that couldn't be heard. Looking across at each other as they walked, pushing their bikes, they broke into a fit of laughter.

"Maybe you didn't hear as we were so distant, Francesco will have a light in the window to guide you back."

"Thanks, I didn't hear."

The breeze was blowing her hair as they walked, each with their own thoughts. Their eyes met in one of many stolen glances, there was nothing of the fugitive in his easy smiling manner. The laughter was readily switched on.

"Do you ever get depressed about all this? Sleeping in stables, begging for food?" she asked kindly.

"Depressed! Good Lord no. I don't beg, I merely ask. If I had to beg, I'd rather steal, but people have been so kind. They realise the danger of helping a fugitive like me, the consequences for them could be catastrophic. I know of several farmers who have had their homes burnt to the ground and livestock taken away for just such compassion. Anyway, between you and me, I secretly enjoy the adventure: I go anywhere I please and do almost anything I want. Never in my life have I been allowed those luxuries. No barbed wire, no guns, no shells, no bombs. I don't have to carry out senseless, pointless orders. My job is staying alive and I'm good at it. I'm never depressed."

She listened with such genuine interest, hanging on to his every word; he was flattered by her attention.

"This is a wonderful evening," she remarked casually.

"Weather-wise, or good-to-be-alive, as I feel, kind of evening?" he asked.

"The good-to-be-alive kind, I think," she said smiling.

They had stopped walking. A fresh playful breeze blew a tress of jet-black hair across her face, veiling her eyes as though bringing down the curtain on act one. They had reached the olive grove. Turning to face each other, two bicycle spaces apart, both had one hand on the handlebars and the other on the saddle, leaning forward, their faces almost touching.

A fleet of bombers droned overhead, silhouettes in a darkening sky, labouring their way north, pregnant with death and destruction. In a world gone mad, bent on senseless slaughter, two unimportant little people stood alone in the wondrous delight of first love.

He simply leaned forward as she instinctively inclined her head, placing his lips on her lips; their first experience. They allowed each other to search at will: lips, eyes, ears. She let his lips play around that oh so tender swelling as if massaging the contusion with magic lotion. "Shall we park the bikes?" He suggested.

"If you wish."

In that moment, a convoy of German transport travelling south on the road just 30 yards away invaded their dreams and broke the spell. Daytime travel was a nightmare, the RAF swept the roads clean of most traffic; anything that moved was a target.

"I think it's time for you to leave. I enjoyed having your arms around me, however briefly. We can try again, maybe next time we won't be interrupted," she said.

"They won't bother about me, you know, I'm very small fry."

"We'll play safe, she said, and enjoy tomorrow."

When they kissed goodnight, he felt her tongue touch his.

It was so full of promise, he told himself he was reading too much into her action, she was a lady highly esteemed, wherever she went people treated her with the utmost respect. He was flattered by her attentions but he couldn't forget the thrill of the moment. It was a first time experience, for them both. He peddled off into the darkness without fully realising what had happened.

Riding a bike on a rutted track in the dark was anything but fun. Twice he hit the ground before deciding to walk. As he breasted the hill, he saw the light in the window. With a wild whoop, he jumped onto his cycle and made straight for the light like a homing pigeon.

*

Chapter 6

Lying between white sheets and wearing clean underwear in a room to himself was a luxury that had to be experienced to be appreciated. Sleep was a joke, he just wanted to lie there and soak up the pleasure, to review this wonderful day in retrospect. What he actually did was black out, falling into a deep sleep where the day's events came back to him in a tangled web of dreams all intertwined in confusion.

He awoke to the sound of a restless rattling of chains and the sympathetic commiserations of Francesco's voice. One of his animals must be in some distress. Except for another bed, the room was completely bare; not a picture on the wall, not a rug on the floor. Exactly what he wanted: space to exercise and get fit, to be able to feel the pleasure of breathing from the bottom of his lungs again. He swung out of bed on that fine March morning. Dressing hastily in his new clothes, he ventured through into a deserted kitchen. The top section of the stable door was open as the sound of voices drifted through to him. Walking across and resting his arms on the lower door, he was enthralled to see two small feet sticking out of the rear end of an ox while Francesco and Maria were assisting at the birth. Actually, they were letting nature take its course with a pat and a kindly word to the mother. The animal replied in a low-pitched moaning moo.

"Should we give a gentle pull to help it along?" he heard Maria ask.

"No, I'm sure she'll manage herself," Francesco replied.

He watched in wondrous awe as the head of a calf appeared, quite suddenly, as though it had been ejected. There on the floor lay the wet, slimy, steaming creature. Francesco began rubbing it clean with handfuls of straw while Maria attended to the head. The mother turned and joined in the cleaning of her offspring. All attention was focused on this brand new, stupefied, bewildered, bundle of life. As though he had called to them, they turned in unison, looking towards him and beckoning him to join in the rejoicing. Smiling happily, he walked into the stable, congratulating them on the happy event. They had increased their wealth by 25%; they had four oxen, now there were five.

"Have you seen anything like this before?" Maria asked.

"This is the very first! I am grateful to have witnessed such a miracle. It was a scene I'll remember always. There were feet, then a head and suddenly, this living creature. I would like to see him have his first feed."

Moving towards the kitchen, Maria said, "We all need our first feed."

"Open that tin of English coffee, Maria," Francesco called after her, "by way of a celebration." Looking at Jim, "This can be a double celebration: you, Rosanna and the calf," he added.

Actually, it sounded like a triple. He wondered why he had said 'you and Rosanna'. Did it look so obvious? He was flattered, but surprised.

"Will he feed before breakfast do you think, Francesco?"

He remembered once seeing some piglets being born; they wasted no time at all and didn't need any signposts. This little fellow was completely lost and, unlike the piglets, he was in no hurry.

"Come, let us have breakfast. He'll soon find where to go for his."

The kitchen was permeated with the aromatic odour of percolating coffee. He had seen one miracle, the birth of the calf, here was another: on the table sat a tin of coffee from a Red Cross parcel while the nearest prison camp had been 60 miles away; it could only happen in Italy.

After a most invigorating cold bath and shave, he stood in front of the mirror, putting the finishing touches to his appearance with the comb.

Francesco framed himself in the doorway. "Caught you!" he laughed. "Did you enjoy your bath?"

"Luxury indeed, Francesco. I must compliment the padrona. I didn't expect en suite."

"Now's your chance, she's here. Come and join the welcoming party."

Restraining an impulse to rush out and meet her, he simply followed his host outside just as she was pulling into the yard, driving a handsome bay pony around 12 hands high and drawing the most elegant tub-shaped rig done in polished oak.

Taking her hand as she stepped down, his heart shifted into a higher gear.

"Jim," was all she said, making it sound like a caress.

Greeting Maria with a hug and a kiss, she led everyone around to the pony.

"I want you to meet my Brunita. Isn't she beautiful? A little fat maybe because she doesn't get enough exercise. I'm afraid to take her out; some high-ranking German officer might take a fancy to the whole outfit. He would quite simply take it off me; a present for his wife or daughter. I would be left with a useless slip of paper."

She had a most impressive and captivating manner of embracing everyone as she spoke.

"Do you like my Brunita?" she asked.

"It was love at first sight."

Maria told her about the calf. She gave a little cry of joy, nibbling her fingers.

"I really must see him," she said.

As they moved towards the stable laughing and talking, the pony followed, pulling the trap. Rose turned, nudging Jim, she pointed to her pride and joy.

"Look at my Brunita. She wants to see everything," she said, kissing the muzzle and rubbing its head. "You won't get through the door pulling that, my little darling. Francesco will release you later, then you can spend the whole afternoon eating hay."

Lifting his gaze above the pony's head, he knew what he was looking at, but there was no reason for it. Taking her arm in his hand he asked, "What do you make of this, Rose?"

She looked at him and followed his gaze, giving a little sigh of dismay.

"I don't like it, but I can deal with it," she replied as Maria and Francesco joined them apprehensively.

She placed a comforting hand on Maria's shoulders. They were looking anxiously at a German Opel three-ton transport truck approaching.

"Hide in the stables, Jim," she said calmly, "and whatever happens, don't attempt any heroics."

He moved into a stall and stood in the shadows, out of sight. Selecting a vantage point, he watched two soldiers alight from the truck. One was a sergeant, carrying an MP-40 sub-machine gun as though they slept together. He was a hefty man, built along the lines of a carthorse, accompanied by a private who was unarmed and less formidable in looks but a threat nevertheless.

They held no terror for Rose as she walked boldly to meet them, followed somewhat less fearlessly by his hosts. He was getting his first view of her rear: squared shoulders, straight back and a well-rounded bottom. She looked like a feast. He was patiently awaiting an invitation to partake. She walked towards them so vigorously it looked as if they were in danger of being knocked down. The soldiers touched their caps respectfully on her approach. Words were spoken and all appeared to be going smoothly. Francesco lead the way towards the house; so far so good. The danger signals went up when the sergeant tried slipping his arm around her waist. Evading the move gracefully, with the minimum of fuss, she didn't appear to be perturbed but the move set an alarm bell ringing in his ears. He moved swiftly towards the adjoining doors to the kitchen, placing them strategically just an inch ajar, providing him with a wide view of the kitchen table; the usual target of scroungers. He had a sick feeling that these boys had other things in mind. He moved away as they entered the kitchen laughing boisterously and talking just a little too loud. How was he going to prove himself worthy of this woman? The odds weren't in his favour. The moment of truth was fast approaching and he had no clear idea, no plan; he was clueless. Wringing his hands in anguish and moving furtively again towards the adjoining doors, he weighed up the situation: it wasn't impossible. Both soldiers sat with their backs to him, pouring wine into their faces. Francesco was kept busy with the wine jug while Maria nervously served plates of bread, cheese and salami. Rose sat opposite, seemingly unflustered, conversing with them in German and sipping her wine with cool assurance. Maybe food was all they wanted, he thought doubtfully. The gun was lying on the chair next to the sergeant's right hand. He was desperately searching for any small chance. Stealthily moving away from the door, he looked for a suitable weapon while the calf was enjoying his first feed on earth. Normally, he would have enjoyed the spectacle but his mind was racing in spiralling circles. Picking up a stout wooden shaft, he tried a couple of practice swings. Should break a couple of heads, at least, he thought, praying that he wouldn't have to use it. The laughter was booming louder, the talk more bombastic. Moving back to his observation post, he was just in time to see the sergeant making his first move. He reached across the table and grabbed Rose's hand. She smiled as if she was enjoying his touch, keeping up the conversation in congenial spirit, while her warm, tender hand was held in that vice. He crouched behind the door, admiring her courage while he himself was falling apart.

Shaking with fear, throat like sandpaper, an awful pissy feeling playing around his crotch: Jim was a mess. How on earth was he going to justify any right to kiss this fearless Amazon, to caress her body or hope to fulfil the promise in her eyes, when just three yards away she was being man-handled by a gorilla? She managed to slip her hand free. Standing up, she calmly moved back from the table. He was filled with admiration, she showed no visible signs of fear. The sergeant, inflamed with lust, reached across to grab her. The other soldier made a half-hearted attempt to restrain him, receiving a punch in the face for his efforts. He backed off meekly. There would obviously be no trouble from that quarter, which only left King Kong. Making to move round the table towards her, his movements were clumsy and without timing, in vino veritas. He stumbled over the chair, knocking the gun to the floor, which nobody noticed as all eyes were fearfully upon the sergeant. Stealing a fleeting glace at Rose through the door, she of everybody taking part in the drama was most calm. Well, it's now or never! He was sure he had spoken aloud.

Without further thought, he opened the doors and sprang across the floor, swinging the club in one singular movement. The shaft connected as the victim instinctively turned his head. The blow smashed across his ear and cheek like the sound of a butcher chopping meat. The vibrant impact transferred through the shaft into his arms. Exhilaration replaced fear. Almost in the same movement, he aimed a second blow at the other soldier who was already scrambling under the table. The club connected with a chair, shattering the back, sending it spinning towards the stable doors.

"Dirty bastards!"

He heard someone shouting, not realising it was he himself. Flinging the club at the soldier under the table, he grabbed the gun. Fingering the trigger in his haste, he released a burst of fire. From screaming chaos, the whole room fell silent. Only Maria's sobs could be heard. Everyone stood petrified. There were pieces of masonry on the floor and bullet holes in the wall just 2 ft from Rose. She stood motionless, the pallor of her face the only sign of emotion, while they looked at each other for an eternity.

"You missed," she said, with a tremor in her voice.

The smile she offered died on her lips.

"Clumsy wasn't I," he replied by way of an apology, "I'm usually very good with these things. The safety catch should have been on. I can't find it; it's got to be somewhere. We'll have to do something about this fellow," indicating the prostrate sergeant, "or he'll bleed to death. And what about our friend here under the table?" he said, kicking the soldier's foot as he waved the gun, beckoning him to come out.

He complied immediately, placing his hands on his head.

"Ask him where the safety catch is on this thing or tell him that I'll shoot his balls off."

"I'm not sure about the German for 'shoot his balls off'," she smiled, "but I will ask him about the safety catch." After conversing with the soldier, she turned back to Jim and replied, "The soldier said something about a bolt lock."

"Bolt lock! Ah, I really should have found it without asking. Well, well, what will these Germans think of next. You take it and keep an eye on him," he said, handing her the gun.

"I can't use this!"

"You won't have to, but I bet you could," he chuckled.

He watched her wave the gun at the soldier while speaking to him. The soldier then sat on a chair and began removing his boots, cap and tunic. Jim could only look at her in admiration.

Turning the stricken soldier to a half prone position, he gasped, "God! Look at this man's face. It looks like a raspberry tart. Francesco," he called, "towel and a dish of water please. Maria, do you have cognac and clean bandages?"

Soaking the towel in the water, he held it to the wound. Taking the brandy and strips of cloth which Maria offered, she enquired, "He's not dead is he?"

"No Maria. You're alright, aren't you, you dirty old man? Why didn't you just go to a bordello and save us all this trouble?"

"Do you think we can move him, Jim? I have a plan that could straighten out this mess. We don't want any repercussions or reprisals."

"Get thinking, Rose. Whatever you say, I haven't got a clue."

Covering the man's eyes with the towel, he poured the spirit onto the raw flesh, causing the unconscious soldier to jolt reflexively.

"That penetrated his subconscious alright. I felt it and I was only pouring. Let's take a look at his eyes. God, it's like looking at a dead fish. Tell that soldier I need some help, Rose."

The man complied smartly with her request and they managed to prop him against the wall in a sitting position, the private supporting him while Jim bandaged the wound.

"Well the bleeding's stopped. I'll leave one eye uncovered in case he wakes up and thinks he's dead." He was actually enjoying himself. "This fellow will do anything you want, Rose. He's still not sure of getting away with his life."

"I want to talk to him for a few minutes," she said. "Can you drive the truck?"

"I think so."

He watched with admiration as she took command.

"Francesco, bring Brunita and the trap to the door. Take care of the sergeant, Maria." She called the soldier over and began questioning him and giving instructions. After two or three minutes conversing, she dismissed the soldier and called Jim. He obeyed without question, the same as everyone else, with no idea of what she had in mind.

"Here, take this gun, Jim, I don't like it at all."

Francesco reported back, he had the pony and trap ready and waiting outside. She ordered the soldier to help with the wounded man and Maria volunteered too; she wanted them out of her house. Struggling with the 15 st hulk, half dragging him to the door, they eventually got him outside.

"Now then, you!" it sounded like a command, "put on this tunic and cap. There, let me have a good look. You are the most handsome German I have ever seen."

"Good fit, isn't it," he laughed.

"Now listen carefully to what I want you to do. Take the truck and follow the road north for maybe 6 or 7 km. Keep your eye on the clock and check the distance. Turn left when you reach the river. After less than 1 km, you will cross the bridge. Are you following me?" she asked.

"Oh yes, I'm following you, but I hope the RAF don't follow me!"

"Once across the bridge, follow the road for 4 km. Now listen carefully, because this is the one place you can go wrong."

"I'm listening carefully, Rose. This is my life we're playing with. Now what about you? How will you get rid of this headache? Why not put them in the truck and I'll drop them off along the way"

"Just do as you're told," she tapped his nose with her finger. "Do your job and I can promise that everything else will work out alright. Now, further instructions, 4 km from the bridge and 2 before you reach the village which you will see as you are travelling, keep looking to your left, there will be two tar barrels, one at each side of the entrance to a good dirt road. Take that road for 2 km and don't worry if you think that you are in the middle of nowhere, because you will be. You will have the mountains in front for perhaps 1 km, and then the road will swing north. One km further on you will see three houses at two o'clock. Park the vehicle as close to the ravine as possible. Three fig trees will indicate the spot. Oh and get rid of the cap and tunic or you will scare them to death. They will probably hide when they see the truck. Go to the middle one of the three farmhouses. Elvira and Bruno Rea are the occupants; Elvira is my life-long friend

from childhood. Just say Rosanna sent you and a welcome is assured."
She pulled him towards her by the lapels of his tunic, kissing him full
on the lips, just as Maria entered the kitchen.

She neither stepped back nor looked embarrassed, just stood there
looking into his face; nor did Maria look surprised.

"Ready when you are, Rosanna." She looked at Jim, "He's a
good-looking German, isn't he," she laughed.

"Just five more minutes, Maria. I'm giving him his instructions."

"Yes, I can see that!" Maria said, turning to leave the room.

Taking his arm, she led him into the stables.

"Let me introduce you to some of my friends. This is Palomella.
How are you today, my dear? I've brought a friend to meet you. Jim,
this is Palomella."

"Delighted to meet you, Palomella."

"And this is Capponola, isn't she beautiful?"

"Indeed she is," he replied, looking into her face and joining whole-
heartedly in the cow play.

She lowered her voice,

"Giardina, my favourite. I wouldn't like the others to hear."

He whispered a reply, "I won't breathe a word. They'll never get
to know from me."

Laughing together, enjoying the cattle show, "Viola and her little
darling." The bewildered calf stood by his mother.

"What a beautiful baby, I would love to cuddle him. Has he had
his first feed, I wonder?"

"I can assure you, Rose, that he has. He was nuzzling while the
soldiers were guzzling."

"I feel happy. Everything must go well because I have faith in
you. You love animals. They are beautiful, aren't they?"

"Well, I enjoyed the cow carnival and I've never seen more
contented cows. In fact, I enjoyed the whole guided tour, it was a
very pleasant diversion."

She smiled, holding his arm close to her breast.

"That basket Maria brought into the kitchen was a picnic hamper.
I had the time and the place all planned." They walked outside, arm
in arm. "Just a few final instructions, when you reach your destination,
let them strip the vehicle of whatever they need, then dispose of it

into the ravine." She held out her hand, "Goodbye, and please come back safe. We'll meet by the oak trees, one week from today, at noon."

"Why a week?"

"Just to be safe. I would like us to have our picnic. Trust me."

"I do trust you. Implicitly. There is no one else I can turn to."

Looking across at the rig, he shouted out loud, "Bloody Germans!"

"Bloody Germans," she echoed.

Their laughter was infectious. All but the sergeant joined in the merriment as he lay, still unconscious, in the rig that appeared low on its springs.

Giving an exaggerated salute, he turned toward the vehicle. Everyone returned his farewell, even the soldier; he was happy to be alive, whatever the outcome. Climbing into the cab at the wrong side was the first mistake. All eyes were on him, increasing his anxiety to get moving. Everything was in reverse order: steering wheel on the left, gear lever on the right, where the hell was the starter! He was searching like a blind man. At last he found the right button, there was an immediate response as the engine sprang to life. He was on his way. With half an acre in which to turn the vehicle, he almost hit the well. "Whoops!" he said to himself, laughing, "I nearly stopped their tap." Waving nonchalantly as he straightened out the vehicle, he began grinding through the gears.

"Hell," he said, "I'll be lucky to reach the road at this rate."

He got the truck moving smoothly, but running on the wrong side of the road; only realising this when the wheels of Italian commerce in the shape of a mule pulling a huge cart came towards him on the same side.

*

Chapter 7

Gradually getting the feel of the vehicle, he began shedding his anxieties. A staff car approached at speed, he kept his eyes on the road as they passed. He was completely ignored; not even a sign from the driver. Six km on the clock, and moving like a dream, he approached the bridge spanning a swift flowing river. Spring was a half moon away. He passed a convoy of five vehicles dead centre of the bridge travelling south; each truck had a lookout scanning the sky. A wise and necessary practice since allied planes dominated the sky and controlled the roads. One of the lookouts acknowledged him in passing and he duly returned the compliment. Putting his foot down to negotiate the hill, he almost planted the vehicle into the embankment as he overshot the bend.

"Who the hell is the enemy here?" he said, fighting to get the truck back on an even keel and keep the speedometer at a steady 30; she only told him to get there, it didn't matter when.

With the village in his sights, he began his search for the tar barrels marking the turn off. He eventually caught sight of them from the corner of his eye, someone had thoughtfully added an extra daub of whitewash. He turned in on the road to nowhere, feeling more relaxed, letting the vehicle roll along with the mountains in front that wore large brown patches on the lower slopes.

The movement of the vehicle lulled him into reverie. He had weathered a bad winter with little difficulty, had met with exceptional good fortune, and was still in excellent health. A month here, a week there, countless one-night sleepovers; there was always shelter over the next hill, and there were countless hills and countless valleys reaching from the mountains to the Adriatic. Villages clung to each hill top in parallel chains, sprawling up the hillside in desperation.

Some just looked as though they had been put there without thought. He roamed at will enjoying his tenuous freedom. In summer, Italy was a wonderland of sunshine and breath-taking scenery: gently flowing streams meandering through sun-lit valleys and hazy illusions hanging curtain-like between earth and sky. In winter, he ploughed through snow-covered countryside when the rippling streams became raging torrents and the wonderland showed another face. He had graduated from straw beds and stables to his own room, from rags to warm clean underwear and brand new clothing. And now he had found a woman like the one he had seen a hundred times in his dreams, the kind of woman that every man was desperately looking for. He couldn't believe his luck.

The track swung north with the mountains on his left. The three farm houses were exactly where she had said they would be. Pulling up between the gnarled fig trees, just 10 yards from the edge of the ravine and 100 from the buildings, he dismounted and walked to the edge, inspecting the drop. It was ideal for pushing German vehicles over, he was going to enjoy himself. Turning to walk back, he detected movement around the farm yard. Doffing cap and tunic, he threw them into the cab and picked up the weapon. What a handy little gun, he was becoming quite fond of it without having fired a shot, except by accident. Navigating a straight course to his objective, he found the place deserted. They must be at home: where could anybody go from here? He felt a presence in the house and knocked on the door but got no reply, then tried the other two houses with the same result. If fear was the reason, the well was obviously the favoured spot, he could be seen from there. Someone would be brave enough to approach. Within minutes, an old woman draped in black came towards him carrying a jug and glass. All he could see of her as she poured a glass of wine was a walnut face and veined hands.

"Tedesco?" she asked, handing him the wine.

"English," he replied. "Please don't be afraid. I would like to speak to Elvira Rea, I have a message from Rosanna Verde."

"Rosanna Verde! You know Rosanna?"

The old lady was delighted.

"Follow me," she said, and lead him towards the house.

The magic word 'Rosanna' opened all doors. Elvira hurried to meet him, lest she get pushed out. They formed a ring. He was encircled. Trapped. Holding out his hand to Elvira (he knew her without any description. She was about Rosanna's age and height, maybe a couple of stones heavier), she took his hand, smiling.

"I'm Jim Corner. Rosanna and I have had a rather unpleasant experience with the Germans at Casa Rocco."

With her eyes on the gun, she asked, "Did you shoot them? Is that why you're here?"

He was sure she wanted him to say yes.

"No, I injured one. This is his gun and that is their vehicle. Rosanna sent me here until it is safe for me to return. The truck is to be pushed into the ravine when you have taken from it whatever you need."

His last words caused a stir of excitement. She was giving him a thorough physical examination with her eyes, trying to connect him with Rose, while the other ladies were already match-making quite unashamedly.

"We would be delighted to have you stay. You are most welcome. This is my husband, Bruno."

He shook hands with Bruno who was about 2 in shorter and 2 in wider than his wife. He became involved in handshakes all round, even with a one-year-old child who had been brought to meet him. The old lady kissed his cheek, she had first claim.

"My husband wants to know when you would like to strip the vehicle," Elvira asked.

He could see the men waiting for the word go.

"Now, if they will be so kind. Sooner the better; it might attract aircraft."

It was about to attract spanners and screwdrivers. Within seconds, he was the only man among a half a dozen women. Bruno was organising the demolition squad while Elvira screamed her own orders at him, laughing good-naturedly. She took him by the arm,

"You've started something here, haven't you. They are locusts; there will be nothing left when they are finished. Come, let me serve you refreshments. Will coffee be alright? It's our own brand."

All the ladies invited themselves; this was a special occasion.

They talked quite openly as the throng moved amiably towards the house, speculating.

"He looks a bit young for Rosanna," one said while another felt his arm.

"He's solid enough," was her verdict, "I think they make a pair."

They were discussing him as though he wasn't there.

"Don't heed them, Jim," Elvira turned to him, smiling, "they are match-making. What else would a woman talk about here? How is Rosanna? We heard that she flattened two German soldiers and they left their mark."

"How did you hear about that way out here? It only happened a few days ago. She's fine though, a little bruised."

There was a scraping of chairs as they claimed their vantage points around the table, shuffling as close to Elvira and her guest as possible.

"Thankfully we are isolated here, but news filters through. Don't be surprised at whatever you hear in the next few days. You would also be wise to ignore half of it. Look at the welcoming committee," she indicated to the ladies, "it would appear that everyone wants coffee. What they really want is to hear something meaty about you and Rosanna. They'll have the two of you walking up the aisle in less than an hour."

He could tell that he was about to experience a rather severe interrogation.

"How friendly are you and Rosanna?" Elvira asked, point blank.

"I'm a friend. The same way you are, no more. She doesn't encourage men, but then you probably know more about that than I do."

"She has fought one or two off, and dismissed a couple of opportunists mistaking her generosity. She hasn't discouraged you. Where did you get those new clothes?" she asked.

"Rosanna bought them," he replied briefly.

This set off a buzz of speculation around the table. They were satisfied with the grilling so far. There was no need to fire a broadside; the hostess was doing a good job.

"You will probably have observed that my clothes are superior to my station," she smiled slyly, "Rosanna and I shop at the same store.

She wears them first. Once I could wear them straight from her wardrobe, now I have to get busy with needle and thread. Each year I use more thread."

Everyone joined in the laughter.

"Well the extra weight looks good on you."

"I'll pour this coffee over you? Since when did fat look good?"

"Comfortable," he corrected.

Indicating a pretty young woman at the table, she said, "This is Maria, she hasn't taken her eyes off you since you arrived. I'll give you fair warning since you'll be with us for a few days, she's looking for a boyfriend."

"Fighting them off will be your problem, Maria. Not looking for them," he said.

"There are no young men of my age. They are all away fighting the war," she said.

"They will be back within the year and you can have your pick," he assured her.

"Do you have a wife?" she asked.

"No."

The audience were hanging onto this youthful intercourse.

"I'll bet you've done it to lots of girls."

Six pairs of ears waited for his reply. Six pairs of eyes were upon him. He could feel them thinking, "Give us a juicy bone to chew on."

"Haven't you?" she persisted.

He was waiting for Elvira to come to his rescue, but she too was listening, full of interest.

"I didn't realise Italian ladies pursued this line of conversation," was his reply, appealing once again.

Maria was mildly chastised and promptly dispatched to report on the men's progress with the vehicle. After another couple of hours of questions and answers, Bruno arrived with a timely rescue, his face beaming with pleasure.

"Ready for the big drop, Jim," he said, rubbing his hands with glee. "Everyone is invited, ladies, the show's on the road."

They all marched out in carnival mood, the lady of the well labouring along, pleading for an arm to lean on. Nobody took the slightest heed, all were anxious for a front seat at the cliff-top drama. One didn't see a vehicle plunge into a ravine every day, only at the cinema. Detaching himself from the happy crowd, he waited until the old lady doggedly caught up, offering his arm for support with exaggerated chivalry.

"Allow me, Signora. Or is it Signorina? May I escort you to the fair, then afterwards, who knows."

She laughed, exposing a perfect set of gums with not a single tooth to spoil the effect. Pulling his arm tight to her bony frame, she giggled, "Who knows indeed. There's still a couple of good romps left in me. I could surprise you."

"I'll bet you could too."

"Now that we are going steady, we should be on first names. My name is Anna, I already know yours, young man. Since you will be staying here a few days, I would like you to call and take me for a stroll. I am treated too kindly by some, as if I was 100 years old. The rest act as though I am a five-year-old moron. Now if I were to be courted by a handsome young man, and I'm sure Rosanna wouldn't mind, maybe there would be a change of heart. We would at least make them look."

"Indeed we will, Anna. Indeed we will. I will look forward to that, walking arm in arm, just the two of us."

The little gathering turned as one, welcoming their approach, while Anna repeated the whole scenario word for word, like a schoolgirl. Walking her into the spotlight, he stepped aside, bowing with exaggerated gallantry, making her day.

Tilted at a 30° angle, ready for the big drop, teetered the skeleton of the truck that he could hardly recognise anymore. Every detachable part had been taken off and loaded into a cart with as much again lying on the ground for a second trip. Nothing saleable was overlooked. The salvage would bring prosperity to the tiny community; every nut and bolt would find a buyer. Bruno took Anna by the arm while everyone merrily joined in for the final heave, all wanting to be there at its demise.

The truck simply disappeared over the edge. It brought cheers and laughter that almost drowned the crunching, echoing crash as the ravine claimed its share of the spoils. The fortunes of war were hauled away to be shared, stored and eventually traded. This was a profitable day for the residents of Via Viale. He was particularly pleased with his contribution to their good fortune plus a donation to the war effort: one less enemy truck.

*

Chapter 8

A pleasant voice hailed him from the cart: "Captain Jim," a boy called, waving his stick, showing off his skills with a team of oxen.

"My son has just promoted you," Elvira smiled, "Captain is a more worthy rank."

Italy of 1944 had the best grapevine in the world. News was wafted through the air without the aid of telegraph, heliograph, radio or transport. Some rumours were credible; indeed most carried a semblance of truth. While Jim had simply driven a truck a few kilometres with orders to get rid of it, actually trading it for a week's board and lodging, Captain Jim on the other hand had single-handedly ambushed a German vehicle, killed four soldiers, driven 50 km through road blocks and check points, eventually arriving in this vicinity, specifically to gather secret information that he would duly radio back to London. At present he was arranging an air drop of special equipment.

Listening to Anna's tales of her courting days had been a revelation and a pleasure. He could only see her as she was now, but in her youth two young men had pursued her, both competing for her hand in marriage. She had laughed, danced and made eyes at more than a dozen others. Hard work had taken its toll; she was 70 and looked 90. She had willingly told him of the life and loves of Anna Ambrosini. A life of toil ahead and an irrepressible zest to live it to the full, she had grasped at it with both hands and both suitors, experiencing intimacy with both lovers, several times, before making her choice.

"Indeed," she laughed as she related the story, "I was never sure which of the two was father to my eldest son. There were no doubts about the other three."

Returning from their walk on the third day (they never went more than half a kilometre), Dante, Elvira's son, came running breathlessly to meet them, clearly excited.

"Captain Jim," he called by way of warning, "Signor Rossini is waiting for you, and he has a gun."

Anna was anxious for him. "Maybe we had better continue walking," she said, alarmed.

"No, I think we can even up the odds. Dante, you know where I keep my gun because you've been playing with it."

"Captain, I haven't touched the gun."

He was clearly lying.

"Never mind, it's in my bed. The magazine is hidden in the pillowcase. Just bring them here without being seen."

He watched the boy hurry away. He had been practicing and getting a feel for the gun himself and had concealed it in a certain position under the bedclothes. It had definitely been moved. The boy promptly returned with the gun and magazine wrapped in a towel.

"Thanks for the warning, Dante." He took the gun and magazine, slipping it on in a single movement.

"He's talking to two men beside the well. Watch him Captain," Dante warned.

"You stay here with Anna. Look after her."

"Oh Captain, come on!" This was a military operation and he fully intended being there at the kill. The policeman was going to die.

"You won't miss anything because there will be no shooting."

He approached, gun at the ready just in case. The men at the well saw him and waved as he approached. The policeman turned, smiling, holding out his hand, greeting him like an old friend.

"Captain Jim," he beamed good-naturedly.

Jim took the hand, there was no reason not to. With pencil moustache, large nose and a larger stomach, he looked exactly like an old-time stage villain.

"I've called to see if you are comfortable here. I can fix you up with more convenient quarters and supply you with much of the information you seek: ammunition dumps, petrol stores, whatever target you want."

"Thank you, Signor, I'm truly grateful. We can have a serious discussion about this at the weekend. Assuming of course, that my orders stand. I could be summoned north at a moment's notice. You understand of course, all secret information would have to be confirmed but I am grateful for your offer. Your name will not go without mention. What is your name, sir?"

"Rossini, Captain. Alberto Rossini. Please call on me if you need anything. My office is in the village."

"I will, Alberto. Goodbye and thank you."

The Fascist rode off on his motorcycle. He would have to be of some use to the Germans to rate a motorbike: the man was obviously looking for a bolthole. Dante and Anna had appeared on the scene.

"Ah, Anna, will ten minutes give you time to prepare the coffee? I am really looking forward to it."

"How about a drop of cognac in it?" she asked with a sly wink.

"Will that not kill the taste of the acorns?" he asked.

"That's the idea," she replied, chuckling as she walked off.

He and Dante walked into the house together.

"Hello Captain, been courting?" Elvira laughed, her strong arms up to the elbows in dough.

"That looks good, Elvira," he said, looking at her generous figure and handsome face with pleasure.

"I'm trying to tempt your appetite," she replied. "When you first came, I thought I was feeding a pig, now you're not eating at all. Maybe Rosanna isn't eating either I hope, then I can look forward to a couple of good summer dresses on her next visit."

"Why should she lose her appetite?"

"Why should you? You can't wait until Friday, can you?"

He waited for her to continue the conversation, but she wasn't forthcoming. He walked into his bedroom. Now that the boy had access to the gun, he was anxious to find a new convenient hiding spot. Looking around the room, he decided in the meantime to carry it with him.

Walking back into the kitchen, he watched her cutting the dough into loaf-sized portions.

"I don't want Dante playing with that gun," she said, "and if you hide it here, he'll find it."

"Yes, I know. I'll ask Anna if she'll keep it safe for me."

"By the way, where have you two arranged to meet?" she asked.

"Friday at noon, by the oak trees. She may not be there," he added.

"If there is a thunderstorm at noon on Friday," she said, "Rosanna will be standing under the trees with two umbrellas and dry clothing for you. You can bet your life on that."

"Well, nobody knows her better than you," he said hopefully.

"Not even her mother. If she said she'll be there, she will be."

Elvira was hanging out the washing as he returned from his morning run.

"Good morning, buffone," she called, laughing heartily, "Rosanna has found herself a clown. You are crazy."

Laughing as he ran past her, into the stables, he emerged carrying a bucket. She laughed as only a jolly, plump person can.

"Now he's going to drain the well. Maria..." she called. Maria was at the well drawing water. "I thought you were interested in him when he first arrived."

"Interested in this clown!" Maria replied, balancing a large pitcher of water on her head like a stage juggler. "He prefers old women."

"Older ones anyway," Elvira agreed.

Watching Maria with open admiration, her beauty was free from the Hollywood influence: no make-up, just natural beauty, long eyelashes and features a film star would envy. Their eyes met in the friendliest of smiles.

"Maria," he said, "you are the most beautiful girl I've ever seen."

"How on earth would you know? You've never even looked!"

"Ah, but you never caught me looking. A man would have to be blind not to look at you."

"Buffone, you are crazy," she echoed Elvira's words, obviously delighted with the compliment though.

Everybody in the community thought so too, since they had watched him running and skipping every day with more than amused interest. He had been teaching the three youngest children to skip. One little girl of eight years or so had caught on, delighting her mother and causing a little jealousy among the others. Were it not for the restlessness within him, this was the happiest time of his life. He was welcome in any of the houses and always at ease with his ever considerate host and hostess.

The following day, Dante and he went out riding on the two donkeys.

The donkeys didn't appear to have any owners. They just roamed at will around the countryside, coming into the farmyard to shelter at night in a lean-to alongside carts, ploughs and other miscellaneous farming equipment. Wherever they happened to be, two thick crusts of bread brought them ambling towards the donor. They didn't object to being ridden so long as they moved at their own pace, which was slow and stop, particularly if they happened upon anything edible. The cool fresh day was peacefully silent. The war must be going on in some far off land, not just 40 km south of these snow-clad mountains. Only the plodding, scraping shuffle of unshod hooves broke the stillness, along with Dante's insatiable curiosity for guns.

"How many Germans have you killed, Captain," he asked.

"Oh, two or three I suppose."

That sounded reasonable.

"Only two or three!" He was disappointed.

"Three is an above average number," Jim explained as simply as possible. "Think about it; if every soldier killed three enemy soldiers then the war would be over long ago. All the artillery, tanks and aeroplanes that account for two thirds of the casualties wouldn't be necessary. But if you think I haven't done enough, then I'll resign."

"Resign? Does that mean that you won't be a soldier any more?"

The prospect seemed to delight the boy.

"Their loss, Dante, not mine."

"Good," he was grinning like a split melon, "Then you could come and live with us. We have plenty of food here and you'll be safe."

"That's the best offer I've ever had. I wonder what your father and mother would say?"

Their fiery steeds had spotted a patch of green shoots and lumbered their way towards them. The riders would have to sit through their lunch break or get off and walk, which is what Dante decided to do. Slipping off the rope halters, the steering mechanism that rarely had any desired effect, they strode back home together.

"Do you attend school?" Jim asked.

"I've resigned," he replied seriously. He liked the word. "I'm nearly 12, and I read and write quite well. There is no school anyway, nobody goes anymore."

"Have you got books at home?"

"Of course."

"Will you read for me sometime?"

"I'll be glad to because I'm a good reader," he said confidently.

He was a very amiable boy, never a complaint, and gentle with animals too. That was the first thing he had noticed. He regarded them as friends, as equals.

"Are you going to stay with us then, Captain?" he asked.

"I have to leave on Friday in any case. I'm still a soldier you know, I have to obey orders. I haven't resigned yet."

"I heard Mother say that you could stay as long as you want."

"We'll see, Dante. We'll see."

As they walked towards the house, a bicycle was placed precisely beside the door.

"I'll bet it's your 12th birthday, and somebody's bought you a bicycle, Dante."

"That's the mayor's bike," Dante said casually.

"The mayor! Does he visit often?"

"Never, he probably wants to see you. That's what they all come here for."

"Well, let's find out then, shall we?"

They walked into the house, Jim's hand on the boy's shoulder. The mayor was sitting having a glass of wine. He got up immediately and went through the 'hail fellow well met' procedure.

"Captain Jim! I've heard so much about you, I had to call and pay my respects. Tomasso's my name, I'm mayor of the town. Village actually, and very tiny."

"Tomasso, I'm very pleased to meet you and flattered by your visit."

He glanced at Elvira, she was smiling.

"Actually, Captain, I came with a dinner invitation: my home this Saturday evening. Such an occasion will hardly alter the course of war. There will be a feminine companion," he added. "You might have no reason to return here until Sunday."

"That indeed sir is a tempting offer, if only the invitation could have come sooner. With all respects, I must decline. Duty calls and I have an important rendezvous at 12 noon, Friday. A meeting, sir, which could decide the course of events. Lives are at stake."

Elvira, intent on having her two-penny worth, interrupted with, "One for sure, maybe more if the captain fails to keep his appointment. The location is the key to the secret."

The mayor looked from one to the other. If he was being secretly informed about the course of history, it was time to get in his plug. "Captain," he shook the hand of opportunity, "I wish you every success in your mission. I'm sure the town will have a favourable mention in your report to London."

"That, Tomasso, I promise. What is your full name by the way?"

"Bandini, Tomasso Bandini."

"Maybe I could mention you by name?" he suggested.

"That, Captain, is more than I would ask, but since you insist, I accept."

Turning to Elvira, he said, "Signora, my visit has been a pleasure indeed."

On that note he left, happy in the knowledge that he had achieved his purpose. They looked at one another, he and Elvira.

"You are a fraud," she said, smiling.

"And you are my accomplice," he replied.

Elvira poured two glassed of wine.

"To the meeting," she said, holding up her glass, "may it be fruitful."

"By the way, whose lives are at stake?" he asked curiously.

"She laughed, "Well, you never know, you know."

*

Chapter 9

Friday brought mixed feelings. The excitement and anticipation was overshadowed by the pain of leaving. It seemed everyone had gathered around the well as on the day he arrived, a fearful stranger with a gun. Now, a week later, he was surrounded by friends, most of them in tears. Shaking hands all round, he could sense the depth of feeling in each contact. He kissed Maria on the lips as a tear fell down her face. In that fleeting contact, he felt a warm tenderness awaiting some fortunate man. She was a hard-working, cheerful girl, Maria; not at all the way she presented herself that first day. Standing all forlorn and weeping unashamedly was his lady of the well. Taking her in his arms, he squeezed her slender frame fondly; it was like holding a bundle of sticks. Anna's daughter-in-law, a lady he had spoken to not more than two or three times, hugged him, declaring that Via Viale would never be the same without him. Turning, he walked away. After he had gone 50 yards, Dante caught up with him.

"Mamma said I could walk with you to the road."

He put his hand on the boy's shoulders and they walked off together.

"Can I carry the gun?"

"Yes, of course," he replied, snapping off the magazine and handing him the weapon.

"Now tell me what you'll do if we meet some Germans?" he asked the boy.

"I'll give you the gun, and do what you do."

"You'll have to be fast, I'll run."

"You wouldn't run!"

"Wouldn't I? How do you think I've stayed alive all this time? An intelligent soldier only fights if he has to. Sometimes it is prudent to run."

"Let me walk to the bridge with you," the boy asked, tears shining in his eyes, ready to brim over.

"This is far enough. I'll take the gun now."

"I know why you're crying: because we didn't meet any Germans. That's it, isn't it?"

The boy agreed with a curt nod, unable to speak.

"I knew it. I knew it. You were looking for a fight, weren't you?"

The boy nodded again with his head bowed, tears on free flow.

"Come on now, let's shake hands man to man."

Dante looked up, starting to smile through wet eyes, and wiped his nose on his sleeve before holding out his hand.

"You wouldn't cry whatever happened, would you?" the boy said, continuing to use both sleeves as handkerchiefs.

"I'm crying now, it's just that there are no tears, so we had best go before they start falling. We'll stand back to back, when I say go, walk 20 paces, stop, turn and wave. Ready…go."

Counting aloud…18, 19, 20, they turned, waved, and called goodbye. He watched the boy wipe his face with his sleeve, turn, and walk off.

Standing on a hill overlooking the bridge, with a good field of vision, he realised that the gun would be a problem. The bridge was his only access and already two vehicles were crossing with their lookouts scanning the skies; it was a beautiful day for strafing. Across the bridge, the main road running parallel with the river was no problem. He merely had to walk across and take an adjoining dirt road into the country. Calling at a nearby house, he asked the farmer for a half sack of straw. He duly obliged and extended his hospitality to wine, bread and cheese; a sack of straw seemed such a meagre offering.

"I thank you for your offer, but I only need to conceal the gun. You understand?"

Taking the half sack of straw, he placed the gun inside.

"How would you carry it? I want to keep my finger on the trigger," he asked the farmer.

Actually, he knew how he was going to carry it, but the man had been so obliging, asking his advice might give him a feeling of importance; a way of thanking him.

The bridge was deserted. Crossing without incident left him a little deflated: all that planning and unnecessary precaution and not a German in sight. The bastards never turn up when you expect them.

Taking the first dirt road out of the valley and into the country, he spotted a vehicle pulled into the roadside, half hidden by the budding foliage. the bonnet up and the rear end of a soldier stuck to the mudguard, head and shoulders buried in the engine. The visible part of the body was the fattest arse he had ever seen. Unseen, he watched the mechanic completely engrossed in his task, his posterior simply inviting a boot. Emerging from the bushes came another, hitching up his trousers and fastening his belt. He did exactly as anticipated, slapping those huge buttocks with his flat hand. The soldier must have sensed a presence because he looked up and, seeing an interested spectator, waved. He then attempted further fun by pretending to kick the objective, but at that point the head and shoulders emerged from the engine, lashing out with an oily rag. The clown danced out of range and cast a second glance at Jim for further approval. Smiling back, he waved and continued the climb out of the valley, leaving the comedians to their horseplay.

According to the clock on the vehicle he had delivered to the little community, which was probably changing hands on the black market at this very moment, he still had 7 km to go, probably less than six across country. Time was no problem, he had allowed for any unforeseen delay. He stood on the top of the hill looking out on the valley, listening to the sound of silence. Everything had gone so smoothly. There was no likelihood of meeting any bad men today, so he pulled the gun from the sack and hid the sack and straw under a nearby rock, in case he might need it on a return trip. Striding along light-heartedly, drunk with joy, it seemed the only outlet was song. So he sang.

Arriving at the bridge early, he was surprised and elated to see her there. She was not alone. Spotting him almost immediately, she waved and walked calm and sedately to meet him, accepting his outstretched hand with a warmth of feeling in the handshake.

"I've missed you," she said simply.

"How are you, Rose?" was all he could find to say.

"At this moment, I feel good."

"So do I. So do I."

After all the rehearsing on how he would greet her, he was tongue tied. Alvaro came forward to greet him.

"Thank you for giving up your time, Alvaro, and please give my regards to Anna; tell her that I am looking forward to paying you a visit."

"That will please her. She talks about you often."

"Really? I'm flattered."

"I'll bid you goodbye and leave you two alone, you must have a lot to talk about."

With that, he walked off.

Picking up their bicycles, they rode off together in an easy silence. This was not at all like the first time, there was only a strong attraction then. Since that time, they had endured an ordeal and come through it with a healthy respect for one another. The experience had cemented implicit trust and a depth of feeling. They paused at the olive grove, without having spoken a word.

"Shall we linger here a while?" she asked, "I've become quite fond of this little spot."

"Me too, I remember kissing a beautiful girl here. It was my very first kiss."

"Would you like to kiss her again?"

"Very much. Do you think she would mind?" he asked with a discerning smile.

Both bicycles hit the floor at the same time. They were instantly locked in each other's arms, lips together. She had her arms around his neck while his were around her back. She was teasing him with her tongue and the flush of excitement rushed to his thighs. He felt an overwhelming desire to stroke her bottom. His hands began playing around the mechanism that triggered off the jiggle in her walk. She didn't object. With their faces just an inch apart, she smiled mischievously. He was conscious that his feelings were getting out of control.

"Naughty!" she said, as they broke from the clinch.

They walked the rest of the way slowly, pushing their bikes; there was so much to discuss.

"How did things work out at your end?" he asked. "No kickbacks? Because they take each defeat, however small, as a personal insult.

At present they are suffering a lot of insults. Each defeat feeds their malice against the underdog giving them a spiteful incentive to put the boot in. It's their way of taking revenge against the top dog."

"I delivered the casualties to the first transport vehicle I met, deliberately keeping clear of the main road until we were almost at the river. Instinctively, I must have been following you. Their story was that partisans had attacked them. The soldier agreed whole-heartedly with this. He was really very practical and assured me that the sergeant would go along with it. If the truth was revealed, he would lose his rank, and I did threaten them with the truth. They would have to explain how two soldiers were overpowered and robbed in the process of attempted rape. A rather embarrassing situation, don't you think?"

"I do. And there's been nothing more said?"

"Not as yet, but in the interests of your safety, we have moved your bed into a furnished cave; wall to wall straw. You don't mind sleeping there, do you?"

"I don't mind if you think it's necessary."

"Merely a precaution. Your bedroom is approximately 1 km from the house, in the first foothills. There is a small fireplace in the shape of a half tar barrel and wood should you feel cold. Oh and one more luxury, very important to you, just 10 yards to the left of the cave, there is running water. A towel and soap has been provided," she smiled, "are there any other questions?" she asked.

They arrived at the house, and any doubts he had entertained about a welcome were quickly dispelled. Maria kissed him and drowned him in tears. She had been haunted, she said, by fears of more visits from Germans. Now that he was here, she felt safe. He remembered someone else had said that. It seemed that everybody felt safe with his presence except himself. Francesco, unassuming and sincere, greeted him warmly.

"Glad to have you back," was his welcome.

The scene was a replay of the first visit: Rose with a consoling arm around Maria, Francesco with a welcoming hand on his shoulder. As they entered the house, the setting was identical: large wood fire, snow-white cloth, food cooked, table laid. It was a step back in time. Only the mood had changed; they were old friends now. Their lives had been overtaken by events and he found himself with a reputation he could well do without. The Germans made short work of anyone with a reputation and he had no desire to became a framed photograph on his mother's sitting room wall. There were plenty of reasons not to play the hero. The primary one was sitting opposite him, playing footsie under, and eyes across, the table. They were having a wonderful time. It had all been done a million times before, but it was new to them. Flashing glances over the rim of a wine glass: old stuff, but a very pleasant game for first time players.

"Tell us about your stay at Via Viale," Francesco asked. "There wouldn't be much left of the truck to dispose of. Bruno is very clever with his hands. He'll probably build a new model with the parts and sell it on the black market," he chuckled good-naturedly.

"What was left would hardly have made a shelter for the hens. Now that you mention it, I spent a whole week there and never saw one single part of that vehicle again."

Francesco laughed, tapping his nose knowingly.

"Did they ask how you came about the vehicle and the gun?" Maria enquired.

"I told them the barest outline of that episode but it was enough for them to make up their own story. It was probably discussed and chewed over after mass on Sunday. I had visitors from the village wanting to meet Captain Jim of British Intelligence."

He was looking at Rose, she was smiling at him, wine glass at her lips.

"That's how reputations are made," she said. "Here in Italy we are short of heroes, so we invent them. The mayor, Tomasso Bandini, would be one of your visitors, seeking some reflected glory. One of the others is an easy guess; it would be an active Fascist seeking to ingratiate himself with the British. Having picked the wrong side, he is looking for a way out."

"Well you are right on both counts. The other was Rossini; he wanted to trade information. The mayor gave me a more tempting offer: dinner and a female companion for the evening, and the night. All this for a mention in Captain Jim's report to London. I don't even know where London is. I've never been there! They were asking a man with no bank account for a £10,000 cheque. I gave them one each to make them happy. Everybody won."

He was intoxicated by the warmth of friendship, the intimacy, the pleasure of being listened to with interest. It was good to be home again.

Later that evening, Jim escorted Rose back to her home before making his own way to his cave for the night. He pushed her bike with the gun in the shopping basket while she walked by his side, holding onto his other arm.

"Would you like that picnic we promised each other? We could light a fire and cook salsiccia tomorrow. Would you like that?" Her enthusiasm was contagious.

"How about salami, cheese and wine?" he said excitedly.

"Prosciutto and a flask of coffee, English coffee. We'll make it a feast." A feast was how she looked to him. He was trying to read something into her words. "By the way, you didn't tell me very much about your visit to Via Viale. Didn't you enjoy it?"

"I was treated like a VIP and I loved every moment."

"You could've stayed. Why didn't you?"

"Ah, this is my opportunity to test your feelings. I missed you in a way that I couldn't understand. I was lonely among friends. You know what I'm saying?"

"Yes, I think I do." They had crossed the road and were approaching a large oak tree. "This tree is a favourite landmark of mine. You can see the outline of my home just 100 m from here. Do you see it? Over there," she pointed.

He nodded and, moving closer to her, they kissed as they did that first time, searching with their lips, lingering, careful not to excite.

"I'll be at Maria's at noon tomorrow," she said, before walking off into the gloom, pushing her bicycle.

He waited for her to reach the gate as she faded slowly into a dim shadow. She must have known he would be watching her because a distant silhouette waved a white handkerchief. He then turned and followed the directions they had given him to his cave, while throwing the 9 lb weapon from hand to hand like a toy. At one point he turned swiftly like a hare and dropped to one knee, calling out, "Bang!" like a schoolboy. Another German bites the dust. His happiness was too much to contain.

The white-shrouded mountain was a clear guide as he walked light-headed towards his hideout, as though on air. Rose had described the cave perfectly: 10 ft deep and almost as wide, furnished with a bed and thickly carpeted with straw. There was a fireplace at the entrance built from a cut away tar barrel raised on a brick hearth and a supply of dry kindling lay just inside the cave. The water supply was by way of a small cascade just outside the opening. The rock there had been worn smooth and the water, 2 ft deep in a small pool, was crystal clear. Continuing its flow downhill, it joined the stream and wound its way through the valley. It was an ideal setting for a love scene in a film.

*

Chapter 10

The sun tried hard to sneak into the cave, succeeding in part. Awakening to greet this most promising day, he leapt out of bed and began preparing for whatever it had to offer. Picking up the towel and soap (an expensive luxury: his was home-made) he made his way to begin his ablutions and make himself presentable for their meeting. Fearlessly, he put his head under the cascade with breathtaking reaction. Just five minutes ago, the water was mountain snow. He was more than usually numbed from the neck up but persisted with his toiletries in the interests of hygiene. Returning to the cave, he dressed quickly, removed the gun and made up his bed ready for the night. With a final check, everything was prepared to receive his guest. Gun in hand, he ran the kilometre. When he arrived at the farm, he received a timely greeting from Maria and Francesco. Choosing a length of rope, he measured it for size, cut a strip for skipping, then filled a sack with straw and soil and suspended it chest high from the tree in the yard. He was about to begin an extensive training programme, watched occasionally by his hosts with puzzled expressions. When he began kicking the bag, they laughed hilariously. Before war broke, interrupting his plans and tiny ambitions, he had reached blue belt status in the Japanese martial art of Ju Jitsu.

He was left with an hour to spare; maybe she would come early. After checking the old alarm clock on the shelf over the fireplace for the tenth time, Maria informed him of her approach. Both pointers stood at 12 as she entered the yard; could anyone be more punctual? The pony and rig looked immaculate. He took her hand as she stepped down, stumbling into his arms. She smelled of lavender as they made a big show of staying on their feet in the ensuing clinch with her cheek smooth and fresh against his. The dulcet tones of laughter chiming in his ear, Maria shook with laughter.

"You would have flattened him caro," Francesco chuckled to Maria.

A pleasant harmonious feeling prevailed as they gathered around the pony discussing its well-being.

"Leave the hamper in the trap. I'll deliver it to the cave," Francesco said. "When we return, Brunita can spend the day in the stables. She likes that, don't you?" he said, patting her.

"I hope you are hungry. I have some surprises to share," she said eagerly, flirting openly.

"Well, he's had no breakfast," Maria said. "He's been kicking that bag all morning."

"Kicking a bag? Are you angry about something?" she asked.

"No, no! It's just a whim. When I've mastered the technique, I'll give you a demonstration."

"Then I have something to look forward to. Let's take a walk through the stables. We should see a difference in the calf."

"These farms," he asked as they walked along, "are they profitable? The methods are rather primitive."

"They pay their way, no more. No one will ever get rich. On the other hand, no one ever goes hungry. Basic food such as bread, cheese and flour are mostly unobtainable in large towns. One must find a source of supply through devious channels and at a price."

As they entered the stable together, Jim whistled, "Gosh, that calf has grown in a week! The poor old cow's having a rough time. Is he sucking that thing or chewing it?"

She smiled, "The animals are on a mixed hay and straw diet and he isn't getting enough milk."

"Remember the last time we came through here, Rose? That was a day."

She turned, smiling into his face.

"Is a woman likely to forget the day she was almost raped. And fell in love for the first time with her champion. You look surprised! Surely you knew. A 34-year-old spinster doesn't usually flirt so outrageously."

There was a clip-clop of well-shod hooves. Francesco appeared at the doorway, fighting the pony good-naturedly.

"She's keener to get back than she was to go," he said laughing.

Giving the pony its head, she made straight for the vacant stall and began champing at the hay on offer.

"The fire will be ideal for cooking, grilling, or whatever you like."

Maria appeared in the doorway. They were dispatched rather than took their leave. They might have been going on a ten-day trip. The air was fresh and clean on this beautiful afternoon. He began teaching her how to breathe.

"Fill the lungs, pause, expel slowly."

"I must have been doing this wrong all these years," she laughed, "how on earth have I survived?"

When they reached the cave, he took her hand.

"There is something I've always wanted to do. Come with me to the waterfall."

"Something outrageous, I suppose," she said sarcastically.

"Let me sing you a love song. I've never had the nerve, the girl, or the time and the place to do it. This is the chance of a lifetime. I have the scenery, the weather, the waterfall and a beautiful girl. There will never be another opportunity like this."

"A love song, with a gun on your shoulder? Has Hollywood thought of this, I wonder?" She was laughing at him.

"I'll put the gun down. I want both hands on your hips, yours on my shoulders. Try keeping a straight face. The cameras are on us. That's good, no laughing."

She resisted the urge to laugh in his face while he, after a couple of failed attempts, began his song *By a Waterfall*, a song from a Dick Powell film.

After a verse and chorus without pause or interruption, she looked at him without laughing.

"That was very pleasant. I wasn't really sure what to expect but I liked it."

"There's lots of ice cold water if you feel inclined to pour it over me. Screen lovers singing into each other's faces always gave me the urge to pour water over them. How did you feel?"

"Well, I'm not sure. Though it was very good. I enjoyed being sang to!"

"It was something I've always wanted to do, but wouldn't dare risk doing it again. Thank you for being a willing listener. Let me escort you to lunch. May I take your coat?"

She wore a red cardigan that contrasted with her hair and highlighted her strong physical qualities.

"Here, let me offer you the best seat in the cave. It cost me the earth, you can see where I scraped it away; and a place to put your feet for extra comfort."

"I like it," she smiled. "An outdoor fitted kitchen. Admirable. I love these cut-away tar barrel fireplaces, so chic. Glowing embers, smokeless fuel." A playful breeze contradicted her little quip. She wiped her eyes and coughed. "Well, almost."

The hamper fascinated him. It reflected her appreciation of style and taste. Flask, bottle and glass strapped to a padded lid with compartments for each food selection, wrapped and packed in starched-white serviettes. He had no idea how her family lived but she was obviously in a higher league. She knew exactly what each wrapping contained and chose it as needed.

"Attend to the wine and fill the glasses," she told him while spreading sausages along the grill.

The basket created a party spirit. The smell of cooking tickled his olfactory nerve, reminding him that it had been almost 24 hours since his last meal. She tapped his hands playfully with a fork as he picked a sausage from the grill.

"They will taste better cooked. You should be opening the wine."

"It is open, but you've only brought one glass," he mumbled through a mouthful of hot sausage.

"You deserved to burn your mouth!" she said, smiling.

Pouring the wine, he held it to her lips while she sipped, eyes sparkling across the rim. Holding up the half sausage, he watched her bite into it. Each little intimate action stimulated their senses; he was reading more into her actions than was actually intended.

"This is your first picnic," she said.

"How did you guess?"

"Because you are behaving like a little boy."

"It's fun though, isn't it?"

She smiled, and fed him a slice of salami by way of reply. A carefree mood developed. Everything they did, each touch, brought a thrill of delight. The coffee, a loving cup of pleasure, spurred the intimacy they shared. He held his desires in check, quite unsure about how to begin without giving offence. Elbows on knees, cups cradled in both hands, facing each other, they flashed messages of encouragement, willing the other to make the first move. The bold front he had shown was beginning to wilt. His ego, he knew, would never survive a rejection. Suddenly, and quite out of the blue, as if she had read his thoughts, she held his hand. They stood up looking into each other's eyes. Without hesitation, this heavenly creature asked him to leave and join her in a couple of minutes.

"I would rather not undress in front of you. Not at this stage."

He simply walked away in numbed surprise, moping around in a daze until finally gathering enough courage to present himself at the entrance. She was lying in the bed just a few feet from him. The sight of feminine garments neatly laid out on the straw sent a wave of desire rushing through his body. Moving to the bedside, he stood looking down at her well-rounded shoulders and strong, sturdy arms outside the sheets. Her handsome features framed in a halo of raven black hair against the off-white pillow. She was the feast he had hungered for laid out waiting for him to indulge. Undressing with her eyes full upon him, neither one felt embarrassed, that had been replaced by eager anticipation. Pulling the covers aside revealed both breasts, large gently curved orbs with firm pink nipples. Could anything on earth be more beautiful than these deposits of soft, silk smooth flesh? When he cupped them in his hands, a charged current raced into his thighs. Feeling the warm soft expanse of her body against his body, breathing in the exciting animal smell, she had him trapped in a tangle of arms and legs while her lips crushed his lips. The cave suddenly exploded around them.

Some little time after those overwhelming moments, they lay looking at each other with a new awareness. There was nothing surprising now in caressing each other in places which might have shocked them both just a week ago. No words were spoken; none were necessary.

*

Chapter 11

Lying next to Rose with his head cradled in one hand, Jim gazed into her dark eyes and smiled dreamily. Then he slowly pushed himself forward to kiss her lightly on the lips, before jumping out of bed and declaring, "Come, let us go to the stream and cleanse our bodies in the font."

With her eyes full upon him, he snatched up the towel and wrapped it around his middle, then held out his hand, beckoning her.

"Really!" She made a clicking noise with her tongue. "I'll follow. Please allow me my modesty."

"Don't be too long, the sun is about to hide behind the mountains, and Rose, this water is cold."

The cool mountain air stung his body and the rocky earth was hard on his feet. The water fell onto his flesh like ice needles; this was punishment. He decided to call it off when he spotted her approaching, picking her steps carefully, one hand holding the swagger coat together, covering midway between knees and thighs. Her legs, long and sturdy, mesmerised him. When he called, she lifted her gaze and waved. This handsome, noble-looking woman was reasonably well off and must have had a wide choice of suitors, yet she chose him to be with. The thought left him puzzled and flattered.

"Have you bathed already?" she asked.

"No, I've been waiting for you."

Throwing the towel aside, he sat down fearlessly in the freezing shallow pool. There was room enough for two in the rock font, the desire to have her sit naked next to him prevented him screaming, the water numbing his body from the waist down.

"You look fresh and clean sitting there."

She tested the water with her foot.

"Oh my God!" she cried.

"It's wonderful really!"

He had difficulty keeping his teeth from rattling.

"Come in, come in," he cried, patting the water with his hand.

"Alright, just turn your head."

He felt her flop down beside him. She screamed and, scrambling to her feet, submerging his body under the cascade of ice water. He jumped up breathless, speechless. Standing naked in the pool, she held the towel in front of her, laughing.

"Turn your back while I put on my coat, or I'll walk away with the towel."

He obeyed, shivering helplessly and teeth chattering. As he stepped out of the pool, he began jumping up and down in front of her, swinging his arms violently, along with other swinging pieces. She was doubled up with laughter while holding her coat together, never neglecting her modesty. She threw the towel at him.

"Freeze there where you are until I dress," she smiled and walked off.

He stood outside the cave drying himself, waiting longer than necessary before venturing, "May I come in?" his hand held, as if about to knock on a door.

Fully dressed, she turned a cheerful face, a smile playing on her lips.

"Come in, buffone. Come in and make yourself respectable."

"Elvira always addressed me by that name. I know what it means."

"It means clown, and it fits," she said, like an endearment.

Taking him by the arm as he finished dressing, she inspected him closely.

"Allow me," she began combing his hair. "What size hat do you take, it must be bigger than average."

He chuckled, "Size seven. Heads don't come much bigger than that."

"I thought so," she smiled, holding his face between her hands. "You need a hat: your hair is a definite give away. My, you have a lot of scars! Do they hurt?" she inquired with a note of concern in her voice.

"Not any more," he replied as he reached his hands under the sheets, searching among the bedclothes.

"It's behind the bed, on the straw. I didn't fancy a gun in my back with you on top of me," she quipped. Then, turning slightly more serious as she spoke, "I have something to ask you. You are invited to my home tomorrow. My parents wish to thank you. You will come, won't you?"

"I'd be delighted, but how did they find out? You didn't tell them."

"I had to tell them the truth. They heard so many rumours, hearsay scattered about in the wind and all totally incorrect. As they heard it, you came out quite well. A hero in fact, Captain."

"Captain!" he laughed. "You told them the truth though? A similar incident could occur and I might not be up to it a second time."

As Rose readied herself to leave their secluded mountain hideaway, she proposed plans for the next day.

"You don't mind going to church?" she asked. "If you would rather, we'll meet after mass."

"I think I would like to go. Years ago when attending mass, to look as if I was praying, I would read the gospel of St Matthew through several times until I could quote from the verses with some authority. Yes, I am actually looking forward to hearing mass with you."

"I will take care of the necessary precautions: Fascists and sometimes German soldiers attend. I'll wait for you on the church steps. In the event of any danger I won't be there, in which case meet me at the oak tree near my home. Are you happy with those arrangements?"

"Happy indeed, to put my safety in your hands. You are the only person on earth I would trust."

They sat looking into each other's eyes. It was good just being together. He had to fight his hands to keep them from touching her.

*

Chapter 12

He walked briskly into town along the dirt road with the gun concealed in a sack. All roads led to church on a Sunday. He greeted everyone he met: men, women, boys and girls, all dressed in their Sunday best. The day promised everything. The piazza opened up quite suddenly as he entered from a back street. The church dominated the square with little groups of people standing around talking. It was a happy scene. His heart lifted joyfully as he saw her waiting on the steps. All else disappeared from view as he ran towards her waving joyfully. She stood straight and proud, her face aglow beneath a wide-brimmed hat, beckoning him. They stood a moment appraising each other in silent admiration.

"You look very handsome. The sack though is an ugly necessity."

"I didn't want to scare the priest," he smiled at her. "You are so beautiful."

She shook her head, smiling, and took his arm, leading him into the church. Several conversations were taking place but they all ceased abruptly. Heads turned and all eyes focused upon them as she ushered him into a rear pew on the extreme left. The occupants, two young women, volunteered their seats. The precautions had obviously been pre-arranged. Nothing had been left to chance. The talking started up again with increased volume.

Throughout the service, they sat closely. When standing, they leaned against each other. Whispering an apology, she stepped out to join the communion queue in the isle. It was then with his eyes on her back, that he saw Anna stand behind her dressed in her finery, a black hat covering the bun. Small and chic, she looked like a young woman from behind. He watched Rose all the way to the altar, watched her being served with the communion host, and followed her journey back to the pew. His eyes never left her. He saw little else. Once the service was over, the congregation shuffled out noisily. One of the young women who had given up her seat hailed them from the aisle. Having left before mass ended, she returned to report that the coast was clear.

Outside, people gathered in groups, socialising: Sunday service was the highlight of their week. Each group greeted her with obvious respect, acknowledging the captain. He was stuck with the rank and could do nothing about it. Everyone was aware of what had happened a week ago. It had all been chewed over and dissected. Given a little time, they would also know what they did at the cave yesterday.

Anna, waiting outside, greeted them with genuine pleasure. "I'm so happy to see you both. Would you accept an invitation to my home and eat with us? I want to hear the truth for a change. All these rumours!"

"What have you heard?" Rose asked.

"Conflicting stories. One, that the captain here," she smiled, "saved you from a fearful ordeal, another that he was too late. Which is true?"

"He got there in good time, I assure you."

"Well done, Captain. By the way, who promoted you?"

"Dante Rea," he laughed.

"Then it's official! Congratulations. Now, about dinner?"

"I'm taking him home. No, no, nothing like that, Anna. My parents want to thank him, that's all."

"That's all! They have plenty to thank him for."

"They are aware of that. We promise you a visit as early as possible."

"Please make it sooner. I won't keep you, your parents will be anxious to meet the captain."

"Ciao caro. Captain," she laughed, shaking her head.

Everyone greeted Rose as they strolled out of the square. Even the Fascist policeman standing near the barber's shop waved an acknowledgement.

"Is there anybody in town you don't know?"

"I am the school teacher and old enough to have taught some of these early teenagers. People trust me with their children's welfare. I know everybody."

"They respect you as well. One can always judge that by the warmth of the greeting," he said with pride.

"I think they accept you too. The incident that you prevented proved the cautious ones right; those who sent their teenage daughters into the country for safety."

"But it happened in the country."

"An isolated incident. The danger lies in the towns where soldiers are billeted or go for a night out, perhaps on one of their 'voluntary enlistment' raids. While looking for young men, they might stumble on a pretty young woman. You've seen what the consequences could be."

As they approached her home, he began to get a little nervous. Pausing at the drive, she watched him take it all in.

"This would make ideal headquarters for a German general. You've been very fortunate."

"That was one of our fears."

"Well you're safe enough now," he replied confidently.

Her home faced south, surrounded by a 2 m circular wall grading gently to 1 m at the front, which completed a full circle, broken only by an arched gateway.

"The nearest I've been to anything like this is a seat in the cinema; a Mexican hacienda in a cowboy film. I would like to be around to see your flower garden a month from now. Isn't that Brunita with her head over the stable door? And a double garage! What mystery lies inside there?"

"A car and the trap."

"A car! Really?"

"Really. It's standing on blocks. The wheels are buried elsewhere. A precaution: they take anything. If they can't carry it, they drag it."

The paved driveway ended at the porch in a large sweeping circle. Her father came out to greet them.

"Give me your bag," she said, "I don't want them to see the contents."

Papà shook hands most amicably. He was a tall man, beginning to stoop with age. He led them through into the kitchen where her mother was wrestling with a cooker on low pressure. Another handshake. She only took her eyes off him to attend the cooking.

"Do you have these problems in your country?" she asked, her eyes boring into him.

"I wouldn't know. I've been away these last five years, but I'm sure they do."

"We would like to thank you for helping Rosanna," she said sincerely. "We hear conflicting stories but Rosanna told us the truth in less detail."

"I think her story will be correct. She was the intended victim. Did she mention how her plan worked afterwards? That was most important. The consequences could have been disastrous. I don't understand how so many people know so much about it."

"You will find that this is a land of hearsay and rumour. A secret isn't secret for very long."

Rose returned to the kitchen with a list of items and figures. After a brief discussion with her mother, she handed him the list.

"Will you check these figures?"

Scanning the list, he came up with the total at once.

"But you haven't had time," she said, surprised.

"Well maybe I'm wrong. Let me double check."

"You are correct. I'll bring another set," she said, leaving the two together, to return almost immediately with a second slip.

Running his eye down the bill, the answer came as quickly again.

"Where did you learn to do that?"

He was watching her mother watching them both, wondering if she instinctively knew something.

"I used to clerk for a bookmaker."

"You kept books? How clever! You didn't tell me this?"

"The subject never came up."

She was impressed by his flair for figures.

"Were you paid well in your profession?"

"Hardly a profession! Yes I was paid well and I only worked six hours a week."

"Just six hours a week? That's all you worked?"

"More than that. I was good with a shovel too. Now there is a talent. Your mother hasn't taken her eyes off of me yet," he said in English.

"Are you afraid of her?"

"I would be if we were alone. On the other hand, she looks so much like you."

"You said that in reverse. Can I be of any help, Mamma?" she said, taking plates and dishes into the dining room.

He volunteered, but his help was refused, he was ordered to sit. It had been some years since he had enjoyed the intimacy of a close family circle: the warm laughter, the soft comments, and the obvious bond of affection.

"Eat!" Mamma coaxed.

He apparently wasn't filling his mouth full enough.

"Do you have property?" her father asked, bringing him into the conversation.

"Sir, I have nothing."

"You prefer cash perhaps?"

"I prefer it, but I haven't got any."

"I used to worry about money until I discovered it's not important," Papà said.

"Oh I agree it's not important, if only it wasn't so damned necessary. Having said that, for the past three years I've never given it a thought. The last money I handled was Egyptian piastres. I don't even know the rates of exchange."

"Then you must be a happy man," Mamma smiled, "we feel indebted to you. Have you anything in mind you would like?"

"You are not indebted to me. That I proved myself to myself was reward enough. It was most important. I have Rosanna to thank; her display of courage inspired me."

"I was terrified," she chuckled.

"So was I."

Papà took him into the parlour while the ladies cleared away the dishes.

"How were things at Via Viale? You spent a week there didn't you?"

"Everything was fine. It was a happy time. Most of the inhabitants had never seen a German soldier. I enquired how three farmhouses boasted such an exotic name. Nobody seemed to know."

"Many years ago, a natural avenue of trees grew there. They are long gone now, cut down for firewood and never replaced. Cognac?" he asked, pouring out two glasses.

"Yes please."

He very rarely touched spirits and Papà was generous.

"Salute."

"Salute," he replied, downing half the measure in a single gulp. The fire began in his throat, and burnt its way down. He coughed and spluttered before it smoothed out into a warm glow.

"Cognac isn't your drink I see."

"This is fine. I drank unthoughtfully. I'll enjoy the other half."

"There's more if you so desire. You are a man who has travelled freely. Your experience allows you freedom of movement. You appear to go where you please without fear."

"Not without fear, but I go wherever's necessary. If it's a courier you're needing, I'm available."

"An escort actually."

"For yourself? Surely the Germans wouldn't bother you."

"No. This involves walking 14 or 15 km. Neither my wife nor I are capable of such a journey. Rosanna suggested you might escort her. It involves staying over a couple of nights."

"She suggested?" he asked, both amazed and delighted.

His heart skipped a couple of beats. Two nights! Did Bruno ever fix that door on the bedroom?

"Will you?"

Would he!

"Might it not be wiser to go by pony and trap?" he suggested, just as Rose and her mother came in from the kitchen to join them.

"She might return home with a slip of paper. No, it's not worth the risk."

"It might be both pleasant and interesting. Yes, I would be honoured to escort her."

This appeared to be such a heaven-sent opportunity that she hadn't even hinted at, but had secretly engineered. When he looked at her, she smiled impishly.

"Your bath will be hot in an hour," her mother informed him.

"We'll leave you in Rosanna's care. Don't let him go before we return," she said as they took their leave.

"They insisted on staying but I finally persuaded them to take their nap. Come with me." She reached out her hand and took his, leading him into another room.

He suddenly realised where they were. She watched while his eyes took it all in. Done in rose pink, a dressing table with triple mirror ornamented with most of the vanities he expected: brush and comb, spray perfume, an obscure tin, a secret jar, matching drawers, comfortable bedside chair and the bed, so personal, so luxurious, so inviting.

"Do you like it? Sit down, we can talk freely here."

"About the journey, why didn't you ask me?"

"Because I don't want them to know the way we are. I asked them to ask you, knowing you would come."

"This is so comfortable. I like it; you have good taste."

She smiled, "You don't have to whisper, no one will hear us. Come," she patted the edge of the bed, "sit with me."

The intimacy of her nearness was an overwhelming temptation: the tantalising smell of perfume, her full face, those avid lips just inches away. He felt as though he was being pushed from behind. He placed both hands on her hands where they rested in her lap; he had to touch her somewhere. He was in a fever of excited emotion while she looked so composed.

It happened as in the cave, but more deliberate, more adventurous. They made new discoveries, something more than the last time. Afterwards, they lay in each other's arms. Not a word was spoken. The whole magical, emotional turbulence had been transmitted in wondrous silence.

"Your bath was ready an hour ago."

"Would you run the water and get in first?"

"Maybe I should, since you haven't turned a tap for years, you might flood the place."

Before getting out of bed, she put her hand on his head and turned it.

"Just while I put on my robe," she said.

Cleansed and refreshed, they went into the kitchen to make coffee.

After she had taken her parents a cup each, they sat together sipping theirs.

"When do we start the journey?" he asked.

"Contain your excitement," she laughed. "Not until Thursday."

"Is your mother happy about the arrangements?"

"About you, isn't that what you mean? Well you did save me from a fate worse than death. Yes she trusts you."

"I know of no fate worse than death and I'm certainly not worthy of her trust. I have already broken that."

"Not really. You have a false reputation for boldness. It was I who made you break it."

Mamma joined them, looking huge in a thick dressing gown.

"Did you enjoy your bath?" she asked. "How long is it since you experienced such luxury?"

"Longer than I can remember!"

"You enjoyed your last visit to Via Viale, I'm told. So you won't mind a return trip?"

"I'm looking forward to it."

"Good. I was afraid we might be imposing."

He smiled.

"Excuse us, Mamma, I want him to earn his dinner. Come, I need you to help me tend and feed my Brunita. You can clean out and put down fresh straw."

The pony greeted her with a welcome whinny as they walked toward the stable.

"Does she have Sunday off?" he asked.

"Sunday and everyday. All she does is eat! Look at her tummy."

"There's a couple of hours of daylight left. Let's take her for a spin, she might lose three or four kilos."

"Why not. It's what she needs. It's what you and I need."

Eager to get moving, the pony proved difficult to yoke once between the shafts and even harder to restrain. She left him holding its head while she went indoors to inform Mamma of their intentions. Wearing a coat and carrying a shoulder bag, she came out striding vigorously, face glowing, freshly perfumed, and took the reins.

"Let go of her head," she said, "and jump in."

Once free, the pony tried taking charge but Rose was equal to the challenge, restraining her as he vaulted into the rig, landing somewhat untidily amid merry laughter. After negotiating the first hill, the pony settled and was allowed to go her own pace.

"I'll go over the route you and I will take on Thursday." Handing him the shoulder bag, she continued, "This is to replace that untidy sack. Somehow we will have to make it fit."

While he scanned for familiar landmarks from his previous trip, it was clear that she knew every foot of the road, as did the pony. Only the clip-clop of hooves and the occasional jingle of harness along with the creaking of the trap could be heard on this fine evening. The track ran parallel and at a safe distance from the road. A convoy of four trucks were travelling with motorbike escort. Over her shoulder, he watched the convoy turn towards them following the bend of the road. The road would soon swing right again and they would be travelling alongside each other. She turned in her seat, following his gaze. As though from nowhere, three aeroplanes swooped out of the sky on to the convoy. Suddenly, all around them was the roar of engines, the tearing, raking rattle of heavy machine gun fire. Two vehicles exploded in separate sheets of flame. Men ran for cover, shouting in panic. The pony became fractious and unruly so he leapt from the trap and took a firm grip on the bridle, patting and stroking its neck while the muscles on her withers twitched involuntarily. Meanwhile, the planes climbed out of their dive, turned and came down for a second attack. The motorcycle escort sped down the road trying to escape the inferno. A plane broke formation and followed his progress without firing a shot. Travelling too fast to negotiate the bend, the bicycle overshot the embankment, breaking into two separate parts. The rider flew through the air like a rag doll, all arms and legs, while the bike, handlebars skyward, engine roaring, careered onward and landed only feet away from him. She caught his eye, looking first at the scene then back to him in stunned amazement. It all happened in two minutes. The planes flew off casually, circling the skies, seeking other prey while those left alive began dazedly salvaging whatever and whoever had escaped the shambles. Turning the rig and patting the pony's neck, he jumped into the trap. They were homeward bound and the horse needed no urging. They were half way before venturing to look at one another. Reaching out his hand she grasped it firmly.

*

Chapter 13

The pony had been badly frightened and with the stables in sight, Rose needed both hands to restrain her.

"I'll give her a rub down while you attend to any other needs," he suggested after the pony was unharnessed.

The animal was upset and in need of reassurance. In spite of the ordeal, she ate her food without any coaxing.

"She will be fine. Horses in distress usually refuse to eat. How are you?"

"Still numb. That's the first time I've seen men die violently. It was a nightmare."

They pushed the trap into the garage and lingered in the half light.

"Put your arms around me," she said.

They stood together, lips lightly touching as Mamma came to call them for supper. She froze, and then quickly stepped back out of sight; seeing what she had already suspected came as a great shock. Prudently, she hastened back into the kitchen, trying to compose herself; to act as though she had seen nothing while trying to arrange a table that was already laid and make coffee that was already percolating. In her confusion, she was doing things twice. Listening to the small talk as they came into the house, she quickly glanced into the mirror for any give-away signs.

"Benvenuto," she greeted as they walked casually through the doorway.

Seating themselves at the table, she watched them from her vantage point at the cooker, aware of every glance, each flash of the eyes. She watched their legs make contact under the table. All the giveaway signs that had gone unnoticed during the early part of his visit became sexual acts. She had to force herself to be polite.

"Did you have a pleasant drive?" she asked.

"Mamma, it was awful. We witnessed the most dreadful carnage. There was an air attack on a convoy and it was quite upsetting."

"You will be used to atrocities?" she asked as though he was responsible for the whole chaotic mess.

Neither of them detected any bitterness.

"Nobody gets used to that. It's a risk that every soldier has to take, but if he's lucky, it happens to someone else. Everybody hopes to make it to the end of the war, and I really hope that can't be very far off."

"Shall I wrap some food to take with you?" she asked.

"Thank you, Signora, but no. I suspect I have a flatmate. We'll let him find his own food."

"You mean someone is sharing your cave."

"Something. He only wants a warm place to sleep. At night I hear the rustling of straw while he makes himself comfortable but in the morning he's gone."

"It could be dangerous. Does it not trouble you?"

"He only wants to share with me, not evict me."

"On our return, I'll have Francesco move you back. It appears safe to do so now. You should be in a house," Rose said.

"If you wish, but I am comfortable."

Mamma was trying to read the coded signals they were sending and receiving with their eyes, messages in the clearest of black and white. There is nothing more obvious or more naive than first love, whatever the age.

Fearing Rose might ask him to stay the night, she suggested he leave for his own safety. Completely engrossed in each other, neither one detected any anxiety in her manner.

"Thank you, Signora, it's time I made a move. Give my regards to the signor. It's been a pleasure."

Rose picked up the shoulder bag wrapped in a towel.

"Let me walk you to the gate, it's a lovely evening." Spring was less than a week away.

As they left the house, Rose passed him the concealed weapon, saying, "Take this. The towel is a camouflage to keep Mamma's eyes off. If she saw what was in there, she would have a heart attack."

They stood apart at the gate; silhouettes would be clearly visible from the porch.

"You will come tomorrow?" he asked.

"Yes, of course. Tomorrow and tomorrow, how could I not come?"

"I'll wait for you at the tree and we'll ride back together."

"As you wish. Will cheese and wine be alright for a small celebration?"

"Ideal, but what are we celebrating?" he asked.

"We'll think of something. I'm sure it's going to be a lovely day."

"I'll be there at one. Come when you can, I'll wait."

They reached out and held hands.

"Until tomorrow," she said, "goodnight."

"Goodnight."

*

Chapter 14

Each day, she taught an almost empty classroom. They were hazardous times. A spring offensive was imminent and people kept their children at home. The tree proved to be an excellent observation post with a wide view of the road and a clear picture of the surrounding countryside; her home too was clearly visible. He could watch and wait without being seen.

Making himself scarce and comfortable, he was at least an hour early. This was as good a place as any to be. Surprisingly, she was early too. He watched her freewheel down the road from town, his heart beating just a little faster. Making his presence known, she waved and came to meet him.

"Hello," she smiled, "have you been waiting long?"

"Since last night!"

"So have I," she said, smiling. "Can you wait another half hour, I'll try and make it 20 minutes?"

"All day, if you want; I don't mind so long as you are there at the end."

"Twenty minutes," she said, pedalling through the gate, turning to give an assuring wave.

After a short wait, he watched her return towards him. Picking up his bike, he joined her as she rode along. She told him about her morning and about the children that didn't attend as opposed to the few that did. Apparently, German soldiers had been in town yesterday evening. Everyone hid behind locked doors. They had manhandled Salvatore the policeman when he tried to intervene in their loud merrymaking.

"Is that the man who waved to us after mass?" he asked.

"Yes, that was Salvatore. We attended school together. He was always gentle and amicable. He looked fine this morning when I saw him in conversation with someone. I bid them good day and went on my way. Would you like to rest here at the olive grove?" she asked. "If you wish."

A farmer driving a pair of oxen, accompanied by his young family, stopped to talk as they were passing by. He listened as she chatted away to the children, her voice so clear and refreshing. Two were of school age: 10 or 11. Diplomatically, school was never mentioned. They had been in the fields since dawn and were hungry so she didn't detain them.

"While I was talking to them, they were looking at you, at the gun. They were afraid and excited. We will have to conceal it."

"I had a similar experience on my way to meet you. I agree, we must do something about it."

"Shall we walk or ride?" she asked.

"Ride I think, I too am excited."

"Then let's hurry, I will calm your turbulence while you fulfil my urgency. I didn't realise that this could become addictive, at least not for beginners."

They shared bread, cheese and wine; the hour of fulfilment; the calm, serene aftermath of togetherness; the physical cleansing in the pool by the waterfall. The adventure was repeated again and again during the two days following, each time more ardent, less discreet. He awoke early and sprang out of bed eagerly: Thursday had arrived with all its expectations. Grabbing soap and towel, he punished his body at the cascade and dried himself off, tingling with health, picturing her as she was yesterday, her face radiant, soft brown eyes smiling into his as he lay on top of her in an ecstasy of uncontrollable bliss. There was no place in his mind for anything else. Her image dominated all his waking moments. He could imagine no greater thrill than the thought of going to sleep with her, and then to wake up feeling her at his side.

He dressed, made up his bed and picked up the travel bag that she had searched for on the black market, and probably got stung buying. It was ideal concealing what was intended with easy access. He might even be mistaken for the new postman. With a last nostalgic look around the cave, he sadly left his hole in the hill where he had experienced joy, happiness and extreme pleasure with the overriding knowledge that she had shared each fulfilling moment with equal bliss. These were the happiest days of his life.

Francesco and Maria greeted him as they did every day with cheerful affection.

"I'm moving your bed back today," Francesco told him, "you realise that you have company up there?"

"I know, he must be afraid of me, he only comes in at night. Perhaps it's a she looking for a place to have a family. Move me out as soon as possible Francesco—live and let live."

"Somebody should tell that to the Tedeschi. Sit and have some breakfast. We won't be seeing you for a few days so let's talk of pleasant things."

"I would love to! I'll be back on Saturday night. Keep a light in the window for me."

For the fourth time in four days, he waited by the oak tree. In that short time, the surrounding countryside looked greener; the brushwood was beginning to leaf. Only the oak tree seemed bare, but on closer inspection one could see signs of spring. She waved without seeing him, knowing that he would be there. He joined her as she stopped at the gate, as they had each day.

"I'm a little late," she said, "I hope I haven't kept you waiting too long. Try this for size." She handed him a black cloth cap. "Sorry, I couldn't get blue."

"Black is my favourite colour." He smiled and tried on the cap at a jaunty angle. "How's that?" he asked.

"Allow me. In this case it's intended to conceal your hair. You are much too conspicuous. There, that's better. How does it feel?"

"Good. Now I can touch my cap to the young women."

"Come along," she said, smirking, "let's not keep Mamma waiting. Lunch will be on the table."

Mamma was waiting on the porch as they pushed their bikes up the drive.

"Benvenuto, young man," she greeted him warmly.

She was particularly hospitable during lunch and when he found himself alone with her over coffee while Rose and her father attended to last-minute details, she asked him, "What are your intentions when the British arrive?"

"I don't have a choice. Report my existence and accept whatever they have in store for me. I expect a pat on the back and a brand new gun."

"Have you had experience with other women?" she asked point blank.

Completely unbalanced, he found himself stammering a reply.

"None! I've... I've always been afraid of them."

"You weren't afraid of Rosanna, yet she is a few years your senior. I also am afraid: that you might go away and leave her pregnant."

He spilt his coffee into his saucer while trying to find something to say.

"I wouldn't do that."

"Figlio, I'm sure you have the best intentions. I know you are sincere, but once you get back home, everything will be different. You'll forget Rosanna. If she's pregnant, you'll never know. You won't even want to."

"Signora, you have no faith."

"Sooner or later you will leave her. You'll have no choice. Going now will save a lot of heartache. She's in love with you but she'll get over it. You both will."

"I don't see any obstacles. If there is any difficulty at all it will be getting back to her, but I'm sure I can. Signora, I'm sorry but I couldn't leave if I wanted to."

Rose and her father came through into the kitchen.

"Ready when you are. I'll bring my case."

Mamma walked with him to the porch.

"I know you will look after her."

"Signora, she's capable of taking care of us both."

He smiled and walked on a few yards while Rose said goodbye. Taking her case as she joined him, they strode off briskly.

She called to each and everyone by name as they passed the workers in the fields; she had a greeting for all and they replied with due respect.

The case was pulling his arms down to his knees as he constantly changed hands. Arriving at the top of the hill overlooking the valley, she took it from him.

"Just until we get to the other side. You can stretch your arms."

"They've already been stretched. What have you got in there? Bricks!"

She laughed, "It will be empty coming back."

The valley lay before them, a patchwork of green and brown tilled earth. Shrubs and trees bursting into life, the river flowing fast and deep, a no-man's-land: yesterday Italian, today German, tomorrow British. They stood together looking out at the garden of Europe. Suddenly, there was that familiar nerve-tearing sound of gunfire. They looked at one another with apprehension, watching the planes climb out of their dive and turn for another strike. He counted the seconds of impact in his mind. Smoke began to rise into the sky just two miles upstream. It was all over in minutes.

Making their way into the valley towards the bridge, they were startled by the sound of further small arms, but this time it was ground fire and much closer. They stopped, aware of imminent danger.

"We'll review the situation, Rose," he said. "That's too close for comfort."

Voices were clearly heard shouting above the raking, tearing bursts. Taking her arm and the case, he lead her off the track and into the trees, slipping and sliding, picking their way through the shrubbery to a safe vantage point. With the bridge in full view, he put down the case.

"Someone is being pursued, make yourself comfortable, we might be here sometime."

"Why do you say that? Do you see something? Someone?"

"On the bridge: two soldiers searching the river at each side. Do you see?"

"Yes, but why are they looking in the river? A person would drown in there."

The shouting grew louder, the voices closer, more excitable, between the bursts of gunfire.

"There are looking for someone. A strong swimmer could negotiate that current. It could possibly be escaped prisoners. Only somebody desperate would chance that water but we are safe enough here. Are you afraid?"

"A little."

"Well don't worry. They won't hang around too long. There will be casualties from the air raid. Just take a look at the sentries on the bridge now."

"I see. They are leaning against the wall chatting. The shooting has stopped."

"They'll soon be leaving, what's left of them." Then he added with a sigh, half to himself, "You know, it will be a great pity to see a bridge like that destroyed."

Rose decided to change the subject, "You and Mamma had a heart-to-heart over coffee. What were you discussing?"

"You and me. She knows."

"She knows because I told her."

"That must have been difficult. I mean, to tell one's mother of such intimacy."

"She asked and I wouldn't lie. What did she say to you?"

"She fired a burst from the hip, live ammunition too. One hit me in the voice box: I was speechless. Here comes what's left of that convoy. They're calling the sentries off the bridge. Give them ten minutes to get well away. Are you feeling alright?"

"I'm fine. Now tell me what she said."

"She was afraid that I would go away and leave you pregnant."

"It's a possibility. I'm sure you fire live ammunition too. Would you?"

"I won't have a choice when the time comes. She asked me to go now." After a slight pause he asked tremulously, "What do you want?"

"You already know."

"It's clear." He reached out a hand as she got to her feet. "Let me take the case. I'll hand it to you if we meet any baddies."

They were the only two people on earth as they crossed the bridge in an eerie silence. Climbing out of the valley and reaching the top of the hill, they moved onto a small dirt track. As they passed some stunted olive trees with thick brushwood around the trunks, he suddenly became aware. The hairs on his neck bristled. Handing her the case so abruptly, she stood quite still. He was already moving towards the warning sign, gun in hand. There was movement in the bushes as he approached; it was only momentarily. As he moved in closer, a man was lying prostrate in the shrubbery.

"Stand up, mate. You'll get yourself shot playing hide and seek," he chuckled with amusement.

A British captain in full uniform got to his feet, clothing soaking wet and shivering uncontrollably. They looked at each other for a moment.

"Get those wet clothes off, Captain. I have a dry vest in the bag and you can have my pullover. I'll have it back when we get you fixed up."

He beckoned Rose.

"Who are you?" the officer enquired, taking off his wet clothes with difficulty.

She put down the case and walked up to him. "Let me help," she said, peeling off the wet shirt.

Jim handed him the vest.

"We are friends. This is my wife, Rose. Here, put this pullover on and as I said, I want it back."

"Rose," the captain said, "I am delighted to meet you. You are heaven sent."

"Feeling warmer now?" she asked, giving him a most sincere smile.

"She's my guardian angel, Captain. You can find your own. This one speaks four languages: English, French, German and Italian."

The officer couldn't keep his eyes off her.

"Your English, dear lady, is a joy to my ears."

Jim turned and spoke to her in Italian.

"You've made a hit, Rose. Look at his eyes. He's in love with you. The first chance I get to show you off and I'm jealous."

"I believe you are, you fraud. 'This is my wife'!"

The captain looked from one to the other puzzled.

"Well, you will be, won't you? I'm asking."

"You've picked a nice time and place to ask! Proposing marriage in the presence of a man in danger of catching pneumonia. I'll give my answer at a more appropriate time."

He turned to the puzzled officer, "A lover's tiff, Captain. We were arguing about the best way to help you."

"Come with us," Rose continued, "I will arrange a night's lodging and a hot meal. We'll also get rid of your uniform for something more country style. My husband will advise you on anything else you wish to know."

"Keep your boots, Captain, they are most important, and your underclothing. All you need for an effective disguise is a jacket and trousers. How are you feeling now?"

"Much better since meeting you two. This is a stroke of luck I didn't expect. I felt I was going to die. Are you operating undercover? How did you come by that MP-40?"

He laughed, "Captain, there is only you and Rose know that I'm alive. Oh yes, and the German sergeant, he won't forget in a hurry. She took the gun from him. He was trying to rape her when I came along and intervened. I wasn't doing very well either. The man was belting hell out of me, she picked up the gun and shot his balls off." He watched the officer looking across at her with sheer admiration. "You know what she did then, Captain? Put him in a horse-drawn vehicle and delivered him to the nearest field hospital. She told them that partisans had attacked him. The soldier didn't dare deny it. What could he say? A woman shot his balls off while he was trying to rape her?"

In Italian she reproached him, "You are a habitual liar. If I marry you, I won't know when you're speaking the truth."

"It's a great story though, Rose. Sounds much better than what actually happened, don't you think? I mean, there is no hero, just the heroine."

They laughed while the officer awaited some enlightenment. As they walked toward a farmhouse, the farmer and his wife watched their approach fearfully from the doorway.

"I was asking my husband to teach you some tricks of his trade. The dos and the don'ts of life behind the German lines. He is an expert. Fearless too, Captain, in spite of his modesty. Let me relate one or two incidents."

"Don't," Jim said with mock sincerity. Then in a more tender tone, "Go and charm the farmer."

They watched her walk up to the couple at the door.

"How did you ever find a woman like that, Geordie? God smiled on you too."

"He did, Captain, he most certainly did. They'll miss her in heaven among the angels and the saints. By the way, how was the water for swimming?

"Geordie, I was nearer death in that river than ever I was in the front line. I couldn't get out; the current was sweeping me downstream. I managed to grab an overhanging tree branch that hit me in the chest and I somehow hauled myself up over the edge."

"How far were you from the bridge at the time?"

"No more than 20 yards."

"You were luckier than you think. There were two sentries on the bridge scanning the river. They got fed up and both of them leaned on the wall at the downstream side, smoking and chatting."

"How could you know that?"

"We were watching from a vantage point, waiting to cross. You heard my wife: I'm an expert. She wasn't kidding you know. For instance, I didn't see you hiding back there in the bushes, I felt you, intensely aware of a presence. It's a sixth sense one develops with experience. Much like a blind man: he can't see, but his other senses are extremely acute. You will realise what I am saying as time goes by. Here's Rose."

"I've made arrangements, Captain. He wants you out of the house by eight o'clock in the morning." Turning to Jim, "Have you advised him on how to cope?" she asked.

"Give me a pencil and paper, I'll write half a dozen tips down. One interesting point, Captain, move 20 or 30 miles north, you'll find the Germans less active there." He began writing. "How long before our lads arrive? You should know."

"Two months at most."

"You'll be just starting to enjoy yourself then, Captain, and they'll come and spoil it all," he laughed. "Here you are," he said, handing him the slip of paper, "stick to those rules and you'll be home on the next boat and don't sneak around, walk openly. So long as you stay in the countryside, the Germans won't bother you. They have more urgent things to attend to."

"Thanks, Geordie. I won't forget you." He turned to Rose, "Or you, Rose, you are an inspiration."

"My pleasure, Captain, I assure you."

He all but kissed her. They parted, having learnt something from each other.

"That was a very pleasant encounter. I rather enjoyed it. In fact I've enjoyed the whole journey, a bit frightening sometimes, but exciting. There's never a dull moment when you're around, Geordie. Why did he call you Geordie?"

"Where I come from, everybody is called Geordie."

"Really. Why?"

"I don't know why, that's just how it is. Maybe it's the dialect."

"You have a dialect! I didn't realise."

"Well it's there and there's nothing I can do about it. Indeed, there isn't anything I want to do about it."

"Very commendable. You are what you are, Geordie," she added, laughing mischievously.

"I recovered my pullover and lost a vest. I still came out of that lot a loser. In fact, you are the only winner I've ever backed. The road looks clear. Let's hurry across and into the country before something else happens."

"I really don't know why I feel safe with you. You make things happen."

Crossing the road to the track exactly at the tar barrels, they walked on leisurely.

"The snow has gone from the lower hills. You know, Rose, the Gran Sasso was clearly visible from the prison camp at Fermo."

"From Fermo? Really! That must be 70 or 80 km."

"It didn't look more than 10. In spring, the sun would spotlight its magnificence; a white shrouded beacon. As summer approached, the snow line would climb visibly. September saw a huge cone, capped with ice cream. From then, the process would reverse: the cream spilling down its slopes until it was clothed once again in a forbidding white shroud."

"Geordie, you are full of surprises. A talent for detail, exceptional descriptive powers and clever with figures."

"And the gun. Don't forget my other outstanding qualities: expert with shovel and gun. Look at those donkeys, eating their way through life and working hard at it. They aren't overjoyed at our visit either."

They had been spotted however and suddenly everyone was there, including old Anna and the baby, the oldest to the youngest. All were gathered to greet them. There were kisses, handshakes and backslapping almost to the point of personal injury.

"I think this has all happened before, you know," he called to her above the noise of the welcome.

He kissed Anna's walnut cheeks, Maria's inviting lips, cooed at the baby, and shook hands with Franca, Bruno, and all. Elvira wrapped her arms around him and he felt pleasantly powerless.

"Can I kiss your clown, Rose?" she called out, laughing in his face.

Everybody congregated in Elvira's kitchen. Giuseppe, Franca's husband, brought in a huge jug of wine with a handful of glasses, a finger inside each. After an hour of chaotic welcoming chatter, Elvira called time and cleared her kitchen and with Franca's help, got to work on a meal for the guests. They worked and chattered happily while Dante dragged him off to his room for a complete report on the military situation.

"Have you killed any Germans?" was the first of a hundred questions.

"Just a couple, with my bayonet. I left that behind, it was covered in blood."

"Both at once! How did you do it?"

"Both and together. Two Germans on one bayonet."

"Gosh! Did they scream?"

"Scream, yes. Complained more than anything."

He was saved by the bell as Elvira called him for dinner. Dante followed, seating himself at the table.

"Not you!" she said, giving him a small flick across the ears. "You've had yours."

"I don't want to eat, Mamma. I just want to hear how Jim bayoneted the two Germans."

"Go away, boy. He talks about nothing but killing. Jim hasn't even got a bayonet."

"He has, he told me," he replied, backing away from the table, "haven't you?"

He looked at the boy and stalled, "I'll tell you all about it later."

Rose looked across at him, smiling, "Bayoneting. Two Germans," she shook her head. "What will you think of next."

"It pleases the boy. What you don't know is they were both on the same bayonet."

They were seated at the table.

"It's a joy to see you, Rosanna, even without what you've got in the case, although I am looking forward to those too. And it's nice to see you eating again, buffone. Did you have any difficulty getting here?" Elvira enquired.

"It's always hazardous travelling, especially with him."

"Risky without him though. He didn't tell us that a German tried to rape you. We heard the details from another source. We're always well up with the news here despite being isolated."

"Oh he's good for my morale, and we had a very pleasant experience today after an enforced delay."

She described in detail their little adventure at the bridge and the encounter with the British officer.

"Wait just a moment," Elvira said. She screamed for Bruno who was busy in the spare bedroom. "Come and listen to this," she called.

With a hammer in his hand, he seated himself with them at the table. She seemed to find more pleasure repeating what she had already described for Bruno's benefit. The account of the journey whetted their appetites and they requested the full story of the rape escape. As she was not forthcoming, the request became a demand. Complying reluctantly with their wishes, he listened to her as the story unfolded, looking back in retrospect. While he only saw the show through a crack in the door, she had watched it all from centre stage. His entry from the wings, the swinging club, the sickening impact, the broken chair, the burst of gunfire and the ensuing, deafening silence. Elvira and Bruno looked at each other in amazed disbelief, then at each of their guests.

"You were here a full week and never said a word about all this. I think I'll make you a bed up in the stables!" Turning to face her friend, "Look at her eyes, Bruno. I only mentioned separate beds and they are filled with fear."

"No, perhaps they are both just tired. They've had an eventful day," Bruno said wryly.

"Perhaps Bruno's right. Come with me, both of you. Let us end this speculation."

She led them into her own bedroom. It was cheerful, comfortable, clean and bright. A pair of oil lamps were burning; an excessive luxury. While Elvira fussed around with pillows and bedclothes, ignoring their reluctance to accept her generous hospitality, he let Rose go on with their joint protest and left the room to bring in the case.

"This is very small recompense for your kindness, Rosanna so let's have no more frivolous objections or I will put your clown in the stables. I thought that would shut you up," she chuckled. "Now, let's have a look in the case."

Leaning on the bed rail, he watched and listened to their easy conversation. The little cries of delight as Elvira picked up and examined each intended gift. A blue satin nightgown made her gasp. She turned to Jim, holding up the dress.

"This is mine after you leave. When you lift it tonight, easy does it, she'll still be in there."

He smiled, shaking his head, looking at Rose, looking back at him.

"There's clean water and a bowl. If you need anything else, call me, but I'm sure you won't. Goodnight both of you."

"Well, shall we take advantage of this stroke of luck?" he said, "I don't want to rush you. Let us have everything free and easy between us."

"Everything is, and you've never rushed me."

"What will you wear to sleep in?" she asked, a smile playing on her lips.

"I have nothing with me. I'll just sleep on you."

"Then you won't mind if I sleep in nothing… that will make us even."

He awoke with his face against her breast, breathing in the warm, exciting animal odour emanating from her body. Nuzzling the nipple with his lips, he felt her body shake with soundless laughter. He peeped at her from under the bedclothes while she looked down from her pillow.

"There's nothing in there," she smirked.

"Just testing. I thought you were asleep. It's daybreak so it must be after seven."

"It's after eight. I've been awake half an hour."

"Why didn't you wake me? I've wasted that half hour sleeping."

"I felt good lying here with you beside me. It was a new experience. But I want you up and dressed before Elvira knocks on the door. She will be bringing us hot drinks, so move. Hand me my night dress, I want to greet her sitting up."

Handing her the nightgown, he dressed hastily. The last thing he wanted was to be caught with his pants down; so undignified. As if she had waited until he was decent, the knock came to the door.

"Come in," Rose called.

He opened the door to see her standing with a tray and three steaming cups of coffee, the kind that had no smell. It had however a certain pleasant taste. She wore a dressing gown that was obviously from Rose's own wardrobe and hadn't stretched at the same rate as her body.

"I'm disappointed. I hoped to catch you two in bed together. He hasn't torn that nightgown I hope. I wonder what Bruna would say to a situation like this. Does she have any idea?"

"She asked me," Rose replied.

"And you told her, I know you wouldn't lie. I would hate to be in your shoes, buffone. Violating her daughter's chastity! She'll never forgive you."

"Time heals all things, Elvira."

"I hope so, for your sake. Pull up that chair and join us. How did you sleep caro? Or would this brute not let you."

She laughed, "He tired himself out. I tried keeping him awake."

They became totally engrossed in themselves, this was their first meeting in two months and there was much to discuss. He envied the bond of intimacy between them. It would be nice to be part of a friendship like theirs with such depth of feeling.

*

Chapter 15

The morning was cool and the sky overcast when they started out after a breakfast of boiled eggs and bread. It was pleasant being together, holding hands, talking, and a now and then a glance of assurance. Where on earth could be more delightful? They passed a wooded area with the rusting skeleton of an old van, discarded kitchenware, pans broken, bottles and crockery scattered around like a tip. Further on towards the town, they encountered a combined orchard, vineyard and cornfield. He asked her about this overworked garden. How could Mother Earth cope with this triple demand? She explained that a peasant could, with care and attention, coax a living from little more than a garden. It may be a profitable hobby or he might have a job and even hire out for seasonal work.

Approaching the village square, she was greeted by name on more than one occasion.

"I want you with me," she said, "where I can keep an eye on you. This time, I'm giving the orders."

"But you always do. Can I have a look around the town while you complete your business? Let me flirt with the laundry girls."

He smiled, indicating the women washing clothes at an ultramodern-styled launderette, bashing and rubbing the garments against the rough stone edge of a large trough in the cobbled square.

"Promise you will do no more than that."

"Scout's honour."

"Scout's honour!" she repeated, shaking her head, "I'll probably be an hour, maybe more."

"I won't let you down, Rose. Do what you have to do. I'll meet you at the church steps."

"Ladies," he greeted, approaching the four women hard at work scrubbing garments against the trough.

They were laughing and giggling like happy schoolgirls rather than work-hardened mature women.

"Good morning, Captain," two of them chorused, nudging one another while they gave each other sly looks, whispering among themselves like children. He was about to enjoy their company, they obviously wanted to talk and he had an hour to spare. One lady mischievously prodded her neighbour, whispering, "You ask him."

A motorbike with sidecar combination and uniformed rider drove into the square. Relieved to see it wasn't a German, but out of habit he automatically reached his hand into the bag with no deliberate intention, simply for the comforting assurance the feeling gave him. It was a uniformed Fascist, they had mostly been tamed but not apparently this one—his teeth weren't yet drawn. Dismounting from his bike, the soldier walked menacingly towards the happy gathering at the well, like a Hollywood cowboy with his hand on his pistol.

The ladies ceased their happy chatter, looking warily at the soldier then towards Jim with awe and wonder.

"Inglese," he called, drawing the Beretta. "You come with me."

This couldn't be real. Something had to be done quick. Shifting the safety catch, he had a mischievous desire to laugh. The pompous ass was going to try to apprehend him and take his gun away. Promptly firing a short burst through the bag, just left of the man's feet, he triggered off unbelievable panic. The policeman dropped his revolver and ran; the washer ladies screamed, left their clothes and made towards the church. The square, busy a moment ago, was completely empty. He stood there asking himself what had happened. Bending down, he picked up the pistol, checking the safety catch and putting it in his bag. He would soon have a bag full!

Rossini came running across the square, half dressed, braces dangling, shirt hanging out of his pants.

"Captain!" he exclaimed breathlessly, "What the hell's going on?"

"Sorry, Alberto, but some clown just tried to arrest me."

"Parenti! Where is the silly bastard? And what are you doing here?"

"Came to see you with some good news. Your name's not on the war criminals list. I thought you might sleep easier as the British will be here in two months."

He was beginning to enjoy the farce.

"Well, that improves my future. Now I want you off the street. Nobody's going to venture out while you are here shooting a gun."

Rose appeared, hurrying towards them.

"What have you done?" she asked, severely scolding him, but there was only softness and anxiety in her voice, concern in her eyes.

"I was told you'd killed Signor Parenti!"

She was clearly upset.

"Rose, sweetheart," the endearment slipped out, "you know I wouldn't kill anyone. I shoot at the legs. It has the same effect, but they don't die. In this case, I hit the cobble stones. I'm really sorry to have upset you."

"Signorina, there has been a misunderstanding," Rossini assured her.

She was plainly relieved.

"I want him with me if you don't mind, Alberto."

"As you wish. I only want him off the streets. Oh, thanks for the news, Captain; it's a relief."

"A pleasure, Alberto. See you in a couple of months."

"I might be looking to you for your support, Captain. Arrivederci."

This was the first time he had seen her annoyed. She allowed him to take her hand, but wouldn't speak. He decided it was best to say nothing although he would gladly have gone down on his knees and begged forgiveness.

Leading him by the hand into a building, probably the town hall, they were ushered into a waiting room. It was warmer outside. He felt the chill of her annoyance more than the room. It was something he couldn't handle.

"You are going to talk to me, aren't you?" he begged.

He couldn't quite believe it was himself asking.

"Of course I'll talk to you. I'm disappointed. You gave me your word." Once again that attempt at severity which melted into repentance. "Perhaps there is an explanation," she added, afraid she was taking her displeasure too far.

Before he could reply, she was summoned into an office. As a further peace offering before she left, "It's only a month old. Perhaps there is something of interest to you," she said kindly, handing him a newspaper.

"Thank you."

He felt much better. All was well again. Struggling to read the written Italian in the out-of-date, censored newspaper convinced him that the war was lost. The Allies were being repulsed on all fronts. The Russians were retreating from Moscow; it didn't say to where. The Italian front line was being held (that at least was partly true) with losses in manpower so severe that it was only a matter of time before the British and Americans surrendered. Air attacks had ceased: manufacturing of planes couldn't keep pace with their losses and they were unable to train pilots fast enough. Without doubt, according to this newspaper, the war was almost over. Despite all this, however, every night more than 500 planes flew north on bombing missions. In the daytime, fighters patrolled the skies, searching for targets. He had never seen one single plane shot down.

She was being ushered out of the office by an exceptionally polite official.

"Successful mission?" he greeted her hopefully.

"I think we've had a worthwhile journey. Now what am I going to do with you?" Her voice was soft.

"Do anything you please."

"Just look at your bag," she said.

The barrel of the gun was sticking out through the scorched tear. Like a schoolboy displaying torn trousers, he looked at the damage as though someone else had done it. Her tender look made his heart sing—all was forgiven. He had known that she wouldn't stay mad with him very long, but it had made him so unhappy. People eyed him warily as they walked out of the square.

When they were clear of the town and past the rubbish dump, she took his arm, pressing it to her breast. This was a newfound happiness. They had experienced their first quarrel.

"Say nothing of what happened in town. We might be gone before they hear about it," she said.

"I hope so. I'm not up to all the questioning. They would want the whole show all over again and in detail. By the way, I have another confession. My armoury is expanding. That policeman dropped his pistol in fright. I have it here in my bag. When I get a chance, I'll examine it more closely."

Their arrival back at the house was awaited with excited curiosity; news of the incident had gone before them.

*

Chapter 16

Their friends came out of the fields, leaving their work to meet them. News of the drama had gone on ahead, carried on the wind. Work ceased and the oxen stood patiently at ease in their yokes. They were surrounded while being bombarded with questions fired in salvos. He gave them a brief outline of events as they had happened, which only served to whet their curiosity. They were escorted home with questions being slung from all angles. Did you? Did he? Who was killed? There was no escape, the barrage was sustained all the way to the well where decisions were made, arguments settled and stories told. With a smile and a wink, she spurred him on. He was happy to see her at ease again. They wouldn't be satisfied until the whole story was told and there were no witnesses to contradict the tale of fact and fiction he told. As he related a chronicle of reckless courage that nobody, with the exception of Rose, doubted for a moment, there were gasps from the audience. When he put his hand in the bag and pulled out the Beretta, it was proof enough. His account was accepted word for word. They were both satisfied and stimulated. The narrator had taken a keen hold of the truth and seasoned it with suspense. He was a teacher reading to a class of infants (that's how she described the scene to him later). The story came to a conclusion in hushed silence.

"But," said someone, unable to contain the uncertainty, "was anybody killed?"

"Nobody," he replied.

Franca called from the doorstep. Her home was their venue for dinner. She had spent the whole afternoon preparing and had judged the time to perfection. Leaving his audience to mull over and discuss the drama at length, Rose took him by the arm.

"I'm sure we can walk these 20 m without incident. I enjoyed your story. You have a flexible imagination and you're not at all predictable. Each time I tried to guess what was coming next, I was sidetracked. You possess a discerning instinct. Could you possibly have the same talent for writing?"

They were welcomed at the doorway. Franca's pleasant face was aglow with pleasure. She wore a brand new pinafore, probably a wedding present taken out of mothballs for the first time. It was as if he was seeing her for the first time. She was a pretty woman and always made him feel special. Her 8-year-old daughter, Gina, his successful student with the skipping ropes and equally alert mentally, welcomed them, also wearing a pinafore. Franca proved more than adequate as a hostess and a skilful cook. Well aware of her culinary skills, Rose had told him to expect something other than pasta or minestrone. Giuseppe proved equally as amiable as Bruno and as generous as Francesco. The dinner comprised of roast chicken, potatoes, corn, beans and erba.

"Beef steak," she explained, "is impossible, but chicken is an excellent substitute and I must apologise for the erba; it is the only seasonal green available."

"Franca, I prefer chicken to beef steak and erba is my favourite vegetable. I haven't eaten like this for over five years, and that is as far back as I can remember."

"I think you are trying to make me feel good."

"But you are good. How can I show my appreciation? Thank you doesn't sound enough."

"It's all I ask. As for appreciation, you are showing that now."

Giuseppe, standing at his shoulder with a jug of wine, charged his glass.

"Taste it," he urged.

Sipping and trying not to make a big show with all eyes upon him, he complimented, "It's very good."

"You would have said that about a glass of vinegar, but I knew you would like it. We have the best wine in Italy," Giuseppe boasted, topping up his glass so full that he had to be careful to avoid staining the spotless white table linen. They were equally generous with dessert. Anticipating his taste, Franca placed a second large portion of apple pie on his plate before he had finished the first.

"I tried to make the dinner as English as possible," she said.

"Franca, we don't have such excellent meals. I've never eaten anything cooked so perfect!"

"Now I know you are trying to be kind," she smiled, and he could see that she was pleased.

Picking up his wine glass he nudged Rose and asked, in English, "Will you help me drink this?"

"Put your glass alongside mine and we'll drink from the same one. They'll excuse me if I leave some."

Giuseppe brought out the oldest accordion he had ever seen, cleverly coaxing pleasant music from its worn bellows while they all joined in singing Italian folk songs. Not being familiar with the words, he hummed the music. The evening came to a pleasant conclusion with a rendering of the wartime international favourite *Lili Marlene*, sung Italian style, again and again.

The next morning, they set off on their return journey. Along the way they encountered a farmer perched atop a huge cart drawn by a lumbering pair of oxen, prompting Jim to suggest, "Let's hitch a ride!"

The driver stopped while they clambered aboard, waiting until they were reasonably comfortable before proceeding on his time consuming journey. They were transported across the bridge in stately fashion, the ungainly vehicle continuing in their direction for a further 2 km.

He delivered their daughter safe and happy; mission successfully completed 48 hours after setting out. He stayed for dinner and listened while she related their adventure, omitting the town incident. They parted with a handshake at the gate before he took the lonely road back to an empty bed. Few people ventured abroad at night; not once in his travels had he encountered a fellow traveller after dark. Tonight he pushed the bike; there was no reason to hurry. Jumping into the saddle, he peddled under the phosphorescent light of a gibbous moon toward the welcoming light in the window.

*

Chapter 17

March gave way to April. He was given charge of the vegetable plot and produced better than average results while Maria laboured alongside Francesco, ploughing, sowing and planting. They produced enough to sustain life with nothing over and above to create prosperity. They became less discreet, he and Rose, as time went by; they courted openly now. The front line was static. The Germans were moving equipment north to prepared defences. The expected offensive was only a matter of days away. All indications pointed to a swift advance by the British and a carefully planned retreat by the Germans. Rumour was rife with everyone expectantly awaiting liberation from the Nazi oppressors, except for the two lovers who were dreading the British coming as it spelled the end of their world together. Each afternoon was spent in siesta at Francesco and Maria's where their privacy was sacrosanct. Their hosts were aware, but graciously chose to ignore. Respect was mutual. Lulled by the peaceful security, whether safe or false, they ceased to care. Their time together was being threatened by his deliverance. They dreaded the morning of awakening to find that they had exchanged one enemy for another. With the Germans, he only had to maintain a low profile. The advent of the British meant he would have to leave this state of bliss. They were in a no-win situation.

On a beautiful day in May, they lay peacefully in each other's arms. Lovers with the added bonus of trust and friendship.

"Does that proposal of marriage still stand?" she asked out of the blue.

"It took you long enough to reply," he said, surprised. "I was afraid to ask again. A refusal would have flattened my ego."

"Well we can't have that, can we? I'd better say yes. I'm

pregnant." She said it with a weak smile. "That should boost your ego."

He tried being as casual as she.

"I didn't think I had it in me!" he said.

"You haven't. It's in me!"

"Well how about tomorrow? We only need a priest. He knows us well enough by now."

"I doubt if he'll marry us tomorrow and when Mamma hears about this, you will be in trouble. She knows I'm innocent."

"Well, let's get married before we tell her."

"Would you like to tell her?"

"No."

He was on his knees searching under the bed.

"Coward! What are you looking for?"

"The glass slipper. I'm looking for my other boot."

"Its over there by the door. If Francesco and Maria are asleep, we won't disturb them."

As they cycled along the track, everything looked greener; the sun more golden; the earth richer.

"This is the happiest day of my life," he said.

"You say that every day. Today is the most shocking. You've had a fright."

"Shocking? Not at all! The gunner is going to marry the princess. And that's not all, they are going to have a son of a gun. The war will be over before he arrives."

"And if it's a girl?"

"The war will still be over. We'll call her Rose Green Corner. If your name had been Rosso instead of Verde wouldn't that have been perfect: Rose Red Corner."

"Mamma would have been happier if your name had been Rosso. She used to say 'I wish you were married to a nice Italian boy'. You are not what she had in mind." They had stopped just 200 yards from her home; it looked like a picture postcard. "Now is as good a time as any to explain the reason why I kept you waiting for a reply. I don't want to leave this beautiful spot, but I will to be with you."

"I wouldn't ask you to, why should you?"

"You mean you will stay here with me?"

"Why not? Wherever I go I'll have to work. I'm starting to make future plans for the first time in my life. I'm going to report my existence and volunteer for the Italian front. But first, I'm going to fix up your marriage allowance and if the worst happens, you will receive a war widow's pension."

"Don't you think we should get married first? Otherwise I won't qualify for either. It's really good of you to make me a widow and inherit your estate. It's nice to look forward to a secure future," she said mockingly.

Glancing at her while pushing the bike, he tripped over a stone, fell and got himself entangled in the frame. Her laughter brought Mamma onto the porch. Watching them behave like children no longer surprised her. He was a regular visitor, though never unaccompanied. Watching him scramble to his feet, she waited to welcome them. She was always polite but he was never sure of her true feelings.

"Welcome, young man." It was always young man! "How does your garden grow?"

That was something he would gladly like to talk over with her but she was already speaking to Rose. Papà on the other hand showed some interest. He was easy and polite, always prepared to offer a drink, which was refused, but he kept asking.

She waited until dinner was almost finished before dropping the bombshell, announcing her condition in a voice as clear as a bell. No stammering, no clearing of the throat. His own was so dry he couldn't swallow; there was no hiding place.

"Mamma, Papà, I'm pregnant," she stated her condition simply.

He waited for someone to drop something, at least a knife or a fork. There was no Italian-style panic. Just silence. Did she say it? He couldn't have imagined it!

"How do you feel about it, caro?" Mamma asked as if she was enquiring about her work.

"Excited I think. Yes I'm really excited."

"And you?" Mamma turned to Jim.

He swallowed the lump in his throat and took a sip of wine.

"I'll feel better when we are married and I find out where I'm going."

"You do have to go of course?" Papà asked.

"Afraid so."

"Where? Do you have any idea?"

"Here in Italy, I'm sure. I'll volunteer for this front."

"Why do you have to be sent to the front? I mean, have you not done enough?" Rose asked.

"What is enough? I'm missing, believed dead. Nobody knows what I've done. I'm readymade material, baptised by gunfire. Here in Italy I'll be closer to you. Soldiers don't fight all the time you know. They do get leave."

"I think," Mamma suggested, "we should all have a glass of cognac."

"Agreed," Papà replied, getting up to carry out her proposal.

He was impressed by their acceptance of the situation: no tears, no fuss, no blame. After pouring each a generous measure, they drank a little toast to the future and settled down to talk things out.

"First of all," Papà asked, "do you have any suggestions to put forward, figlio?"

"Arrange the wedding at the earliest possible date. If we marry before they come, there's nothing anyone can do about it."

"I'm sure that can be arranged in time."

"Well I'm not certain about the rules but I know there will be all kind of obstacles to surmount. When I report my existence, then everything is out of my control; I go wherever they send me. Once we are married, Rose will receive an allowance and, if the worst happens, a war widow's pension. So you see, I'm worth more dead than alive."

"He's already said that once and it sounds worse a second time. I would rather you didn't persist."

"Alright, we target for June 1st," Papà said enthusiastically. "The priest will grant special dispensation in these uncertain times. Of course, it will all have to be secret," he laughed.

"Isn't everything here in Italy," Mamma said. "Tomorrow, everybody will know without being told."

They talked and planned well into the evening. There were so many details, so much to arrange. Papà took him by the arm.

"I'm sure the ladies will excuse us. We're going to choose his wedding outfit."

Papà guided him to their bedroom, which was both spacious and comfortable, revealing the first built-in wardrobe he had ever seen. Papà pushed the sliding door and exposed an array of suits, offering him a choice from a selection of four.

"Luigi, the town tailor, is a personal friend of mine. He will undertake any alterations necessary."

He decided on the medium grey, choosing a white shirt and matching grey tie. A pair of snug-fitting black shoes completed his wedding garb.

"Try on the suit, then we will have an idea how much work we will be imposing on Luigi. You have a head for figures, I understand. Anything else you are good at?"

"A gun," he chuckled. "Now, how does your suit look on me?"

"Not bad. It will look a lot better with a little alteration by an expert. Guns will have no place in society after the war, but I could find an occupation to suit your capabilities."

"What are you trying to say, Signor?"

"We don't want Rosanna to leave us. Neither Bruna nor I expected this. I know you felt her resentment and I hope you understood."

"Signor…"

"Maybe we could dispense with the signor. My name is Giovanni."

"Alright, Giovanni. These shoes are a perfect fit. Anyway, I didn't understand. At first, she was good to me. Then she began to suspect."

"How could she have been otherwise after what you did for Rosanna. She didn't suspect, she knew, we both did."

"Rose has already told me that she doesn't want to leave. You can put your mind at rest, Giovanni. I will do whatever she asks. I want to please her."

"Thank you. Bruna will be pleased. She is secretly worried about that possibility. Shall we go and get their opinion, about the suit I mean?"

Walking into the room, he felt both pairs of eyes on him; he created an impression. Bruna got up to make a closer inspection.

"You are a handsome young man. You make the suit look good. Why are you not Italian," she said, giving him a rare smile.

"I blame my parents, Signora, they were thoughtless."

"Maybe. I suppose I shouldn't blame you for that," she smiled, placing her arm around his shoulder; an uncharacteristic show of affection that had Rose looking surprised. When he caught her eye, she gave him a 'well, what do you think of that?' look.

"Mamma, he's afraid of you."

"Are you? Are you really?"

"I little bit."

"But you're not afraid of the Tedeschi!"

"Well I like everybody to think I'm not."

"Everybody does. I thought you weren't afraid of anything."

"If you ever find anybody who isn't, I would like to meet him."

Rose smiled. She was feeling pleased with their verbal exchange.

"Take off the suit, I'll parcel it up. Tomorrow we'll meet in town and visit Luigi together."

"Good, that affords me an opportunity to have a haircut."

"Then you will need some money."

"Why?"

"Because the man has to make a living."

"I'll have to start giving that some thought. When I report my existence, I'll be rich; they owe me three years' back pay. Almost £300: enough to buy three motor cars."

"They won't be £100 each when production starts again, £300 may only buy one!"

"One will do, we can only use one at a time. I'll get changed and take my leave. Thank you, Signora, you were easier on me than I deserved."

He was well-known in the town, although he rarely visited, and only then to attend mass with Rose. If he was going to live here, it would be prudent to find out who was anybody and be polite to the nobodies. It would be wise to keep a social balance.

The sun was dancing a heat haze on the tarmac as he strode along the road into town; it was great to be alive. People were going about their daily business and he made a point of greeting everyone. His salutations were well received. The barber was sitting outside his shop smoking a cigarette when a German truck pulled into the square and parked at the municipio. Three soldiers and a captain dismounted. A man on a bike called a warning to him as he walked across the piazza to join the hairdresser who was now standing, watching curiously.

"Buon giorno. I would like a haircut. You do have a back door just in case?"

The barber beckoned him inside without speaking. Turning the chair to face the window, he said, "I'm curious, but you have more at stake."

He sat comfortably, enjoying the snip-snip of the scissors and the warm, friendly chatter of the barber.

"I see you often at mass on Sundays with the school teacher."

"You know her? What's your name, Signor?"

"Giorgio. Everybody knows yours, Captain. Signorina Rosanna, your fiancée, I've known all my life."

"She had a black eye when we first met. Maybe you saw what actually happened that day?"

"Look! They are taking men off the street and forcing them into the municipio. God, they treat people like animals, pushing people around. This doesn't look good at all."

The barber stopped cutting and watched tentatively as he sat with the apron spread around him, hair half cut. Watching while the officer strutted around with unbelievable conceit, screaming orders.

"The British are doing the world a favour ridding it of those arrogant bastards," Giorgio said, chopping the air with his hand.

They had disappeared into the building with half a dozen hostages. The square was deserted. Giorgio got back to his work talking in time with the click-click of the scissors.

"I remember the day well," he said. "They came into the town, firing their guns, scaring people to death, kidnapping young men to do their dirty work. Everyone ran in panic, all except the signorina. She waded into the fray fearlessly, attacking two soldiers who were taking a young man hostage. Swinging her briefcase, she knocked a soldier to the ground while she pushed the other and knocked him off balance. The youth escaped. She achieved her goal and her courage spurred the crowd into action, but not before a soldier floored her with a single punch. The crowd began hitting and kicking the soldiers who were struggling now to make their own escape. She had inspired the people. Someone helped her to her feet. She walked away with the dignity of a princess, calm as a summer day."

"That must have been a sight to behold."

She appeared at the window and waved as the Germans came out of the building. They were followed by the six men struggling with a huge desk while the captain screamed orders to the driver of the truck. She burst into the shop as his hair was being teased into style with skill and care.

"You look good," she greeted cheerfully. "That's an excellent job, Giorgio. Can I pay you?"

"No charge, Signorina. We've been watching the Tedeschi steal our antiques."

"What will they take next? They kidnap our young men, violate our women, now they've come for our inheritance. Can't you stop them, Jim?" she added, chuckling.

"I could, but not for an old desk. They can have that. Just look at that dancing captain! His arrogance is unbelievable. Imagine men like that ruling the world."

"God would never allow such a catastrophe. He is English, isn't he?"

"God, you mean? Of course he's English! What else could he be?"

"They think he's German," she said, smiling.

"Jesus Christ, what conceit! Well there goes the desk. They're leaving. Let's wave them off. It will never get out of Italy. Somebody will chop it up for firewood to keep warm during the winter."

"Giorgio," she said, "you must accept payment. It's your living. How are Veronica and the children?"

"They are very well, Signorina. I don't think taking pay for this will leave them either better or worse off. So if you don't mind, I'd rather you didn't insist."

"Very well, Giorgio, we'll accept it as a wedding gift. Thank you."

"A wedding gift? Really? Congratulations! I am delighted."

"So are we, Giorgio," he replied. "Goodbye and thank you. You might see us from your window on June 1st."

"My shop will be shut that day. I'll be at the church with everyone else. Goodbye and good luck."

They left the shop arm in arm.

"You did a good job of spreading the word there. That's better than an announcement in Il Popolo d'Italia."

"Of course, I'm well aware. Now let's take that parcel and have your suit made to fit. You are ahead with your preparations, aren't you? Haircut and now an appointment with your tailor."

Salvatore, the town policeman and a reluctant Fascist, met them as they left the square, although not by accident. He knew their whereabouts.

"Signorina. Captain," he greeted them respectfully. "Can you spare a moment?"

"Of course, a pleasure, Salvatore," she replied cheerfully. "How are Tina and the children?"

She had asked the same question of the barber just minutes ago. To her, everybody was important.

"The children are happy, thanks to your kindness and perseverance. Ours is the only school open. Tina is more worried than I."

"Why? What's troubling her? Can I help?"

She was truly concerned.

"Not you, Signorina, but maybe the captain here."

"What can the captain do for you, Salvatore? I have trouble helping myself."

"The British will be here soon. I'm a Fascist and they might think that I've been helping the Tedeschi."

"Well, have you?"

"No," Rose was quick to defend.

"Then why worry? Everybody's a Fascist. They won't shoot everybody!"

"I'm sure you will find them most understanding. It would be unkind to compare us with the Germans. The British are not interested in you, Salvatore, and since you are well respected in this town, you have nothing to fear. If by any remote chance they do question your loyalty, then I will speak on your behalf."

"Captain. Signorina. Thank you both."

"Just one small detail, Salvatore. I'm a corporal, not a captain."

"That's of no consequence, they will listen to a soldier with your record."

"You think so? Then go home and comfort your wife. Tell her there is nothing to worry about."

"Thank you, Captain. Signorina. Arrivederci."

"You handled that problem quite well. He was visibly relieved," she said as they continued on to Luigi's. "While you and Papà were sorting out a suit, did he ask any special favour?"

"Why do you ask?"

"Mamma was more than usually cheerful this morning. He asked for your promise not to take me away, didn't he?"

"Yes."

"Did he ask for it in writing?" she laughed.

"He made me carve it on the wardrobe door. We are on first names now. I call him Giovanni."

"Progress indeed! When Mamma allows you to call her Bruna, then you will know you are one of the family. We are here, this is Luigi's."

It wasn't a shop as he had expected but a house in a side street, exactly like the adjacent houses except for a sign painted on the wall indicating his trade. As she opened the door, a bell above their heads rattled rather than rang. They stepped into a room with a trestle table for a counter. A man of no discernible age was hunched over a foot-operated sewing machine. Recognising his patron, the machine stopped and he rose to meet her.

"Rosanna! This is indeed a pleasure. Come in, come in."

They were ushered into a tiny room while he called his wife from the kitchen. Seeing her guest, she screamed her name and hugged her, tears flowing freely down the worn, lined face.

"Is this the British captain we've been hearing about?"

Rose formally introduced him.

"My fiancé. We are to be married on June 1st, hopefully."

There were further cries of delight and more embraces; he was caught in the crossfire. A handshake just wasn't enough. Their hospitality was overwhelming. They offered everything but the double bed, and that could be theirs, but only after the wedding. They accepted a glass of wine to toast the occasion, a cause that was still being toasted three hours later.

"Promise you will bring your husband and have dinner with us," they begged.

"I promise. First, let me state the reason for this visit."

While she opened the parcel, Luigi felt the cloth with thumb and finger.

"This is an excellent piece of material. It will be a pleasure working with cloth like this. If you will, Captain, just slip into the shop and put it on. Call when you are ready."

At his call, all three came into the shop. Rose to supervise, Luigi to do the repair work, his wife to advise. Measuring the alterations painstakingly, the tailor constantly kept repeating the maxim: measure twice, cut once.

"This will be my pleasure, and our wedding present to you. If you call tomorrow, your suit will be ready and I guarantee a perfect fit."

"I'm sure it will, Luigi, we are indebted to you," he said, edging towards the door, but was obliged to return and join the conversation. He was asked how life would be when the British arrived. "In a town so remote, you may never see a British soldier."

"We see too many Germans."

"Then you might have better luck with the British. I could be the only one you will ever see."

With that, they were reluctantly allowed to leave.

*

Chapter 18

They sat on the porch in the pleasant warmth of evening having tea with homemade cakes and pastries, discussing the preliminaries to the wedding. Indeed, they had talked about nothing else all week. With just two more days to go, everything was arranged for 11 am, June 1st. Feeling the excitement creeping up on him, he had difficulty getting to sleep at nights while she confessed to the same problem. The British had not as yet arrived, while the Germans were moving so much equipment north that there could only be token resistance when the attack did begin. Everyone waited anxiously for the transition.

"You have chosen a beautiful spot in which to live," she said, smiling as they watched the sun set behind the mountains.

He smiled, "If they will let us live in it."

"What kind of thoughts flutter around your mind when you lie awake at nights. I'm curious, since I'm having the same difficulty."

"You mostly. My mind is so tiny, I can only fit you into it."

"You dominate all my waking hours, 20 a day at present. Even when I'm in control, my thoughts run off at different tangents, but they always return to you, and the baby."

"Mine get out of hand completely. God I wish it was Thursday night! How are we going to get through the next two nights? And I'm not supposed to see you at all tomorrow."

Mamma came out to sit with them.

"Isn't this a most delightful evening? Can I pour you another cup of tea, figlio?"

She could never bring herself to address him by name. He often wondered if she knew it, yet she was always kind towards him.

"Yes please, it's such a pleasure. That was my first cup of tea in nine months, and I drank it out of a margarine tin last time. Soon I'll be drinking out of a mess tin, meanwhile I want to taste the flavour from a china cup and enjoy this wonderful evening, and the delightful company."

Rose turned her head slightly to look him full in the face. Their eyes had developed a quality of understanding, a thought-reading process.

"Your parents will be surprised when next you write home," Mamma said.

She was in a happy mood, eager to talk and enter into the spirit of the occasion.

"They will be happy that I am alive. It's almost a year since I wrote."

"I will write to introduce myself and apologise for stealing you away," Rose said.

"By the time you can send a letter, I will have written and told them everything about you in detail. The thrill of becoming grandparents will have long been moderated. According to my reckoning, ours will be number ten on their programme. However, an introductory letter from you will afford a greater emotional tremor. The personal touch will delight them."

"Ten grandchildren! Mother of God," Mamma repeated, aghast. "We will welcome your parents here for a holiday after the war. We want to get to know them."

"Thank you, Signora. That is exceedingly gracious. You and mother will enjoy each other's company despite the language barrier. Incidentally, she's your equal in size," he told her with a sly chuckle.

"Then I will look forward to our meeting. As we won't be seeing you tomorrow, Giovanni will explain your role at the church. Don't be surprised when you see the ring, it's standard Italian and patriotic."

"Surprised, Signora? It would have to be a steel band."

"It is, Jim. That's what Mamma means by patriotic. Everybody sacrificed their gold to the war effort."

"Well that doesn't astonish me either. A piece of string would do. We'll buy a good one, 24 caret, no less. Remember I told you about all the money I will have to my credit."

"You were going to buy three cars as I recall."

"Two now, Rose. Two and a ring."

She laughed, "Let's go inside and see Papà, then I'll walk with you as far as the tree."

He received instructions from Giovanni while she tried the ring for size. He did the same, his fingers were like puddings but it conveniently fit the little finger. A measure against the ring he intended buying whatever the cost.

The wedding day dawned after an almost sleepless night, his mind a web of confused delight. Their secret rendezvous had helped them through the long yesterday. The old alarm clock had ticked its way past 6.15 am as he tiptoed silently through the kitchen and stepped outside to welcome the golden silence of morning. He felt an uncontrollable urge to hurry. After an extended session with the skipping ropes and a run through a table of exercises, he stripped and sluiced himself with two breath-taking buckets of water from the well, drying himself with the towel, while discreetly examining his body for any flaw which might have developed overnight.

Maria surprised him while he was stealthily making his way back to his room. She laughed while they exchanged greetings and then walked to the stable doors to pass the time of day with Francesco. They had developed a good relationship and he was sorry to leave. He thanked them also for the privacy they had afforded Rose and himself throughout the past weeks.

He dressed and was being examined and inspected. She turned him again and again; touching here, adjusting there, until finally passing favourable comment. At last they set off for the church. The sun shone brightly from an azure blue sky as they walked along the road to town. Salvatore met them at the entrance to the square, assuring a safe passage to and from the church; he had posted three sentries at strategic points. The wedding was a typical well-kept Italian secret: the piazza was crowded. He thought it might be market day but what would anybody have to sell? Heads turned as he walked through the crowd, greeted by people he had never seen before. Up the church steps and through the doors, he stood in the spotlight, looking at a sea of faces all turned towards him. They broke into smiles of approval as he swallowed the lump in his throat and walked the 100 miles down the aisle. Eventually reaching the sanctuary of a vacant front pew, he heard St Christopher whisper 'you are on your own now. This is as far as I go'.

The congregation continued their speculation and discussion while the priest entered the scene amidst the shifting of bodies. A subdued sound of oohs and ahs and of drawn breath resounded throughout the church. Jim stood up, his heart hammering against his ribs. The priest walked forward, beckoning him to the altar rails, indicating where he was to stand. With his eyes fixed firmly to the front, he was aware of a presence at his side. They stole a glance at exactly the same moment. Their eyes met and they allowed each other a fleeting survey from head to toe. She was dressed in a cream coloured two-piece costume with matching Juliet hat and half veil. This magnificent specimen of womanhood by his side favoured him with a smile of approval. He did all that was asked and made few mistakes throughout the ceremony. He watched and listened, particularly to the promise to love, honour and obey. She answered clearly while mischievously looking into his eyes. Then suddenly it was over. She was now his very own for her to do with as she pleased. They procured a duplicate marriage certificate written in English to hand over to the paymaster on his return.

They walked out of the church amidst loud cheers, clapping and cries of best wishes and proceeded towards the awaiting carriage. Giovanni had taken over the reins while Brunita, ten kilos heavier after a month out to grass, stood impatiently scraping the cobbles, striking an occasional spark with her steel shoes. The principal guests followed in equal style, travelling first class in mule-drawn carrozzas. As Brunita laboured up the steep dirt road, panting and snorting, totally out of condition, he leapt from the trap and took hold of the bridle, apologising to Giovanni for his action. She had the little back door open awaiting his helping hand. Together they walked up and over the hill—this was her personal suggestion. The scene was in total contrast to the first day she had brought him here, just three months ago, a tramp with shoulder-length hair. Mutually attracted strangers then, now husband and wife.

Tables were laid on the grass space between the houses, brilliant-white linen reflecting the afternoon sunshine while women fetched, carried and laid the places. The traffic began to build up behind: the two carrozzas carrying passengers followed by guests on foot. Anna, who was sharing Mamma's carriage, quickly caught up before they were overwhelmed by force of numbers.

"Mia caro, you looked radiant," she greeted. "My eyes were upon you the whole time. And look at the prince! Can this be the bundle of rags you dragged in here not so very long ago?" Placing her hand on Rose's stomach, she laughed, "He didn't waste much time did he?"

"Maybe I rushed things a little. I was afraid he might walk away and leave me."

"I guessed his intentions that first day." She patted his face with her hand. "You didn't look so handsome then."

They were suddenly encircled by well wishers, suffering some superficial bruising until Anna rescued them again, ushering her charges into the cool of her kitchen where fresh water and towels were laid out. She had anticipated their every need.

"You look fresh, Rose. Did you sleep last night?" Jim added.

"Hardly at all. I was thinking of you. Did you sleep?"

"A couple of hours, no more."

"Perhaps we will sleep tonight. Will you let me?"

They smiled at each other.

"I'll let you do anything you please. We did sleep at Elvira's, remember?"

"Every detail, and since you will allow me to do as I please, then I must reciprocate."

"I hoped you would."

"You knew I would."

He was helping her into her jacket when a small crowd of people burst into the kitchen: Anna, Papà and Mamma proceeded by Elvira, Dante and Franca. Everybody embraced everyone else.

"We missed the ceremony. Those bloody soldiers kept us waiting two hours at the bridge. Caro, you look positively beaming. God what a beautiful outfit, will it ever fit me like that? And look at that clown! Will he make me pregnant if I kiss him? We all know what he's done to you."

"Bruto," she said, putting her arms around him, "I'll risk it."

Music drifted in from outside; a raucous voice had found the only outlet to a few glasses of wine. The smell of lamb roasting on a spit floated on the breeze as they stepped outside into a scene from a Hollywood musical extravaganza. The leading players made their way to the table amidst cheers, light-hearted banter, and the odd coarse joke.

Late in the afternoon, the wine had taken its toll. Overcome by drinking, dancing, and the heat of the day, some of the guests were stretched out in the shade sleeping off the effects while the die-hards continued dancing and singing. An out-of-tune couple held each other up while singing a duet. Later, the principal guests sat in the cool of Anna's kitchen discussing the day's events over coffee, real black market coffee.

"You didn't drink at all," she said.

"You noticed," he smiled. "I need a clear head. I want to feel what I am doing tonight. But you didn't drink either."

She laughed. "While you are doing what you feel, I want to feel what you are doing. Mamma is looking at us very inquisitively."

"Then tell her."

"If I do, she'll lock you in the stable with Brunita."

"If you don't, she might die of curiosity."

"We'll have to risk that."

"I was giving some thought to the bridge. They are preparing to blow it."

"Are you sure?"

"What the ladies told us confirms it."

"Then perhaps we should accompany them. Help them find a crossing point. The river can't be so high at this time of year."

"I don't fancy swimming fully clothed. Maybe you can charm the sentry on the bridge."

"He might get other ideas."

"Then I'll be on hand to remove his testicles; without anaesthetic."

"That would be painful."

"Not for me. You had best ask if they need us."

All eyes were curiously on them while they had been talking in English. Apologising, she asked, "Would you like an escort as far as the bridge?"

"I would," Franca replied promptly.

"You mean both you and him?" Elvira was more cautious.

"If you wish."

"We had already discussed asking him, so we thank you and we'll all sleep easier tonight."

"That's settled then. If you will excuse us, my husband and I would like to take our leave."

Her announcement brought a chorus of oohs, ahs and a couple of wry comments.

"Thank you," she continued with a smile. "We would like to thank Mamma and Papà, and Anna in particular for her kindness. Francesco, would you prepare the rig please?" With a sly aside, she looked at Jim. "Maria will be riding with us, I'm sure you wouldn't mind walking."

"Whatever you say, Rose."

There was laughter.

"This is an ideal time," Elvira said, "to request the pleasure of your company at Via Viale. The invitation is for a week, no less, longer if you choose."

"Say yes, Rosanna," Franca pleaded. "We have been preparing in anticipation, don't disappoint us."

"I'll leave the decision with my husband," she replied, smiling.

"Then you accept," Elvira said.

"If he so desires."

"He so desires, don't you, buffone? Oh my God, he's teetering. Pull another string, Rose, your puppet is undecided."

She had everyone laughing, Mamma loudest of all. She had been watching and listening with pleasure. She liked the idea of Rose being the dominant partner.

"Come on, desire won't you?" Elvira coaxed.

"There will be at least three very special meals that week," Franca threw in the decider.

Actually, he didn't want to end this very pleasant repartee by just saying yes.

"Then that does it. I haven't forgotten the last dinner. Did we thank you for that, Franca?"

"By eating it, you thanked me."

"Here's Francesco," Anna declared.

She got up to walk with them to the rig after having said their goodbyes.

"You'll be leaving soon. Be sure and make this the last place you visit before you go, and I'll expect to see you both before then."

"It will be Anna, and thank you for everything."

"I hope you don't think I paid for all this. I couldn't afford the coffee."

"I'm well aware, but you did afford the time."

"So long as you understand. Let me kiss you both and wish you everything I think you deserve."

She brushed away a tear as she left.

"You will hurry, won't you? I only meant this as a joke, now it's backfired. I'm going to be without you when I shouldn't be."

"It was worth the laugh. I'll hurry away now and maybe get there before you."

He held her outstretched hand walking alongside the rig as they passed him at the olive grove. His possessions were in the trap when he arrived. He only had to dig his bag out of the hay that the pony was eating. They all came out of the house to join him: Maria, drying her eyes on a towel and Francesco with a sad smile. The goodbyes took some time amidst kisses, handshakes and promises. Finally she took his hand.

"Let me take you home," she said as they walked to the trap.

"Arrivederci e presto ritorno," Francesco said with a final handshake.

Homeward bound, Brunita maintained a brisk trot. They looked back at the forlorn figures and waved when they were almost out of sight. Completely alone for the first time that day, looking into eyes filled with promise, afraid to touch, their bodies ached with anticipation.

A double bed was the only alteration to her room. She found space in her wardrobe to hang his one suit.

"You can visit the bathroom first while I undress," she told him.

It was all so strange. He was tingling with excitement but tried not to hurry his ablutions. When finally he was done, he knocked on the bedroom door in case she wasn't quite ready.

"Come in, Jim! You don't have to knock on your own door."

She stood their smiling at him in a most enticing nightdress. He had to keep a firm grip on himself while she looked so calm, so in control.

"You look good enough to eat," he said.

She laughed. "I'll be as quick as I can, then you can eat as much as you like."

*

Chapter 19

The advance party for Via Viale arrived at 10.30. At 11 precisely, all five set off, laughing and talking animatedly.

"Did the brute keep you awake last night, caro?" Elvira asked impishly.

"They both look fresh and alive to me," Franca said. "Whatever they did has done them no harm."

"Will you shut up, Franca? I want to find out exactly what happened," Elvira chided.

"Why didn't you sleep, Captain? Were you making plans to take the bridge?" Dante asked, adding, "is the gun in your bag?"

"Will you stop talking about guns," his mother shouted at him.

At this rate, they wouldn't get to the bridge by evening. He wanted to push on but they were having so much fun that he decided to stroll along at their pace; everybody wanted to talk. Elvira stopped to converse with a couple of passers-by, old acquaintances. She had lived here before she married and moved away. When they finally got going again, he tried to urge them on, but in vain.

"It's obvious what he has in mind." It was Franca this time. "He wants to get back in time for an afternoon siesta."

"I was quite looking forward to that," Rose said, playing their game.

"Of course you were," Elvira replied. "You are tired. This selfish pig probably kept you awake all night."

"Actually I enjoyed being kept awake, but the poor dear fell asleep on me. He tired himself out."

"And left you wide awake. The dirty animal!"

He wasn't going to be let off the hook at all; he couldn't win.

"Ladies," he finally spoke up, "I would like to get back and siesta with her. So please can we get moving?" he entreated.

"Bruto!" they both exclaimed. Rose just laughed.

The valley was a joy to behold with everything in bloom. The earth was green and golden in the afternoon sun.

"This is magnificent," he said. "Imagine fighting a war here in this beautiful land. It's criminal. They just employ a million dumbos like me and turn them loose on each other."

"I didn't realise you felt so. You've never spoken with such passion."

"That's because I've never felt at all. A piece of bread, a lump of cheese and a warm place to sleep and I was happy as a pig in shit, and twice as ignorant. I can't believe I was that person. You breathed life into a dead body and redeemed a bankrupt soul. Rose Green, I love you."

She just stood there smiling. "There are some changes in me I would like to thank you for."

The spell was broken when Elvira remarked, "They have forgotten we're here."

"Sorry, caro, he speaks to me in English and I get carried away."

"You were both carried away. If you don't mind telling us, what were you discussing?"

"Yes, what were you saying?" Franca seconded the request.

"We were debating upon trying the bridge first, or just going ahead and fording the river. What do you think?"

"The bridge first, then the river if we have no choice," Franca said. "I'm terrified of water."

"He thinks they won't allow you to cross."

The bridge was visible between breaks in the trees and shrubbery as they made their descent. The silence so complete, peasants working the land almost a mile away could be clearly heard chanting folk songs while they still conversed in whispers. Choosing a spot with both the bridge and the road along the river in full view, they planned their strategy, hanging onto his every word. They were only going to walk across a bridge but the very presence of soldiers changed that simple act into a military operation. The plan was for them to walk forward and when the sentry challenged, Rose would reply in

German, while he positioned himself in the trees just 20 yards away.

"Just so long as we know you are there," Franca said.

He was already in position as they walked toward the bridge. The soldier came to meet them. He watched as they talked, the soldier giving directions before turning them back. Keeping undercover, he moved with them as they walked down the road a hundred yards or so, feeling their anxiety as they searched for his presence. Moving in the shrubbery unseen, he appeared on the road, 50 yards ahead, sensing their relief as they saw and hurried towards him like lost children.

"The sentry informed us," Rose told him, "that the British are just 5 km behind and they are awaiting instructions to blow the bridge. He said there is a crossing point just 500 m downstream where the river divides with an island centre stream."

"Somebody must be panicking—5 km away! We've walked 7 without seeing a goat. Anyway, we had better take his word for it. Just continue walking down the road and don't be afraid if you don't see me. I'll be seeking out this crossing point, then I'll call you."

Disappearing down the bank side, he searched until he found a likely spot. Wading through the shallows and onto the island, he inspected the waters on the north side. They ran swift but the stream was narrow, no more than 7 m. However, it was dangerously visible from the road. Laying down his bag at a strategic point, he waited until they came into view and beckoned them onto the island. All except Rose had removed their shoes, feeling their way across the stony shallows, laughing and calling to each other as if they were out for a day's ramble. They all gathered around him while he explained the situation.

"Now, it's only 6 m wide, we could jump it in two leaps. Can everybody swim?" There was no reply. "Then I'll have to take you across one at a time. You first, Dante."

His mother removed Dante's clothes, packing them into a bag that contained their night attire while he stripped to the waist, placing his shirt and vest near his bag.

Taking the boy by the hand, they walked to the river's edge. It was clear enough to gauge the depth. He should've had a trial crossing but it was too late now, Dante was shivering with fear and needed some assurance.

"Climb on my back and hold on tight." He felt the boy's nails digging into his flesh. "Relax," he said, "here we go."

Wading in until the current threatened to take him off his legs, he scrambled across, swimming with the stream, completely submerged. Touching the bank side with his hands, he managed to get his head clear of the water and heaved the boy onto the grass verge. The strong current was midstream. He could stand waist-deep here and hold onto the edge comfortably.

"That was easy, wasn't it? You weren't afraid at all." In fact the boy was speechless. "Now I'll go and bring your mother."

When he got back to the island, Rose was standing alone. He looked at her questioningly.

"They are in the bushes changing," she said. "They have decided to cross in their nightdresses. They didn't mind you seeing them in a state of undress. It's only Jim, they said. Now there's a compliment. They trust you with the easy-going simplicity of children."

Water was dripping off his hair, running down his face and falling from his nose and chin.

"Only Jim! I'll feel a lot better when Jim gets them all across. We are too exposed here."

The ladies came out of the bushes laughing and giggling like schoolgirls. Their clothes packed in the small travelling bag. They were both good-looking women and he couldn't help feeling a physical attraction. Particularly towards Elvira with her large breasts jigging as she walked and when she laughed.

"I'm ready for you, buffone," she jested, and they all laughed with her.

"Give me the bag and I'll throw that across first."

He called out to Dante, pitching the bag well clear of the water.

"Now Elvira, you said you were ready. Just put your hands on my shoulders and hold on."

Taking a deep breath, he plunged in with his formidable anchor. She hung on tightly, allowing him to use his arms. He swam with the current and grabbed two handfuls of riverbank as they stood together waist-deep, coughing and spluttering. After several attempts, they were still standing waist-deep, he couldn't get her up onto the bank side.

"Put both hands on the side and jump."

She made a vain attempt. He wasn't sure where to put his hands on a 14 st lady in her soaking wet nightdress. They were getting nowhere and her helpless laughter added to the problem.

"Elvira," he said, "you will have to excuse my hands. They are going between your legs."

"Woo hoo!" she cried.

He bent down, hands clasped between her thighs, his head underwater, heaving and pushing until she scrambled up the bank side.

"I hope I haven't ruptured myself."

"I think you enjoyed it," she said, giggling.

"Elvira, please. Did you?" he retorted.

He plunged back into the stream for the final trip, but as he set foot on the island, he froze. That awful feeling of fear playing around his crotch. Attracted by the laughter, two soldiers walked across the shallows towards them. He moved nearer his bag. The larger of the two, a big fellow, carried an MP-40 slung from his shoulder, his hand gripping the weapon between the mechanism and the magazine. He looked formidable. Making straight towards Franca, he began pawing her at once. The other soldier was armed with a bolt-operated rifle, which looked a bit outdated, and chased after Jim, clapping his hands and shooing him away. As he bent down to pick up his bag, the soldier booted him up the arse, bellowing raucously; he was having a great time. As he ran with bag in hand into the bushes, the soldier turned his attention towards Rose. She stood, waiting, watching, seemingly in complete control of her feelings, yet she must be terrified. The soldiers paid no further heed to him. He was the butt of their joke and of no further consequence. Franca was having a fearful time. The big soldier took his hand off the gun and put it around her waist, his other hand fondling her breasts. The gun between them was a hindrance but he could manage both, that was plain. Franca was in a distressed condition. Rose held her adversary at bay by talking to him in his own language but he was already reaching out and touching her breasts. The big soldier was half carrying Franca towards the bushes. He sat squatted, watching the whole scene, gun in hand, waiting for an opportune moment.

The soldier dragged a terrified Franca towards where he waited. At ten paces, he stood up and touched the trigger, firing a short burst at the big fellow's left thigh and away from Franca. The soldier went down as if he had slipped on a banana skin, taking her with him. Rose's assailant turned quickly, slipping the rifle from his shoulder. Jim wasn't so particular this time, he put a burst of four or five rounds straight between the soldier's thighs, collapsing him immediately to the stony ground, twisting and squirming. In almost the same movement, he grabbed the MP-40 from the big fellow who was sitting dazed, holding his leg. Franca was whimpering with fear, clinging to him, hampering his movements. With a gun in each hand, he dashed across to get the rifle. Rose had already taken it from the man rolling around in agony. Throwing one machine gun aside, he took the rifle and flung it into the deepest part of the river while Rose calmed Franca who was sobbing uncontrollably in her arms. He paused briefly to review the situation. Elvira and Dante were locked together 20 yards from the riverbank where they had run in fear. He beckoned them. They walked fearfully and slowly back, clinging to each other. The big man was just sitting nursing his leg while the other soldier lay moaning, huddled in a ball. He picked up the discarded machine gun and gave it to Rose.

"If they give you any trouble at all, just aim and pull the trigger. Remember it is them or us."

"Trust me, Jim," she said.

"I do."

Placing his gun on the stones, he took Franca by the arm. She was a little more composed, her body heaving now, and then with a sob she clasped him tightly as they stepped into the river while Elvira watched and waited on the opposite bank.

"Just hold onto my shoulders," he coaxed. "Do you feel alright now?" She nodded. "Now don't be afraid. Here goes," he said and plunged in.

She held on desperately, impeding his movements. The other two crossings he had done with one single deep breath. Franca had him gasping before he reached half way. She pushed him under, using him as a float. It proved to be a long swim. At the bank side, he couldn't grab anything that would help him. She was panicking, kicking him under and standing on his back in desperation, trying to scramble out of the water. She was terrified. Elvira, with her impressive strength, pulled her clear of the river. It took more than a minute for him to breathe. He was coughing and spluttering with Elvira leaning over, slapping his back anxiously. Finally able to speak, he gave her some last minute instructions.

"Go as far away as you can before stopping to dress. Is Franca alright?"

"I'll see to her. Take care of yourselves, and thank you."

"Go now," he said.

With that short farewell, he scrambled back to the island. Rose was talking to the big fellow, standing back at a safe distance, gun at the ready. He had no doubt if the soldier mustered enough strength to try an assault she would shoot. Picking up his own gun, he took the one she was holding and exchanged magazines. Then threw the other one into the river along with the rifle.

"We've got to get away from here. Those shots will have been heard miles away."

"This man is asking for the first aid box from the cab of his vehicle. He says it is parked just off the road in the trees."

"Come."

He took her hand and they ran together across the shallows and over the road. The truck was there where the man said it would be. He opened the cab door and the Red Cross pack was looking at him. With both hands full, he pushed her towards the track leading out of the valley.

"Go on ahead as fast as you can. I'll catch up."

He turned and ran across the road to the water's edge.

"Catch!" he shouted to the soldier, but didn't stop to see where it landed.

He paused briefly at the truck intending to put a burst into the petrol tank but on hearing the sound of approaching vehicles he abandoned the idea and chased up the hill after her. Now and then as the shrubs and trees thinned out in places he could see her scrambling up the steep rise. It occurred to him that she would also be visible from below. He pushed himself hard to catch up. The trucks had stopped and men were shouting. Stealing a backward glance at a convenient spot, he saw the comings and goings of men running from vehicles to the river. The sight spurred him on. As he drew alongside her, he pushed her into the shrubbery. Watching the show from about 200 yards, it looked like a training exercise with men running everywhere. Orders were being shouted and the front vehicle pulled away.

"Follow me," he said, "and do exactly as I do. Don't stand up."

"Jim," she said, "I'm going to wet myself."

He stopped, trying not to laugh out loud. He saw her looking at him, puzzled.

"It's only a feeling. I get it sometimes too. It will pass. Come, let's push on."

They crept where the cover was thin and ran where the sun didn't penetrate the trees, only stopping when they reached the top where they stretched out in the shade, lungs burning, fighting to breathe. Neither one spoke for some time. They just lay there enjoying the peace and feeling the security of each other.

"Jim, I just want to lie here and not move at all."

Stretched out on his back, he felt for her hand and squeezed. His body was exhausted but his mind was at work. She lay so quiet and still that he thought she must be asleep. As he turned his head, she was looking at him, eyes wide open.

"I thought you were asleep," he said.

"My mind is so disturbed, I don't think I'll ever sleep again. What a dreadful experience. When that soldier put his hands on my breasts, I thought I was going to be sick."

"You were magnificent! You looked like the Queen of the Amazons standing there with fearless dignity. You were my inspiration. You kept your head when all about you had already lost theirs, including me. I worked by instinct."

"Fearless dignity!" she repeated. "I was terrified. I only wanted to throw up."

"I'll bet that soldier is sorry now," he chuckled, "He'll never have the desire to touch any other woman's breasts, or kick anyone else's arse. I hope the ladies are alright. Poor Franca, what a state she was in."

He lay looking at the sunlight glinting among the leaves, when her face appeared above his face, blotting out the scene.

"Rose, you are so beautiful, I love you so much it hurts."

She kissed his lips while massaging his bare chest. The warm, tingling sensation flowed into his thighs. "We'll have our siesta here now," she said, smiling.

Suddenly the earth shook, the explosion ripped and echoed throughout the valley. They froze, looking at each other in alarm.

"There goes the bridge," he said.

"Then they've gone. Thank God!"

"They're gone," he repeated. "We are in no-man's-land. The German's have gone and the British haven't arrived. It's all ours, Rose, yours and mine." He got to his feet and took her by the hand. "Come, let us explore our inheritance. The lease will be a short one."

They strolled through their no-man's-land with absolute impunity. Sometimes they talked, and kissed once or twice. The journey was free of anxiety. Time had no meaning; it was sheer enjoyment. Sometimes, with his arm around her waist, he tested the mechanical movement of her hips with his hand. Arriving home around six o'clock, they found Mamma and Papà pacing up and down the drive like expectant grandparents in a maternity ward.

"Caro, caro," Mamma repeated as they embraced. "Thank God you're safe. Why is he stripped like that?"

"It's alright, Mamma, he just lost his shirt, that's all."

"Had a bad day at the races, Signora," he laughed.

"Did they get across alright before the bridge was blown?" Papà asked.

"They will all be safely at home by now. But how did you know about the bridge so soon?"

"We heard without knowing what the explosion was. Word got to us about an hour ago. We were so anxious. Your Mamma was ill with worry."

"Poor Mamma," Rose replied. "I'm a big girl now you know. With a husband to take care of me. He does it very well too, so you must not worry."

"Mmm," Mamma replied, looking at him, or through him. "We

have hot water if you wish and dinner will be ready when you are."

"Thank you Mamma, but I must find dry clothing for my husband. You would look after Papà wouldn't you."

"Mmm," was her reply.

Giovanni provided him with shirt, trousers and clean underwear. Once showered and dressed, he felt much better. He had been lucky again. His third encounter had happened on the very last day and he had come out of it well. Even Franca escaped the inevitable and she had no defence at all. Rose, he felt sure, would have put up a fight, and might even have won.

*

Chapter 20

D-Day arrived. They listened to the news on the radio, he and Giovanni, discussing at length the impressive scale of the operation. While the British had arrived here, few were seen in his little corner of the world and he felt no obligation to go out and look for them. Old cars and trucks were taken out of mothballs and appeared on the road; the source of fuel was a mystery to all but their owners. People looked for ways of posting letters to their loved ones scattered across Europe.

Rose and he spent idyllic days and blissful nights, but nothing is perfect, and their joy was overshadowed by the fast approaching day of separation. They decided to extend their honeymoon. While still in control of his own destiny, he granted himself a further two weeks furlough, thus delaying their own D-Day. The sun shone brightly, a gentle breeze played with her hair. Brunita trotted along at her own pace, enjoying the rattle of her hooves on the tarmac.

They leaned toward each other and kissed lingeringly while riding happily along in the rig. Blissfully unaware, wolf whistles and catcalls mixed with loud cheering brought them down to earth. They quickly drew apart.

"Get stuck in, mate, you have plenty there to go at!"

"How about swapping places, pal?"

A complete regiment of artillery were leaguered along the roadside while men gathered around the cookhouse. They had caught the lunch hour.

"Hey, take a shufti at the king and queen of Italy."

"I didn't know Italy had a king!" somebody called, "but the queen looks a bit of alright."

She responded with regal charm: a smile, a queenly wave. Before they had cleared the lines, she had received offers ranging from clandestine meetings to proposals of marriage.

"Strange men in strange lands behave in the most unaccountable manner."

He breathed a sigh of relief as they gained the open road while she was overwhelmed, delighted by the rough good-natured humour. He smiled at her undisguised pleasure.

"That was a delightful introduction. In complete contrast to the master race. 'Hey, mate, you've got plenty to go at there'," she mimicked joyfully as he laughed. Her good humour was infectious.

"That's how they behave in a crowd, meet them alone and you wouldn't get a squeak. It's mostly bravado."

"By the way, where did you learn the royal greeting?"

"I saw a film of your queen riding in a coach and, this is in the strictest confidence, I practiced her mannerisms in front of the mirror."

"You are a queen. More beautiful and much more sincere than our own."

Their bridge, the one where everything had happened, was a sorry sight in its wrecked condition; unnecessary vandalism of no strategic importance. They turned around following the road downstream. The river had subsided since that eventful day just two weeks ago. There were several islands on midstream now and the water had narrowed considerably. The steel bridge lay bent and buckled, the huge crossing girders snapped and sunk deep into the riverbed. The substitute bridge was a remarkable feat of engineering; a RE structure which took the mainstream of traffic adequately. Military police conducted the flow of vehicles with little delay either side. They were signalled to halt and ordered to pull into the side of the road. A red-capped corporal came across to question their destination. Rose bewitched him as he flirted good-naturedly, surprised by her excellent English, while he sat silently, pretending lack of comprehension. The policeman was practically eating out of her hand as she charmed her way over the bridge behind a supply column.

"You are a pleasure to behold and a joy to listen to," he said proudly.

She smiled impishly.

"These English Romeos are so genuinely obliging."

She acknowledged the whistles and wisecracks from passing

trucks with the same good humour. Brunita was superb, ignoring the roar of traffic like a London cab horse. They turned off the highway and travelled west on a smooth dirt road in a relaxed and buoyant mood.

"Sing me a love song, like the one you sang on our first picnic. I'll remember that day all my life. You've learned something about making love since then, Jimmy boy."

"I had a good teacher and enjoyed every lesson."

"You were the best pupil I ever taught," she said, laughing. "Are you sure you won't be embarrassed?"

"I wasn't last time."

"How about the *Shadow Waltz*. The lyrics are particularly good and very apt. The words were written with someone like you in mind."

"The *Shadow Waltz*. Sounds very nice. I feel in a romantic mood. Go on, I'll pay you for the pleasure tonight?"

He began his song to the rhythm of jingling harness, the thump-thump of hooves, and the creaking of the trap; perfect background music. She rewarded him with a smile of encouragement that made him feel good.

"Did you like it? The words I mean," he asked when his song ended.

"Delightful. I loved the words, the song, and the singer. You make me feel so special."

She held his hand. No further words were spoken until they arrived at the well.

The welcoming party were there in force to greet them. It had all happened before but never like this. After the kisses and the handshakes, everyone stood around in horseshoe fashion while Gina came forward with a bouquet. The flowers were just beginning to fade, a clear indication that they had been expected sooner. In practiced and quite discernible English, Gina delivered her well-rehearsed speech.

"Welcome to our home Mr and Mrs Corner."

The sincerity was quite touching. Rose handed him the bouquet of flowers and took Gina in her arms while everybody looked on silently. Someone suddenly remembered they were supposed to cheer.

When next he looked at her, there were tears in her eyes, which she contained with her usual dignity.

While they were being ushered into the house, he detected a lack of questioning that was always a feature during previous visits. This time the entourage were speculating among themselves with childish excitement. Elvira led them straight through the kitchen to the bedroom, the one that didn't have a door. Now it boasted a new blue panelled one. Giving them a key, Elvira stood aside smiling, expectant and excited.

"Will you open it or shall I?" Rose asked.

"You. I'll put my hand on yours."

They opened the door and walked in together.

"Mamma mia!" She was speechless.

"This must have cost a lot of money," Jim said to Bruno who was hovering behind.

The whole community were trying to get through the door.

"A lot of work anyway. It was a labour of love actually. You paid for it all."

"I? I couldn't buy a penny bun!"

"Well you bought all of this, let me tell you how. The total cost: one engine, one petrol tank half full, and four wheels. And there are more parts left to trade should you desire extra comfort," Bruno told him proudly, pulling back the bedclothes to reveal a brand new mattress. "The best," he boasted. "Those chairs are all my own work, my best work."

"The curtains?" Rose asked, walking across to feel the quality. "I love these."

"My donation," Franca called from the crowded doorway, "I would have liked to do more."

"You promised three dinners, isn't that the reason we're here. What more can you do."

"The first one will be ready in an hour. I must fly. Remember, one hour," she called back.

"The dressing table is my contribution." Maria pushed her way into the room. "On loan, I'm afraid. It's something I need to store my biancheria. I live in hope."

"You don't need to hope, Maria. I want to meet the lucky so-and-so when he comes."

"I want him to meet you both. I wish he would hurry," she said, smiling.

"Thank you, Maria."

The ten days they intended staying flew by. They tried reaching out to make time stand still, but time refuses to do that. The sun was high overhead while their room—their neat, tidy little bridal suite—was pleasantly cool. He looked casually out of the window at nothing in particular, simply waiting while she sat in front of the mirror brushing her midnight-black hair.

"Rose," he exclaimed with some surprise. "Come here."

Still brushing her hair, she joined him at the window. They smiled at each other. She took his hand and threw the hairbrush on the bed.

"Mamma must have been missing you," she said, laughing, as they walked out to meet Mamma and Papà.

Rose and Mamma embraced while he greeted Giovanni who was keen to show him around the Fiat.

"How did it perform after all these years?" he asked.

"Like a bird." He could detect the excitement. "Would you like to take it for a spin?"

"I would later, Giovanni."

They had a pleasant, comfortable relationship, he and Giovanni. Arm in arm, Rose and Mamma joined them while Papà was explaining how he got the car back on the road. He had employed a young mechanic from the village who had put it together and had it running in two or three hours.

"I've heard nothing else but that car since yesterday," Mamma complained good-naturedly. "How have you been treating my daughter, young man?"

She had only used his name once, on their wedding day.

"I've done everything she asked, Signora, and she hasn't threatened or raised a hand to me, so I must have done it right."

"He responds to kindness, Mamma, try it. You'll be surprised. He is house-trained, which you already know."

Mamma laughed.

*

Chapter 21

The two weeks' leave he had granted himself became four, then six. It was the end of July and the front line had advanced 150 km north of their paradise. It was time for him to leave or risk being classified as a deserter. Everybody knew him, or of him. It was only a matter of time before the British authorities discovered their secret. Her parents never questioned his intentions while Rose dreaded his departure. During one particular visit to see Francesco and Maria to read the letters they had received from their sons in England, they both decided that he must leave. They stayed awake most of the night making plans. When they kissed, her face was wet with tears.

"This is out of character, Rose."

He reached for the light switch.

"Don't," she called, "I don't want you seeing me like this." Amidst welling tears she asked, "Will they grant you love leave before sending you to the front?"

"Love leave!" he repeated, laughing. "I like it. They might. If I'm sent to the Italian front, I'll steal a couple of nights on my way there. They won't begrudge us that. We've already stolen six weeks and nobody's objected."

"Will you let me drive you to Ascoli Piceno? There must be an HQ or something there where you can report. Perhaps they will send you home and tell you to come back later."

"When it's all over you mean? We'll walk together to the oak trees where it all began. I'll kiss you and walk away."

Next morning, they stood together on the porch.

"What will you do?" she asked.

This was one time she had no answer. He had depended on her for everything, now he was on his own; a forbidding thought.

"What will I do indeed? Without you I'll be afraid. I feel sick already. I'm numb from the waist up; normally it's from the neck up."

"Jim, if you don't come back, I'll die. My life is in your hands."

"If I don't come back, I'll be dead. Promise me you'll claim your pension, then I'll rest easier."

"Yes I will," she laughed while the tears started on free flow. "I don't mind crying, if only one's nose didn't run—it's so undignified."

Mamma came out with a parcel of food.

"You may not need this, but take it just in case."

"Thank you, Signora."

He offered her his hand. To his surprise, she put her arms around him.

"When you come back, my name is Bruna."

"Yes I know, Bruna."

Papà came out to shake his hand, pushing a handful of new military currency at him.

"Take it. As Bruna said, just in case."

"Thank you Giovanni."

Their conversation on the surface was quite normal as they walked to the oak trees.

"You have the letter I wrote to your parents?"

She knew he had, but it was something to say.

"I'll post it with my first letter," he replied. "What did you tell them?"

"I introduced myself and apologised for taking you away. I told them about the baby and promised they would see him or her whenever it became possible."

Standing facing each other as when first they met, she said, "I'm going to cry again. Sorry."

He was washing his face in her tears, kissing her eyes, cheeks, lips.

"We are in a mess, aren't we," he said.

"Here, take my handkerchief."

"No no, I'll use my sleeve. Rose, this is too painful. I'll just walk away and let you enjoy your cry."

He turned and walked off blindly. At the top of a knoll, he stopped, looked back, and waved to the forlorn figure standing alone. He felt an overwhelming sadness.

The first vehicle travelling south left him standing by the roadside. They actually blew raspberries at him in passing. He wasn't doing so well without her. It was time to assert: the next bastards won't pass without knocking me down, and the way I feel I don't give a shit. As a three-ton Bedford approached, he stood square in the middle of the road. The vehicle slowed to a halt and pulled up 2 yards from him. He walked forward and rested his arms on the mudguard. An officer put his head through the open window.

"That was bloody stupid! Who the hell are you?"

"Corporal James Corner, Captain."

"Corporal! Where's your bloody uniform?"

"I lost that two and half years ago sir," he laughed, still leaning on the mudguard.

There was a 30 second silence while the officer scrutinised him.

"Get in. Let's try to make some sense out of this. You do know where you are going?"

"South, Captain. Other than that I have no idea."

"I'll take you as far as Chieti."

"Well that will get me started. Okay, Chieti it is."

He answered all the questions the officer put to him but he could still see the doubt on his face. The officer wasn't at all sure what he had picked up.

"Your story is absolutely incredible, you know. A year behind enemy lines and you look cleaner and in better condition than we are."

"Let me try and make it credible, Captain. I married an Italian girl, we are expecting our first baby in December."

"We've heard everything now sir," the driver came in. "A man running for his life and stops to get married," he laughed.

The officer was busy compiling a mental picture.

"The girl you married, she hid you from the Germans. Is that the way it was?"

"You've got the general idea, Captain. I didn't hide, just kept a low profile."

"This is beginning to get interesting. How did you meet your wife?"

"Briefly, and sparing the details, I intervened when a German sergeant was trying to rape her. He was too big and while he was knocking hell out of me, she picked up his MP-40 and shot his balls off."

The more he told that story, the better he liked it. The driver was laughing and dying to share his humour.

"She blew his balls off and played with yours."

He was enjoying his own wit.

They were approaching the winter front line positions where every kilometre had been won at a cost to both sides. The greatest sufferers were the ordinary people, most of whom had lost everything. Each town and village from mountain to coast over a distance of some 40 miles had been reduced to rubble. It was a heart-breaking scene with families living in makeshift shelters amidst the ruins. On arrival at Chieti he was fed, given blankets, and spent the night in the back of a truck. He had obviously been the subject of conversation in the officer's mess because the next morning he was sent for and escorted to the captain's office. They were travelling companions and now on more friendly terms.

"Good morning, Corporal. Did they make you comfortable?"

"No complaints, sir."

"Good. The colonel would like a word so just stick around a while, I'll send for you. In the meantime feel free."

The colonel must have had an easy day ahead because he conversed with him in the most gentlemanly manner for over an hour, giving him information about a reception centre at Foggia set up for the purpose of dealing with escapees. Transport and escort had been laid on to take him there. During his wait, he received VIP treatment: given sandwiches and Victory V cigarettes for the journey. A couple of soldiers slipped money and more cigarettes into his hand. They also gave him a friendly cheer as the jeep in which he was being transported moved off.

No time was wasted on arrival at the reception centre where he was duly delivered. His clothes were taken away and burnt while he walked through a delousing complex. After completing the sanitation process, he was fitted out with a new uniform, provided with a meal and more cigarettes. Then he was escorted to a marquee, told to choose a vacant bed and rest until the train left at midnight.

Everything was organised in precise detail; even the train departed on time. However, something had gone wrong along the line, because the 100-mile journey took exactly 24 hours. Fortunately, they had been issued with sandwiches and a blanket. On arrival at Naples, transport awaited to take them to their final destination, Salerno, where a hot meal was provided despite arriving at an ungodly hour. The following two days were spent being medically examined and extensively interrogated, writing a letter to his parents, and generally getting settled in. A marquee on the beach, just 20 yards or so from the sea, was his home until a boat back to dear old Blighty became available. This was the beginning of his problem.

After several requests for interviews, all granted without delay, word was circulated among the powers that be they had a crank on their hands. A man volunteering for the front and refusing to go home, while he in turn failed to convince them his home was here in Italy. His only progress was the support of a sympathetic pay master who assured him that his wife's allowance would be given priority and paid from the date of marriage, also informing him of the substantial credit to his account and granting his request for a £50 withdrawal. It cheered him that he had found an important ally, but still all of his efforts failed to convince the higher command that his home was here in Italy. He was all but certified insane. Things couldn't possibly get worse, when suddenly fate took a hand. Walking along the road, eyes downcast along with his spirits, an officer approached and was about to pass by. A respectful salute would be expected but he had already decided that he wouldn't salute another officer until somebody took him seriously. He walked straight past, eyes front; the bastard could do whatever he liked about it.

"Corporal!" the captain called. But the voice lacked severity. They turned and faced each other. "Geordie?"

"Captain," he replied, holding out his hand. "I'm delighted to see you again! You made it, and looking a hell of a sight better than when last we met."

"Thanks to you. How is that pretty wife of yours?"

"Pregnant."

"Well good for you. This is something to celebrate. I hope you are not otherwise engaged because you are coming with me. There is a nice little cafe in town and they have a hell of a menu. I recommend the bread. Let's go, I'm not taking no for an answer. You can tell me about your wife on the way."

"I can talk all day about her. But what about the old army bullshit about officers and other ranks?"

"That didn't apply when I was cold, wet and afraid, so it's not going to make any difference to us now. Tell me, are you taking her home?"

"She is home, Captain, where she wants to stay and I want to be with her. I've decided to miss the boat, that's the only way I'm going to make them take me seriously."

The captain was acknowledging salutes right and left as they walked through the town.

"Does it bother you, Captain, if they don't salute?"

"Hell no. I wish they wouldn't! Here we are, this is the place. It's clean and it's cool, no pimps or prostitutes. Maybe you prefer sitting outside?"

"Wherever, and I'll order the same: whatever."

The waiter was just a bit over attentive. It occurred to him that the captain was no stranger here.

"You've been coming here regularly I see."

"Why do you say that?"

"I think the waiter is working overtime for his tip."

"He'll get the usual: 20 cigarettes. They are better than money. Always carry a packet with you, they can open a few doors."

"I'll remember that. I've been giving mine away to the lads."

The waiter hurried over with a couple of drinks, earning the first instalment on his tip.

"Now what's all this I've been hearing around the base about the crank who married the Italian girl and doesn't want to go home. I never dreamed it would be you."

"It's me, Captain, and I do want to go home; I want to go home to my wife. That's the bit they don't understand."

"I understand, but I want you to stop hitting your head off the wall. I'm indebted to you both, and now it's time to start paying back.

You are aware of course that a captain has about as much pull as a corporal. Less, I sometimes think! However, it happens that I've been partnering the colonel at bridge recently. Do you play bridge, Geordie?"

"A little bit. It exposes too many weaknesses."

"You can say that again, as the yanks would say. Even they know about the Limey screwball who doesn't want to go home. At least this colonel doesn't think he's Jesus Christ—he's almost human. I promise to get you an interview. He will probably have heard of you anyway. You are the first man in the history of this war that hasn't wanted to take the boat home."

"Hey, this is a good drink, Captain, what is it?"

"I don't know. The waiter recommended it after his first tip. I'm glad you like it. Ask him yourself, he hasn't heard you speaking Italian yet. You will have him grovelling. What's your name anyway? I don't even know the name of my saviour."

"Jesus Christ is your saviour," he replied, and they didn't stop laughing all evening. "Jim Corner is mine though, Captain."

"Mortimer Clarke, Corporal."

"Mortimer! Hell's flames, your mother wasn't very thoughtful. I think I'll call you Captain." The laughter grew louder. "Shall we get drunk?"

"Why not, but let's eat first. It takes longer to get drunk that way. This is a hell of a night and it's only just beginning."

"Mortimer," he laughed. "Hell, what a couple of drinks will do. I'm beginning to like your name! Mortimer, I'm pleased I met you. Just wait 'till I tell Rose, she liked you at first sight."

"Did she really? Well I'll let you into a little secret: I fell in love with her too. I'll never forget when she spoke. 'Let me help you captain' she said."

"Come on Mortimer, you're getting sloppy. I hope you're not a sloppy drunk."

"No, I promise I'm not. Hell, just because I'm in love with your wife!"

"Captain, everybody's in love with my wife. I just happen to be the bloke she chose to make love with."

The drinks kept coming, their conversation slurred. They laughed at everything and everybody.

"I'll tell you a secret, Captain. I don't think I've told Rose this.

Have I? I don't know. Whoops! That's one I'll not drink. Never mind."

"Camerata due più bicchiere per favore. What do you think of my Italian, Geordie?"

"It's about as good as mine, you just said another two glasses, comrade."

"I wish it were. That's a big asset in your favour; speaks fluent Italian."

"Flu-hell. Rose said they'll send me to prison for murdering the language."

"Anyway what about this secret you were about to divulge."

"Secret! What secret? Oh, that one. Well, doctors didn't attend births when I was born. The midwife or the woman next door delivered us; I don't know how the hell we survived. You're not going to believe this you know."

"Go on, try me. I'm listening."

"Where was I? Oh yes, Ella, that was her name, the woman from next door. She smoked a pipe and wore a cloth cap. The shawl she wore was kippered with tobacco smoke."

"That must have been hell for you. Did you live?"

"Only just! Old Ella held me by the feet far too long before slapping life into me, consequently the blood rushed to my head and I became a half wit. 'Ella,' my mother called, 'If it's a boy, get rid of the bugger. They are nothing but trouble.' There was I dangling by the feet, waiting to be slapped or rabbit-punched."

"Were you listening to this conspiracy?"

"Every word! That's why I'm so bloody stupid. Ella decreed that I should live. She slapped my arse so hard I couldn't sit for six months."

"Then what happened?"

"She hid me away in the bottom drawer and forgot about the whole thing."

"Just a minute, I need a drink. Did you live?"

"Hell, Mortimer, I already told you I did. They took me out of the drawer 22 years later and shipped me off to the Middle-East, full pack and rifle."

"And a bloody good job for me too, Geordie. I would have died of pneumonia at that river. Let's drink a toast to the midwife, she saved both our lives."

Holding up their glasses, they toasted, "To Ella. God bless her."

*

Chapter 22

He awoke early the following morning, lying on his bed fully clothed, boots and all. It took him some time to realise his surroundings, remembering nothing of how he got there. Stripping naked, he picked up a towel, walked onto the beach and into the sea. It was like wading into a millpond in the cool of morning. As he broke the smooth glass surface, the water caressed his body like balm. He swam using a strong breaststroke. He was a good swimmer but never quite reached competition level. He swallowed a mouthful of seawater and vomited. Feeling a lot better for this, he began to enjoy his swim. God, how he missed her. It was a gnawing emptiness, just like hunger. An incurable ache that only her presence could cure. Maybe she wasn't feeling so bad with the baby growing inside to give her comfort. Rose, Rose. He repeated her name.

He was sitting on the beach writing letter number ten. It was really just a way of talking to her. If they were to be delivered, he would have to do it himself.

"No wonder you want to miss the boat," a familiar voice said, seating himself on the sand. "So this is the poor man's Riviera."

"Hello Captain, good to see you. What tidings?"

"Tidings of great joy. You have an interview in half an hour. It's okay, don't rush, your carriage awaits."

"Mortimer, you are a friend indeed."

"I only hope you don't end up cursing me. The colonel had heard about you. He showed unusual interest when I told him the tale of Rose shooting the German sergeant where it hurt most. That did it. He said he wanted to meet your wife."

"What job is on the cards?"

"You do speak Italian well enough to interpret?"

"I think so, although Rose wouldn't recommend me."

"Can you drive? I know you can handle a gun."

"I can meet all those requirements."

"Well come on then, get spruced up."

"Just a minute, Captain, which front?"

"The Adriatic."

"I'll take it."

"The colonel does the choosing, Geordie."

The great man himself was indeed almost human. At that level, officers sitteth at the right hand of God. Indeed, he showed most interest in Rose, she would have got the job immediately.

"I'm not at all sure what this job implies or why this man needs someone with all these qualifications. However, ours is not to reason why. You appear to fit the bill. You'll be given two days' weapon training, two days' driving instruction, and a day interpreting."

The interview was at an end. The colonel began writing without even looking up. He just pointed with his pen.

"You'll be given all the details through that door."

These senior ranks had a knack of knocking lesser mortals off balance. It must be part of their training. As he walked through the door, Mortimer was in conversation with the aide, also a captain. Everybody appeared to be at least a captain here.

"Well, what was the outcome?" the aide asked.

"He just said I fit the bill."

"Right, let's get to work then."

Mortimer got up. "See you outside, Geordie," he said.

"Geordie!" the aide repeated.

Mortimer laughed. "When a man saves your life, Ralph, you don't stand on ceremony. See you."

"Okay, Geordie," the aide chuckled, "you have a pay book?"

"I have, but it's temporary."

"Let me see," he reached for the book. "Leave it with me. You have an Italian wife I'm told."

"It's all written down there, Captain."

"Right, this slip will get you all you need from the quartermaster's store. The colonel has been most generous with your leave: 14 days plus 6 days travelling; 20 days in effect. Be sure you report for duty on time. Your pass gets you to Foggia, find your own way from there. You will be informed where to report before leaving on the midnight train from Naples."

He was talking and doing things quickly as if he was in a hurry to get rid of him, which he was. Pressing a button, a sergeant appeared at the door.

"I'll hand you over to the sergeant. He'll fill you in with all the details."

To whom, he wondered, would the sergeant pass him on to. Did anybody have time for anyone but themselves at this place?

"Sit down please." At last someone was treating him on level terms. "So you're the bloke who married the Eyetie. Had a rough time I'm told."

"Things seem to be working out alright now, Sergeant. What's the job, any idea?"

"I know everything that goes on around here." He lowered his voice to deliver the next line. "This bugger next door doesn't know his arse from his elbow. If I put his death warrant in front of him, he'd sign it. The silly bugger's fanny struck."

"To be honest, Sergeant, I think I am too. You are referring to the captain? The old colonel appears to be wide awake."

"He is. He has everybody taped; both here and up front. This job, for instance, it's been open for a week. He thinks it doesn't justify the extra skills they are asking. Oh by the way, the driver you are replacing got himself shot."

"Well that's nice to know, Sergeant. About these requirements, it was something the colonel said that made me curious. 'I'm not sure why this man needs someone with all this expertise' were the words he used. If the last man to do the job got killed, then I reckon the job justifies a better man than me."

"You've saved him a headache, Geordie. He couldn't find a man who could speak Italian to combine with the other skills: a driver who could handle a gun."

"What rank is my boss? You haven't told me about the job yet."

The sergeant laughed.

"Yes, I'm sorry. I get carried away talking about this arsehole

150

next door. The job is tailor-made for a man with your experience. Your boss is a major but he hob-nobs with the big lads, kind of a messenger boy. He doesn't appear to do much of anything. As for the driver, they got lost and wandered too near the front line. He had a rifle but it might as well have been a cricket bat, hence the reason for an expert with a gun. The major's looking for someone useful for his own protection in case something similar or worse happens again. Anyway, Geordie, let's get down to the nitty-gritty."

"Similar or worse! What could be worse than getting killed."

The sergeant laughed, he was extremely friendly and informative. Laying everything out in detail and in the clearest black and white.

"I hope I'm making everything clear to you. If there's anything you're not sure about, just ask."

"There probably is, Sergeant, but I have five days to think about it."

"Any time. Report here at nine in the morning. I'll take you to our weapons expert. He's a friend of mine, Geordie, so don't show him up. About the only thing he ever shot was a clay pipe."

"He might know something I don't."

"I wouldn't bet on it. See you in the morning then. Goodbye."

"Bye, Sergeant, and thank you."

They looked at each other for a while. Maybe he'd found another friend. Was it possible to have two after never having any at all?

When he went outside, Mortimer was sitting in the vehicle reading.

"*Keys of the Kingdom.* I enjoyed reading that. It was in the prison camp library."

"You had a library! If I had known, I wouldn't have escaped," he chuckled. "Some of these base soldiers might learn some humility from this book. Right, Geordie, where to now?"

"I have to get kitted out. You'd better go, I'll find my own way."

"Go where? And let you hump a full kit bag! I'm just waiting for a boat home. I'll accompany you to the stores. Jump in."

It was a very short drive, just a couple of buildings away in fact.

"I'll come in with you just for the hell of it," the captain said.

Jim walked up to the storeman and handed him the note. Accepting it, the soldier stood to attention when he saw the captain.

"Can I help you sir?" he asked.

"Yes, you can get the quartermaster sergeant please."

"Right away sir."

He scuttled off through a curtain. The quartermaster came out with a bunch of papers in his hand, trying to look busy. He stood to attention much smarter than the storeman and for longer. Mortimer was playing cat and mouse.

"Sir," the quartermaster said, a bit too loud.

"I would like this man kitted out Q, if you would be so kind."

"Yes sir. Private Roberts, at the double. Come on, man, get a move on."

Jim stole a look at Mortimer; this was theatre.

"I want you to fix him up Q. This is a soldier I'm giving you the honour to serve. You won't get many of his calibre through these stores so make the most of it."

"Yes sir."

"Oh by the way, he'll be meeting his wife next week. She's never seen him in uniform. I want you to help him make an impression. But you know your job, I'll leave it to you."

With that, he sauntered through the stores, pretending to inspect, running his fingers along the shelves while the quartermaster was doing his best to keep his eyes on his work.

He came over to examine a shirt Jim was trying on.

"Mmm, something a little more officer type, Q. I glanced at those shirts behind that curtain, maybe they would be more suitable."

"We'll do what we can sir," he replied, praying that the officer would just go away and allow him to just stuff any old rag into Jim's kit bag.

"Now that's something like it. Q, you certainly know your job. Turn round, Corporal. Very nice. That should score a bit with his wife, don't you think, Q?"

"He looks smart, sir."

The quartermaster seemed to be warming up to his job despite the indignity of having to fit out a corporal personally.

"Now, a good warm winter outfit, Q, and then I think we can commend you to your superior on a job well done."

He was deliberately avoiding Jim's eyes in case they burst out laughing.

"When Field Marshal Alexander asks for the name of your tailor,

Corporal, keep him guessing. Would you and Private Roberts accompany us to the truck? Oh, and carry the corporal's kit bag please."

Mortimer produced a bottle of bourbon whisky, deliberately handing it to the private. Possession was nine tenths of the law.

"With my compliments, gentleman. Enjoy yourselves."

They drove away laughing.

"Where did you get the whisky, Captain? I'll bet that's not the only bottle you've got stashed away."

"You and I have scotch. I bought it off a yank. He had a jeep full, as well as watches and rings; a regular merchant of Venice."

"Can you get me a ring, Mortimer. A good one, I have £40. I want the ring valued before buying. It's a wedding gift for Rose, she's wearing a standard Italian ring at the present, brass I think. If it fits my little finger, it'll be okay. I tried hers on with this in mind."

"Forty pounds, hell Geordie! We'll get two for that. Two of the best. Twenty-two caret." He opened the bottle of whisky and handed it to Jim. "You first, you are the better man."

"The best man usually drinks last, so I accept. Bloody hell Mortimer, we had better give this man the truck back before we start on this bottle."

After taking a swig, he said, "I think you're right. We'll get your kit bag put away safely, deliver the vehicle, then finish the bottle on the beach."

*

Chapter 23

Reporting at the office ten minutes before nine, the sergeant was there to meet him.

"Good morning, Geordie. You're early. I guessed you would be. Shall we go? Deadeye Dick will be expecting you. Your reputation went on ahead so he will particularly want to show you how much he knows."

"Then I might learn something. You know, I don't think I can hit a clay pipe. Though I have shot off a pair of balls."

The sergeant laughed.

"A pair of balls!" he repeated. "Come on, let's get started. My name is Peter by the way. I'll pick you up tomorrow morning if you like."

"Peter, I need all the help I can get."

He was introduced to the teacher and the class. The instructor assembled his pupils, seven in all. He was good and had obviously swallowed the training manual, every word as per the book. He also had a healthy respect for experience. To make a point, or impress the class, he would look at Jim and add, 'I'm sure you will agree with that, Corporal', or 'I think the corporal will bear me out'. His stock reply to this was always 'indeed' or 'absolutely'.

The simplicity of the gun was in its crudeness. Easy to use, effective, and cheap to make.

"Let me show you how it operates." The sergeant was getting into the swing of things. "It breaks down into four parts: barrel unit, main body trigger mechanism, shoulder stock and magazine. Now, someone place this blindfold over my eyes and I'll show you the complete weapon in seconds."

As good as his word, it took him six seconds. Jim had paid particular attention to the blindfold trick, knowing full well that the sergeant was going to use him as a guinea pig. As expected, he was handed the gun.

"Would you like to have a try, Corporal?"

All eyes focused on him and the weapon, throwing it from hand to hand to get the feel. His own MP-40 was minus shoulder stock. Little feats of expertise he had practiced with it were not practical on a complete weapon. Determined to match the instructor, he chanced a well-practiced trick of throwing the gun in the air with a triple turn and catching it at the ready position, slapping the trigger mechanism for effect. There were whispers of appreciation and cries for more from the class. His gamble had come off, but he wasn't so foolish to try again or show off any further.

He began dismantling the gun, taking note of where he placed each part. With the blindfold in position, he deliberately took all the time in the world to assemble the weapon, having made his point. Each piece he snapped into place as the sergeant had done. The snap and slap was the hallmark of an expert displaying confidence.

Throughout the next two days, the instructor never chose him again to follow on after a demonstration, always selecting a less adroit pupil. The sergeant proved himself magnanimous, giving praise for a good effort and on one occasion, with all the class gathered together during firing practice, he said without spite, "You should be teaching me, Corporal."

Then he laughed when the class comic called out, "I'm sure the corporal will agree with that."

Mortimer visited the classroom towards the end of the second day. The sergeant brought his class smartly to attention.

"Carry on, Sergeant. How are they shaping up?" he asked in lowered tones.

"A good class, sir. They performed well on the range today."

"Good show, Sergeant. Mind if I hang around? I might learn something."

"A pleasure sir. We were giving the corporal here a send-off. He's leaving us today."

"Is he any good?"

"He's good. Bags of experience. Ex-POW Spent a year behind enemy lines. He obviously learnt something there."

"Really. I'd like a word with him when the class is dismissed. You see, I've had a similar experience."

"Certainly sir, you have something in common. I'll call him."

"Thank you, Sergeant. I'll wait outside."

"Very good sir. Corporal, the captain would like a word."

"Right, Sergeant, thank you, and goodbye. Goodbye gentlemen, it's been a pleasure."

"I think the sergeant will agree with that," the course jester called.

The sergeant laughed, proving once again he was above resentment. Jim waved goodbye and walked out.

"Hello there, Mortimer. Good to see you. I'm told we have something in common."

"I like to sound them out, Geordie. The sergeant was alright, he spoke generously of you. It's the hallmark of a good man when he talks of a better one without malice. I've looked at two rings, both 22 carats, but he wants too much for them. They're alright for size."

"How much is too much?"

"Fifty-five pounds for the thick one, 45 for the other. I got him down to 45 and 35. He's considering my offer of 35 and 30. I think we'll get them at that price."

"That's a hell of a come down; 55 to 35! I can manage that amount easily. I think I owe you that much. You've paid for everything and I haven't spent a penny."

"It will take a hell of a lot more than £35 to square my debt to you."

Peter drove up in a jeep.

"Well this is a stroke of luck. There are two orderlies out looking for you, Captain. The old man wants to see you."

"I can't imagine why since it's our bridge night. I'll see you tomorrow, Geordie, we're going along the coast to a village where we can eat fish and chips and have a drink. Will you come along, Sergeant? We can both keep an eye on him. Rose might send us a letter of thanks."

"Glad to, Captain. Jump in both of you. How was the crack-shot sergeant today, Geordie? He told me how you had upstaged him in front of the class, without bitterness I might add." Taking a corner without due care and almost hitting an oncoming vehicle, he shouted into the rear view mirror, "Bloody Yanks!"

"Bloody Limeys would be more appropriate," Mortimer said.

Arriving at the office, Mortimer dismounted. "Tomorrow night, Sergeant, I'll drive."

They all laughed.

Peter met him the next morning.

"The driving instructor's a good bloke. I'll have a word with him, he's expecting you."

"Does everybody get this treatment, Peter?"

"Not likely! They find their own way. You'll be surprised how many silly buggers get lost. I'm here today because I had to have a word with you."

"Had to?"

"Well, requested. Captain Clarke and myself will run you to Naples when you leave. He won't be seeing you before then. The colonel had a private word with him and the outcome was a friend in the ranks is totally unacceptable and bad for discipline. The captain asked permission to run you to Naples, the colonel had no objection and I was invited."

"Thanks Peter, I'm not surprised."

"He's getting the rings today. I'm liaison officer."

On arrival, Peter introduced him to the driving instructor who looked at him intently.

"I never thought I'd ever meet a man who refused the boat back to Blighty."

"It takes all sorts, Sergeant."

"There aren't many of your sort. Anyway, my job is to find out if you are up to standard. Between you, me and Peter, you are even if you're not. I'll take you for a test run and if you are as good as I expect, I'll leave you to practice on your own."

The test was rigorous and the left-hand drive didn't help. He was corrected on several occasions. When they got back from the drive, the sergeant handed him a list of faults.

"That was a good effort, the left-hand drive caused you most difficulty. I'll leave you on your own to practice what I have written.

We will have another run tomorrow and I will expect some improvement."

During the afternoon, Peter came with a choice of two plain 22-carat gold rings. He felt a strange excitement as he slipped them on his finger (he had already given Mortimer a rough measure with a piece of wire).

"The broad band £35, the finer one £30. That's a lot of money, Geordie."

"I've got a lot. Let's go and find out if they are genuine, shall we?"

As they drove towards town, Peter criticised everyone else on the road.

"Look at that bloody idiot. The way some of these Yanks drive! Our own are no better."

"Getting hurt will keep them out of the front line. That's the only explanation. It's tough up there."

"It isn't putting you off. You are going up there for a second, hell no, a third helping. I bet some of those Germans will know you by now," he laughed. "Oh and by the way, don't blame the colonel, he had to say something. Mortimer told me he was most apologetic and very understanding. A man, he said, who owes his life to another can never repay the debt. His words."

"Peter, he would have lived without my help. I didn't save his life."

"That's not the way he sees it, and I'm inclined to believe him."

"If we hadn't met again, I would have forgotten the incident."

"But he wouldn't. Anyway, the jeweller is around here somewhere. Keep a lookout. Here we are, this is it. I'm coming in with you, I want to hear how good your Italian comes across."

"Do you speak any, Peter?"

"Six words, maybe ten."

"How will you know how good mine is then?"

"Don't get technical. I can listen can't I?"

The jeweller was a man about 55 years old; just the age to know something.

"Buona sera, Signor," he set out to impress Peter. "Will you give me your opinion on these rings. I'll pay for your expertise of course."

He had taken the jeweller by surprise. Few soldiers made any effort at all with the language. Here was a man speaking it, and quite articulately. Picking up the rings as if he were handling the crown jewels, he replied, "Where did you learn to speak Italian?"

"I'll double your fee if you guess correctly," he laughed.

"Give me time, give me time. These are good quality rings."

"They are genuine then?"

"Absolutely."

"Are they worth 20,000 each, allied currency."

The jeweller took a pencil and paper and did some sums.

"On the black market, yes."

"Is there any other market?" Jim laughed.

The old jeweller chuckled. "Not really," he replied.

"How much would you pay for them? I'm not interested in how you would sell them."

Weighing one against the other, he replied, "Ten thousand for the heavier one, a little less for the other. They are both good. Your dialect, it's from the Adriatic side."

"That's close enough. How much do I owe you?"

"Nothing. It's a pleasure to hear a soldier speak my language. Not many even try."

"My wife is Italian." He couldn't help mentioning her name to anyone who showed an interest. "We live near Ascoli Piceno."

"You live here in Italy!" He called his wife. She screamed from somewhere in the back of the shop and came waddling in with a dish and tea towel in her hand. "This British soldier lives near Ascoli Piceno. He married an Italian girl."

It took all the diplomacy he could muster to get away without offending their open-hearted kindness. They made him feel good; he was accepted. He and Peter were offered a glass of wine to toast the occasion. He put 600 allied currency on the counter.

"Thanks for your time, Signor," he said. "It's been a pleasure."

They walked out of the shop followed by the old couple asking them to come again.

"Come for dinner. Eat with us."

"Thank you, Signor e Signora."

As they drove away, Peter glanced across at him. "I was impressed," he said, "you never had to search for a word."

"I did, but I covered it up with little words that fill in gaps like but and however. If you get stuck with Italian, you can play ping-pong with words. You appear to be keeping up the conversation—they do it themselves. It's a wonderful language. Well it must be, because my wife teaches it."

"She speaks German and French too. I heard that by the way. The captain told me."

"Did he really."

"She made an impression on him alright. He told me everything that happened. How you two came along and saved him. How about a couple of beers?" he suggested as they arrived back at the camp.

"Where on earth can you get beer?" he asked.

"I'll settle with the captain, then I'll bring half a dozen bottles and we'll sit on the beach. How does that sound?"

"Sounds great. Here, take the £40. He should get three bottles of whisky for a fiver. Hell, that's almost three weeks' pay. Be sure he spends all of my money for a change. I've been here five weeks and spent nothing. I forget that I'm back in the world of finance. Do you realise I haven't handled a penny piece in almost three years! The paymaster reckons I have £300 in credit. I didn't realise there was that much money in the world."

"You've earned every penny, Geordie."

"I've had the shit scared out of me but I never thought about pay. It was something one had to do. It's a strange thing, fear. I always felt as though I was going to piss myself during the first few minutes of the action. Anyway, I always managed to preserve my dignity. After the panic had subsided, I was as good, or better, than they; whoever they were. Tell Mortimer not to forget the whisky, Peter. I want a bottle for Giovanni, that's my father-in-law, he's a good bloke. Her mother's nice too, but I'm never quite sure how I stand with her."

"Well you're not supposed to like your mother-in-law. I think I must be an exception."

"Well good for you, Peter, because in 30 years that's exactly how your wife is going to look. You have nothing but happiness to look forward to. I can see Rose then, each time I look at her mother; she's 15 st. I can just imagine the pleasure with 15 st of Rose wrapped around me."

They both laughed at the prospect.

"You are worthy of every ounce. I'll be on the beach with the nectar in one hour," Peter called as Jim jumped from the vehicle. "We'll drink to all that flesh you have to play with. I usually have to search round the bed feeling for my wife."

They stayed for a while, laughing and discussing that prospect. Jim was leaning over the seat helpless with laughter.

"Remember, when you find her, Peter, the sweetest meat is nearest the bone. See you on the beach. Bye."

"Bye Geordie."

On the final day, he spent an hour with the official interpreter and his course was completed. He handed in his bedding, less one blanket that he kept for the train journey; those cattle trucks were dirty. Then drew his Sten Mark II plus two full magazines from the armoury. Peter had all his papers and leave pass with written permission to withdraw from his credit whatever reasonable sum was required. He took £50. The afternoon was spent on the beach swimming and lazing around, planning his journey with joyous anticipation. With luck, he could be with her by six or seven o'clock the following evening.

A Yankee sergeant came to the marquee looking for the guy with the Italian wife. His tent mates pointed him out.

"You the guy with the officer, pal?" he asked, handing him a gift-wrapped cardboard box, in as much as it was sealed and tied with string. "Don't get it wet," he added.

"How much do I owe you?" he said, knowing full well that it would be already paid for.

"Your buddy settled the bill. Bye, and good luck up front."

He knew instinctively what was in the parcel. Only a man who knew the score would think of a gift like this. It would contain tea and coffee, something he should've thought of himself. Now he had a present for everyone: the ring for Rose, whisky for Giovanni, and tea and coffee for Bruna. He felt a thrill of excitement. He numbered the letters that he had written from one to ten; his heart was in every line.

His friends arrived at the marquee with transport before eight o'clock. He was surprised how pleased he felt about meeting Mortimer again.

"Let's check the itinerary," the captain greeted. "Travel route, guide book, kit bag, gun and ammunition—you won't need those. I've done some checking on your boss. If you ever get near the front line, then you will have lost your way," he laughed.

"His last driver got himself shot."

"He shot himself cleaning his rifle."

"I could do the same."

"Be sure you don't shoot yourself in the balls. You have a big beautiful girl to please. Now let's get loaded. I'll take the kit bag. Better carry his gun, Peter, in case he does shoot himself."

Bidding a fond farewell to his tent mates, he walked out to the vehicle.

"I see you were wise enough to keep a blanket. Now you have two. I brought one as well. You won't be travelling first class!"

"Those cattle trucks have square wheels too," Peter said, "You should be alright, there are only 50 men for a dozen trucks."

After a ten-mile drive, they arrived at a small fishing village. Mortimer had obviously been there before because he drove straight up to the restaurant. He was well received too, commanding a lot of attention. The sort that comes expensively. He must be a hell of a bridge player. He always had an idea of what the opposition held in their hands, thinking out moves before the next card was played. Jim tasted his first fish and chips for five years. The meal was better than anything he could remember, although he hated being unfaithful to Franca. They drank two bottles of wine between them that added to the pleasure. If only there had been more time, but then when is there ever? While they drove along, it occurred to him that no one had paid the bill.

"I didn't see anybody pay for all that," he remarked.

"You enjoyed it didn't you?"

"Like nothing else on earth."

"Then don't concern yourself with the bill. What you need is a full night's sleep, worry about that."

They pulled into the station with ten minutes to spare after checking in at the RTO He was about to leave them to find space in one of the trucks but Mortimer kept a tight grip on his arm. The transport sergeant came by shouting orders left and right to men passing by with rifles and kit bags.

"Sergeant," Mortimer called.

"Sir," the sergeant said smartly.

"See that this man has a truck to himself."

"Absolutely impossible sir. I have officers sharing a wagon."

"Well then, you've just lost yourself a bottle of whisky!"

"Just hold on a moment, Captain."

He walked to the last wagon and evicted half a dozen soldiers with their kit.

"What the hell's going on here?"

A sergeant wrestling with his full pack and weapon complained as he was pushed towards another truck.

"Sorry for the mix up, Sergeant," the RTS apologised. "The rear wagon is reserved for six mountain rescue dogs and their handlers. You can share with them if you wish."

"Not bloody likely," the disgruntled sergeant said, searching for a not so crowded wagon.

"Wait beside the rear truck, Captain," the RTS told him in passing while going about his organising.

"This is my address, Geordie." Mortimer handed him a thick envelope that he stuck in his kit bag. "Careful you don't lose that."

"I won't, I have one for you here," he said, handing him an envelope. He pulled out another and handed it to Peter. "I've put enough money in there to buy your wife a good present."

"I hope there isn't any money in mine," Mortimer said, knowing there would be, but it wasn't worth spoiling the evening arguing about it.

"Why the hell would I put money in yours. You must have been printing your own!"

"I typed out your file," Peter said, "and sent it onto Foggia. Don't be surprised if they give you the MM when you get to the front. Didn't I tell you that arsehole would sign anything?"

"I hope you haven't typed me a reputation I can't live up to."

"I think you'll find it satisfactory, and so will the reader."

The transport sergeant blew a whistle. He was lifted into the truck along with his kit bag. The engine screamed, the link chains tightened, the wagons shuddered and moved off slowly. They were shaking hands as they walked alongside. The engine gathered speed and he watched the two soldiers wave until they disappeared out of sight.

He was wide awake and ready to go as the train rolled into Foggia on time. There was the usual melee of soldiers milling around with rifles, pack and kit bag, wanting to know what happened next. The transport officer and a sergeant ordered the soldiers into some kind of line while five transport lorries stood by. Names, ranks and numbers were called; ten men and their kit to each vehicle. Within half an hour, he was the only one left standing.

"Why the hell are you still here?" the sergeant barked.

"My name wasn't called."

"If your name wasn't called, then you shouldn't be here at all. What is your bloody name?"

"My bloody name is James Corner," he answered, looking straight at the safe job sergeant.

"Bloody smart-arse eh!"

"Bloody smart soldier, Sergeant."

"Right, bloody smart soldier, let's have a look at your travel documents."

The officer spoke for the first time. The sergeant had just about dried his lungs up.

"Are you the man with the Italian wife?" he asked.

"Yes sir."

They looked at each other for a moment.

"Alright, Corporal, come with me."

He followed the officer, struggling with kit bag, blankets, gift box and gun. He was led into an office where a corporal clerk was sifting through some papers.

"Is Corporal Corner's file handy?" he asked the clerk.

"I have it here sir." The clerk gave him the dossier.

164

The officer read through the document, glancing at Jim.

"Can I see your leave pass and general orders, Corporal?"

Jim handed over his travel orders. The officer took them then picked up the file for a second reading. Maybe he wasn't convinced. What on earth had Peter put in there?

"Are those two officers ready to leave, Corporal?" he asked the clerk.

"They are waiting at transport, sir. The driver should be reporting in any time."

"Hold him when he reports in, I'll have a word with the officers. Excuse me, Corporal," he said politely, "you are about to have a change of luck."

What the hell was in that file, he thought, when the officer left the room. He turned to the clerk.

"What did he mean, I'm about to have a change of luck?"

"For the better I would say. It couldn't get much worse, could it? A year behind enemy lines and straight back up there." The clerk sounded sympathetic. He thought his luck had changed six months ago, the sympathy was belated. "How did you survive through such a hell of a winter?"

"It wasn't as bad as that you know Corporal, I did get married."

The officer came in with the driver following.

"If you are ready, Corporal, the driver has orders to drop you at your door. Enjoy your leave."

Christ, another human being! he thought, while gathering up his belongings. He didn't think that there were more than two.

"Here mate, I'll take your kit bag," the driver offered.

"Thanks."

Another surprise.

"Best of luck, the clerk called."

My, my. All this at a transport depot! Things are changing. The driver stowed his kit bag.

"You ride in the front, Corporal, those two kids can sit in the back."

"Kids?" he said. "I thought they were officers."

"One pippers. Boys straight from college. Wait 'till you see them," he laughed.

The transport officer must have given them a brief summary on their fellow traveller. They considered themselves in exalted company and shared their rations open-handedly. The laughter began ten miles into the journey and didn't stop, though they did stop to buy a bottle. What they really wanted was whisky, but having no idea how impossible that was, they settled for wine. He deliberated over giving them the whisky out of his kit bag when the driver suggested they exchange the spare petrol can for a bottle of whisky. A wild proposal since the purchase of either was well nigh impossible.

"Can you replace the petrol and the can?" he asked the driver.

"No problem. Replacing the whisky is the headache; and drinking it will give you one too," he said.

The prospect of a drunk driver when he was so near to Rose was daunting, but he listened with glee to their coarse banter and wild laughter. He even accepted the wine and put the bottle to his lips without drinking. They were approximately five miles from home when he made the proposition.

"I'll give you a bottle of whisky and a pound for the petrol," he told the driver.

"Make it two pounds and two bottles and you can have the jeep as well!"

It had occurred to him that a two-gallon can of petrol would be far more valuable a present than a bottle of whisky. Taking the bottle from his kit bag and 400 in military currency from his pocket, he handed the bottle to the officers and the money to the driver while directing him along the road to town, putting his hand on the steering wheel while the driver took a swig of whisky from the bottle. They were less than a mile from home and already half the whisky had gone. The house was a thrilling sight. While the hilarity was building up to a crescendo in the jeep, his heart was beating faster, making him behave very much as they were, albeit without the aid of the whisky.

The jeep pulled up at the end of the drive. While he was gathering his kit together, the driver was happily unstrapping the petrol can.

"This will lighten the load," he laughed.

There were handshakes all round before they drove off shouting cheerfully, loud enough to be heard in town. He was left standing by the roadside in full view of home, knee deep in kit bag, blankets, gift box, petrol and his Mark II; clearly visible from the house.

*

Chapter 24

He waited until all three came to the gate, watching her walk hopefully to meet him, not at all sure. He waved and she came running clumsily in her sixth month of pregnancy. Rose paused momentarily as they stood just a yard apart appraising each other. They stepped forward burying themselves in each other's arms, kissing eyes, nose, and lips, repeating each other's names over and over. She felt so good to hold again and there was much more of her now. Over her shoulder he saw Bruna and Giovanni standing, watching.

Finally they broke free, she with a hand on her chest feigning breathlessness and with tears in her eyes. Picking up the presents, he shook hands with Giovanni and presented him with the can of petrol.

"Nine litres, Giovanni, with my compliments. I can get more."

Papà performed a most uncharacteristic dance of joy while everyone looked on laughing. Then venturing the unthinkable, he kissed Bruna on the cheek while handing her the present.

"There's 20,000 lira in that box at black market prices."

"That's a very good reason to keep it," she replied.

Turning back to Rose, her face glowing with joy, he put his hand inside his shirt and unhooked the large safety pin, removed it, then took the ring from his shirt pocket. Losing the ring would have meant losing his shirt, that's how he explained it to her.

"I remember not so long ago you did lose your shirt!" she laughed.

"Give me your lovely hand," he said, kissing her lips.

"You already have my heart and I've given you everything else."

"Then it's time I gave you something."

She placed his hand on her swollen belly.

"You gave me this. Keep your hand there and he'll kick with excitement, he behaves the way I feel."

He felt movement while they looked at each other with a strange emotion. Taking the metal ring from her finger, he replaced it with the gold band then raised her hand to his lips. The whole tête-à-tête had taken place in English. Bruna and Giovanni stood by watching with curious interest. Picking up his pack and blankets, they all walked towards the house: Rose admiring her ring, Bruna happy because her daughter was happy, Giovanni gripping his petrol can.

As they stood alone together in the bedroom, her arms around his neck and his hands on her hips, their lips touching, she asked, "Will you forgive me?"

"I'll try. What do I have to forgive you for?"

"Behaving like a schoolgirl rather than a teacher. I was terrified that I would never see you again."

"I can't forgive you for that. If you don't see me again, then you know I'm dead! Don't forget your war widow's pension."

"I won't," she laughed. "Speaking of pensions, I had a cheque delivered last week. It's here in my drawer, payable to Mrs Rose Corner. It took me some time to realise who that was. Here it is, the sum of £12. What is it for?"

"It's two months' marriage allowance. You will receive another one shortly, or maybe a book of cheques payable each week. The pay clerk kept his promise. I'm really happy with that."

"I'll receive money each week for being your wife! What about you, do you have enough?"

"I have so much, I want to share it with you. You remember the captain we helped that day at the bridge?"

"Of course, how could I forget!"

"He gave me his home address, I have it here with me. You can write and thank him. Without his help, I would have been on the boat back to Blighty. We became firm friends. He pulled all sorts of strings for me, for us. A word of warning though: be careful when you write, he's in love with you, and he's your educational level."

"It's strange, I could never attract a second glance, then when I meet two Englishmen they both fall in love with me. There must be a reason for this fatal attraction. By the way, where is Blighty?"

168

"It's the place every soldier serving abroad dreams about: home. They sing a song called *Take Me Back to Dear Old Blighty*. I'll sing it to you sometime."

"Of course, how stupid of me! I'm so excited I'm not thinking properly. You are the reason, you know that don't you?"

"That's how I feel, sweetheart, and you are the reason." They kissed tenderly. "I have a letter from him. It's here with his address enclosed. Just a minute, I'll find it." He looked in his kit bag. "Here it is."

"He must have a large address, it's a very thick envelope," she chuckled.

"It certainly is." Opening the envelope, he pulled out a bundle of money. "These are the notes I gave him to buy the ring. There's £40 here! I should've known when he handed me the envelope but we were at the station in Naples and the train was about to pull out."

"There's a letter enclosed, read it," she urged.

"You read it, Rose."

She began, "My dear friend and your charming wife, don't be offended at this my first instalment on the debt I owe. I cherish the day you both drifted into my life, a pair of ministering angels bringing not just hope when hope had been abandoned, but comfort, kindness, guidance, and assurance. At the risk of being moved by my feelings towards you both, I will write no further on that chapter in our lives. Let me wish you the happiness I feel you both deserve and may the gift of this ring bring that joy to you. God, I didn't realise how sloppy I am. Your word, Geordie, you brought it to my attention that first day we met in Salerno, remember? We got blind drunk. Whoops! I'm telling tales out of school, but you can forgive him that one slip, Rose, because he talked about you all night then accused me of being sloppy when I told him I was in love with you too. Don't ever forget me! Mortimer Clarke."

They stood looking at each other; she with the letter, he holding the notes.

"Your wedding ring looks so good. I wanted to buy it for you."

He watched the pleasure in those cream-splashed coffee-coloured eyes.

"I'm delighted," she said. "With the ring, the letter, and the money."

"If you are delighted, Rose, then so am I. Let me give you my letters." He pulled out the bundle tied with string and gave them to her. "Love letters! They are numbered one to ten. They say everything that I feel. I missed you. It was such a painful experience being so far apart. I'm the postman because I wanted you to get them personally."

"Well! My very first love letters. I like the way they are tied; you do things in style."

"Next time, they'll be tied with rose-coloured ribbon."

She kissed him.

"I like string much better. Can I show Mamma?"

"Yes why not, she won't be able to read them. I love the scent of this room, it smells exactly like you."

"Then I'll have it disinfected. Don't be too long, I know Mamma is preparing something special for dinner."

She looked so beautiful.

"Tell her I'm looking forward with pleasure and anticipation to whatever she is preparing."

He felt so happy standing there in the room that he lovingly shared with her, revelling in the sheer joy of just being able to reach out and touch her. Outside, it began to rain. It poured like he had never seen rain come down. Gazing out of the window, he watched the parched earth trying to absorb it all at once. The ground was so hard that the water stood in pools.

"God," he said to himself, "what a lucky man. Home and dry."

His presence at dinner could just possibly be the reason for the festive atmosphere. Her eyes attracted his like magnets. Her advanced pregnancy had a hypnotic effect on him. Her heavy body held a special attraction—there was more of her for him to love. He was aware that Bruna was speaking, telling them the gift box contained two kilos of coffee and the same amount of tea, while she had hoarded just enough from her exhausted supply for this special occasion. Tearing his gaze from Rose, he politely replied to Bruna, telling her how the box came into his possession and rebuking himself for his lack of thought. He told them how Giovanni's present was originally a bottle of whisky.

"I hope the petrol was a good exchange?"

170

"Nothing on earth could have been better or more timely. We now have 100 km of motoring," he beamed.

"I'll get more."

"Don't get yourself into trouble, please. I appreciate it, but it's not that important."

"It's alright really. I'll get it without stealing," he said confidently.

He was a man of means with over £70 in his pocket and £200 to his credit. Enough to buy two new Morris 8 motorcars, and some to spare.

They lay awake laughing and talking well into the night as the rain continued, enjoying each the other until sleep eventually enveloped them. He awoke to a brand new experience, she was holding his hand to her stomach and he could feel the life in her womb twisting, turning, moving.

"Lively, isn't he?" she said smiling.

"That's amazing! Did I do that? Why do you keep saying he? It could be she."

"You did it alright and I say he because I'm selfish. I want two boy friends: one to love and one to love me."

"I'm selfish too, but I want you to have what you want. Can I get up and make you a cup of tea?" he asked, eager to do something for her.

"You can hand me my nightdress and put on your pyjamas, then get back into bed and wait."

He scrambled around doing as she asked.

"Now what do we wait for?" he was curious.

Suddenly there was a knock on the door. They heard Bruna request permission to enter.

"That's what we were waiting for. Now let me see if you are decent," she said, adjusting his collar, patting his pyjama jacket into shape. "Come in, Mamma," she called.

Bruna entered carrying a tray, bidding a pleasant good morning and looking quite pleased with herself.

"How has he been behaving this morning?" Seeing a look of surprise on his face, she laughed, "I don't mean you. I already know how you behaved."

"He's been active this morning, Mamma. Jim thinks he might be a she."

Bruna smiled.

"It's possible. But all the smart people, the knowledgeable experts, predict a boy."

"All except Anna," Rose laughed. "She doesn't care what it is so long as it's a girl with golden hair."

"If he or she inherits your brain, Rose, I don't care if it's a girl with blonde hair or a boy with black," Jim replied, hand once again rubbing her belly.

Bruna laughed, possibly in agreement.

"For how long do we have the pleasure of your company?"

"Eighteen days, Bruna. Then I must go away to fight the foe—they can't do without me."

"But I have to do without you," Rose pouted.

"I report to a town called Ancona."

"Really?" Bruna said in surprise. "I have a sister living there. I must write her a letter; there is so much to tell. We've been out of touch for so long, she will be delighted with the news."

"If it is at all possible, I'll visit her, but will I be welcome? Maybe she has a foreign prejudice too."

"Mamma has no bias, she just thinks everyone should be Italian."

"Perhaps her grandchild will strike a balance then," he said, laughing.

"She might ignore the English half. I do hope he isn't blond," she laughed with him.

Mamma, bemused by their exchange, interjected, "I refuse to be drawn into this verbal chicanery. And you, young man, are welcome here so long as my daughter is happy. Any decline in your affections towards her or sign of neglect, you're out! Now if you don't mind, I would like a private word with your wife."

He kissed her forehead, "Just an affectionate gesture to seal our friendship, Bruna."

"Elvira was right, you are a clown," Mamma mocked him.

*

172

Chapter 25

After breakfast, Jim and Giovanni took the Fiat and an empty two-gallon can onto the road at the end of the drive.

"We might be wasting our time. No more than half a dozen military vehicles use this road," Giovanni told him.

"Six vehicles at two gallons each. Fifty litres would be a profitable day's work. The car won't run without petrol you know."

Sitting in the car talking with Giovanni was a pleasant experience. Maybe Bruna was as amicable under her hard exterior? Was it a defence against the foreign intruder?

A three-tonner approached after an hour's wait.

"Watch the technique, Giovanni," he boasted, getting out of the car with the empty can.

He was in luck. The driver, an artillery gunner, pulled up in front of him.

"Having trouble mate?" he asked.

"Out of petrol! Can you help?"

"I might spare a couple of gallons. Is that your Fiat?"

"My father-in-law's," he replied.

"You married an Eyetie! Christ, you didn't waste any time! I bet you speak the lingo."

"A little bit. I wasted a lot of time. I've been here two and a half years, one and a half as a POW. Fill this two gallon can and I'll give you ten bob."

"Ten bob! God, that's expensive motoring isn't it. Five bob a gallon. I hope we meet again," the driver chuckled.

"I can afford it. Thanks for helping me out of the shit."

"You've bought your way out. Christ, ten bob! Thanks mate."

He said goodbye to a happy man. They had just returned to their post with the can empty again when his next business deal approached: a corporal and a driver. The transaction was completed once made. He gave them ten bob each, showing off in front of Giovanni.

"Bloody expensive motoring, mate!" the corporal said. Exactly the gunner's words. "Can you afford it?"

"Hell yes, I'll be voting Tory at the next election," he chuckled. He decided to let the next vehicle pass when he spotted an officer's cap in the cab but it stopped anyway and the officer addressed him.

"Can I help you, Corporal?" he asked.

Saluting smartly, he graciously declined the offer hoping that the truck would move on. The officer was insistent.

"Do you have a pay book? Or some form of identity. We do have deserters you know."

"Really sir! You're giving me ideas. It would be easy for me, I speak Italian," he laughed, producing both leave pass and pay book.

"Don't be too clever, Corporal."

"I apologise, sir. That was out of character."

"Are you having problems?"

"Just ran out of petrol sir, that's all."

"Give him a gallon," he ordered the driver. "Is that your Fiat? Where did you get the petrol to run out of in the first place?"

"I married an Italian girl. The car is my father-in-law's and it's still possible to buy anything in this country, at a price. We must have been running on paraffin oil," he laughed.

"Married! Hell, Corporal, you haven't had time!"

"You wouldn't believe how much time I've had. I'm well into my third year. I was a POW here."

"You must be one of those chaps on the run behind the lines. Had a rough time I believe?"

"Sometimes. I was lucky."

"Shouldn't you be on the boat home? A friend of mine made it too. He escaped while on his way to Germany. Now the lucky bugger is on his way to Blighty. Stevens," he called to the driver, "fill his can."

"Thanks, Captain. This friend, would it be possible that I have met him?"

"Hardly likely. His name was Clarke. I took over his job."

174

"Captain Mortimer Clarke is my friend. I met him, my wife and I, ten minutes after he escaped. He was just about to catch pneumonia after swimming a river that was running faster than him. We fixed him up with dry clothing. Could it be the same man?"

"Really! Did you hear that, Stevens," he turned to the driver, "the corporal here saved old Mortimer's life."

"I'm listening, Captain. It reads like a book," the driver said.

"Saved his life! That's how he put it too, but he would've got by without my help. I have his address here in my pocket. I'll be writing to him soon. Would either of you two want a mention in my dispatches?"

"By all means, Corporal. Tell him you met George James."

"Don't forget me, Corporal, Arthur Stevens. I was there the day they bagged him."

"Well this really will be something to write home about. I can't wait to tell my wife. Mortimer was in love with her, you know."

"He didn't get married here by any chance, did he? Anything's possible. Well this is a story for the mess tonight. Corporal, I hope we meet again."

"So do I. Goodbye gentlemen and thanks for the petrol."

Two happy men put the Fiat back into the garage when suddenly the heavens opened. It had been threatening all morning but had very kindly held back the floodwaters until their profitable enterprise was complete. The rain came down like ice bullets, splintering on the driveway. It was impossible to walk the 20 yards from garage to house without getting drenched, so he and Giovanni spent a most interesting hour leaning on the bonnet of the car, facing one another. He listened intently to his father-in-law relating intimate details of his daughter's childhood.

He created his own image of her as he listened to Giovanni, picturing her at each stage of the story from a plump happy little girl to a buxom, intelligent teenager. He pictured the rose bud, whose sweet fragrance he now enjoyed, bursting into exquisite bloom. He was sorry to see the rain ease and a little sad as Giovanni stopped talking abruptly when Bruna called them from the doorway.

"Giovanni, it's been an informative conversation and a very

profitable day. I thoroughly enjoyed the last hour, listening to the story of my wife."

"It was a pleasure. I'll never have a more interested listener. Its a great comfort knowing that your feelings are genuine."

"You will never know the mountains I climbed to get back here. I was all but certified insane. But I forgive them, Giovanni. How could they know the treasure you, Bruna, and I share?"

"How indeed," Giovanni said. "Sufficient for us that you do. I never doubted your sincerity."

"Thank you."

"Mother of God! Are you both insane," Bruna greeted as they walked into the house.

"You see what I mean, Giovanni. Now Bruna doubts my sanity," he laughed and hurried on through to their bedroom.

He found Rose sitting in the chair with his letters spread out on the bed in numerical order. She looked up at him, smiling as he entered. She was waving a letter.

"Number six," she said, "and I've read it six times. It gets better each time. You poured your heart into this one. I love every word." She handed it to him. "Let me hear you say what is written. Go on, read it."

"I don't have to read it. I can repeat it. I remember writing it."

"Well, go on, recite it. It will give me great pleasure."

He repeated the letter word for word, just a little self-consciously. "Did I overdo it do you think?"

"Not at all. I'm still listening. Please go on."

She looked at the letter as he spoke.

"Who could doubt such sincerity? Almost word for word."

"I remember writing it on the beach at Salerno, with the sea as calm as a mill pond. It was a beautiful day but my heart was a lead weight and the sun scorched my back. Walking into the sea soothed my body, but not my spirit."

"Strange, I was suffering the same symptoms then. Now we are together, we can forget the pain and the loneliness."

Bruna knocked on the door calling them for lunch.

"Coming, Mamma," she answered as she gathered up the letters in the correct order and placed them neatly in her drawer. "Number six, I will keep in a special place." Placing her arm around his shoulder, she said, "Come, let us enjoy tea and fresh baked bread. Then afterwards we can lie on the bed, listen to the BBC news, and enjoy each other."

"Could anything on earth be more inviting or so exciting?"

*

Chapter 26

They spent the first five days in and around the house attached by an invisible cord, never more than two or three yards apart. News of his return had spread around the province, everyone knew. There were those who were surprised. Indeed, more than half the people never expected him to come back at all. Anna paid a visit on the fifth day. She was plainly upset, having expected them to call, worried lest he had come home wounded and unable to visit.

"Anna," he said with deep regret, "please accept my apologies. Is there anything we can bring with us tomorrow? Some compensation for being so inconsiderate."

"Bring yourselves, that's all I ask," she said, "and since mine is the first house you will visit, there is no need for an apology. You were quite right to spend the first few days together. Indeed, if you wish to be alone further, I can wait."

"Tomorrow it will be Anna," Rose said decisively. "Now we'll have coffee. Let us share the wealth Jim brought with him. After which we insist on escorting you home. I've decided the walk is exactly what we need."

"Since you've decided, caro," Anna chuckled, "I can't imagine anyone else objecting." Placing a hand on his shoulder, she asked, "May I kiss him? I've never had the pleasure of kissing a soldier."

"Help yourself Anna."

Already everything had taken on a new meaning. They were greeted by a beautiful sunny day with not a cloud in the sky. A gentle breeze played in her hair. It was a morning created especially for them. He was standing to attention in a soldierly-like manner while Bruna delivered a cautionary word.

"Stay on the country road and avoid all military traffic, and don't put your wife under any unnecessary stress or anxiety."

Saluting smartly, he asked, "Any other orders ma'am?"

Giovanni stood by, smiling.

"I'm entrusting you with my most treasured possession and I detect a tone of insolence," Bruna said severely. "Watch your step or you will find yourself sleeping in the stables."

"Both of us?" he laughed, opening the car door and helping Rose into her seat. "Your most treasured possession is in good hands, Bruna. I'll pay for any damage."

"With your life you will pay," she said, more severely.

"Bruna," he laughed, "the car isn't worth that much! It can be replaced," he said, tongue-in-cheek, looking towards Papà while Rose sat in the car smiling, radiant on the sunny September morn. He kissed Bruna on the cheek and whispered sincerely, "Have no fear."

Joining Rose in the vehicle, he engaged gears and drove off. They waved goodbye as if they were going for a month rather than a day. The Fiat responded to his touch, giving the feeling that it had just rolled off the assembly line rather than what it was: a resurrected 1935 saloon car. It had revolutionised the European car market in its day, but its day was almost ten years ago and three of those years had been spent in a garage standing on blocks with all four wheels buried in the garden. Being one of only half a dozen cars in the whole province, it was widely known and easily recognised.

Arriving at Anna's, they were greeted by a large welcoming party. Most were a little in awe of the uniformed soldier at the wheel, but the feeling was soon dismissed and the ladies shepherded Rose into the house for a pre-natal interrogation. Anna greeted him with a kiss.

"Mother of God!" she exclaimed, "whatever happened to those golden locks. Why did I not see that yesterday? Let me take your arm and we'll rescue your wife from the wise women in the temple of knowledge."

"Tell me, Anna, how do you happen to be more articulate than the other ladies of your generation?"

"I don't just happen to be, your wife taught me. My generation never attended school therefore illiteracy was the norm for the farmer and his wife. Rosanna, God bless her, persevered and finally broke through the barrier of ignorance. I now read quite well and enjoy it, although my writing is just out of the infant stage."

He looked at her for a moment.

"Anna, let's you and I do a little courting in the stables. I want to hear more about your literary accomplishments. What have you read?"

"Well," she said, beginning to enjoy the interest shown in her secret passion, "I read *Piccole Donne* written by an English lady."

"Louisa May Alcott was the lady's name. She is American though. Did you enjoy it?"

"I read it through several times. I'm also in the habit of turning back the pages and reading a passage that interests me again. Alas work was long, hard, and also necessary, which left little time to read. I would fall asleep and we never had any electricity—there were all kinds of obstacles."

"Alvaro must be proud of you."

"Oh he is now, but not while I was studying," she laughed.

"Was he jealous?"

"No, not jealous. I kept him waiting. You know," she was giggling, "he wanted me in bed with him."

"I don't blame him, you are still pretty even now. I'll bet you enjoyed yourselves in bed, Anna."

"Cheeky! I know you do. Rose missed you so much while you were away. Don't let them keep you parted for too long. She needs you more now at a time like this. You should be together."

I'll tell them about that, Anna, they should know better. It's been most enlightening. I've enjoyed our talk. Shall we join Rose and the gynaecologists at the clinic?" They laughed together.

They found her in conference with the pre and post-natal experts answering their very personal questions while bewildering them with a few of her own: was the baby lying properly, was she having problems with her water. He couldn't believe what he was hearing. Yet to her it appeared to be a natural line of conversation and exactly what she expected.

"What does the father want?" they asked as if he wasn't there.

"Well he wants me most of the time," she replied, laughing amidst a chorus of giggles. "But why not ask him, he can speak."

Heads turned, putting him in the spotlight.

"Oh a boy or a girl, either will do," not quite sure what he was saying.

"And they are my sentiments," Anna said, "we will all be wiser after the event. Are you staying to eat, caro? If not, let me offer you some refreshment."

"Thanks, Anna. A glass of wine would be nice. He'll have the same."

"I rather thought he might," Anna laughed. "I'll ask him though." She put her hand on Jim's shoulder and looked into his face, smiling. "He can have a choice."

"Wine please, Anna."

He listened to the conversation, sipping his wine, a little more relaxed, watching Rose and silently agreeing to everything she said.

"But seriously," one of the ladies turned to him, "would you like a boy or a girl?"

"I want Rose, and I'll accept whatever she gives me," he replied, smiling.

Rose was obviously in no hurry to leave. Had it not been for Anna, the day would have been spent there and he didn't mind at all. He was just beginning to feel comfortable watching her facial expressions, the way she talked with her hands. When they conversed together in English, she rarely used her hands.

"I want a firm promise for Sunday," Anna said as they prepared to leave.

"We will see you at mass, Anna," Rose said. "We will walk home and spend the whole afternoon here with you and Alvaro. Ladies, I thank you. We will continue our conversation on Sunday," she said, taking his arm and walking out through the door.

They walked to the car escorted by the ladies who were still calling advice through the open car window as they drove away. Both were completely relaxed in a feeling of absolute freedom as the Fiat gained the open road. They were silent, contented. As they drove along, listening to the hum of the tyres and feeling the breeze through the open window, she took his hand, caressing it for a while and then carefully replacing it on the steering wheel.

"If anything were to happen," she said, "Bruna would never forgive you for my selfishness. You haven't told me you love me since this morning."

"I'm sorry, but everybody was talking about babies lying at the proper angle inside a womb and asking if you were still getting through the day without wetting yourself. I didn't feel it prudent, but I love you always." He looked across at her and they enjoyed a laugh together.

They joined the queue of military vehicles waiting to cross the bridge.

"Who would believe that terrific bang that shook the valley only took out the centre arches. We thought it was the end of the world. Will we ever forget that day!"

"I'll remember that all my life, I rather think Franca will too," she replied.

The line of traffic began to move. The MP on duty waved them on. She gave him one of her special smiles and a wave that he acknowledged chivalrously. For a woman who had just graduated from virginal spinsterhood, she was mischievous to say the least. As he was about to discover.

Two three-ton transport lorries laden with troops moved slowly over the bridge. Jim followed behind at a respectable distance. She impishly leaned across and kissed him then sat back and waited, listening for the outcome of her action.

"You lucky bastard!" the lads shouted.

"Go on mate. Get stuck in. She's asking for it."

"Hey pal, can I have what you leave?"

She was laughing with delight while he slowed down dropping further and further behind the truck.

"What on earth will you do next?" he asked.

"I couldn't help myself. That's what you said that first day you kissed my cheek."

"I remember. Were you really annoyed then?"

"Actually, I was delighted, but I had to pretend! A 34-year-old spinster being kissed for the first time. I was determined the next time wouldn't be just on the cheek. When it did happen again, we had two bicycles between us, remember?" She kissed him again. "You lucky bastard," she giggled.

"You are aware of what you're saying, aren't you? It isn't at all ladylike you know."

"Of course I know, but I like saying it. I embarrassed you didn't I?" she said, smiling.

"No, not embarrassed. You did surprise me though."

"Pull in," she said, "we are in luck," indicating a three-tonner coming towards them. "I want to see how you fill up at these petrol stations on wheels."

Pulling into the side, he reached for the can and stepped out, flagging the oncoming vehicle to stop.

"Having trouble mate?" the driver asked.

"Out of petrol," he said.

"No problem," the driver said. "Whoo-hoo! What have you got in there? I wouldn't mind being out of petrol with her. She's a bit of alright. I could do something for that myself."

She looked at him, smiling, as if she couldn't understand a word but took it all in.

"If you look closer, you'll see I've already done it. Now how about some petrol before she drops it here. I'm on my way to the hospital. Fill this and I'll give you a quid."

"Sorry, Corporal. Hell, I didn't realise it was that serious. Here you are, take the petrol and keep your money. I'm only pleased to help."

"Thanks mate, but I want you to have the quid."

"Okay." Feeling a bit guilty, he put his head in the car window. "I hope you will be alright, lady. The best of luck," he said, climbed into his cab and with a final wave, drove off.

Jim returned the can to the back of the car and then climbed into the front seat with a huge grin. Driving along, he spotted the two tar barrels and turned in, letting the car roll along at a steady 30. With the houses in sight, she asked him to pull up.

"Let's have five minutes together," she said, "before we are overwhelmed."

"When this war is over, we'll spend the next 50 years together. Have you thought of that?"

"You won't be so eager to make love to me then, will you?" she laughed. "I think you should practice more."

"Oh I will. Now that I have your permission."

Peering through the windscreen, he saw the little gathering waving; some with handkerchiefs, others violently flailing their arms.

"We've been spotted. They're hailing us."

"So I see. Push on and blast the horn. Let them know that we are happy to see them."

She was being helped out of the car before it stopped. The ladies crowded around examining, touching, and advising her. The children were apprehensive at the sight of a soldier in uniform, aware of his identity but afraid to approach. Gina broke the spell, greeting him in the English that she had practiced for the honeymoon presentation.

"Welcome to our home, Mr Corner," she said.

"Thank you Gina," he replied, holding out his hand, which she took without hesitation.

He joined the crowd around the well. Franca was the first to greet him.

"I really must kiss the soldier," she said while everyone laughed.

"I would be careful, Franca, you can see what he's done to me."

"With a kiss?" she asked.

"Well it started that way."

"Never mind how it started," Elvira called. "Just let us know how it happened and the way it finished."

Rose was taken indoors amidst merry laughter while Jim was left with Bruno and the children. They were all full of curiosity having never seen a British soldier. They were in awe despite knowing him so well. That feeling quickly vanished and they were soon playing in the car, practicing at the steering wheel, and switching the lights off and on. Some just sat back in the seats. He let them do exactly as they pleased.

"Do you know where we can buy flowers?" he asked Bruno.

"Flowers! What good are flowers? They die in a week and your money's gone."

"I would like to buy some. Can you help?"

"It's your money. I can take you to a nursery, but they are very expensive."

"That's alright, let's go. Gina, tell Rosanna we're going for flowers, will you?"

"Can I come?" she asked shyly.

"I wouldn't dream of going without you, but ask your Mamma first."

He watched her scamper away barefooted giving him an extra

purpose to his errand. She was back almost immediately and scrambled into the car. He watched as she sat back in speechless wonder, trembling with excitement. He had known the child all these months and this was the first time he had really seen her. Bruno and Dante were his only other passengers. The rest, for reasons of their own, decided to stay at home.

"I want to buy shoes and socks for the children," he said as they drove off.

"Now you're talking sense. Shoes won't die like flowers," Bruno chuckled.

"Oh I want the flowers too."

"That's alright. If we buy the shoes, you won't have enough money for flowers. It's all black market dealing and they won't even be new," he warned, "Drive into the village."

Bruno directed him to an ordinary-looking solid stone-built house. The shoemaker could be seen at work through the window as the car pulled up outside his door. He ceased his labours and came to greet them. A soldier driving a car was worth investigating—there could only be large profits from any transaction. He ushered them into his workroom littered with old rubber tyres. They trod on offcuts while the remains of a sheet of good leather lay in a corner; several pairs of old shoes cluttered the table. It was difficult to imagine making a purchase at all, but he had learned not to be surprised at anything in Italy. Slight of build, his ageing body withering on its frame, the cobbler didn't exactly instil confidence. However, after friendly introductions and a request to examine his products, the skill became evident as he produced from nowhere a dozen assorted pairs of children's shoes in various sizes, well-matched and skilfully put together. When he asked about socks, the cobbler called his wife, sensing a good deal. She bid them welcome and smilingly excused her necessary departure to acquire the socks. While Gina and Dante were trying the shoes for size, Bruno and the cobbler began bargaining. He watched Gina weighing up one pair against another.

"Take both pairs Gina," he said, half listening to Bruno and the cobbler.

"I like this pair best. Two pairs would be too expensive."

"I'm rich, Gina. Money doesn't matter."

"How many pairs do you want?" Bruno asked.

"Just hold it a moment, Bruno." Dante was stamping the floor wearing a pair of boots with another pair in his hand. "Are they comfortable?" he asked.

"I like both pairs, but I'll take the ones I am wearing."

"Take both," he told him, turning to the shoe-maker. "How many pairs do you have for sale, Signor?" he asked.

"These are all I have available at the moment. If you care to call back in a week, I'll have a wider selection."

"These will be fine. Bargain for the lot, Bruno."

They both looked at him, the cobbler almost rubbing his hands with glee.

"Are you serious?" Bruno asked.

The lady of the house returned with the socks wrapped in newspaper. She pushed a pair into his face, apparently to smell.

"Brand new," she said, "and all very good quality."

Bruno took and examined them, counting ten pairs, smelling and fingering each sock.

"They are new. Do you want all of these too? They are different sizes."

"Better than army socks," the woman said, "you might want a couple of pairs for yourself."

She smiled showing her three front teeth: two up and one down.

"I might, Signora. Thanks for the thought. Alright Bruno, we'll take them all."

Bruno was beyond surprise by now. He just smiled with amusement.

"It's your money, I hope you have enough," he laughed.

"Here you are Gina, choose two pairs of socks. You do the same Dante."

He watched Gina remove her shoes and measure two pairs against her foot. Dante just picked up two likely looking pairs. Bruno made his final offer while the cobbler and his wife had their heads together doing some mathematics.

"Get ready for the shock, 2500—three months' wages, Bruno said. "Now we can forget about the flowers."

He paid with pleasure.

"Thank you, Signor e Signora. I'm obliged."

He was more than happy with the deal. They piled into the car with a bag full of shoes and socks, the children carrying their own. They couldn't risk the thought of losing them in the bag.

"Now let's go and fill the car with flowers, Bruno."

He listened to Gina reading the newspaper that was wrapped around her second pair of footwear.

"First I think we shall buy some books," he laughed soundlessly. This was fun.

"Books!" Bruno gasped, putting his hand to his forehead.

"Children's books, Bruno. Don't say you can't eat books, they are food for the mind."

"This is madness. Another month's wages. Do you realise what you are doing?" he laughed.

"Yes, I'm blowing four months' wages. Where I'm going I might not live that long."

They arrived home after a successful day's shopping. Gina tumbled out of the car struggling with her load excitedly: shoes, books, and flowers. She ran straight to Elvira's, realising that everyone would be there. Dante followed with books and shoes but Jim caught him by the arm.

"What about your mother's present?" he said, handing him the bouquet.

Gina in her excitement had alerted the whole community. They streamed out of the house, making a beeline for the car. Bruno was busy trying to tell anyone who would listen how much money had been squandered, but nobody listened to him. Everyone came to claim their present. It was Christmas in September. A large bouquet of flowers for each household with shoes, socks, and boots for the children. Happiness was evenly spread. The donkeys eeyored their approval. Joy was building up in his chest, pushing against his rib cage, creating a pleasant ache as he handed out the gifts. Some were comparing presents while the women were fitting shoes and socks on the children.

Rose stole up on him as he watched the carnival atmosphere.

"You are enjoying yourself, aren't you?" she said.

"Hello sweetheart. I have your present here. Let me get them for you." Reaching into the car he brought out a most impressive bouquet.

"To my darling Rose with all my love. I mean every word, however sloppy it may sound. These endearments are beginning to slip out naturally now. It seems to be easy for me to tell you how beautiful you are here and now."

"Am I really?" She put her hand on the bump. "Even like this?"

"Swellings become you. I remember a most attractive swelling on your cheek when we first met."

"Someone's always knocking me around it seems." She peeked into the car. "Is the other bouquet for a lady friend?"

"Indeed it is. It took six months for us to get on first name terms."

"Well she'll kiss you for the flowers. You've found her weakness. We will be here until it's dark I'm afraid. They've arranged a dinner and sing-song during your absence. Put the flowers in water and join us. Oh, this is their way of saying thank you for that day at the river, a favourable comment would be in order."

The tables were placed to accommodate everyone. Laid with ivory-white linen, dinner sets probably seeing daylight for the very first time, and crystal glasses never used (and probably never would be again); bottom drawer treasures for very special guests. They were all delighted when he told them he had never seen a spread like it.

"In England, they eat like this every day," Franca said knowingly.

"You would be surprised at just how humble our meals are," he replied.

Giuseppe sat at the end of the table with his ageless accordion creating a true party spirit, obliging anyone with a request tune. Bruno was a natural clown. His antics brought Rose close to premature delivery. Wine flowed freely, oiling tongues and vocal chords.

After the feast, they moved outside for dancing and no one was exempt, that included expectant mothers. Elvira made light of her 14 st, stamping, twisting, and twirling to the music. Her large breasts swinging freely, slapping against her body while she revelled in the dance, expressing pleasure with each partner. Franca joined in with joy and enthusiasm, shedding her inhibitions in lively and surprisingly rhythmical gyrations. He partnered both with equal satisfaction.

Having once paid ten guineas to learn ballroom dancing with less than average success, he always felt foolish on a dance floor.

Consequently, he could never relax, but here everybody just stamped their feet and felt free. One was unlikely to stand on his partner's toes. He sat back enjoying a flash of thigh or a titillating glimpse of panty, feeling the warm, cheerful, light-hearted atmosphere. They were respected and made to feel welcome.

The party spirit prevailed. Everybody did whatever it took to preserve the special welcome up until the goodbyes. They all insisted on one more visit before his tour of duty took him away. Franca placed the flowers lovingly and gently in the car, Bruno covered the recessed headlights to comply with regulations, Elvira had an arm around them both while Gina stood by, ready to deliver her farewell speech in well-practiced English. Headscarves and pinafores were already being placed to moist eyes when they finally took their leave.

*

Chapter 27

He drove with care, picking out the smoothest ground. When they hit the tarmac, he gave all oncoming traffic a wide birth while she sat comfortably relaxed.

"How are you feeling after your over-exertions," he asked. "You gave our son a good bouncing around."

"I feel fine," she laughed. "I must have tired him out; he hasn't moved since."

"It was good, wasn't it? I enjoyed Elvira's frolics. She must have lost seven pounds. Franca too will be a couple of pounds lighter."

Across the bridge and out of the valley, he moved into the country road.

"Sing me a song," she requested lazily.

"How about a duet?"

"Alright, I'll follow you."

"*Take Me Back to Dear Old Blighty*. You come in a line after me, then I'll repeat with you."

They sang and laughed the rest of the journey.

"I love that eye-tee-tiddly-eye-tie bit! You are easy to follow," she said.

"When I know where I'm going," he laughed.

As they pulled into the drive, a familiar figure stood on the porch.

"Did you see what I saw?" he asked.

"She has probably been there a couple of hours. I wonder when I'll be grown up," she sighed. "Poor Mamma."

"Maybe when her grandson arrives she will concede."

"I'm afraid not. She will have two children then."

"At least it takes the weight off my back. I hope you don't grow up."

After they had put the car to bed, Bruna met them on the path as if she had just stepped out for a breath of air. She was quite taken by surprise when Jim pushed the bouquet into her hands and she allowed them to escort her into the house, one at each arm. The flowers both intrigued and excited. She set about arranging them immediately while asking Rose about her day. He watched while she worked with obvious delight, placing the most elegant stems in pride of place, each bloom in order of merit. She possessed a keen inner eye. Finally, the more fragrant blossoms were arranged strategically to fill the room with their own distinctive perfume. She turned to look at him, obviously seeking an opinion. He made a circle with thumb and index finger.

"Does that mean you approve?" she asked.

"More than that, Bruna. I would like to congratulate you. You have turned an ordinary bouquet into an exquisite floral display with natural skill."

"I've already accepted you into the family, there's no need to go overboard."

Rose came in accompanied by Giovanni, each carrying a tray. One with tea, the other laden with torta and home-baked goodies.

"Was he going overboard Mamma?" She looked at the flowers. "I don't think so. The arrangement is as good as he says, maybe a little better. He gave due credit, no more." She turned to him, "So you've finally been accepted! How does the alien regard his family membership?"

"I'm overwhelmed, it's a bit premature," he said, laughing. "I was prepared for a ten-year probation."

Giovanni regarded him with a smile.

"Shouldn't we look at the other side of the coin? How well were you received by your own people when all was revealed?"

"With amusement I think, certainly without animosity. I was referred to as the man who married the Eyetie."

"Did they not envy you?" Bruna asked seriously.

"I'm sure they would, Bruna, had they known my wife. I am lucky don't you think."

"That's a silly question. You get the first prize and want me to confirm your luck."

"Well at least we agree on the prize-giving."

Actually, they were beginning to agree on a number of themes.

He impressed her with his general knowledge of Italy and his aware-ness of the people; the outcome of a full year's experience fresh in his memory. Bedtime was usually before ten o'clock. Tonight they laughed and talked well into the following day, learning more about each other. He and Bruna gradually cemented their friendship.

"We'll walk to church. I need the exercise." It was Sunday and they were preparing for mass. "How do I look?" she said, standing in front of the mirror, viewing herself sideways.

"Beautiful. A bit out of shape, but on you it's becoming."

"Becoming," she repeated, shaking her head, smiling. "Come, let me take your arm."

Bruna was on the porch waiting to see them off.

"How does she look, Bruna? She won't believe me."

"What did you tell her?"

"That she was attractively curvaceous."

"That's a fair assessment. Take good care and don't tire her."

They stood by patiently while Rose suffered some imaginary adjustments to her clothing and the odd light touch to her hair. After the inspection, they walked off, turning to wave on reaching the gate.

"Dear Mamma," she sighed.

"Dear Mamma indeed. Entrusting her treasure to a foreigner; one scarcely worthy of the privilege."

"You consider it a privilege then?"

"I consider it an honour, and I can understand her anxiety. Imagine you and I entrusting our daughter to some alien. The thought is terrifying."

As they approached the town, they encountered acquaintances, greeted friends, and passed the time of day with all. Among them were girls in their Sunday dresses and recent school-leavers who still addressed her as Signorina. In the piazza, people stood around in groups chatting and conspiring. Salvatore approached in uniform. They were delighted to see him looking contented and at ease.

"No political problems, Salvatore?" he asked, shaking his hand.

"Everything's as it should be. Signora, a pleasure to see you. I had news of your return, Captain. Before they send you away again, will you do us the honour of eating at our table? Veronica suggested I ask."

"We could happily fit that into our programme, Salvatore. Veronica as yet hasn't met my husband. We will look forward to the visit."

"She's seen him, Signora, on your wedding day. She also knows your name. Signor e Signora Corner isn't it?"

He pulled out a notebook and pencil repeating the name as he wrote.

"Salvatore, it still sounds strange to me," she laughed. "Try not rolling the R and it comes out easy."

Touching his cap in a salute, he bid them farewell, repeating their name.

There was no sneaking into church through the side door. This time they displayed their presence, occupying two seats near the front in full view of the congregation where everybody scrutinised her condition, weighing it against his time of arrival in the community. In spite of conjecture, she was respected and highly regarded. Everyone without exception wished them happiness. He watched as she made the short journey from pew to altar to receive communion, rewarding the congregation with a full frontal on her return. She knelt to pray and he did the same, to thank God personally for his good fortune. While in a begging posture, he had in mind to ask for a safe return plus a 40-year security guarantee to enjoy his luck. He tried, but it appeared the line was engaged—everyone was ringing the same number.

"Ite missa est," the priest announced.

The opportunity was lost, he had dithered his chance away.

"Rose," he said, "I am too late."

"Too late for what?" she asked.

"Too pray for a wish."

"Why didn't you ask while you were on your knees? It's standard procedure."

"The line was busy! I kept getting the engaged signal. There were evidently lots of other more important requests."

"My prayer I'm sure was duly noted. I asked him to send you home safe. We can only wait for his answer."

"Really, I'm pleased I didn't deliver my entreaty. He'll listen to you, you are a close associate. I remember seeing your wings that first day."

"You clipped those, didn't you," she said, scoffed.

But no one could possibly hear above the shuffling of feet as people filed out laughing and talking noisily. Anna joined them in their pew.

"You used to reprimand the children for exactly this kind of behaviour," she said, smiling. "This man will answer for his sins come Judgment Day."

"Judgment Day, Anna, is exactly what we've being praying to postpone," he said as they made their way down the worn steps.

The piazza was crowded with colourful groups: young girls flashing eye signals to the boys of their choice, older women enjoying a chit-chat, and men discussing the coming grape harvest. After shaking hands with half of the townsfolk, they made their way to Anna's house, greeting people as they went.

A sudden instinctive warning registered somewhere in his sixth sense as they crossed the footbridge.

"Something is not quite right, Rose. I must take a look. Excuse me, Anna."

Walking casually downstream to the thick shrubbery, he began to feel foolishly dramatic. On turning to walk back, a dishevelled German soldier emerged from the bushes, hands on head, awaiting his approach. He signalled to him to drop his hands; it was an undignified posture. The soldier fell in step with him. Neither spoke, just looked at each other as they walked to join the ladies.

"This then is your premonition," Rose greeted his return. "He reminds me of someone I met here six months ago."

"Really, did I look as bad as that? Anna, you remember the day she dragged me to your home?"

They laughed while the soldier looked on.

"However you looked," Anna said, "she couldn't keep her eyes off you and you could see no one else. I do remember wanting to mother you. I have no such feelings about this man but he is some mother's son and in need of help."

"Well go on, Rose, you're the interpreter."

She conversed back and forth with the nervous soldier for several minutes until finally she turned back to Jim to explain the predicament.

"He's been watching you," she said. "Both of us in fact. How did you not get one of your presentiments then? He has been living in your cave since June. Eating whatever fruit and veg was in season. He was afraid to give himself up, fearing that he would be shot."

"That's three months' rent he owes me! What's the going rate for a furnished cave? I did leave the straw."

"We'll discuss that over lunch. Bring him along, he can sleep in our stable tonight. Tomorrow we'll find some higher authority. I don't like the idea of you just handing him over to a passing truck."

"Whatever you say, but we'll leave the stable door open and give him a chance to change his mind. The last thing I want is a German companion."

The stranger was well received by the little community. All the neighbours crowded into Anna's kitchen. He was, however, but a ten-minute wonder. Rose was their attraction, their main interest. She and what she was carrying. A topic they could get their teeth into (even those without teeth).

"We will take him into town tomorrow. There must be someone of authority who will accept him and provide the necessary protection. Then we will have a day on the town, spend some money, and do some shady deals on the black market. I'll test my bargaining skills. We will walk arm in arm, you and I, through the park, hire a carriage, eat in a restaurant, and visit the cinema."

Anna laughed, "Test your bargaining skills! They will charge you treble and make you think it's cheap. It will be like taking candy from a child."

"Not if you are there to keep an eye on him," Rose told her.

"No, no. I've never ridden in a car before. I couldn't possible go. Besides, he won't keep his eyes on the road, they'll be on you."

"I'm a very good driver Anna," he laughed, "and I will keep my eyes on the road if you come along. We'll call tomorrow at eleven o'clock to pick you up and then deliver you safely back home before dark. You don't want to see us cheated do you? Rose can't haggle and I'm new to the game."

"Please share our pleasure, Anna. Jim will buy anything you want: flowers, perfume. I know a good restaurant, we will eat à la carte, or whatever is on the menu."

"I don't know," Anna said, but she was wavering.

Rose had made the outing sound exciting. Anna looked to the neighbours for support but there was no support forthcoming; any one of them would gladly have taken her place. With this realisation, she finally made the decision. A childish excitement began stirring in her breast.

"Is it safe in the car? What will I wear? And those British soldiers are no better than the Germans."

She was excited at the prospect while still looking for a way out.

"I'm a British soldier, Anna."

"No, no. You're different. Your wife is Italian—you are one of us."

"I feel as you do, Anna, but they are still going to take him away."

"If he intends spending money he needs someone to look after him or he will be cheated. Who knows, I might even enjoy it. In my whole life I've never been further than our own village. I'm both thrilled and scared."

"I promise to keep both eyes on the road, Anna. Rose and you will sit in the back. Our friend, the German here, will sit in the front with me. And I don't want to look at him do I."

"Promise you won't turn your head. Those army trucks are much too big to hit."

"Anna, you will have a day to remember."

After bedding down the soldier in the stable with his two army blankets and a pillow that Rose insisted he should have, he hurried back to their room to find her in bed with the window half open, the mild September breeze caressing her face and arms. He stood at the bedside watching her in the evening light.

"What are you looking at?" she asked.

"You. You looked so peaceful. I was afraid you might already be asleep."

"Would I do that! Come to bed, I've been waiting for you."

*

Chapter 28

The day began with the sun drying up the dew-covered grass. Odd puffs of cloud hung suspended in an azure-blue sky. A world of sunshine and joy away from the war-torn front. This was a different planet. He let the old Fiat roll along at a steady 30 for Anna's peace of mind. Taking a quick backward glance, he saw her chatting away excitedly like a child on her first trip to the seaside. When they had called to pick her up she was all ready and waiting, along with the rest of the little community, gathered there to see her off on the adventure. The soldier sat anxiously silent in the front. Jim had taken him a tray of bread and cheese and a cup of tea for breakfast hoping he wouldn't be there. Not only was he there, here he was riding to his destiny in style. Into the valley and across the river via the bailey bridge, they cruised along unhurriedly while he kept a keen eye out for a suitable hand- over point for his prisoner. Approaching two vehicles parked off the road facing in a southerly direction, he pulled up opposite and watched for a while. An officer and four men were laughing and talking over mugs of tea and cigarettes.

"Does that scene look secure to you, Rose? Safe for a hand-over I mean."

"Well they look friendly. Yes, I think he should be safe with them."

The decision made, he beckoned the soldier to follow him as he got out of the car. Their approach was watched with amused interest. Saluting smartly, he introduced himself.

"Corporal Corner, sir, with one that got away."

"At ease, Corporal. Where did you find him?"

"He found me. Got left behind and was afraid to give himself up. If he's going to be a hindrance, I'll take him further afield."

"No problem, Corporal, assure him he'll be alright with us."

"My wife speaks German, sir, and she's waiting in the car, anxious for his welfare."

"Your wife! You don't let the grass grow, do you."

"On the contrary, I let too much grow. She's six months pregnant and I've been here two and a half years."

"Got yourself a wife and a car! The war's been kind to you."

He laughed as the other four soldiers began taking an interest.

"My father-in-law's."

"I'm curious about the two and a half years."

"I'm a leftover from the 1943 chaos. Bagged in Libya in 1942."

"Then you should be back home in Blighty."

"And here I am back home in Italy with my wife. I'm due up front in 11 days."

"Enjoy your 11 days, Corporal, and don't keep your wife waiting."

"Thank you sir."

"Bye gentlemen."

He patted the German on the shoulder and bade him auf wiedersehen, then turned and walked back to the car feeling relieved and light-hearted. Getting into the car, he looked at her.

"I'm sure he'll be alright," he said, "but the next German wishing to surrender will have to catch me first."

She laughed. "Well let's go in case he gets homesick."

They had a wonderful carefree journey singing a couple of verses of *Lili Marlene* and a tuneless rendering of *Mamma Dare Me Cento Lira*. An air of excitement prevailed as they drove into the town.

"Rose, this is medieval," he said with surprise.

"I'm glad you like it. The walls, what's left of them, date back to the Roman era. The Ponte Di Cecco was built by the Romans. You are looking at history," she told him proudly.

On a smooth walled face, was a life-sized portrait of Mussolini in one of his conquer-the-world postures. It had been smeared with paint and used as a target for every type of missile. Painted across the noble Roman features in bold English capitals were the words: HE WOULD RATHER F— THAN FIGHT. They spotted the graffiti at precisely the same moment. Their eyes met.

"The Romans didn't do that," she said with a sly smile. "Unfortunately it is true," she added, "but let's look further. There are so many interesting sights to see, so many wonderful things to do."

They parked out of the sun under some trees beside an old carriage. In the shafts was a still older horse with lowered head, asleep and dreaming of sunlit meadows and clover fields. Two boys of 10 and 12 years came up to him while they were still taking in the scenery.

"You have cigarettes, gum, chocolate? We will show you the town."

He knocked them a little off balance when he answered in Italian, "I have neither, but if you want to earn some money, you can stand guard over the car for a couple of hours. I'll give you 50 lira each and the same when we get back."

"Okay, we watch."

"Nobody will steal the car!" she said.

"I wasn't thinking of the car. Someone might syphon off the petrol. Do you think we should hire this carriage? I feel a bit guilty about disturbing the horse. He might drop dead and then we would have his death on our conscience."

"We are in no hurry. I'll tell the cabbie to let the horse go at his own pace. No faster than a walk in case the obvious happens."

His sympathy for the horse prompted him to strike a bad deal with the driver who was charging him double for the hire. It seemed reasonable to him but not to Anna. She tore into the cabbie like a tiger, shaming him, very reluctantly, into knocking 25% off.

"The price," Anna emphasised, "not the time."

The noble steed put one leg in front of the other and took up the slack. The carriage creaked and groaned on its uncertain springs. The wheels turned and they were off on their sightseeing tour of the town. Rose lay back on the worn leather seat, filling them in on any interesting point that the cabbie considered unimportant (there were many).

On one street corner, a woman sold flowers. Unable to resist the coloured display of dahlias, carnations and chrysanthemums that delighted his eye, he asked the cabbie to stop and he jumped down. Taking Anna by the hand, he helped her out.

"I want you to bargain for these, Anna, while I listen and learn how it should be done. We want two nosegays and two large bouquets of every flower on the stall."

She was as sharp as Bruna and the vendor knew she would have to settle for just an average profit. He stood aside, an interested spectator. Two young girls stood by the stall admiring the flowers while enjoying ice cream cones.

"Excuse me, ladies, where did you buy those? They look delicious." Surprised at his command of Italian, they stared at him for a moment. "Can I have a lick?" he asked, smiling. The girls began giggling, jokingly holding out their cones. "I'm flattered. Would you allow me to buy you another one each?"

Declining the offer and thanking him, they pointed out the shop, even quoting the price. He watched them walk away giggling and turn to wave to him.

"Anna," he said when the deal was struck, "ask her to keep them in water until our return. There will be an extra 50 lira for her trouble."

With a wave and a smile at Rose, who sat watching his flirtations and smiling, he went off in search of ice cream cones, looking among his small notes and counting out the correct amount as near as possible—expecting no change. Purchasing four ice cream cones, he put the money on the counter, thanked the lady, and hurried back to the carriage. Rose and Anna were busy pinning on their posies, laughing and giggling just like the two girls with the ice cream cones. They gave a little cry of joy when he handed them the treat. The other two he gave to the cabbie and the flower seller.

"Where's yours?" Anna asked.

"I have a pocket full of money and the only thing I want is Rose."

"Well she won't charge you," Anna quipped.

The flower seller wanted her money in advance as insurance against them not returning.

"The whole lot, including your tip, is 300 lira. Pay 100 now and the balance when we collect."

"Hell's flames, 15 bob for flowers and I'm supposed to be enjoying myself," he exclaimed as he handed the vendor a 100 lira note.

"Come on, Jim, that's not like you. Pay up and look pleasant."

They had cast off all care. He jumped back into the carriage. The cabbie tickled the old horse with his whip. It responded willingly, taking the strain and actually breaking into a trot of his own accord; there was life in the old nag yet. Through a pleasant avenue of trees and into the park, they passed a beautiful stretch of flower gardens not quite at their best, though still soothing to the eye. Rose lay back completely relaxed, looking at him through half-closed eyes while Anna took in everything, looking from right to left, afraid of missing out on the slightest detail. The driver was nodding in his seat. The horse plodded his weary way with an occasional snort, ridding his muzzle of pestering flies. Passing a fruit and veg market comprised of hand barrows and carts, he asked the driver to stop again.

"Take the bit out of his mouth, I'm going to buy him a few carrots."

He purchased the carrots from the nearest stall. They were badly wrapped in a sheet of newspaper so he was obliged to balance the bundle from vendor to consumer like a juggler. They took turns feeding the horse, who enjoyed the attention as much as the feast, obviously having difficulty chewing through teeth that were worn with age.

"Anna," he said, "take this 100 lira note and buy him a cabbage. It will be softer for his mouth."

"A hundred for a cabbage!" she said aghast, "how much did you pay for the carrots?"

"A hundred," he told her as if the price was in order.

"Ladro!" she screamed and stormed off ignoring his out-stretched hand offering the money.

Rose looked at him smiling while they listened to Anna tearing into the trader and mustering support from the other shoppers. She returned with two cabbages. They enjoyed the horse's pleasure, helping him to the tastiest meal of his humdrum life.

When they returned to collect the flowers, Anna asked him for 200 for the vendor and the agreed price of the carriage hire. "If we are to eat at a restaurant, the way you spend we won't have enough to pay the bill." She turned to Rose, "I can see him having to wash up as payment for our meal. Keep an eye on him, caro, don't let him out of your sight. He has already promised a week's wages to two children just for sitting watching the car. I only hope they haven't sold it on the black market. The man is completely irresponsible."

"Better do as she says, Jim. You can afford to take your wife and friend to dinner, can't you? It's a fairly high-class restaurant."

"Let me take account of my assets," he said, pulling out a bundle of notes. "I'm new at budgeting you see, Anna. First, let us provide for our immediate debts: flower money and cab fare. Here take 1000 just in case."

Rose sat laughing while Anna took the roll of notes out of his hand, peeling off the required amount. She pushed the wad back at him.

"Put that away," she said, shaking her head wearily, "before the wind blows it away."

"There's no wind to blow it, Anna," he smiled.

"Do you need a wind? You can blow it yourself without help."

Anna collected the flowers and settled the account then climbed back into the carriage before the old horse had drawn a second breath. Back at the car, the cabbie not only looked for his tip, he asked for it. Anna dismissed his request abruptly.

"You were hired for two hours. You've worked one hour and 45 minutes. Your tip is the 15 minutes' bonus."

That was her final word, he was sent on his way. She proved herself an excellent accountant. Time was balanced against money. The boys too hung around for their tip on top of their wages.

"Pay them exactly what you promised," Anna told him, looking on keenly, guarding against the likely event of him giving extra. "How long is it since you handled money?" she asked and without waiting for his reply, "you never did handle any, did you? It didn't stay in your hands long enough."

"Anna, I stand corrected. Now let us find a jeweller. We can spend a lot of money there. I want to buy you each a necklace and perhaps a bottle of perfume. Will you allow me to do that, Rose?" he asked as he got into the car.

"Perfume," Rose agreed, "if there is any available. As for jewellery, it's pointless looking. Even the trashy stuff is far too expensive. Drive on, I'll direct you," she ordered.

Quite a few shops were open for business with nothing on display and nothing obvious to sell. She guided him to the perfumeria where the proprietor greeted her.

"Ah, Signoriii…na," pausing in his greeting when he saw her condition. She brushed aside his apology. On display were a few bottles of doubtful quality perfume and empty atomisers. She was obviously no stranger here. He led them through into a room of mirrors where expensive perfumes were arranged in a huge glass cabinet. This room had most certainly been kept under double lock and key during the German occupation. They would have cleaned him out in an hour, simply taking his whole stock away in a truck, leaving an IOU to be honoured when they had conquered the world.

He enjoyed the respect she was shown. The man didn't push any sales talk. He knew that she knew what was good and what was better. Neither did she inspect and reject but simply decided on two rather expensive perfumes and made her choice.

"I would like you to take two bottles, Rose—one for your birthday and one for Christmas."

She looked at him, smiling.

"It's really expensive you know. But since you intend washing up for your dinner, I'll take two."

"I'm a good washer-upperer. Anna, you take two bottles also. Drive Alvaro wild tonight."

"I can do that with a bottle of lavender water. He doesn't need inducing."

"Good for you, Anna, you've still got what it takes."

"I've got what he takes," she laughed.

"Let's go mad. Go on, take two bottles."

"One bottle, thank you. I was 19 years old when a young man last bought me perfume."

"Did he kiss you, Anna?"

"Yes," was all she said.

"Then I'm hoping for the same treat."

"Your wife will give you all the kisses you want. Can you hear him, Rosanna?" she asked.

"I'm listening," she replied.

She touched her ears and wrists with the perfume glass stopper before putting it under his nose.

"Does it please you?" she asked, "I want to be sure, I'm using it as a temptation."

The proprietor was standing by, listening and smiling.

"Rose, I wish it was tonight," he replied in English.

She glanced quickly at the shopkeeper who turned away with an even broader smile.

"You do realise he speaks English?" she said. "No matter. I'll take it if the smell appeals to you."

"Absolutely," he said, not caring at all about his little faux pas.

"Then pay the man and we'll settle with each other later."

"How much do I owe you?" he asked in English.

The answer came back promptly in the same language.

"Your bill, sir, comes to 2200 lira."

"If I had come in alone to buy, would it have been double?" he asked. Without waiting for a reply, he turned to Anna. "You are right, Anna, I do need some protection."

"Only from yourself. That's not money you're spending, it's just pieces of paper."

"You may be right. I used to be more careful with pound notes. Would you have charged me double, Signor?" he asked, laughing.

The shopkeeper glanced at Rose.

"A little extra maybe," he smiled.

"That's honest, and deserves a reward. Take the six pounds and have a drink on me."

"Thank you sir! I will look forward to another visit." He turned to Rose, "Signora, my congratulations."

"Thank you," she replied with just the right amount of charm.

The shopkeeper walked with them to the car, actually opening the door for the ladies. Jim stood by until the man had exhausted his courtesy.

*

Chapter 29

The fragrance of her perfume permeated the car.

"Have you spilt the bottle, Rose?" he asked.

"I hope not, at a thousand a shot! You said the smell was stimulating, isn't that the reason you bought it?"

"I don't need a stimulus. I can love you with or without."

She smiled, her eyes fixed on the windscreen navigating their course.

"Take the first turning on the right and, unless it's been moved, the restaurant should be straight ahead. The sun is smiling upon us: we will eat outside. Is that alright with you, Anna?"

"Today is the best day of my life, I agree to anything."

"Anna goes to town," he acted flamboyantly. "There's more to come. After dinner we will visit the cinema."

"A rare pleasure indeed, but I must consider my family."

"As you wish, Anna."

The restaurant boasted a car park: a bombed plot of waste ground alongside the garden cafe. She received a similar welcome here as they were ushered to the table of their choice. He had brought along a packet of English cigarettes to guarantee the best service and attention, which she was already attracting by her presence, but he placed the cigarettes in full view of the waiter anyway. Today they were in luck, there was chicken. He chose from the menu, ignoring the prices.

"Chicken salad for me, Rose, and whatever you choose for afters. The choice of wine I'll leave with you."

"As we have no other choice, I think he will enjoy chicken breast with almonds?"

"Sounds delicious. Have a double portion; one for yourself," he said, laughing.

"He might not eat all of his, we'll have one between us," she replied. "The sweet is straightforward: ice cream or torta. We've already had ice cream so we are left with torta. We are not spoilt for choice. Anna, stop looking at the prices."

"Can I have half a portion?" she asked, "these prices terrify me."

"You can, but they will charge the same."

"I'll have the same as you, caro."

"Let's punish her, Rose, and order a double helping. This table is ideal, I can keep an eye on the car and you."

Anna laughed.

"If anybody tries to steal a couple of wheels, he'll deal with them. He'll probably give them money and the wheels."

The cigarettes had the desired effect. The waiter was on hand to cater for their every need, putting the finishing touch to a most enjoyable day. Rose drank more wine than usual while Anna had stopped looking at the prices. In the prevailing mood, whatever they said invoked frivolity. Their pleasure was his delight. He added a 50 lira note to boost the tip as cigarettes meant nothing to him, he could never quite understand their power of purchase or the value placed on them. The bill neither surprised nor shocked. On a day like today, it would have been cheap at double the price. He tried hiding it from Anna without success. She stormed at the waiter, demanding to see the proprietor while he and Rose looked at each other, smiling.

"Don't let her little outburst disturb you," she said, "it's the climax of her day. She's really enjoying herself. You will probably end up with a rebate."

Anna duly appeared happy and smiling carrying two bottles of wine followed by an apologetic proprietor seeking assurance of their satisfaction. None of the other customers bothered to watch the display, behaving as if it were a daily occurrence.

He drove back at a steady 30; there was no reason to hurry. Getting home before dark now appeared to be the least of Anna's worries. They were laughing and giggling, discussing his bargaining skills with each other.

"A hundred lira for a handful of carrots. This from the man who was going to do shady deals on the black market! He even let the cabbie take him for a ride."

Rose couldn't speak for laughing.

"Have you two opened those bottles?" he asked, taking a quick look over his shoulder.

"Eyes front, Captain," Anna shouted; Rose was rolling around in fits of laughter.

"Hey," he said, "take it easy back there or you will bring on a premature mishap."

"Just keep your eyes on the road. I've delivered scores of babies. I'm the unofficial midwife of the province, but this one I especially want to bring into the world as I feel responsible."

"Look at that golden sky across the mountains. Was there ever such an evening! Tell me, Anna, how could you be responsible for our baby?"

"Because I sat there watching you two eyeing each other knowing full well what was going to happen. I encouraged the affair when I should have sent you packing."

They joined the line of traffic waiting to cross the bridge.

"In those days I had nothing to pack, and in any case you and I were attracted to each other. You noticed that, Rose."

"I did," she said, adding fuel to the fire.

"You know that she came to my room that first night and sat on my bed."

"Listen to the man, he asked me to sit with him and for a half hour your ears must have been on fire. He talked about you the whole time. Isn't that true, bricconi? He asked the most personal questions."

"Well he knows everything there is to know about me now, don't you? I'm carrying living proof."

"There's still more I want to learn. Shall I take the country road?"

He had already pulled off the tarmac.

"You've taken it anyway before we could reply. Is this his usual conduct?"

"You mean doing what he pleases before asking permission? Sometimes he doesn't ask at all, he just does it."

"And that annoys you, doesn't it?" Anna observed, rocking with laughter.

"I'm asking now: may I have permission to get back on the road before reaching town? We do have to turn off at the bridge don't we?"

"Did I detect a hint of sarcasm in his tone? You are too lenient with him, caro. No man ever dared speak to you in that manner. Whatever got into you?"

As he swerved just in time to take a sharp left turn, he called behind him, "Hold onto your hats, ladies, and that lump, Rose, in case it goes bump. I promised Giovanni to test the car springs. Whoops, is everybody alright back there? I'm new at this driving lark, Anna, but I am improving don't you think."

"Mother of God, he tells me this now when I'm almost home. Thank you, Santa Maria, for your protection."

"Amen to that, Anna. Here we are, get off your knees. Didn't I do well? Careful how you go. You've been away so long the dog might not know you."

"Keep that man under control, caro. There are clear signs of disobedience."

He jumped out of the car and ran around to open the door, helping her step down.

"You will come in for a glass of wine? Don't end the day so abruptly. I'll even allow him to come too."

"It'll be a pleasure, Anna. Well," she said, "I'm waiting! Are you going to help me out? I realise I'm only your wife."

"My wife," he said, helping her down, "you are my princess."

"Clown," she chided. "Reach inside and get the bottles off the seat and don't forget the flowers."

They spent a whole day of their ever-dwindling supply of days visiting Maria and Francesco, reading the letters from their sons in England, a privilege reserved especially for Rose. It gave her great pleasure making the 20 or so badly written lines read like a storybook, dictating from her heart the feeling missing in the words. A good memory was most essential because the letters were read again and again by request.

"But surely they realise those few lines could never contain the story you relate," he said, bemused.

"They probably do, but does it matter when it makes them happy? I write the replies myself in the hope of making their sons happy. All it costs is a little time."

"We don't have much of that left, do we; together I mean."

"I'm afraid not, but when we've fulfilled our obligations, there will be four days left. I want us to spend them so close that we will have difficulty breathing. Dolce far niente. Would you like that?"

"Rose, you are reading my thoughts."

"Then that's how it shall be."

The days went by so quickly. They were preparing to go to their last Sunday mass together. He longed to share her spiritual beliefs, find pleasure in her faith, but however hard he tried, he felt nothing. Often, in sticky situations, he would whisper the name of Jesus. It was only a word, no more. His plea was never headed, why should it be. The shells burst all around, bullets thankfully winged their way past or plopped harmlessly into the earth, but the fear prevailed. Strangely, going back to the front line didn't bother him. That was a chance he had to take and he felt capable of handling any situation. What troubled him most was the dreadful empty feeling of separation, thinking of her every waking moment, walking around as if there was a hole in his chest.

She was viewing her swollen body in the mirror as she did every Sunday. She always viewed herself sideways, trying to smooth it flat with her hand.

"Three more months at this rate and I'll burst," she said, smiling. "Take a good look at what you've done. Pleased with yourself aren't you?" He laughed with her. "When you come home we're going to practice caution. It's all live ammunition you have stored away in there," she said, patting his thigh playfully. "I'm going to learn how to dodge the bullets, maybe you can teach me, you are good that."

"Bruna might teach us how. After all you're an only child."

"She will teach you how, by putting your bed in the stables, and we don't want that, do we? We are going to have two children so we'll use the time between one and two practicing birth control with impunity. If you make me pregnant during practice, we will have achieved our objective and the experience will hopefully have taught us a lesson."

"Whatever you say."

"Now, get down and tie my shoe laces; I have difficulty bending.

These little things I shall miss most of all, and the big things, and the wonderful things."

"Bruna will take my place. I'll take comfort knowing you will be in good hands."

"Nobody will ever take your place."

"I sincerely hope not. We are talking about a stand-in, to fetch and carry for you. I'm sure Bruna will fit the bill admirably, she's made for the job."

"And you can be sure she will do it. Now get up," she laughed.

"Give me a moment, I'm not finished worshipping."

"Well finish and cheer me up, I'm getting that awful feeling already. Wear your wedding suit today, discard the uniform."

"An excellent idea, if only you could do the same. You look like a princess. They get pregnant too you know. I have never seen a princess but they all looked beautiful in the story books."

"Come," she laughed, "I'm beginning to feel better; keep it up."

She called through into the kitchen as they passed. However, Bruna was already on the porch waiting to greet them. She practiced her imaginary adjustments to her daughter's clothing while Rose winked at him over her shoulder.

"I saw that! He'll probably be laughing behind my back." She turned to face him, "I entrust her to your care but you don't deserve the privilege."

"Bruna, that's my most treasured possession and tomorrow I'm handing her over to your charge. I trust you will take good care of her, no one else I know is worthy of the honour."

"I think I am equal to the task since I nursed her eight years before you were born and 26 before you arrived."

"Then I think I've made a wise choice, Bruna. Thank you, I can go with an easy mind. You are all heart and there's plenty of you."

"Just let her lean on you and don't hurry. Walk at her pace."

"I will do exactly as you say, Bruna; she is also my pleasure. I will look after her today, you do the same for me tomorrow."

"Bye Mamma, we'll be back for lunch."

They kissed a friendly farewell. Rose gave a sly nudge with her elbow. He wasn't quite sure what she was implying but, taking his life into both hands, he too kissed Bruna on the cheek and was surprised at the fond reception.

"You don't do that very often, do you. Have you a favour to ask?"

"Just an expression of affection and eternal gratitude, Bruna. Thank you for everything, including my wife."

She watched them walk off arm in arm with apparent disregard for tomorrow.

*

Chapter 30

Under the pretext of visiting a relative in San Benedetto, Giovanni insisted on driving him to the coast road where all northbound vehicles would afford a lift. As they drove through the countryside, it was a pleasure to see the towns and villages untouched; the bridges had been blown but that didn't make anyone homeless. The journey was also made more entertaining by his father-in-law's account of Rosanna's tender years—tales that he had heard before but that sounded better at the second telling.

"She once got angry with me. Her wrath lasted five minutes," Jim shared.

"That's a long time for Rosanna to stay angry. She probably intended teaching her husband a lesson. Just letting him know who's boss."

"We weren't married then, but she made me crawl. I was actually begging forgiveness and, as if it had never happened, we were kissing five minutes later."

"Glad to hear it. Watch your step in future. She's a good teacher if you are an obedient pupil."

"I wouldn't dream of disobeying her," he said, laughing. You can assure Bruna of that."

"Bruna offers her prayers for your safe return."

"Really! I'm both surprised and flattered." He paused and then changed to a more serious tone, "Father-in-law, in the unlikely event of anything serious happening, I would like you to ensure that Rosanna receives all the benefits due to a war widow. The pension would amount to twice her teaching salary. Promise you'll follow up that request."

Giovanni looked at him, "I do believe you're serious. We really shouldn't be discussing anything so morbid."

"Talking won't change anything either way. You will be a

grandfather long before I return. This is a difficult country for warfare. I'm surprised our soldiers have progressed so far through these continuous hills and valleys."

"You may be home to enjoy the event with us."

"Giovanni, I'll settle for just being alive and reading the letter she will write an hour after her delivery, however weary the experience leaves her."

"Indeed she will, and I'll take pleasure posting the news the same hour."

"I can't ask more than that. Just pull in at the side, Giovanni. Whatever fate lies ahead begins here. My next lift won't be nearly so pleasant."

Parked at the roadside, they sat in silence, neither in any hurry to make a move. Some little time later he broke the silence.

"She could have done a hell of a lot better. You know that."

"Denying it would be less than honest, but in Bruna's words, whatever your shortcomings, where could she have found someone to treat her with the same respect?"

"Really, tell me more. I have a particular inclination towards Bruna's lore."

"You just said she could've done better. I agreed. Bruna said she could have done worse and again I agreed. Need I say more?"

Dragging his kit bag from the back seat, he said, "Tell Bruna I'll be back."

"She will look forward to it. Take care of yourself."

He flagged down an oncoming vehicle. The driver was alone and going all the way. His luck was holding.

Making one or two enquires on his arrival, he eventually found his reporting point; an imposing building even by Italian standards. The obliging driver took his leave only when it was confirmed that he was expected. He stood in the foyer after reporting his presence, surrounded by his earthy goods, as soldiers of various ranks were coming and going. Some acknowledged while others ignored. Just when he thought he had been forgotten, a door opened down the hall and a sergeant called, "Corporal Corner?"

"Yes, Sergeant."

"This way."

"How about my kit? Will it be alright here?"

"Best bring it in or somebody might break their neck over it. Come in and take the weight off your feet. There's a chair." Checking his documents, the sergeant looked at him. "I see you married an Italian girl. Very interesting indeed."

Italian, not Eyetie, Jim thought to himself.

"I don't suppose you're in any hurry to get up there?" he asked.

"If I arrive when it's all over, that will be soon enough."

The sergeant chuckled. "I'll inform my superior then find you something to eat and a place to sleep. Tomorrow we will finalise the arrangements. The truth is, I want your advice."

"My advice? You're kidding. Nobody has ever asked for that. Not in my living memory. Everyone was always telling me what to do. But go on, this is interesting."

"I'm courting an Italian girl seriously and I would like to marry her."

"So what's stopping you? Won't she pass the test? I don't foresee any other difficulty."

"Nothing like that." He was obviously in a dilemma. "It's me."

"You. I'm afraid I don't understand."

"Do you have problems, Corporal? I mean being married to an Italian. Already I'm getting snide remarks and we are only courting. Would it have adverse effects on my career as a soldier?"

"You are creating a lot of obstacles, Sergeant. Marry her and you will be looked on as I am: the bloke who married the Eyetie! That's as much thought as anyone will give you. Nobody's interested. I have a big problem though, Sergeant, a big one. Last night we almost broke the bed. My wife is a big girl you see. We parted less than eight hours ago and already I'm as lonely as hell. I miss the stimulation of her mind, the satisfaction of her body, and the sheer joy of her company. My biggest worry is getting knocked off at the front and leaving these earthly joys behind, perhaps for someone else. Even when I'm talking about her, as you see, I'm carried away on a cloud of emotional excitement. That, Sergeant, is love. Seek and ye shall find."

The sergeant nodded thoughtfully and responded with a grin,

"Come with me and I'll arrange a meal and a place to sleep, then I have a date with my own stimulation and satisfaction."

"Don't keep her waiting on my account, Sergeant. If I'm successful in your case, I'm going into business after the war giving advice to the lovelorn: 'Complete satisfaction or your money back'. Make my first case a success, Sergeant."

"You are as mad as we expected. Here, let me take your kit bag. You can sleep in the office truck. I'll inform the driver then we'll go and eat."

After tea, the sergeant brought a couple of blankets and a pillow. Jim looked at him in surprise.

"What, no sheets?"

The sergeant walked away chuckling, only to return with one white sheet and an apology.

"I don't believe this. Show me where I can fill my water bottle, but don't wave your hand over it because I would rather have water."

"Come, I promise pure water. By the way, you can keep that extra bedding. It will see you through the winter. We'll call it payment for advice."

"Thanks, Sergeant. Have a good night."

There was nothing left to do so he went to bed early. Surprisingly, he blacked out when his head hit the pillow. No dreams filtered through his weariness.

Struggling out of his coma in the morning, he was somewhat disappointed: usually she was centre figure. Her influence sparked off fantasies out of focus. Sometimes vivid, always humorous, all quite unreal, but she was always there. Hearing someone moving about the vehicle, he looked over the tailboard to see a man jobbing around outside.

"Morning," a pleasant face greeted, "I thought you were dead and decided to let sleeping dogs lie. You came with a reputation for being mad. I'm here to show you around the wash, shave and toilet area then escort you to breakfast. Those are my orders."

"Thanks, mate, what's your name?"

"Smith, 502."

"Come on Smithy, your mother didn't christen you 502!"

"John. She was a snob."

"John Smith! I love it. Okay John: towel, soap, razor and toothbrush. Ready when you are."

"Bring your mess tin and utensils. Afterwards we'll go straight to breakfast."

They each brought a mug of tea back to the truck and continued enjoying each other's company. The sergeant came along unnoticed while they were enjoying a chat and a swig.

"Morning gentlemen."

"Morning, Sergeant," they chorused.

"Hope you had a successful night, Sergeant."

"Thanks to you, Corporal, yes. If you call at the office in ten minutes I'll have your papers ready." Turning to John Smith, he continued, "He'll be riding in number three truck. Help him with his kit, John."

With that he walked off.

"He was in good form. John! Does he usually call you that or was it for my benefit?"

"He's trying to impress you. He's playing with an Eyetie you know."

"Couldn't find a better playmate. I married one."

"Yes I know," the driver answered casually.

"How could you know? I'm only passing through."

"Corporal, everybody knows. Word went around here two weeks ago that some daft bugger had refused to get on the boat for Blighty."

"Really!" Jim laughed. "The man must be mad."

"Well I admit to being one who thought so. You were being discussed at breakfast and I agreed with one man's comment: anyone who refuses the boat back to Blighty must have a very good reason. I think you have."

"Thanks, John, that's generous. Let's get my kit stowed and ready to travel then I'll collect my papers."

The office door stood ajar, the sergeant was waiting for his call.

"Come in, Corporal and close the door. Take a seat and give me the benefit of your experience."

"I assume your fiancée said yes?"

He smiled, "Yes she did."

"Then I'll give you the benefit of my experience. Do whatever your wife wishes and you will have nothing but joy ahead."

The sergeant laughed. "Corporal, meeting you has been an unexpected pleasure."

"So I've heard. Everybody here was expecting to meet some kind of idiot."

"We were, but I was intent on sounding out the idiot. In these circumstances, he might know something I didn't."

"And did he?"

"Oh yes! A lot more. By the way, I've given the transport driver a haversack to fill. Since I'm still responsible for your welfare, allow me to see you on your way."

They walked out of the building, through the vehicle park to the awaiting truck.

"This haversack, Sergeant, what will they fill it with?"

"Tins of food of course."

"Why? Don't they feed us up there?"

"Take these." He was handed 40 cigarettes.

"I don't smoke, Sergeant."

"With all your experience you still have a lot to learn, Corporal. Forty cigarettes and a haversack full of food will buy you anything."

"Will they buy my way back to my wife?" he asked sardonically.

"I'm afraid they will only buy you a bit at somebody else's wife."

"Then they are of no use to me, Sergeant."

"Take them just the same. You will soon discover their true value."

"Thanks, Sergeant. And I was giving you advice!"

"Selling, Corporal. And it was cheap enough at the price. Here we are."

They arrived at the transport vehicle where he was introduced to the driver and a corporal whose job he never did discover, but they both proved amiable, obliging, and hospitable. Two men who had the war taped to a fine art, having accumulated every possible comfort a soldier could fiddle: sleeping bags, thermoses, hip flasks and a bottle of cognac. The driver winked at him.

"Strictly medicinal purposes," he said.

They had cups, saucers, plates, books, and magazines. The truck was a home from home. As yet he had not been introduced into the larder but they packed his haversack so generously it weighed more than his kit bag. This accumulated wealth had its problems; there was no way he could carry it without transport.

The first signs of war's destruction began some miles from their destination and gradually became worse. Where resistance had been stubborn and the fighting fluid, whole villages were laid waste and scores of farms were reduced to rubble. People went about their business of staying alive. Some with purpose, others still in a daze, few even managed a smile. All wore some article of army issue clothing. Men, women and children held out begging bowls as the convoy passed by. Many were fortunate; the soldiers were ever generous.

Arriving at their destination, each vehicle was directed to a parking spot. With no idea of procedure, he simply watched and waited. His driver selected an ideal site beside a small wooded copse and immediately prepared a brew while the corporal went off in search of further information. Two hours and several cups of tea later, he returned accompanied by a captain of the RASC.

"Your arrival has been widely broadcast, Corporal, and I'm sure there will be a search party out looking for you. In the meantime, make yourself comfortable. If you are not claimed by tomorrow evening then you are one of my staff. But we'll wait and see what develops."

Dinner was prepared and served. Food was abundant and his hosts liberal. The table was a packing case in the back of the truck, hidden from envious eyes. Fried meat loaf with tinned potato and beans formed the nucleus of the meal, followed by tinned peaches and cream. Coffee touched with cognac completed the splendid repast. His hosts indulged themselves further, smoking a bow-shaped cigar that smelled like tarred rope, but they enjoyed it. His bedroom for the night was the cabin of the truck and he was in good company. A picture of Betty Grable and her million dollar legs was pasted on the rear of the cab, though he only spotted it on awakening.

The smell of cooking greeted him as he scrambled out of his blankets to be welcomed with five-star treatment. Hot water in a peach tin was provided for the luxury of cleaning teeth, washing, and shaving and it proved ample. Breakfast was equally indulgent: tinned bacon and fresh eggs preceded by porridge flooded with tinned milk.

218

If his prospective employer failed to find him, he could spend the rest of the war in copious luxury travelling up and down the leg of Italy. His dream, however, was short lived, shattered by the advent of the captain.

"Your services are required, Corporal, and incidentally, your presence has been noted and duly acknowledged. Come with me and I'll fill you in with the details on our way."

"Do I take my kit, sir?"

"No I don't think so. Pick it up later." He climbed into the jeep excited and apprehensive. "A Major Oliver will meet you here at the provost's office, that by the way is our destination. They need an interpreter on a minor case before the major arrives. They were delighted to have someone on hand who could cope with the language."

They proceeded through an arched entrance and down a tree-lined drive towards a large building that had been subjected to some harsh treatment. Bullet holes scarred the walls and two huge gaps from heavy calibre shells were in evidence and under repair whilst windows were being replaced. The captain led the way into a large room where three military policemen sat around a desk conferring seriously while a woman and two children (a girl of 10 or 11 years and a youth somewhat older and taller than his mother) stood sobbing and weeping. The sight of a soldier armed with a Mark II terrified them further. The sobs became louder. The woman was pleading and shouting for mercy.

"Shut up, you silly cow," the provost sergeant shouted.

She immediately toned down the whimpering, cowering in fear. He stood by at a loss, watching. This was something new.

"The corporal will help you out with the language, Sergeant, if you wish to proceed."

"Thank you sir," the MP replied. "Corporal, I want you to get what you can out of this little lot: names, places, articles stolen, and most important of all, who bought their ill-gotten gains. Well go on, get cracking."

"Do you intend imprisoning them, Sergeant?"

"Hell no! That means feeding them. Just get what information you can."

As he approached the trio, the weeping and sobbing grew in

volume. The woman fell to her knees pleading for their lives. It was disconcerting and not at all what he expected. He wasn't quite sure where to start and all eyes were upon him. Putting his hand to her elbow, he asked, "Please get up off your knees, Signora," in her native tongue.

"You're not going to shoot us?" She began to calm down a little.

"I'm here to help you," he said, realising that the Germans would probably have shot them, and they had just recently left.

She grabbed his arm and hung on with both hands. So far so good, the boy too was comforting his mother while the girl clung to her. Giving a half glance to his audience he felt he was making some progress. Turning to the little girl, he asked, smiling, "What's your name?"

"Giulietta," she muttered, showing half her face, the other half buried in her mother's coat.

"Why aren't you at school, Giulietta?" He was trying to win her confidence.

Looking at him in surprise, she showed him all her face, wet and smudged. "There is no school. It was bombed," she replied.

Her fear, like the school, had also gone.

"My wife is a school teacher you know Giulietta."

Her mother still clung to his arm making it impossible to shoot if such were his intentions. He patted her on the arm.

"Feeling better now, Signora?" he asked.

"You won't shoot us?"

She almost wanted it in writing.

"I only want to know what you stole and how you disposed of it. They know you stole something."

"Signor," she looked at him defiantly, "I am a widow with two children. My house was destroyed. We live in a cellar with no electricity or water. Of course we stole, how else can we live?"

"Tell me everything. I might persuade them to set you free."

"You won't tell them all I tell you?" she asked. His arm was imprisoned against her breast. "If you let us go free, I'll pay you back some other way."

He smiled, "That really won't be necessary, Signora."

He felt embarrassed despite the fact that the onlookers had no understanding, but they might catch onto the signs.

"Talk freely. I'll only tell them what you want me to say."

"We took blankets and pullovers."

"How many, Signora?" He was unable to free his arm without breaking the trust.

"Six of each. We sold them to Ernesto and Luigi."

"Six of each! My, that's a lot. They will imprison you for that. Let's make it three. Do you have enough blankets to keep you warm at night?" he asked.

"Let us go free and you can come and spend the night with me. I'll keep you warm and make you happy."

He just ignored the offer—she was scared out of her wits. The sobbing had stopped but the tears flowed freely.

"Did they pay you in food or money?"

"Both. Two kilos of rice, some bread, and 200 lira. We won't go hungry for a week."

He was overcome with pity. He tried to pull his arm away but she held it fast.

"My arm please, Signora."

"If you let us go free. I'll wait for you in the car park."

"You must release my arm before I can help you."

She reluctantly let go and he turned to face the audience, relating to the sergeant the information he thought was important.

"These are scapegoats, Sergeant. Three blankets for a handful of rice. Could anything be more pitiful?"

Now he was pleading on their behalf.

"Don't be a bloody fool, Corporal, we are supposed to deter these pitiful bastards. Lock them up where they can't steal. The Germans would have shot them. Anyway, your information was quite adequate. By the way, what payment did they receive?"

"Rice bread and 200 lira. They're living from hand to mouth in a cellar."

"You don't have to plead for them, Corporal. I want to get rid of the buggers. Just scare the shit out of them and make it plain that next time they'll be shot."

"Right, Sergeant."

As he turned, an officer standing at the door was looking straight at him and he knew instinctively who he was. The sergeant called the room to attention.

"Carry on, Sergeant," the major said, acknowledging the captain and taking the chair that was offered.

"Alright, Corporal, complete your job and get rid of them," the sergeant ordered.

He had already taken a quid's worth of lira from his pocket. The girl and her mother were crying quite audibly, appealing to a higher authority—they still weren't sure. The boy comforted his mother and displayed a quiet dignity. Maybe he had been directing his questions to the wrong person. Pushing the money into her hand, he looked at the boy.

"Next time you steal… I'm speaking to you, son." The boy merely lifted his eyes and stared at him. "If you get caught, you'll get shot. Giulietta," he said, smiling at her, "I might not be here to save you, but I know that you won't steal again, will you?" She smiled through the tears and shook her head. "Good girl. Take your mother and brother. You are free to go."

All three dashed out of the room before someone had a change of heart, creating a receding echo of sobs.

"Everything is prepared and ready, sir," the sergeant said. "Here is a list of missing articles and we have three men in custody."

"Thank you, Sergeant." The major walked over and sat on the edge of the desk, the paper still in his hand. He looked at Jim. "Are you Corporal Corner?"

"Yes sir," he replied, rather casually.

The major didn't appear to mind although he commanded great respect from the military police staff.

"Well don't go away. We've waited too long already for your arrival," he smiled. "Take a chair. You might learn something."

Equal or not, the major didn't talk down, not to him or anyone. When he smiled, he flashed even teeth, displaying a couple of gold caps. There was a lot to like about the man and it made him feel much easier. He had spent a lot of time imagining what manner of man was to control his destiny.

Occupying the vacated chair beside the captain, he sat down to watch an expert at work. The thieves walked in with an air of bravado that changed abruptly when the provost sergeant dropped one of them to his knees with a blow to midriff. There was no evidence of rebellious behaviour but the action had the desired effect. The major simply ignored the incident, concentrating his efforts on the other two while Jim focused attention on his new boss, sizing him up. His job was to deter theft, seek out corruption, and protect the interests of his country. He was doing it efficiently and effectively. Drastic measures were sometimes necessary. It occurred to him that the thieves would think twice about doing another job before they got out of here. He had a lot to learn if this was a typical day's work. Three sorry looking prisoners were marched back from whence they came. The major and the sergeant had their heads together in serious discussion. Suddenly they broke into laughter. The major, in lighthearted mood, gave precise and clearly defined orders before taking his leave. Jim stood up as he approached. The man looked him straight in the eyes.

"A very interesting show, sir," the captain said, "and quite successful I'm told. The corporal read the script otherwise it would have gone over my head."

"Glad you enjoyed it, Captain. They are not always that easy. If you are ready, Corporal?" he turned to Jim.

"His kit is in one of my supply wagons, sir. If you would follow me, it's probably on your way."

"After you, Captain."

They called goodbye to the provost and walked out Indian file.

"You drive, Corporal, since that will be among your duties."

Was he being tested already? The vehicle, a 15-cwt Bedford, was a welcome sight with fitted canopy for protection against recent rains and future snows. Arriving at the supply lines, his hosts helped load his kit and, in addition to the bulging haversack, they pushed a large tin of oatmeal and four cans of milk into the back of the truck. The captain and the major chatted like old friends. Goodbye handshakes were all the more sincere, since their friendship was short-lived and they would probably never meet again.

*

Chapter 31

As they drove past an artillery regiment leaguered in reserve he glanced at the major for some indication.

"Those low buildings at two o'clock," he said. "I suppose you're often asked the $64,000 question?"

"Strange as it may seem sir, not many people do. It's something nobody can understand so they don't ask. Everybody comments but usually they just write me off. I'm the silly bugger who married the Eyetie."

"Does it bother you?"

"Hell no! Secretly I enjoy it. But I'll tell you, my wife wanted to stay in Italy. It was my desire to please her, that's all there is to it."

"Would it surprise you if I said that I understood?"

"It would sir, unless by some coincidence you find yourself in similar circumstances."

He felt the officer looking at him. He didn't see the smile on his face.

They drove into a large stable yard. The boxes were being used as officers' quarters and the large building converted into a mess. He followed the major into the harness room furnished with a homemade filing cabinet, table, and a chair occupied by a soldier with a field telephone at his elbow. He didn't get up, but looked keenly at Jim with engaging interest.

"Anything demanding attention, Jonesy?"

Jonesy! He noted the familiarity.

"Nothing that can't wait sir."

Sir! It didn't cut both ways.

"Corporal Corner, this is Jonesy. I'm not sure what his mother christened him."

"You have called me every unprintable name during these last five weeks and three days, we'll skip the hours. I'm delighted to meet you, Corporal. Your shoulders look broad enough to share his wrath."

"Things were never that bad, Corporal. If he got a rollicking, it was deserved."

"Weren't that bad for him because he pushed the overspill my way."

"You will learn not to heed him but he's usually there when we need him. May I have your travel documents? Thank you," he said, accepting the envelope. "Jonesy, find him a place to sleep and a bite to eat."

"I'll sleep in the truck, sir."

"You will be cramped, but if that's your choice then by all means. Since you are in charge of the vehicle perhaps it's a good idea."

"I'll fix him up, sir. When you're ready, Corporal, dig out your mess tin and we'll enjoy eating alfresco," he chuckled. "Do I call you corporal or what?" Jonesy asked on their way to dinner.

"What, if you like, but my name's Jim."

"I know your name, I've read your file. I hope you're as good as it reads, Jimbo. Claude expects a lot."

"Claude?"

"Our boss. He's alright. If he had two glass eyes it wouldn't stop him seeing and he's as sharp as a razor. By the way, if you are sleeping in the vehicle, I'll show you where to park. Some of these officers are like schoolboys after a couple of drinks. You married an Eyetie eh? Claude's involved with one, I'm not sure how seriously, but she has a very bad track record."

"You're a favourite backer then?"

Jonesy laughed. "Indeed, boyo. I stick to my wife. I don't accept any outside rides."

"Wise man. My wife is the only ride I've ever had."

"And a hell of a shag she must be. Kept you here in Italy didn't she," Jonesy laughed. "But it's good to hear a man brag about his virginity rather than how many women he's shagged."

The lunch of Bully Beef stew with rice for afters, accompanied by a floorshow, proved a rare treat. The duff sergeant came in for some playful criticism.

"Who called the cook a bastard?" a joker called.

With a perfectly timed improvised twist, a wag answered, "Who called the bastard a cook?"

Amidst laughter, the duff sergeant acknowledged his critics like a boxer who had just won a contest. It was a pleasant good-natured exhibition of camaraderie and it put him in good spirits to meet the major.

"Corporal, come in. Bring that box up and take a seat. Did anyone inform you of your duties?"

"To be honest, Major, I didn't really care what they entailed. I just wanted to be as near to my wife as possible, she's pregnant by the way. I assure you, whatever the situation, I'm capable of handling it."

"Well that's very comforting since we will be called to the front on occasion and possibly be involved in dangerous situations. Does that worry you?"

Jonesy had said he was sharp and he could feel his eyes searching.

"Danger always bothers me, Major."

"That's a definite reply. Only a man with experience could be as honest."

"I won't let you down, Major, but about interpreting, won't I be involved?"

"I'll pass all the jobs onto you that involve no security risk. You will be invaluable to me, but you'll find that it's a thankless task. When you hinted that our circumstances might be similar, what exactly did you mean? I'm curious."

"Only someone similarly involved could understand my reasons for being here at all. But that apart, with my experience I would eventually find myself in some front line after a month's leave at home. So why not this one."

"I'm quite sure you would, and why not be near your wife. About the similarity you mentioned in our present situation, we might discuss that another time. Your opinion could be interesting. By the way, we don't usually pay thieves for stealing and if you are called upon to issue a warning, try a little severity, otherwise you handled the case quite well. By the way, when is your wife expecting?"

"The middle of December, we think."

"I'll try to get you a couple of days' leave when the baby is born. You should be with her then."

The suggestion was thoughtful, quite unexpected, and a favour he would never have asked for himself. It proved the inherent quality of the man that revealed itself in the weeks that followed. They were off to a good start.

Jonesy was the anchorman. He made life comfortable with his creative ideas and a knack of pulling rabbits out of the hat. He advised Jim on packing in a limited space to attain maximum effect and furnished him with a sleeping bag. He did his shopping from an exclusive source on behalf of Gina, Claude's fiancée. Stealing could only be curtailed; the black market flourished with the sale of army issue food and clothing. 'If you can't stop the thieves, buy back the goods. It's only money' was Jonesy's maxim. He and Jim exchanged confidences, spent the evenings playing cribbage, writing letters, and talking over cups of tea. Indeed the highlight of their day was tea and snack before retiring. Claude usually slept at Gina's. All in all it wasn't such a bad war.

He transported the major each evening, returning to pick him up at 08:00 the following morning from Gina's villa just two miles away. He made friends with Angelina the maid one morning while waiting for the usually prompt major. He was asked into the kitchen for tea and their friendship developed. He was privileged by virtue of having an Italian wife who was pregnant. Angelina had an insatiable curiosity. It was like talking to a ten-year-old child, she was so charmingly naive. Aware that all their conversations were relayed word for word to Gina (and God alone knew where else) he began calling ten minutes early and Angelina brought his tea to the truck where she stayed chatting.

One morning, Gina accompanied Claude to the vehicle. Angelina liked sitting in the passenger seat asking questions and listening to his detailed romantic replies. It was like telling fairy stories to a child. He stepped down from the vehicle and stood awaiting their approach, surprised at the tingle of excitement she stirred within him. If he had seen her before, it must have been on the screen at the cinema. She was a vision in a silk dressing gown that must have come from the wardrobe of a Hollywood studio. His pleasure was two-fold when

Claude introduced her in Italian. A woman of Gina's class and experience would most certainly speak English.

"Corporal?" she repeated with distaste after Claude had presented him. "His name is Jim," she winked. "I get all my information from Angelina. Corporal indeed! I've heard so much about you, Jim, we really had to meet. I've watched from the window while you flirted with Angelina. I didn't realise you were so good looking."

"Gina, I was supposed to say that," he replied courteously.

She was beautiful and easily the most charming woman in the world. Her eyes were the outstanding feature in a delightful, smiling face that radiated warmth and friendliness. Dark hair fell to her shoulders in a mass of ringlets.

"I've listened to so many stories about your wife, I feel as though we have met. As you see, I've come prepared with pencil and notebook. If you would be so kind as to give me her address, I must write and tell her that she married the best looking man in Italy."

"That won't be necessary, Gina, I've already told her myself."

He was rewarded with a merry laugh as he wrote her name and address with Gina looking over his arm.

"Mrs Rose Corner," she repeated, clasping her hands gleefully. "We are going to be such good friends, she and I. And as time goes by, you will both come to visit and bring the baby." She turned to Claude. "Darling, I feel so excited."

Jim looked at this vision of beauty and joy. Having learnt all about her past from various sources, he hadn't expected anything so delightfully charming, deciding there and then that the truth was a lie. She was much too nice a person to be the whore described to him. There had to be some other explanation. Claude stood aside, eager to go yet reluctant to break up this newly established friendship. Jim sensed the restlessness that Gina was probably ignoring and held out his hand to say goodbye; it was immediately disregarded as she kissed him on both cheeks.

"Good friends don't shake hands in Italy, Jim. You disappoint me."

They drove along in an uneasy silence that troubled him. It wasn't usual.

"Pull in at the side, Corporal. I would like a word."

"Something I've done, sir?"

"No. Wouldn't I correct that on the spot?" They sat for sometime without speaking. "How much do you know about Gina?" the major asked.

"I speak Italian sir, after a fashion, but enough for them to trust me. In her case, I don't believe what I've heard."

"Thank you, but it won't go away."

"Nor will the Germans. God they're a bloody awful race. It's the presence of one German in her past that makes everything look worse than it really is. Is she pregnant?" They were sitting half turned in their seats facing each other.

Claude looked at him, smiling. "Now we find ourselves in similar circumstances. You couldn't have known this six weeks ago. It's not something that can be swept under the carpet. The problem grows daily."

"How far have you gotten with the preliminary arrangements? Gina appeared quite content."

"We've talked it over and are in complete agreement. Preparations begin at Christmas. Gina has spoken to a priest who will be happy to perform the ceremony with or without permission."

"That's grand, Major. You did a better job than the Germans and the Italians: you got her pregnant."

"Her words exactly!" he laughed. "Drive on and let's discover what the day has in store."

"Yes sir. I'm delighted, we are going have a good day and a hell of Christmas: our baby will be born and you'll be married."

"Your baby will be born. One thing at a time, Corporal."

The office was actually Claude's sleeping quarters that Jonesy now occupied. The telephone was manned 24 hours but it rarely, if ever, disturbed his night's sleep. Since it was a harness room, there were a number of assorted pegs attached to the walls and Jonesy made use of each one. No job was too big and small tasks were treated with the same industrious effort. Claude was catching up on his paperwork, Jim doing a spot of maintenance on the vehicle. Everything revolved around the office. He was replacing the last plug when Jonesy called him for a cuppa. He walked into the room while wiping his greasy hands on a filthy rag. He usually came in for some good-natured ribbing, being the youngest of the trio. He actually enjoyed it—they liked him.

"Look at the state of that man sir." Jonesy was building up for a few laughs.

Claude looked up from his work. "Make him drink his tea outside," he replied, smiling.

"Bloody hell sir, it's cold out there."

"What do you think, Jonesy?" he enquired ponderingly.

"I think you are far too lenient with him, Major," he said, looking at Jim standing inside the door, cleaning his hands cleaner. "Okay, come in," he repented.

"Thanks, Jonesy," he replied gratefully, "how about a couple of the major's biscuits."

"Anything else, boyo?"

"Give him the packet. I have a favour to ask."

"Bloody hell, I'm being paid in biscuits."

"That's about all you're worth, Jimbo. You go everywhere with that gun stuck to your back. Who are you going to shoot?"

"Somebody for sure, Jonesy, before this war is over. A good boy scout is always prepared. I've done it before you know and, regrettably, I know it will have to be done again."

"It might never happen, Corporal. Be at the provost's office at 14:30, I'm relying on you to deal with this case impartially."

"Can you trust him, sir," Jonesy continued the playful banter.

"He's learning, and getting quite good: he doesn't pay the thieves for stealing now and he is expert at turning down offers from the ladies. What was the professional term for those bribes, Corporal? Your own words."

"Fanny for freedom, sir, but it's only been offered twice."

"Oh I like that!" Jonesy said. "And what's this about paying thieves, sir?" he pressed the point.

"He can be forgiven that one. It was his first day and he was thrown in at the deep end. However after refusing the ladies' offer to let them go free, he paid her."

"Oh I don't believe this," Jonesy was having a field day. "How did you and your wife get together the very first time? She was a virgin and I can't imagine you pressing your advantage."

"I must admit it puzzles me too. How did it happen, Corporal? You can spare us the details, just the introduction if you'll pardon the vulgarity."

"It happened the only possible way. We just did it," he said, smiling.

"Go on, boyo. At least take us to the bedroom door."

"Not quite that far. There was no bedroom. We did it in a cave by mutual consent and every day thereafter for the next five months. Did I eat all those biscuits?"

"Every one, you greedy bugger," Jonesy chuckled.

"Sorry gentlemen. I'll get cleaned up and attend to that job." He sensed them smile as he made his exit.

The major disliked denunciations. That's how their love affair began, when Gina was the victim of one such vendetta. Her two accusers both had husbands in a prisoner of war camp. Claude pointed out that Gina's husband had died for his country, and that in all probability theirs would return unharmed. For her protection he'd arranged an armed guard over the following days.

The new provost sergeant was of the same opinion as Claude about people who denounced their neighbour. He spent little time on, and gave short shrift to, the complainants.

"Okay, Corporal. We've got that out of the way. I want you to have a word with our new criminal element next. These two, wait 'till you see them, wrapped themselves in pullovers and walked off as cool as a summer breeze. They almost got away with it too. Right, bring them in Bob," he told his assistant.

The mother and daughter were brought in sobbing and crying. He wasn't at all surprised. Indeed, he had expected them. The crying ceased temporarily when they saw him through a veil of tears standing by the desk.

"Mamma, it's the nice man with the gun," Giulietta said with relief.

"Ever seen this pair before, Corporal?" the sergeant asked, laughing.

"If I had, Sergeant, they wouldn't be difficult to remember." He approached the criminals, "Signora, would you mind continuing to cry a little louder. You too, Giulietta. No, no, don't overdo it."

"Go on!" the sergeant said. "Scare the shit out of them. Make a job of it. What the hell can you do with these!"

"Sergeant, you are making me look like the school bully." The woman had hold of his arm again, pleading. "More tears and pleading, ladies," he urged, "I'm supposed to be scaring you."

They had read the script and knew how to turn it on. Their pleas were heart-breaking.

"Okay, get rid of the buggers, Corporal, before the little girl wets the floor. Will you stay for a cuppa?"

"Yes thanks, Sergeant." He turned towards the pair, "Now when I shout, I want you both to run for the door, and please don't let me see either of you again. Go away!" he shouted, a little louder than normal.

The staff had a good laugh as they scampered outside. He sipped the tea and talked longer than he should have, delaying his departure, but to no avail. They were standing by the Bedford when he walked into the car park.

"Signora, Giulietta," he touched his cap, "I do hope you haven't been stealing from the truck."

"We wouldn't steal from you, Signor."

"You don't have to is what you really mean. I'm an easy touch." He took two of the four tins of Bully Beef from his haversack and before he could make the offering, they were snatched from his hands. Hunger has no conscience. "How did you know my vehicle?" he asked

"We know where you park, and you sleep in the back of the truck. I will come one night and stay with you," she looked up at him demurely.

"Signora, don't even think about it. I will have you locked up."

He made to climb into the cab as she put her hand on his arm.

"Will you give us money for bread? We are hungry." She wore her most appealing look.

"Why don't you go stealing somewhere else?" he said, fishing in his pocket, bringing out two notes.

"Somewhere else!" she repeated angrily. "We live here. The British wrecked our village. Where do you expect us to go? They killed my husband. Should we starve?"

She was so angry that he was taken aback and a little embarrassed. His hand automatically returned to his pocket.

"I'm sorry, Signora. Take this, it should keep you for a week," he said, handing her a quid's worth of lira. Jumping into the cab, he drove away quickly. "God!" he said to himself. "This couldn't possibly happen a third time."

The regular flow of letters from Rose was his greatest pleasure. She wrote every day, each one a love letter in serial form that he read and re-read, looking forward to the next episode. They were read in the most unusual places, this time he was parked outside of a very ordinary looking house, complete and untouched. The major stepped out and told him to wait and catch up on his clerical work. In his letters to Rose he had mentioned Claude and Jonesy.

"Your superior," she wrote, "must be a very exceptional man. You are not easily impressed. He also must be intelligent enough to realise that you couldn't scare crows, yet you are dealing with the criminal element. I became extremely excited when reading that we will spend two whole days together when the baby is born. Indeed I can think of little else. I am relieved however that you can't see me in this grotesque condition, but then you would lie and probably say, 'sweetheart, you never looked more beautiful'. Don't ever stop lying or I'll never be sure of your love, and please remind me of that in your next reply."

*

Chapter 32

The Germans had counter-attacked with some success. He was enjoying a most rewarding sleep, one in which he was having the best of both worlds. Rose had visited his dreams and touched his lips. In the depths of slumber he was aware it was only a dream but he felt confident she would make a return visit; maybe this time she would stay and he could hold her in his arms. Jonesy was shaking him by the foot.

"Wakey wakey Jimbo." He sat up startled. "An urgent call-out, boyo. Be ready in five minutes."

"I'll be there in three," he replied, slipping on his boots.

"It must be important, they have sent an escort to guide you."

"Guide us where? What's the time anyway?"

"Where is up front and the time is 02:00."

"Okay Jonesy, I'm ready now. I'll just void my bladder in case I do it in my pants when we arrive."

Claude jumped into the truck happy as a sand boy.

"You've probably heard this line a hundred times at the cinema." He pointer a finger, "Follow that car," he said, chuckling.

"I hope you're as happy when we get there sir. You must have had a premonition. Why did you sleep here last night?"

"Don't be personal, Corporal. I'm sure you and your wife have off days."

"Off days sir, but never nights."

"Keep your mind on your work," Claude chuckled. "And for God's sake don't lose our guide." Jim could feel his elation.

The last mile across rough ground and without lights was hazardous at best, except for the brief glow of gun flashes. The front was alive with action. Even brigade headquarters was well forward, possibly within enemy artillery range. They stopped near a group of official-looking vehicles all as busy as beehives. Claude was ushered towards a huge canvas structure erected between two large vehicles standing tail to tail. A light became visible when the canvas flap was lifted to gain admittance. Jim settled down for a long wait, happy in the knowledge that he was in a reasonably safe spot. He watched the activity going on around. Particularly among a group of eight soldiers armed to the teeth standing beside their transport vehicle, talking in undertones and in a strange language. He began to wonder if they had been misguided but the outbreaks of subdued laughter assured him that all was well. He learned later that they were Polish commandos.

A courier appeared out of the hive and came towards him.

"Come with me please," he said.

"Me? Are you sure?" he asked, surprised.

"Corporal Corner?"

"Yes."

"You. Follow me."

Jumping smartly from the vehicle, somewhat puzzled, he followed the escort into the pulse of operations. His heart stopped. The array of brass was awesome. He had inadvertently entered the kingdom of the Gods. Except for a captain and an Italian farmer, the major was a junior ranking officer.

"Is this your man, Claude?" a great white chief asked and without waiting for confirmation, "Come here, Corporal," he said.

He approached the lord high executioner with knees knocking while the aides, brigadiers, and colonels watched his advance. It was painful indeed.

"You speak Italian I'm told." Again no reply was necessary. "Can you read a map?"

This time he waited for an answer.

"Quite well sir I think," he replied, his throat like sandpaper.

Never in his service had he encountered the powers of warfare.

"Take a look at this and tell me what you see."

God almighty! he thought, shaking. The map was in such detail and so clearly defined that a child could read it; he described what he could see, aware that a simple mistake could be possible amidst all this omnipotence.

"Well done. Excellent," the great man said. "We have a job of some importance and the major thinks you are the right man."

"If the major thinks so sir, then I am."

"Good man. Good man. You will be responsible for a dozen peoples' lives. Don't let them down. Do you understand."

"Yes sir," he replied, trembling.

"Captain," he called.

"Sir," the reply came smartly.

An officer stepped forward looking like a walking time bomb. Literally armed to the teeth except the knife was in his belt.

"We've found your man. Take him aside and give him his orders."

"Yes sir. Over here, Corporal, I want you to sound out this farmer. I'll tell you what we want to know as you progress. This is Signor Valente, he owns the farm we are going to clean up," he stated directly and dispassionately.

He had learned the basics from Claude: first, get his trust, then make it known that you are on his side.

"What's your name, Signor?"

"Silvano Valente. I hope these people don't intend destroying my farm. They are all unapproachable and none of them speak Italian."

He had raised his voice loud enough for the war lords to fall silent and shoot piercing glances, almost changing him to a pillar of salt, but the farmer was undaunted. He had found someone he could talk to and intended driving his objections home. Claude broke ranks and came to his aid.

"Can you handle him, Corporal? He's much too audible."

"I can sir, although I would appreciate your presence."

"Carry on, I'm with you."

"Take it easy now, Silvano, otherwise I can't help you. Calm down. What is the situation at your farm?"

"The Germans just walked in, took over, and locked my whole family in the cantina."

Jim turned to the captain.

"I'll ask him what I think you want to know, sir, while you consider what is important."

"Go ahead, Corporal, keep me informed as you proceed."

236

Claude stood by allowing him to employ his own methods; they were mostly what he had learned from him.

"Now Silvano, there are 12 in your family, is that correct?" He waited for the farmer to do his sums.

"Yes 12, that's right, 12 is right."

"Now this is important. The ages of the oldest and the youngest, then we'll know how to proceed once they are free."

"My brother's child, 3 years old, and our parents, both 68."

He translated each answer to the captain who simply nodded, making mental notes.

"How did you escape, Silvano?"

"I was working just 30 or 40 m away from the farm. They never saw me."

"How many Germans and how were they armed? Tanks? Self-propelled guns? Half-tracks? Any heavy weapons?"

To the farmer's knowledge, there were a dozen well-armed men and three vehicles of various proportions carrying two heavy calibre guns. Filling the captain in on this information, he wanted to be specific and threw in some extra questions.

"The cellar door, is it locked?"

"Just with a broken padlock, entry is easy."

"Is it below ground level?"

"No, it's a straight walk in."

"I don't think you need my help," Claude said and left to join the heavy brass.

"I think we have the full picture," the captain said. "I'll want you and the farmer with me, Corporal. I'm told you can handle that Mark II. Don't get trigger happy because I don't want it used, except in the event of something going drastically wrong. There will be sentries. My corporal and I will deal with them silently and clinically." He produced a torch from nowhere, "Take this, you will use it twice. Once to be sure the wine cellar is cleared and again on your way back, at this building," he indicated a farm on his map. "You will encounter a patrol. Flash twice to signal your approach. We don't want to lose the hostages once they are free. They are your responsibility, get them back here safely and that completes your job.

You won't need to fire a shot. Just one more thing, my men are all Polish. There will be a corporal and two privates in our party. If you need to ask a question, direct it to me. Is that clear?"

Claude was once again at hand and it was a comforting feeling among all the unapproachables and cut-throats.

"Is there anything you're not sure of?" Claude asked solicitously.

"I'm sure of everything, Major, except getting back, but I'll stick with Al Capone here," he chuckled, indicating the captain.

"Corporal," the captain turned to him.

"Yes sir."

"Be sure the farmer knows what is expected."

He discussed the situation further with Silvano who appeared in no doubt. At this point he told him of a sentry near the wine cellar.

"Why didn't you mention this?" Jim asked and informed the captain.

"That's alright, Corporal. I expected it. There will probably be another at this point," he fingered the map. "My sergeant will deal with him. I'll dispose of the one at the cantina. That's when you do your job. Silence is the key. Come, we'll get started."

He approached the Great Man, "Permission to leave now sir?" he asked.

"Whenever you're ready, Captain. Oh, and bring back two prisoners. The highest ranks possible."

What he really meant was bring back whoever is still alive.

Silvano stayed so close they might have been handcuffed. He had no faith in the Poles, they didn't speak Italian. The main party split at the foot of the hill. It was to be a two-pronged attack. The sergeant and four men to take the farm from the south side, the captain and three other ranks made up their party. Watches were synchronised. That's what he must get himself, he thought—a watch!

Artillery duels in the thick of the fight lit up the night sky. Theirs was by far the quieter sector. They passed the farm where the patrol was expected on their return journey. The deep valley and the night provided excellent cover and soon the silhouette of the farm buildings became visible against the sky. The commando corporal went forward to reconnoitre while they waited. On his return there was a whispered conversation with the captain and they all moved forward together. By instinct, the captain found a depression at the edge of the farmyard providing ideal cover. They were a few minutes early and the wait was an eternity. The sentry was clearly visible, leaning against a tree, smoking a cigarette, the glow partly hidden in a half-clenched fist. Grinding the stub underfoot, he set off for his last stroll on earth. Walking casually and slowly, he looked down at his feet within three yards of where they silently lay.

Jim felt a movement, saw a shadow, heard a sharp intake of breath, and watched the limp body being gently lowered to the ground. It was his signal. Moving swiftly across the yard, Silvano following, he removed the lock and opened the door. There was a hint of panic until the farmer calmed the terrified hostages. His wife threw her arms around his neck. Silvano led her outside, whimpering; there had to be some theatre. Love is a strange phenomenon. The others followed while the captain stood at the edge of the farmyard urging them into the valley. Jim shone the torch around the cantina. Once he was satisfied, he caught up with his party, pushing the old couple forward impatiently. It had all gone so smoothly.

Moving swiftly to the front of the column as they hurried into the valley, he offered words of encouragement in passing, promoting confidence. As they approached the expected patrol, he flashed the signal, receiving an acknowledgement in kind. They were in position and ready to move forward as their party filed past.

"The flight into Egypt!" a joker remarked amid muffled sighs of relief.

When they reached the cart track running parallel to the valley, he thought his troubles were over. Suddenly a thundering explosion split the darkness and lit up the night sky. The staccato sound of a machine gun was drowned in a storm of bursting grenades and small arms fire accompanied by a series of blasts. Artillery fire was momentarily absent while Polish vengeance had its fill.

His flock, so orderly and obedient, suddenly panicked, scattering in all directions, but Silvano held onto his wife. He looked like losing the remainder of his charges in the Promised Land. The ignominy of reporting back with one out of 12 hostages spurred him into action. The brother carrying the three-year old, accompanied by three other children, returned to the fold. Six out of 12: things were beginning to improve. Ordering them to stay put, he went in search of the rest while the holocaust trebled in volume. The heavy stuff had joined the action. Artillery shells twisted and screamed overhead while gun flashes illuminated the sky.

He walked in an arc away from the farmyard battle towards the firing guns, sweeping the ground with intermittent signals from his torch, fearful of attracting infantry fire. Before long he was rewarded with the sound of a woman's voice calling nearby. Shining his torch in the direction of the voice, he breathed a sigh of relief on seeing a small fat lady approaching, shepherding her party of three children and the two old people. Herding them together, he tried a new tough line, threatening to shoot the first one that strayed. Bullying and coercing with surprising results, everyone remained silent.

The Cube, as he christened the little fat lady on realising her outstanding qualities, provided an invaluable assistant. He asked her to lead the party in a direction between two gun batteries that were discharging their swishing, screaming destruction. Expecting objections, she surprised him by accepting the duty with enthusiasm and zest while giving out orders of her own. The column followed fearfully in rag-tag order but made progress as Jim walked up and down the line urging them onward. Everything was going according to plan until he heard the raised voice of the Cube arguing fearlessly as the column came to a halt. He raced forward to investigate.

She was screaming abuse at a lieutenant who was actually laughing at her while the rest of the patrol he led were giving her encouragement which she didn't really need. Jim intervened and declared his mission to the officer who was now being assisted by a sergeant, but she was a match for them both.

"Corporal, I'm delighted to see someone on our side," the officer chuckled. "This little fat arse is scaring the shit out of me."

"Doing a bit of slave trading mate?" one of the platoon called. "How much for the fat one."

"Put a sock in it, you daft bugger," the sergeant shouted, but the laughter continued.

"I rather think we are off course, sir, but there was no choice, they were afraid of the guns."

"We all are, Corporal. Let me know your destination and I'll try to help."

"Excuse me a moment, sir, while I reassure them."

He walked up and down the column explaining the situation, partly for their benefit but most of all to show off in front of the patrol and the officer in particular. They were all suitably impressed, as he had intended. Explaining his purpose and goal, he was immediately informed how far he was off course.

"But if you continue on your present line, you should reach the coast," the officer laughed. "I'll send a guide. Who do you suggest, Sergeant."

"Collins, sir."

"Collins," the officer repeated. "Corporal, you have a capable assistant."

The sergeant obviously knew his men and Jim was grateful for the choice. Collins was a carbon copy of himself in build and stature and was obviously keen to do the job well.

"You take the lead, mate, since you know where you're going. It will give me an opportunity to keep this lot under control. Oh, better share it with the little fat woman here, she might think I'm downgrading her. Let's keep her happy, she's been a great help."

Collins laughed, "I would love to put my arms around her but they're not long enough."

The woman was aware that they were talking about her so he had to think of something to say.

"He says you look exactly like his wife."

She was delighted and the soldier had no idea why she was so pleased so he left it that way and began herding the flock.

The battle at the farm had ceased. Two fires, clearly visible, were evidence of the outcome. The column stopped, turned, and looked anxiously, speculating on what was burning. All agreed unanimously that the farm was intact. The guns were searching for targets. The counter-attack was contained, the enemy had ran away to fight another day. Collins kept them on course, steering them safely towards their goal. He and the fat lady had become good friends on the march. He spoke a dozen words of Italian that had earned him an invitation to visit and eat at the farm. Claude was waiting anxiously when they arrived.

"Corporal, I'm delighted to see you. Is everybody accounted for?"

"As they say in the army, sir, all present and correct."

"Put them in the duty truck." He indicated a three-tonner. "See that they are made comfortable. You'll find a tarpaulin and a half dozen blankets. Stay with them until I discover what happens next." He turned and walked into the hive.

The children were soon asleep while he listened to the adults speculating on their destiny. After much discussion with motions put forward and moved, they unanimously decided to go back if the Germans had gone. He sat listening to their various opinions and their fears of what they might find on their return. Would the winter food supply still be intact? How had the livestock faired? Each one nurtured a secret fear while the children slept untroubled.

Claude returned at daybreak. "We are taking them back, Corporal. Put the farmer in the cab with the driver and me. You follow in the 15 cwt. It would appear that you have accomplished a thankless task."

"I didn't make many friends either, sir, and by the way, they had already decided to go back themselves."

A journey that had taken two hours of hazardous marching was surprisingly just a ten-minute drive. A bloody and gruesome sight awaited their return: bodies appeared to be everywhere. Actually there were nine, lying in the most grotesque positions. On inspection, each body was riddled with bullet holes. The Poles didn't intend being hampered by prisoners. There was no evidence of their own casualties. Two more bodies were discovered in the stables, lying beside a badly wounded ox.

"Whatever happened to the two prisoners they were supposed to take back, sir?" he asked.

"Oh they brought them. I interrogated two very fortunate, terrified, and bewildered privates. The highest ranks possible—that major lying there committed suicide, the Poles said."

"I can see that. He certainly did it the hard way, sir. I can count eight bullet holes. Polish vengeance, Major: a thousand eyes for an eye. The Germans are still leading the atrocity league by a wide margin though. Personally, I couldn't do this but I think they really do deserve it."

"Corporal! You surprise me, but then you have the experience." The family were already at work stripping the bodies. "I'm going for a burial party, expect me back within the hour."

"What about this desecration, sir?" he asked, indicating the body-searchers.

"Does it matter? Let them get on with it. Compensation for the damage—there isn't a window left in the building and they've lost an ox. I'll be back as soon as possible." And with that he drove away, leaving Jim to watch the farmers play strip-the-corpsy.

The three-year-old was out viewing the dead bodies with interest. He walked across and took her hand. She was looking at the sentry who had bullet holes in his chest. They had even shot a dead man.

"Why is he lying down?" she asked.

"Because he's tired," he told her. "Shall we go and leave him to sleep?"

He noticed the corpse wearing a wristwatch. He lifted the hand and removed it. The little girl laughed.

"If you can't beat 'em, join 'em!" he said in English, laughing with the child.

"Are all the men asleep?" she said as they walked back across the yard.

The fat woman was having a great time removing a treasure trove from a dead soldier. The little girl left him and ran to join her mother.

The major duly arrived with a truckload of men armed with picks and shovels. He stood by while Claude delivered specific orders to the sergeant in charge. The major commanded respect and brooked no nonsense. He ordered that the bodies be taken away and buried 50 yards from the farm in graves 3 ft deep. He duly made a note of each man's identity before internment. The operation took sometime and it was well into the afternoon before they returned to base; neither had eaten since yesterday.

Jonesy walked across the yard, greeting them with mail.

"This will brighten your day, boyo," he said, handing Jim a letter.

This was always an excuse for some good-natured mickey-taking that they nearly all enjoyed.

"Shall I order you a meal, Corporal or would you rather eat your wife's words?" Claude asked, smiling.

"Feed the brute, sir." Jonesy took his cue. "Love will fill his wife's belly but it won't fill his."

Jim put the letter in his pocket unopened. "I'll eat, sir. Jonesy's right," he smiled at each in turn.

"I've been considering a present for his wife," Jonesy intimated, "I feel we know her that well."

"Well I'm in complete agreement," Claude said, "What did you have in mind?"

"Well sir, I was considering a nighty with a fur-line hem."

Jim listened curiously, there was a punchline coming soon. As though his line had been rehearsed, Claude said, "Why just around the hem?" playing the straight man.

"When he goes home on leave, sir, it will keep her neck warm."

"That's a very practical thought, Jonesy, and I know just the place to get it: a black marketeer who wouldn't dare refuse my request in his own best interests. I'll set the wheels in motion. Would it be acceptable, Corporal?" he asked, smiling.

"Well, sir, she usually takes hers off, but we've never done it in winter. I'll ask her."

"Asking will spoil the surprise," Claude said, laughing, "I'm sorry we can't lunch together but military etiquette denies us that pleasure. I will arrange with the cook to prepare a meal for you in the kitchen."

"Thank you sir. A true peasant is happy with the crumbs from his master's table. The kitchen will be fine."

After lunch, he stole away into a quiet corner to enjoy reading the letter.

"My darling…" He pondered over the two intimate words, savouring their full implication, then read on. "The joy of meeting you when you come home has made our son unusually excited. I am being kicked further out of shape. Answering your letter immediately was the only outlet for my own emotions. I would like you to share a ridiculous experience with me. While writing this epistle, Mamma called me for lunch. Ten minutes later, receiving no response, she came searching only to find me trapped in our comfortable bedside chair. My absurdly distorted body had become wedged—I was a prisoner of love. 'What has that dreadful husband of yours done to my baby!' she cried with some annoyance. (Oh by the way, she blames you for the dreadful weather we are having at the moment too.) 'He loved me, Mamma,' I replied, 'and this is the outcome. Did it not happen to you before I came?' 'I didn't get stuck in a chair, and besides, your papà is Italian.' I'll leave you to find the logic in that rhetoric. Fortunately though, I'm surrounded by people who care, and blessed with a husband who loves me so much. If my arithmetic is correct and we calculate from the afternoon I seduced you here in my bedroom, our baby will arrive about the 18th and you might be with us by Christmas. That's wishful thinking of course, but it gives me an exciting feeling. Remember how I had to inveigle and tempt you that afternoon. I believe Mamma's presence in the house caused you some anxiety. You had no such inhibitions that evening we spent in the stable—YOU ANIMAL!"

He read and re-read the letter at least half a dozen times. When at last he checked his newly acquired watch, it was almost time to deliver Claude into Gina's arms. Whatever reason had kept him from her last night, tonight they would be eager to forgive, forget, and make a meal of each other.

After dispatching the major, he enjoyed the evening cuppa and snack with Jonesy, but after falling asleep over a game of cribbage, he was forced to retire early.

While threading his way through a web of dreams, in the misty shadows of his mind there appeared a tangible presence. Awakening to the sound of a canvas flap being pushed aside, he detected the outline of a head poking through.

"Can I come in, Signor?" the head called. "It's cold out here."

Realising with certainty the owner of the voice, he didn't need the aid of his torch.

"What on earth do you want at this hour?"

"To sleep with you of course and repay some of my debt." She said it as if it were the most natural thing on earth.

"How did you get through the picket lines? There are three sentries out there. God knows what would happen if you were caught. You wouldn't need to ask if you could sleep with them. Here, take this blanket and sit in the cab, I'll join you in a moment."

Hastily putting on his boots and overcoat, he scrambled out and went to join her, finding her sitting in the driving seat.

"Move over, Signora," he whispered, "I'm going to drive you home. Kneel on the floor and rest your head on the seat. I'll cover you with the blanket. If a sentry spots you, he'll want a half share, and he'll probably want the bottom half."

Obeying each request like a child, she was actually giggling as he drove slowly and apprehensively through parked vehicles and sleeping men, breathing a sigh of relief as he reached the road.

"Left or right?" he asked. "Quickly!"

"Left I think."

"You think! Come on, sit up and find out."

She obeyed, talking excitedly. A heap of stones by the roadside that had once been a farm reminded her of happier days. She proceeded to relate a story of her girlhood, laughing and giggling as though she still was a child. He wasn't fooled. Before this night was through he would be poorer, both materially and financially. The journey took 15 minutes, a two-hour walk. What, he wondered, were her intentions? Sex maybe, profit certainly. He pulled up alongside a massive heap of stone and rubble that on closer inspection was the remains of a village laid to waste. Whatever misery lay under this all too familiar scene, she invited him to share hers. Yet during the short journey, he had been fascinated by her carefree laughter.

"Where among these ruins do you live?" he asked.

Taking his hand, she led him up a cleared pathway, down a flight of four steps and pulled open a badly constructed canvas door made from a vehicle canopy. She dragged him inside. Putting her arms under his coat she began kissing him and pressing her thighs against him until she felt the response. His hands beneath her coat, he began massaging her hips and stroking her bottom. The thought of Rose left him drunk with desire. Her hand unbuttoning his flies brought him down to earth as he realised Rose would never do that. Gently pushing her away, he hurried outside through the door using the truck as an excuse for his reluctance. It was a fact however that, unattended, the vehicle and its contents would disappear without trace in less than an hour.

"That's no problem," she said, following him outside, "Marco will sleep in the back. We'll lift Giulietta into his bed then spend the rest of the night together."

"Signora, I don't even know your name. We shouldn't be doing this."

"Why not?" To her it was all so simple. "My name is Catarina, my husband is dead and your wife isn't here. I don't know your name either but why shouldn't we love each other?"

"My name is Jim and you, Catarina, are very naughty. Pretty, but naughty."

"You think I'm pretty and you like me," she said. Taking hold of his wrists she felt the watch, "I've always wanted a watch. Will you buy me one?" she asked, placing his hands on her breasts. No bigger than tennis balls, they didn't excite. Compared with the large shapely deposits Rose had to offer he might have been playing with twin hooters on a child's pedal car.

"Catarina, I'll get you a watch off the next dead German I stumble across. First let me give you some food."

Putting his hand in the back of the truck he brought out two tins of meat and enough oatmeal to last a week.

"Thank you," she said, kissing him. "Bring more tins tomorrow and some rice, then stay and eat with us."

"Catarina, tins of meat don't grow on trees. I'll need time to find a source of supply. It's not like buying from the corner shop you know."

She laughed like a child. "Tins of meat don't grow on trees! I know that. If they did, I wouldn't have to steal and we wouldn't have met. Oh, Marco asked me if you could let him have a hammer, saw, and screwdriver. He's going to fix a new door."

Laughing louder than he should (people would be trying to sleep somewhere under that heap of rubble), he reached into the toolbox.

"Here you are, Catarina, hammer and screwdriver. Sorry, I have no saw. Why the hell I'm doing all this I don't know. If I wanted a woman, it would be cheaper to look elsewhere! You are far too expensive."

"Expensive!" she repeated. "You can love me any time for nothing."

"Thank you, Catarina, I'm flattered. I'll bring more food in five days and if you come visiting again I'll hand you over to the sentries."

"I won't so long as you come here. Give me some money to buy bread. Five days is a long time without bread," she said, stroking his face with her free hand.

It seemed his hands were never out of his pockets whenever she was around.

"Here you are. Your hands are already full. If you have a spare one anywhere, grab this 400. I've started buying trouble now! Addio Catarina." He jumped into the cab.

"Jim, I love you," she called.

"Hell I wish you didn't, Catarina," he said, driving away quickly in case she asked him for something else, chuckling to himself, "Poor Bastards!"

*

Chapter 33

He couldn't believe his inability to find a source. With everything the wide boys wanted—money, cigarettes, and petrol—he still failed to make a contact. It had to be done discreetly. Standing last man in the breakfast line, the duff corporal, an addicted chain smoker, was tapping the man ahead of him for a fag.

"Duffy," the man said, "you could have one with pleasure but I hate having ash in my porridge."

"Fussy bugger," the corporal grumbled, "I suppose you hate fag ash in your porridge too mate!" he said to Jim, laughing.

"Duffy, I love it. I couldn't eat my porridge without." Looking about him for eavesdroppers, he said, "I can let you have 60 for a few tins in a haversack."

"Where the hell have you been hiding? Call after dark, but I would love a smoke now. My tongue's hanging out."

"I'll bring 20 after breakfast, the rest tonight. Would you like to make it a standing order."

"Corporal, it's on for as long as we are here."

"Good, then I'll see you, Duffy."

With a good selection of groceries, he made his first delivery, though somewhat indiscreetly. When he returned from Catarina's, Claude was waiting impatiently and showed his irritation.

"I know you don't have a bit on the side, Corporal, so where the hell have you been?"

"Sorry about this, sir, I've been making enquiries about Christmas shopping."

It was a spur of the moment excuse.

"Well I hope you were successful. Don't let this happen again without permission."

"Yes sir."

Least said, easiest mended. There would be no such mistake next time. With a good supply stored in the back, the duff corporal must have been smoking cigarettes two at a time. After trading 160 in five days, at breakfast that morning he asked for a deposit on the next pick-up. Maybe he was in training for the World Chain-smoking Championships.

Reluctant to make a delivery after dark—Catarina was beginning to look prettier with each visit—fate took a hand when the major ordered him to drive to the Questura. His silence was a clear indication of how serious his feelings were. Whatever was troubling him could only concern Gina. On arrival, Claude sat silently for a while then seemed to make up his mind.

"Have you made any progress on the Christmas shopping or was that an excuse for something else?"

Jim laughed. "It was an excuse, sir, but I guarantee a bumper Christmas hamper."

"If you don't, you won't see your wife."

Claude was in one of his rare moods.

"I will sir, but if I didn't, you wouldn't do that."

"Don't be so sure," the major said sternly, looking at his watch. "Be back here at 15:00," he ordered as he stepped down.

"Yes sir."

Three o'clock! He had an hour and a half. Claude's threat couldn't be serious, but it still disturbed him. Driving to the forno, he bought three kilos of bread. It was 50 lira a kilo for Italians, he was charged double.

"God, 15 shillings for three loaves. How the hell could they live without stealing."

He found Catarina cooking over a cleverly made fireplace built out of the rubble. Marco had an exceptional natural ability and a wonderful creative imagination. He and Jonesy between them made him feel inadequate. The children ran to meet him, looking for a similar treat to the last visit when he had brought K-ration sweets. Catarina welcomed him with a lingering kiss, mischievously putting her tongue in his mouth, laughing at his surprise.

"My mouth is as clean as your wife's," she said, flashing an ivory smile. "I've scrubbed my teeth every day with the soap you brought.

Are they as white as hers?" she asked, showing him a clean, even set.

"They are, Catarina, and you smell nice too."

"I hope so. I've washed every part thoroughly. Some parts with painstaking regard," she laughed.

The family were enjoying life despite their circumstances. Since food, their chief concern, was plentiful, laughter came easy and Catarina had paid attention to her appearance.

"Am I as pretty as your wife?" she asked, fishing for compliments.

"Just about." And she was too. Indeed, this was a land of good-looking women. Rose, Gina, Angelina, and now Catarina was beginning to look prettiest of them all, probably because she was available. "Come and see what I've brought," he said as they followed him excitedly to the truck.

He watched with pleasure as they searched through the groceries, aware that the children were looking for sweets while Catarina searched for soap. Sensing their disappointment he asked, "Would you children care for some sweets? I've eaten so many I'm sick."

He revelled in their delight as he handed them the packet.

"I don't see any soap," Catarina said, almost in despair.

"Because I have it here in my pocket," he laughed, watching her face light up.

Soap was the most valuable bargaining commodity on the black market. Anyone who could afford soap had enough to eat. This family were eating better now than at any time in their lives.

"I'll see if the food's ready and we will eat," Catarina announced happily. "But Jim, we only have three plates and three spoons, you will have to share mine," she apologised.

"I don't mind if you don't. What are you serving?" he asked.

"A special treat. Rice with meat stew."

"I'm afraid eating off your spoon will sweeten the meat, Catarina."

She laughed delightedly as they sat down to eat.

"Then you have the first spoonful."

"No, you taste it. It might be hot and burn my mouth."

"I'll blow on it," she said, smiling, her eyes sparkling as she spoon-fed him, her face getting closer with each spoonful.

He was beginning to feel her nearness in his thighs while she caressed him with her eyes. Giulietta interrupted their love fantasy.

"Have some of mine, Jim. Mine isn't sweet."

Before offering the full spoon, she blew on it, her own mouth crammed with rice, then pushed it into his face.

"Yours is delicious, Giulietta. Much better than Mamma's."

"Is it really?" She was delighted. "But it's the same!"

"I know it's the same, but yours was flavoured with choice pieces from your mouth when you blew."

Catarina laughed loudly. She too did it with a full mouth and without moving her plate. Taking the plate and spoon from Catarina, he began feeding himself with gusto while they all laughed loudly.

"That is exactly what is needed to add taste. I've been in Italy for three years and I've just discovered how Italians flavour their food."

The laughter attracted a neighbour whom he had seen moving in and out of her dugout, tempted by the smell of cooking. Seizing an opportunity, she asked to share the joke. It was painfully obvious that laughter was a stranger in her life.

"Ah, Margarita, bring a bowl and spoon. Share our food, we have enough," Catarina invited with benevolence.

Excitedly accepting the kind offer, the neighbour could easily have broken a leg scrambling over the rubble in her haste, seating herself next to Jim.

"Benvenuto Signora," he greeted, "Mangi bene."

Thanking him through a full mouth, her spoon operated like clockwork from bowl to face; she was eating like a hungry greyhound. The rice was going straight down without being chewed. This was probably her first meal for days. Her husband was in Greece and she had received no word for two years, she told him. Wolfing down her rice and a large portion of bread, she appeared to be looking around for more.

"Would you have my bread, Signora, I've eaten too much rice. I do hope you don't mind."

She didn't mind at all but thanked him with the bread already in her mouth. Hunger is a cruel bedfellow, a companion with whom he had had intimate experience.

"It will be all over in six months," Catarina said with authority. She was repeating what he had already told her on his last visit. "Will you take a loaf of bread for tomorrow, Margarita? Jim brought three loaves and I bought one."

Catarina was a kind-hearted human being.

Will you take! It was like offering her hand to a starving wolf. As well as accepting the bread, Margarita intimated that she too might be prepared to trade her assets for food if he so desired. Allowing the hint to go over his head as though he didn't understand, he looked at his watch. Happily, it was time to go. Kissing Catarina and Giulietta, he shook hands with Marco and their hungry, enthusiastic guest, pushing two 100 lira notes into her hands.

"Buy yourself some bread, Signora. They will charge me double. Ciao everybody."

"Hurry back, Jim," Catarina called, waving as he ran to the truck. Driving away as quickly as he could, the last thing he wanted was another 'fanny for food' invitation. Catarina was as much temptation as he could handle. She was beginning to disturb his sleep. Indeed, he had made love to her in a dream that made him feel guilty and unfaithful. Now he was giving money to anybody. He felt like a total abstainer swimming in a vat of whisky.

Jonesy was teaching him a tried and proved method of birth control.

"Maybe you had better use French letters until you gather experience. Follow the instructions to the letter, then you can throw away the French ones. Enjoy each other with impunity."

"We always enjoyed one another. I was lucky, she got pregnant."

"Luck had nothing to do with it. A pair of morons can produce children. The trick is to avoid having them."

"Well I'm aware of that. What I really mean is that if she hadn't got pregnant, though it wasn't intended, her mother would have chased me by some means. All's fair in love."

"And war? How about war?"

"War is an outrage."

"Well there's your answer. Don't fire live ammunition indiscriminately. Hell Jimbo, a machine gunner should know better."

Claude walked into the office carrying a sheath of papers and a map.

"Morning gentlemen."

"Morning sir," they echoed.

"Teaching the expert to shoot, Jonesy?" Claude asked with a dry smile.

"To miss, sir. He is just as effective with that weapon between his legs."

"Well I'm sure your advice is time-tested and proven, but they'll work it out between themselves. Before we proceed with the orders of the day, how much do I owe you for that shopping basket, provided I have enough money to pay."

"Settle with the boyo, sir, he held up a convoy."

"Really," he laughed. "You took my threat seriously, Corporal?"

"No, but it inspired me to greater effort, and a bigger basket. As for payment, it's my Christmas gift to Gina."

"Thank you! That is exceedingly generous. She has written to your wife by the way."

"Well that's payment enough, sir."

"Good. Now we'll get on with the duties. We move on January 5ᵗʰ. There's the map, check it. 'X' marks the spot. That's the bad news."

Jim scanned the map.

"Well sir, the bad news isn't so bad." To him it was a blessing in disguise; Catarina was getting prettier with each visit. "What's this other 'X' marking in the hills?"

"That is the substance of the good news. Your presence is requested at Casa Steffanelli. You are both invited to Christmas lunch. The 'X' indicates the farm where you will collect the main course. You will probably have guessed its origin."

"Well sir, kid goat is traditional. I presume that is what I'm collecting."

"It is. Do you like goat meat?"

"Never tasted it, sir. Last Christmas I spent in the mountains on a ten-day diet of dried figs. I remember having recourse to go to earth three times a day. I'm going to enjoy this though, goat meat can't be bad and the company will be top class. Yes sir, we both accept."

"You will accept alright, Corporal. Gina is inviting. I'm ordering."

Jonesy laughed, "You're a hard task-master, Major. We are volunteering."

"Good. Well, on your way, Corporal, I want you back at 16:00

today—the 23rd. Collect me at 08:00 on the 27th. I'm declaring a four-day holiday. We are only accepting calls from HQ. A relief has been arranged for Christmas Day, 10:00 to 18:00. Any questions? No? Alright, Corporal, get a move on."

The day the infantry regiment pulled out, the duffy, sporting three stripes, pressed all his surplus supplies upon him.

"It's mostly rubbish, Corporal. Sort out what's edible."

"Thanks, and congratulations, Sergeant. Next time we meet I hope you've kicked the smoking habit. Take care of yourself."

"And you, Corporal."

They shook hands and said goodbye. It was now also time to say goodbye to someone with whom he had become dangerously fond. She was becoming an irresistible temptation, dominating his thoughts and tormenting his emotions. The break would be difficult, he would cushion the pain of leaving her with a generous supply of food for the final delivery plus a fiver and his watch. It would ease her anxieties for the immediate future and maybe see them through the winter. Having enjoyed keeping the family happy and free from want, he experienced a feeling of relief. He was beginning to see her quite differently from the day she cowered from him in the provost's office. Hungry people are only interested in food, how they look is not important. Catarina had been struggling to feed her family for a few weeks before he came along and the unequal struggle had taken its toll. It was easy then for him to reject what she had to offer. He was filled with pity for her and the children, but now with enough to eat and no worries about where the next meal would come from, she was a different person. With the aid of a tablet of soap, she had become clean, pretty, and desirable. She was also considerate and kind. He enjoyed kissing her and knew with some certainty that his resistance was becoming fragile. Having inherited his mother's code of ethics, adultery was unforgivable; a gross insult to one's partner and a sin against the commandments.

Marco was skilfully building while his mother and sister were mixing cement and carrying stones. Work ceased on his approach. Since his advent, the village had come to life: building was in progress. Two men with mule and cart were cleaning a road through to the square. Now he could drive the truck up to the door. Catarina placed his arm around her waist as he stood surveying their work.

"Where did you learn to do that, Marco?" he asked with admiration.

"His father was a stone mason," Catarina answered for him. "He enjoys the work, don't you figlio? We have enough sand and stone to build, we only need cement and wood, and maybe some government help." She wore a headscarf and smiled broadly at him, showing off her freshly cleaned teeth. With no food problems, she smiled often. "Come, let us see what you've brought today," she said excitedly.

"I've done the Christmas shopping. You will all have to help carry it in."

With the box safely inside the cellar that was their home, Marco and Giulietta began sifting through the contents giving little cries of delight as they selected a tin to suit their taste while happily crunching sweets.

"You will stay and eat with us. We have bread, wine, and a tin of your choice to go with it."

"Catarina, it will be a pleasure. Bread and wine—sounds like a communion feast."

They ate inside, seated on the edge of the beds with their plates on the floor. Marco sat by the door keeping an eye on the truck. They were laughing and talking in party spirit with all the joy that a full stomach and a cup of wine could generate.

"Where on earth did you get the cement, Marco?"

"We stole it of course," Catarina replied while everybody laughed.

"Good for you. Keep it up, but don't get caught because I'm leaving the province," he said casually. The laughter ceased abruptly. There was a moment's silence. "Oh I'll be back to see you with a full truck load of food."

Already Giulietta was crying. Catarina removed her headscarf and her hair tumbled out. She wiped her eyes and nose with the scarf. Marco gathered up the plates and the cups; the party was over. Just two minutes ago the place was alive with laughter. Life was gay and joyful. He'd stopped all that with one sentence. A feeling of guilt stole over him. They all stood up, Giulietta leaned against her mother sobbing, her thin body heaving and falling. Catarina stroked her daughter's head obliviously while dabbing at her own eyes. She was surprisingly calm and stood proudly.

"You won't come back," she said with emphasis. "This little girl here talks about you all day long as if you were a god. I've been expecting this but hoped it wouldn't happen just yet. Marco," she indicated the boy, "wants to be the man you are. You already know that I am in love with you." Wiping her eyes and nose on the scarf, she smiled through her tears. "I'll never forget how fearsome you looked the first time, standing there in the Questura with the gun on your shoulder. I was so terrified I wet myself. Down on my knees begging for our lives. Remember?" He nodded and smiled. "How could we know then that you were such a gentle man?" Blowing her nose on the scarf once more she smiled, "I'm sorry, this must be so embarrassing for you."

"You know, that's exactly what my wife said when she cried."

"Do I look like your wife?" she asked.

"You are certainly as pretty."

"I think you are just being kind. You will never believe how many times I've made love to you on this bed. Probably the same time you were making love to your wife in the back of the truck. What a tragic waste. We should have been doing it together. Eventually we would, if you didn't have to go."

"I'm sure we would, Catarina, I actually made love to you in a dream one night. We did do it together."

"Except that I wasn't there."

He peeled off his watch and dug into his pocket for the fiver's worth of lira. Pushing them into her hands, he said, "That will keep you going for a few weeks, maybe until the end of the war. I might come back one day with my wife and child when the village has been rebuilt."

"That's a wonderful thought, but I'm afraid that's all it is. She must be very special, your wife. I would like to meet her."

"She is special, Catarina, but so are you." He squeezed her arm. "Meeting again is not such a pipe dream you know. We only live 200 km away—just a four-hour drive—I want my wife to meet you. Didn't we almost commit adultery you and I, although I wouldn't tell her that because she's much too big for you. Goodbye Catarina," he said, kissing her lightly on the lips.

"Arrivederci Jim, don't forget us," she implored through the tears.

"How could I Catarina?" He kissed Giulietta. "Don't get caught stealing," he said, shaking hands with Marco.

He drove off without a backward glance.

*

Chapter 34

The farm was neatly tucked away in the hills and had escaped destruction; it was untouched. He compared their extreme good fortune with that of the villagers as he drove up a steep cart track leading to the house. Parking the vehicle 30 yards from the farm, he walked up a hill that could only be negotiated by a team of oxen in their own laborious time. The whole family came out and watched his approach. The farmer, accompanied by a curious daughter, walked tentatively to meet him.

"Signor Sacco?" he asked, smiling at the pretty girl by his side.

She smiled back, looking around her as if she were the stranger.

"Yes, what can I do for you?" he replied, observing him closely.

"Major Oliver sent me to collect the kid coat for Signora Steffanelli."

His Italian put them at ease immediately.

"Of course! Will you come into the house? We will be eating in an hour or so, you are welcome to sit with us."

His knowledge of the language was good enough to open a few doors and inspire trust. Glancing at his wrist, only to find that the watch wasn't there, he asked, "What is the time, Signor?"

The question fired off a relay of requests. From farmer to wife to a hidden voice from within the house. Information was returned via the same route.

"Three o'clock," the farmer said.

He had already heard three voices repeating it.

"Thank you for the invitation, Signor, but I must decline, with great disappointment I might add. I would love to eat at your table and look at this beautiful face," he said, smiling at the pretty girl, "but time forbids me to stay."

"Do you have time for a glass of wine and a piece of salami?" the farmer asked while the young lady smiled a welcome.

"I do indeed, Signor."

Walking between his hosts to the house, he was met by the farmer's wife. She was broad of hip and heavy around the chest with traces of beauty still lingering on her pleasant face.

"Where did you learn to speak Italian?" she asked, escorting him indoors to the table.

"Here in Italy, Signora. My wife is Italian; we live here."

The owner of the voice that had called the time of day from within served the wine, standing behind him as she poured. He turned in his seat, trying to look at her face.

"Thank you, Signorina."

But she had already turned away.

"What's your name?" Mamma asked.

"Jim, Signora."

"Jim! Just that?"

"It's all I need," he replied.

"We have a son who is a POW in your country," she said sadly.

"What a lucky man! He is in the safest, most generous place on earth."

"Will he be hungry?" Papà asked.

"Hungry, Signor! He'll probably come home ten kilos overweight."

"They say it's cold in England," Mamma said, drying her tears.

"Never as cold as it was here last winter. While your son was warm and well fed in Britain, I was cold and hungry over here. Ironic don't you think? But let me put your minds at ease, of all the millions of young men on earth missing from their homes, your son is among the most fortunate."

"But we haven't had a letter for 18 months," Papà said, not convinced.

"Signor, nobody has had any letters, but I'll tell you this confidentially, POW mail has just arrived in this country. It will take a week or two to sort and deliver. You will have a letter within a month."

He was a convincing liar and it had the desired effect. Tears were dried and handkerchiefs put away.

"Did you really marry an Italian?" the shy girl asked. "British soldiers have only recently arrived. You haven't had time."

"That's what everybody says, Signorina. We met in March of this year, married in June and expect our baby any day. Is that time enough?" he asked, watching her mind race against the clock.

The reason for her reluctance to look at a stranger became evident as she turned, her pretty face radiating pleasure, complimenting him with a full-frontal view. Nor did she turn away when his eyes focused on the purple birthmark covering the whole of her cheek. But it didn't detract from her beauty. A man in love would enjoy kissing that coloured flesh. He pulled his eyes away immediately and looked into hers.

"It's exactly nine months from March to December," she said, laughing gleefully, "Oh you were naughty."

"What do you think, Signora?" he asked Mamma.

"You both were," she replied, "it takes two to play at that game. Eat," she said, pushing more bread and salami at him.

"Why can't you stay and dine with us?" Papà asked.

"Because I don't have the time, Signor, and I'm terribly disappointed because I see you're having polenta and that's my favourite dish. I always enjoy carving out the map of Australia when eating polenta and I love forking up those delicious lumps of pork fat. When I look at these two pretty girls, I'm being punished, Signor," he said, laughing.

"Forget them," the signora said, "tell us about your wife."

"I'm afraid to talk about her, Signora, because I haven't got the time. To describe her would take all day and part of the night."

"Is she pretty?" the youngest daughter asked.

"Very. But not quite as beautiful as you, or your sister," he added, looking at the older girl, "all Italian girls are pretty."

"Are they prettier than English girls?" the young one asked, full of curiosity.

"Reluctantly, I must admit they are. Though English girls are pretty, I think the signorinas have the edge."

They were both delighted.

"I've poured him too much wine," the older one said, laughing.

"You both looked just as pretty before I drank the wine. It hasn't changed anything. My visit has been a pleasure and a delight but I must collect what I came for and take my leave. Signor e Signora, your son will be home long before I am."

"We want all the young men back home together," Mamma said.

"That will be difficult, Signora, but I'll see if I can arrange it. Now if you will excuse me, I must be back within the hour."

"I'll carry the carcass to the truck," the farmer said.

"Perhaps Signora Steffanelli would like some eggs," the older girl said.

"And a piece of salami and some prosciutto," Papà called back.

Ham, eggs and sausage! This was inverted social benevolence; the order of society was being turned upside down. Papà placed the carcass on the passenger seat, wrapped in a clean white cloth along with the ham and salami. The eggs, in a peach tin, were placed on the floor. The carcass looked pitifully small; it would be like eating the seed corn. The family bid him a fond farewell, pressing him to return and eat with them one day. Leaning across from the driving seat to secure the tin of eggs while the shy girl arranged the rest of his shopping, his face brushed against the purple flesh; smooth, warm and silky. The contact was accidental, short-lived, and exceedingly pleasant.

*

Chapter 35

They spent a lazy day lounging around the office reading, writing letters, talking and drinking tea. Jonesy possessed all the wisdom of his 35 years with an added bonus of the ability to comprehend and place situations in their perspective. They played cribbage and poker, Jim won £5000 and Jonesy paid up on the dot with an IOU.

"Or maybe you would rather have a cheque?" Jonesy offered.

"No, it's alright, this is the same value. Besides, a bank would probably question a cheque for that amount."

"Probably. What will you do with the money?"

"I'll buy 50 cars and start a hire car business."

"Jimbo, you're a shrewd man, but it's ten o'clock and time to put your gun to bed. Santa will be here in two hours. Don't forget to hang up your stocking, you never know what you might find in the morning."

"I'll find my feet because it's too cold to take them off. Goodnight Jonesy."

"Night boyo. Sure you can find your way?"

Since the reserve regiments had moved up the line, the truck had been parked just outside the office door. Taking off his boots, he rolled into the sleeping bag and stayed awake just long enough to hold a two-minute conversation with Rose before drifting away on an intricately woven carpet of dreams. He tried to hold one particular flight of fancy, aware that he was dreaming. He pictured her in mystic vision, even touched her. She was easy to visualise, not finely trimmed like a racehorse, but built solidly like a steeplechaser with full chest designed to hold a stout heart and a broad beam for the purpose of leaping to the defence of the underdog. He held and carried her image through until he felt himself being shaken by the foot: Jonesy's standard method of wakening him.

"Wakey, wakey boyo. Santa's been. He left you this," he said, handing him a letter.

"Thanks Jonesy."

The letter was thin, not like her usual epistles. This had to be it. Feeling the excitement rise, the adrenaline flowing like a drug, he avidly tore the envelope and read the opening lines.

"My darling, you have a son. He was born at 11 am on 22nd of December. I intended writing immediately when he arrived but he wore me out getting here and shortly afterwards I fell asleep. Already he is exposing my weaknesses. You tell me that I'm perfect. Well, you'll be happy to learn that our son is, physically. Mamma said he couldn't have been more perfect if his father had been Italian.

"Faithful, trustworthy, competent Anna delivered, washed, dressed, and placed him in my arms. I felt safe throughout in her care. The doctor did arrive eventually but both Anna and I were pleased he was late. Before weariness overtakes, and I feel it creeping up on me, let me say that I adore you. Please hurry home and be with us. James is waiting to greet you. You may be afraid to kiss him, but don't be afraid to kiss me; our germs are compatible. I'll rest now and write at length and in much more detail with a full description of our son. Farewell my love—don't die with happiness. Your friend, lover, and wife, Rose."

He couldn't contain himself. The news had to be shared. He stripped and tortured his body under the cold tap, shaved, and prepared himself for their special occasion. The ice-cold water did nothing to suppress his emotions. Jonesy would have to be the victim; there was nobody else. He stood at the office door grinning like a moron. Jonesy, reading a letter from his wife, looked up.

"Well, what is it? Boy or girl?"

"Boy! But how could you know."

"Only a first-time father could look so idiotic or behave so ridiculous. You've been sitting under the cold tap on Christmas day. Come in, we'll have a cup of hot tea to celebrate. By the way, where's my cigar?"

"I did buy two bow-shaped ones: one for you and one for Claude. Will you smoke it?"

264

"On this occasion I'll try. I can light it and throw it away when you're not looking."

They were ready and waiting when the relief arrived.

"Gentlemen," Jim greeted, "we are pleased to see you."

"What are our orders, Corporal?" they asked smartly.

"Orders? Oh yes, those things! Don't do too good a job because we like ours. In fact if you make a balls of things I'll bring you back some Christmas pudding. But what you really do is record all calls and act only on the ones from HQ. One of you will have to follow us so that in the event of a turnout you will know where we are. Incidentally, if there is a turnout, you'll both find yourselves in an infantry regiment up front. Any questions?"

"No questions, no turnouts, Corporal," they chuckled.

"What are your names?"

"Signalmen Blake and Thompson, Corporal."

"The ones your mother gave you, and not so much of the corporal."

"He's Bob, I'm Tom. I'll be following."

"Let me put you right, Tom. It's less than two miles and there's no way you can get lost. String along behind and keep your eyes open. Okay? Right, let's get on our way."

"Boyo, you are a regimental bastard," Jonesy chuckled as they drove off.

"Too much has happened since the 'yes sir, no sir' days. The important thing in life is getting back to our wives in one piece, don't you agree?"

"Absolutely. Nothing is of greater consequence."

"Besides, I'm keen to practice that method of birth control you taught me."

"It's foolproof, but then your wife isn't a fool is she," he laughed.

"Jonesy, she possesses the wisdom of Solomon, the diligence of Churchill and the courage of a tigress. A man once put his hand up her skirt and she belted hell out of him. A German soldier tried pushing her around and ended up flat on his arse. The day she was about to be raped by a big, ugly sergeant, she stood in front of him fearlessly. And would you believe, another bastard tried to have a go at her the day after our wedding. I put the MP-40 to good use on that occasion. If he lived, and I sincerely hope he did, he will never have the urge to touch another woman's tit. I put a short burst between his thighs and doubled him into a ball. I apologise to his wife."

"You are full of surprises, boyo. I must hear that story over tea and biscuits some night. The major and I know your wife personally by now. Since she is such a fearless Amazon, in your own words, how did you find the courage to put your hand between her thighs?"

"I never did! She would've chopped it off."

"You stuck something between her legs. She's just given birth to your son, and she hasn't chopped that off."

"I rather think she was saving some of that for later. Jonesy, we did it by mutual agreement. We were first-timers you know, experimenting."

"Hey, why are you stopping?" Jonesy asked in surprise.

"I'm not. I always crawl around this bend, and the next one, just before we get to the villa. Now and then I've met a truck coming the other way at 50 and the driver usually claims all the road. I'm always prepared to give. This wide grass verge by the side is for the faint-hearted."

"Well that's okay. Let's get back to your wife."

"God I wish I could."

"I wanted to say, she was 34 years old when you did it. Others must have tried before you."

"I've already explained to you what she did to them. But her best friend did tell me in confidence that there were one or two would-be admirers who never got past the school gates. She's a teacher you know."

A three-tonner approached right on the next turn as he had already described. He quickly pulled off the road and onto the verge.

"I'm beginning to see what you mean, boyo," Jonesy gasped.

"All's well. Are you fit to carry on?"

"Yes but I'll keep my eyes shut the rest of the way. Tell me when we get there but take your time, there's a lot more I want to know about this mating. For instance, with do not touch signs written all over her, how did she happen to fancy what you had between your legs after rejecting all the others?"

"Call that a fluke of nature. I was a tramp with hair hanging over my shoulders, shirt in rags, and jacket fastened with a safety pin at the back. I washed every day and bathed in a river or stream twice a week, and remember last winter was the worst in living memory, but my clothes ponged; there was nothing I could do about that. Along comes a princess, waves a magic wand and hey presto, within two days I'm made respectable. She even allowed me to kiss her."

"You dirty bugger!" he laughed as they drove through the gates.

"Go and ask Tom if he can find his way back."

"Yes Corporal, but don't put your hand up her skirt before I get back."

On his return, Jonesy said, "he'll be alright, he said he could find his way blindfold. I hope he doesn't try. You haven't locked the bedroom door? I want to know more about the princess and the tramp. The baby is big news but my wife and her friends will need something with a thrill to it to discuss on her coffee mornings. Bear in mind that Mrs Lewis is a war widow and Mrs Griffiths' husband is in France. They want romance Jimbo; the actual time and place of conception. Something they can take to bed with them on those lonely nights."

"Well I've already told you the first time it happened in a cave. You can also tell them that I might have fluffed that one if she hadn't taken control. The second, and very much improved, performance took place in her bedroom. We tested the guarantee on the bed: it passed the test most decisively. One exciting evening we took advantage of an empty stable, I think the atmosphere changed us into animals. We tossed, bounced, and rolled in the hay. After we had dressed and composed ourselves, she commented wryly, 'I didn't realise hay exerted such a turbulent sexual influence. Now I understand the unwholesome implication behind the expression, a roll in the hay.' That will give them food for thought. You can also add that we became victims of merciless desire. She dominated all my days and nights. Even she had difficulty concentrating on her work. We lived only for the feel and touch of one and other. Fortunately we found a permanent love nest. The farmer and his wife where I stayed had two POW sons in Blighty. They turned a blind eye when every afternoon we would hurry there like two drug addicts anticipating their first fix of the day. I'm sorry, Jonesy, that's as far as I can take you. The very thought of those afternoons together has my thighs rebelling against idleness."

"I can understand, boyo, with all the temptation around, but it's the same for our wives."

"I'm sure it must be, but that's enough stimulation for your wife's coffee morning. What do you think of the villa? It's worth a few half crowns isn't it. There's not even a bullet mark. How many houses will you find not battle scarred? Gina's husband was a soldier you know. A major, I believe. He caught one very early on in the desert campaign, poor bastard. Fancy dying so young and leaving a wife like Gina around for somebody else. The thought terrifies me. To be killed and leave Rose for someone else to enjoy! The rotten bastard might not treat my son right."

"Bloody hell, boyo! You haven't gone yet. Anyway, how do you know so much about Gina?"

"From the maid. What she couldn't tell me, I got from the local police. They know everything about everybody. She has done her fair share of whoring since her husband died. The last lover did her reputation no good at all—he was a high-ranking German officer. Had it not been for Claude she would've suffered the fate of Mary Magdalene."

"He wants to marry her you know." Jonesy thought he was revealing a secret. "I haven't seen her, but she must be something special to attract Claude. He's too intelligent to get himself trapped between her thighs. There's no way they'll get permission to marry. Who vetted your wife, Jimbo?"

"I did, and her mother examined me. If Rose hadn't been pregnant, I would have been vetoed on the spot for violating the chastity of her unerring daughter."

"Isn't it surprising she didn't shop you to the Germans. That would have ended the affair," he laughed.

"Not Bruna. She's above that. We are now the very best of enemies. She'll never forgive me for stealing her daughter's affections but she likes the way I respect her baby. Here come our hosts to greet us, and no wonder, we've been sitting here for 20 minutes, they must have thought we had stage fright."

"Boyo, just look at that woman."

"I am looking, and I've seen her before."

She came towards them, hair beautifully groomed, wearing lipstick in a vain attempt at gilding the lily, her ample breasts very much to the fore. Wearing a cardigan loosely around her shoulders she looked like a film star. Greeting Jonesy like an old friend, she enquired after his wife and daughter as if she knew them, completely annihilating him with her charm and personality. Claude stood by her side watching his staff being seduced.

"Jim," she said, switching to Italian. "I've written to Rosanna and despite what you said, I had to tell her she has the best looking husband in Italy."

He laughed, "Incidentally, we now have the prettiest baby in Italy: a boy."

"Mother of God!" She clenched her fist and put it to her mouth, chewing her knuckles. A tear escaped down her cheeks. "I'm so happy for Rosanna, and for you too Jim. What a wonderful Christmas present." Angelina waved from the kitchen doorway. Gina saw him lift a hand in acknowledgement. She turned and called excitedly, "Rosanna has had her baby: a boy!"

Angelina shrieked joyfully and did a series of hops and skips as she ran towards them, throwing her hands around his neck and kissing his face.

"A boy!" she repeated. "And Rosanna? Is she well?"

"I think so. She wrote the letter when he was just two hours old."

"Wrote a letter two hours after giving birth!" they chorused in amazement. "Mamma mia, how she must love you."

"Well, she said that too," he chuckled.

"You lucky, lucky man."

Gina took him by the arm, linking the other in Jonesy's. She walked between them towards the house. He had Angelina hanging onto his other arm.

"Are you excited?" Angelina asked, bubbling with joyful vivacity.

"Let's just say I have a song in my heart," he replied, smiling.

"A song in your heart!" Gina repeated. "We want to hear it. Claude plays the piano. So do I," she added proudly, "but Claude is good. Did you hear, darling, Jim is going to sing a song to relieve his excitement."

"Now just a minute, Gina, I didn't say that. I want to share my joy, but singing I do for my own pleasure. You wouldn't like it."

"Corporal," Claude said, "you will sing, I will play and we will let the audience judge our worth. Now that is an order. Incidentally, I was told you had a fairly good voice. It was Jonesy who let that slip."

"He's worth hearing, sir. Sixpence and a song will get him a pint in any pub," Jonesy said, laughing.

"Oh dear, what have I done," Gina said, joining in Jonesy's laughter. "You will forgive me, but now I'm secretly looking forward to hearing your song."

As they entered the house, Angelina's mother was busy laying the table and checking seating arrangements. It was comfortably warm from whatever source of heating they had. Angelina introduced her mother, Elena. Between them they had prepared and cooked the meal. They were now ready to serve and enjoy their work. Elena, a widow since the Abyssinian campaign, showed an obvious attraction towards Jonesy. They enjoyed discussing the war, the weather and the food with her ten words of English and his 20 of Italian.

There was whisky and cognac, but with his spirits sky high he needed no help from a bottle. He sipped wine from a crystal glass.

"Are you enjoying that pasta, Jim?" Gina smiled, watching him wrestle with a twist of spaghetti.

"It's delicious but I'm not handling it very well. It's been so long, I lack practice. Pasta with Rose was never so difficult."

"Perhaps she is having the same problem. You have been in Italy so long that you are almost one of us."

"Our friend Anna made that same remark. She delivered the baby you know. On one occasion she said, 'Those British soldiers are no better than the Germans.' When I pointed out that I was one she laughed and said, 'Nonsense, you are one of us.' So what am I doing here?"

"What indeed, Corporal," Claude replied. "I asked myself that question: what am I doing here?"

"Why should you ask yourself that sir? You who are saving the government thousands of pounds. I'm speaking metaphorically of course, but I was under the impression that we were doing a hell of a job, the three of us."

"Jim, he is a little boy who wants to fight. Tell him how foolish he is."

"I would love to, Gina, but he's my boss."

"You have an easy conscience, Corporal, you've already done it. The war is almost over and I haven't fired a shot in anger."

"You fired one or two broadsides at me sir, and in anger."

"Words of wisdom, Jim, he's jealous of you because you are a fighting soldier." She had him down as some kind of superman. All the ingredients were there: he carried a gun and had the good sense to have married an Italian. "I don't know why I love him so much. He's such a clown. Is everybody above the rank of corporal an idiot?"

"They must be, Gina. When I had my intelligence test, they wrote on my report 'cannon fodder', gave me a gun, and said 'shoot!'. At last I had found my level."

"You are too modest."

Angelina served the sweet: torta with peaches and tinned cream.

"Will you tell your mother the dinner was delicious," he whispered. "And that this is my favourite dessert."

Angelina was delighted and screamed his compliments to her mother who acknowledged in an even louder voice while Jonesy was diving into a double portion of sweet; he was doing alright with his dozen words of Italian.

"I was about to compliment her," Claude remarked, "but I'm sure you've done it for us all. She's certainly stimulating Jonesy's appetite."

"Just his appetite sir?"

"I sincerely hope so," Claude smiled. "Yes, I'm sure. He's no fool."

"Would you like more dessert Jim?" Gina asked.

"Thank you, no. I'm rather pleased Elena didn't take a shine to me. I am so full, but somebody will have to help Jonesy out of his chair."

She lowered her voice, "When you meet Rosanna next week, speak kindly of me. I do so want us to be friends."

"Why would I not speak kindly Gina? You're my friend. I don't have many of those and none like you."

"Because you know everything about me, about the things I've done."

"I know that you have had a great deal of sadness, that men are attracted to you because you are a desirable widow, and I think that the major is a lucky man."

"That's what I hoped you would say even though I know you're just being kind."

"But I'm not. I'm speaking the way I feel."

"Thank you."

They began leaving the table and settling down with drinks. Claude walked over and began tinkling the ivories with obvious pleasure and a fair amount of talent.

"Come on, boyo," Jonesy said, "don't let the side down," he laughed, waving his glass with Elena almost sitting on his knee.

"Well, in for a penny." But he was favoured by a friendly, enthusiastic, well-fed audience. "*I know why and so do you*," he read the music over the major's shoulder, "very pleasant indeed sir."

"It was popular back home just before I left. Make yourself familiar with the words and we'll give it a try."

"Why not, this could well be my swansong. I'm considering retirement after this one."

Claude ran through the music a couple of times while he hummed the words.

"I think I have it sir, so whenever you're ready."

He began confidently, the music pleasant to the ear, the words easy on his tongue. Encouraged by a nod of approval from the pianist and a smile of reassurance from Gina, he felt confident and in good voice. He was enjoying himself.

When they called for an encore, he allowed his ego to take over, but when they asked for more he decided that enough was enough. Claude's fingers were dancing along the keyboard, one tune running into another, then he began flirting with Lili Marlene. Jim took up the English version while the major joined him in German, soon they were all singing in a babble of languages. It all became hilarious with everyone getting entangled in words, the Italians holding the advantage 3, 2, and 1. The whisky and cognac were doing an admirable job. They had all reached the margin where you either stop or look for a more colourful horizon. Gina kept within bounds, she suggested coffee and took him by the hand.

"I need help and you are the most capable," she said, possessing the enviable ability to celebrate happily in sobriety.

"Because I intend enjoying the pleasure of your company. One can only do that when sober."

"That's a dubious pleasure. A few months ago you could have bought it." She smiled rather wistfully and handed him a cup, "Try that for taste. Is it your fifth or sixth coffee today?"

"Sixth probably. I'll know for certain when I break out in a rash, but it is delicious."

"I haven't seen you drink any yet."

"I know it's good because you made it, and I don't believe what you just said about me buying your time."

"Jim I enjoy the manner you adopt to make me feel worthy. Has Claude told you about our baby?"

"He has and I can't tell you how happy it makes me feel. Rose, I know, will be delighted and she will probably send you some tips on motherhood since you are pen friends. Tell me," he asked, "are you going ahead with the wedding?"

"January 2nd, and if no one else comes, we want you there."

"I'll be there, Gina, and so will Rose, in spirit. Here let me carry that tray."

"Thank you. Outside of the priest and a couple of officials at the Municipio, you are the first to know."

"That's good because we both know that they won't tell anybody! Why didn't you just announce it in the national press."

She laughed, "Come, let's take the coffee through while there is still time to enjoy it."

*

Chapter 36

It was after seven o'clock when Claude ushered them out to the vehicle. He stood by supervising their goodbyes until they were finally on their way, well over an hour late.

"That was the best day I've spent in Italy," Jonesy said.

"Mine too since I left Rose, and Gina admitted to it being her best for years. They are getting married on January 2nd by the way. Claude will tell us about it when he gets back. We are both invited."

"Well done, Claude. The big boys won't be pleased though. He'll probably get the sack and that might make us redundant," he laughed.

"I'll stand a wish with that. One thing's for sure, he'll never make colonel but I don't think it'll worry him too much." They pulled up at the office door. "Well, home again jiggidy-jig. I wonder how the lads have enjoyed their Christmas."

They found the two soldiers involved in a friendly argument over a game of cribbage.

"Good evening gentlemen, who's winning?" Jim asked.

They each pointed a finger at the other and chorused, "He's been cheating."

"Well who won then?" he asked again.

"I did," Tom said, laughing.

"Well you are the one that's been cheating because I don't know any other way to win. Is there anything to report that we can't ignore?"

"The provost's office want an interpreter at 10:00 tomorrow. That was the only call."

Catarina immediately sprung to his mind.

"Thanks gentlemen. You are free to go or stay, whichever you please."

"We'll be on our way, Corporal, if you don't mind."

"As you wish."

When the soldiers had gone, Jonesy brewed up. It was what he always did at this time. He showed no visible effects of the half dozen whiskies he had drunk. Tea and snack was a practiced routine, the usual highlight of their day, and today was no exception. Indeed, they had more to talk over and enjoyed their chat until the whisky began to take effect, making Jonesy sleepy. When they retired, he was pleased to be alone with his own thoughts. There was so much to think about. How could a man be this happy? Sleep was out of the question, the day after tomorrow he would be on his way home to see his wife and son.

It seemed he had just fallen asleep when he felt Jonesy shaking his foot with the usual call, "Wakey, wakey."

"Why? Is the war over?" he called from inside his sleeping bag. Surely this had to be a joke.

"They've sent for you to finish it," Jonesy replied, laughing. "I'll fill you in with the details over a cup of tea."

"Okay mate," he said, struggling out of his fleapit.

He pulled on his boots, grabbed his overcoat and then did what he always had to do on getting out of bed. By the time he ran into the office, Jonesy had prepared everything with his usual efficiency.

"Take Claude's gear to the truck and check that he's fully equipped."

"Fully equipped! Why? Where are we going?"

"You're going up front. Where else would you be needed at this hour."

"Puts a damper on the Christmas spirit, doesn't it," he replied, carrying the equipment out to the vehicle.

"Okay, what now?" he asked on his return.

Jonesy handed him a mug of tea. "Here, drink this and check your destination. There's the map and your reference. Apparently it's some farm buildings they didn't quite destroy on their way back to Germany. They've returned to finish the job off."

"What would the war lords be doing so close to the front?" he asked, checking the map reference. "If they've counter-attacked, we'll never reach this place, I hope."

"Wishful thinking, Jimbo. Claude will be there looking for glory. Your job is to get him back for both our sakes."

"I don't know what he's looking for because Gina can provide him with all the thrills he needs. The daft bugger thinks he's Harry Faversham; he's terrified of a white feather. They can give me a pillowcase full. You know Jonesy, normally he would be certified."

"Like you said, boyo, you and I are the only sane people on this earth. How's the tea?"

"Delicious. I want to stay here and drink tea all night. By the way, did they give any reason for this outrageous urgency?"

"A very weak one. Apparently they've captured a high-ranking officer," Jonesy said, smiling.

"They couldn't send him here, that would be too easy, wouldn't it. It's the ulterior motive that worries me because if there are any spare medals, Claude will be trying to win a couple."

"It worries me too," Jonesy said.

"Yes, but you're here! I'm driving the silly bugger."

"Then it's time you weren't here. Wake him up gently because he'll probably be lying on Gina's nightgown. Get him back safely."

"Do you want it in writing!" he chuckled. "Bye Jonesy."

"Bye, boyo."

He had to hammer on the door for a response. Claude appeared after two or three minutes wearing a dressing gown that must have cost at least a tenner. In that moment, he promised himself one equally as good, whatever the price. Gina stood at his side, a vision in pink; they might have been film stars waiting to make an entrance.

"Corporal!" the major was surprised while Angelina and her mother hovered fearfully in the background, each wearing a coat over their nightdress. "Come in, come in," Claude said. "What is so urgent at this hour."

"I'll make coffee, my darling. You are obviously going somewhere. Will you have a cup Jim?" she asked.

"Please Gina."

"Then I'd better dress and prepare," Claude said.

Did he detect a quiver of excitement in his voice or was it imagination?

"Take the map sir, you will need to check it for accuracy. Oh and your pencil torch."

Claude thanked him, taking the stairs two at a time. He turned to the ladies standing like immovable statues.

"Sorry to scare you ladies, but as you see it's only me."

"How were we to know that? You terrified us."

"May I ask where you are going?" Gina called from the kitchen.

"Forward I'm afraid. Our people our holding a high-ranking German. That's the reason we've been given."

"That's a bit weak don't you think? The officer probably speaks English anyway. There's more to it than you've been told I'm afraid. Here's your coffee, Jim," she said, handing him the cup. "A dash of cream, I think I remember you saying, makes it look the colour of Rosanna's eyes."

"Did I say that? I must be in love, Gina."

"Take care of him, Jim. He is a little boy playing war games. Did you see the excitement in his face? Watch for the signs when he comes down."

Claude appeared at that moment, jumping down the last two stairs.

"Whenever you're ready, Corporal," he ordered, before reaching the floor.

Gina glanced at him. You couldn't miss that, her eyes seemed to say.

"Jim is drinking his coffee and you will spare a moment to do the same. It's cooled, all ready to drink," she said handing him the cup, pushing it into his hand.

He drank it to please her but couldn't get it down quick enough. Taking the cup away, she put her arms around his neck.

"You are a big boy now, my darling. Please don't do anything foolish."

They kissed while Jim turned and walked to the door. He stood holding the door handle, looking back at them. Angelina and her mother stared entranced as though watching a love scene at the cinema.

"Life has just become worth living after those cruel years and it's all because of you, my darling. If you don't come back, I won't want to live at all."

"Wait at the truck, Corporal," he ordered. He didn't mind Angelina and Elena witnessing the drama.

"Jim," Gina called, still holding the major close, "use your knowledge and experience. Please take care of him."

"Come now, angel, he's laughing at us." Claude was just a little embarrassed.

Standing undecided at the door, he wanted to acknowledge Gina but the major had ordered him to leave. He walked outside, closing the door behind him.

They made excellent time along the Via Emilia but on reaching Forli, traffic problems began slowing up progress. Vehicles seemed to be moving in every direction. Tempers became frayed as each man's mission became more important than his comrade's. Glory boy officers looking for promotion and seeking medals were charging forward to get into the action. Only Claude kept his head while all about him were shouting theirs off. The road became so cluttered that it was only possible to follow the visible object in front.

"We'll have to get out of this confusion," the major said while scanning his map with the pencil torch. "There's a track to the left just up the road. Stop at my signal."

"That should be easy sir, we are barely moving. But taking a left turning among this lot is quite another matter."

"Just keep your mind on the job and your eyes on me. I'll make it easy."

The change of direction was charged with incident and accompanied by shouts and curses. The major calmly held up the southbound traffic and called on him to pull across and off the road, but the officer in the armoured car behind was equally ambitious. He ordered his driver to push him off the road. Witnessing his dilemma, Claude calmly walked towards the armoured car and proceeded to trim the bullying lieutenant down to size while nothing moved and nobody spoke; everybody listened to Claude.

"Just pull across and onto the track please, Corporal," he said with exaggerated civility while he climbed into the cab, chuckling to himself. "Now we have room to manoeuvre so let's go to war."

Fortunately they were moving away from an artillery duel. With visibility limited to 20 yards, it was difficult to imagine what their targets were. They arrived at a sector that was menacingly alive with infantry digging in, tanks manoeuvring, and armoured cars queuing for positions. It was an awesome spectacle.

"Stop here, Corporal, and wait while I seek further information. In the meantime, roll back the canopy. We will need a full field of vision come daybreak."

Claude returned within an hour just as Jim was beginning to hope that he had gotten lost.

"Right on target, Corporal, our objective is about a mile forward," he said, almost rubbing his hands with glee.

"Are you sure sir? I thought it was a mile the other way."

The major laughed.

"It's bloody cold with the canopy back sir and I'm already shivering with fear."

"Excitement, Corporal," he chuckled.

"Fear sir. An old acquaintance that ne'er shall be forgot. It's crawling around my crotch as it's done many times in the past. When this lot opens fire, it will grip my balls like a vice."

"Well I know for certain, Corporal you won't let me down."

"I'll give you that in writing because I promised Gina I'd keep an eye on you, but that doesn't stop me being afraid. I can do both."

"Well you know more about that than I so let's go and do what we have to. I need the benefit of your experience."

He was relishing the situation.

"You know, Major, you are having the time of my life as well as your own," he said, trying to add humour.

They were moving along at ten miles per hour, passing tanks that were using the terrain to their advantage with only gun turrets exposed, armoured cars sitting in wait ready to spring into action, infantry digging in. It was the longest mile of his life. The farm, or what was left of it, seemed to be large by Italian standards and stood framed against the approaches of dawn, awaiting its final destruction.

They pulled up beside a jeep parked alongside what were once the stables attached to the house. An officer left the vehicle and came to meet them.

"Major Oliver sir?" he asked, "I'm captain Simpson. A counter-order was sent but you had already left. The brigadier said that you would get here somehow. I was left behind to meet you. The Bosch are busy manoeuvring to advantage less than a mile away. My driver and I have been listening apprehensively for the past three hours. I suggest we leave at once."

"Thank you, Captain. You have chosen an ideal spot. You may leave but the corporal and I will stay a while and see what develops."

"Since my orders were to wait and escort you back sir, you won't mind if we stay too."

My God! Jim sat in the driver's seat, stunned into silence. Father forgive them for they know not what they do.

"What weapons are you carrying, Captain?" Claude asked.

What the hell is the daft bugger up to?

"I have a pea shooter sir but my driver keeps a good supply. What do we have in the way of arms and ammunition, Smithy?"

Smithy, he thought, listening to the adventure boys. This was another wartime amateur. He deliberated on who was worse: the death or glory amateur or the smart-arsed professional.

"I have an automatic rifle, a good supply of ammo, and a dozen grenades," the reply came back.

*

Chapter 37

It was breaking daylight on Boxing Day morning, 1944. Claude and the captain were talking about the good old days at Oxford as though the war was going on somewhere else. Unable to believe what he was hearing, Jim climbed down to relieve himself. Smithy did the same and came to stand by his side.

"Mind if I join you, mate? I'm just as scared as you."

"I doubt it," Jim replied and tried to laugh but it came out like a cry for help.

It all began with simple machine gunfire. Then flame-throwing tanks joined the fray right and left of the farm, spewing forth their liquid death. The big guns joined in as armoured vehicles, half-tracks, and self-propelled guns broke cover and raced forward. One tank became a raging inferno, lighting up the arena as infantrymen in the spotlight raced for somewhere to hide. Anything and everything that discharged a missile became engaged in the slaughter. Claude and Captain Simpson calmly planned their course of action while surveying the end of the world through binoculars.

"Here come the company we were expecting, Major. Approaching at two o'clock."

"I see them, Captain. Nice of them to not disappoint us. Corporal."

"Sir."

"Take Smithy and a good supply of ammo to the cover of those ruins. We'll follow behind."

It was a race to see who could get to the safety of cover first. A judge would have awarded a dead heat as they dropped behind the wall, breathless. A gap in the heap of rubble afforded full view of the approaching vehicles.

"Take a good look, gentlemen," Claude said, his voice quivering with excitement, "here comes our target." He seemed impervious to the holocaust going on all around. He had selected his own enemy and was preparing to fight them on his own terms. "This, gentlemen, is the nucleus of an observation post. We are going to save a lot of lives by taking a few. Smithy, take the lookout in the armoured car and don't miss or we'll be missing."

"I won't miss sir," Smithy said confidently, "it's an automatic rifle."

"Good man. Corporal, take the signals truck and escort. I won't tell you how, you've done it before."

"Just a word of warning sir, the lookout is not your problem. There's a gunner inside the vehicle. When the lookout is dead, he'll still be lethal."

"Thanks, Corporal, but I'm well aware. I intend beating him by the element of surprise," he said, pointing to a heap of stones some 30 yards away. "We'll be in position at that point and a simple wave of the hand will be my signal. Ready Captain? Let's go."

They watched the two officers scrambling over the debris.

"Those daft buggers are enjoying this, you know," Smithy said, "Look at them! Like a couple of kids playing games."

"Well the game will soon be broken up. The away team are getting hellishly close. Smithy, I feel like wetting my pants."

"Me too. In fact I don't know whether I have or not."

When Claude signalled from the rubble, Smithy surprisingly beat him to the shot, emptying a full magazine into the lookout while he shared his 32 rounds between the motorbike with sidecar escort and the signals truck. Smithy joined in with his second magazine. The truck went up in flames at precisely the same moment the armoured vehicle exploded. So far, so good. They leaned on the wall surveying the results of their work.

"That's made a few German widows," Smithy chuckled, "I wonder how our bosses have fared."

"Let's go and find out," Jim said, gathering up the spare ammo.

Both officers were lying dangerously close to the burning vehicle, small arms ammunition was flying from the blazing wreckage. They dragged both bodies under cover for closer examination. It soon became painfully evident that they had committed suicide.

Fire attracted fire and shells began raining in. Smithy stood over him while he searched for some sign of life with the major's head on his arm.

"Any luck?" Smithy asked.

"Hell no. The silly sod was going to be married next week. I don't know how the hell I'm going to explain all this to Gina; she's already a war widow once. I promised I would take care of him. How's the captain?"

"Almost cut in half. He was a decent bloke was old Simmy."

The shelling increased in volume, missiles screamed in, exploding with ear-splitting regularity. "What are we going to do?" Smithy asked, "that's the crucial question."

"We take one of the vehicles and make a run for it. You drive, I'll do as much damage as I can with what we've got left."

"Ready when you are, Corporal, let's go."

The farm being the target, they had to run into the fire to retrieve their means of escape but things began to go painfully wrong: both vehicles had been hit.

"Now what?" Smithy asked. "These bloody shells are ours you know," he added.

"Oh I do know, and they hurt just as much as theirs. The cantina: it usually stays in one piece the longest. I think it's consecrated ground."

"Lead the way, Corporal, let's make ourselves sacred before our luck runs out completely."

They reached the doorway of their sanctuary just as a missile exploded behind, showering them with earth, stones, and steel. He felt a searing lump of shrapnel bury into his rump while a lesser ache around his ribs left him gasping. The intense, sickening pain threatened to black him out as he fought to overcome the waves of nausea. They stumbled through the door of the cantina. Seeking support, he leaned against a raised wine barrel and rested his head on his arms. Spasms of pain stoked his fevered body while the stench of cordite doubled him up in a choking cough, sending shivers through his frame as he realised the seriousness of what he had thought was the least of his injuries. His mouth was wet and warm as he wiped his hands across his lips, inspecting the result with apprehension.

"I've been hit in the back and it hurts like hell," Smithy said as he dropped to his knees and fell forward on his face. "Jesus Christ!" he groaned, "I can't get up."

"Here, take my hand. Let me help."

"No, no, it's alright. It's comfortable down here and the pain is receding. I'll be alright in a few minutes."

The shelling continued with unnerving accuracy. Just when it seemed that theirs was the only safe place on earth, the roof came down, showering them with masonry. Wine barrels supported fallen rafters while smoke and dust irritated his lungs, inducing a further bout of coughing.

After a distressing few minutes, he called out, "Are you alright down there Smithy? ... Smithy! ... Smithy, for Christ sake say something."

A new fear invaded his being, adding more pain to his respiratory difficulties. He was alone in this absurd trap. His thick sturdy legs were turning to sponge, incapable of holding his weight as he fell to the floor in a ridiculous heap. He was trying to form a picture of his son in his fevered mind but failed absolutely. Rose on the other hand he could dream up at will. Her image was etched on his memory and stored away in his heart. She was so beautiful, he yearned to touch and feel her, but a great weariness overwhelmed him. He wanted to lie down and sleep for a couple of hours and regain his strength. Tomorrow he would be on his way to meet his wife.

Falling face down in the dirt didn't bother him at all. It was quite pleasant down there. Like Smithy said, he was comfortable. But Smithy hadn't woken up. Everybody was dead except him. He had survived and tomorrow everything would be alright. His strong, good-looking wife would nurse him back to health. They would enjoy each other again. His heart was at peace. The pleasant feeling of weightlessness crept over him. He closed his eyes and drifted off into a deep, deep sleep.

No further dreams troubled him.

* * *